SHE WAS STRANDED ON A DESERT ISLAND WITH THE LAST OF THE RED-HOT CHAUVINISTS . . .

"Woman, we've got work to do," Kyle said.

"Would you stop referring to me as woman?" Skye objected.

He grinned, a brilliant, teasing glimmer in his eyes. "Sorry, it's a hard habit to break. A man needs some form of amusement, and it's fun to irritate you. You hold your own quite nicely. So let's get started. Get out those scissors of yours."

"What do you want to cut?" she asked.

"My pants."

"While they are on you?"

"I'll be happy to take them off," he supplied with evil amiability.

"No, thanks," she retorted, kneeling to plunge her shears into the material of his pants legs. She was keenly aware of his body heat as she surveyed the project. "How short do you want them."

"Pretty short."

"Then don't move. I'd hate to wound . . . your pride."

"I think we both know you'll be very careful, don't we?"

"I'm always very careful." Skye took a deep breath.

"How nice for you. That's something we'll have to see about, isn't it?"

"My, you are exasperating." She had no intention of being a sexually obliging companion for this man simply because they happened to be stuck together. It was a pity, because like it or not, if she was honest with herself, she would have to admit that she was enjoying each touch, his nearness, his masculine laughter.

"I think I'm a lot more than that, lady," he replied.

He was right.

. . . Who knew it would be so much fun?

Praise for this *New York Times* bestselling author:

"Incredible . . . Graham paints a vivid and detailed picture."

—*Los Angeles Daily News* on *One Wore Blue*

"Heather Graham's sense of humor sparkles throughout. . . . Just one more example of why Ms. Graham is a bestselling author."

—*Romantic Times* on *A Pirate's Pleasure*

"Fast-paced, satisfying, combines mystery with sizzling romance."

—*Publishers Weekly* on *Slow Burn*

". . . Showcases Graham's talent for characterization and romantic tension."

—New York *Daily News* on *Devil's Mistress*

NIGHT, SEA & STARS

HEATHER GRAHAM

ZEBRA BOOKS
KENSINGTON PUBLISHING CORP.

ZEBRA BOOKS are published by

Kensington Publishing Corp.
850 Third Avenue
New York, NY 10022

First Zebra Printing: July, 1996
10 9 8 7 6 5 4

Printed in the United States of America

*For my aunt Dee and Uncle George and Doreen,
and very especially for my cousin Ken,
and woodburning stoves and hot tea and long, long
talks during Massachusetts snowstorms.*

Prologue

June 4, the South Pacific

A dozen seabirds, splendid as they soared against the ceaseless green and brown backdrop of island foliage, carried on wild squawked conversations. The sun blazed down on the glistening shoreline; a startled crab danced along the sand in a comical side step.

Suddenly the birds were silent. A light breeze had stirred the trees, and it, too, seemed to stop suddenly.

A strange droning could be heard in the air. Constant for only seconds, it then coughed, sputtered, and choked—a terrible, terrifying sound. The peaceful paradise came alive with screams, and out of the sky fell a burning, billowing lightning bolt of silver.

The silver streak met with the ground at a chilling pace, shearing away the treetops before it finally came to rest. A thicket of high grass cushioned the belly of the aircraft before it skidded and careened desperately down the beach.

The plane held together.

Kyle Jagger lost several precious seconds of time staring ahead, shaking, beads of perspiration racing down his body, so hot, then turning so clammy cold. His heart thundered painfully against his chest; he had held his breath for so long that now each gulping inhalation sounded like the raging wind of an encroaching storm.

But he had done it. He had landed the Lear against all odds, against the fickle winds of the South Pacific, against the hydraulic failure that had threatened them with sure death.

Intelligence and instinct suddenly broke through the haze of his mind. Hydraulic failure . . . hydraulic fluid. He could smell it. It had to be leaking into the plane . . .

Without further thought Kyle jerked off his seat belt and struggled through the small confines of the craft to seek out his single passenger.

It would be a woman, he thought with a mental groan. An unconscious one at the moment. Or at least he hoped she was only unconscious.

Her face was hidden by the wide brim of a beige felt hat; her head was slumped forward. Kyle paused briefly with his fingers against her throat to check for a pulse. She was alive. He hastily unbuckled her seat belt and hefted her surprisingly light frame into his arms, vaguely and disparagingly noting her fragility. She couldn't stand more than five four, and her bone structure must be as delicate as fine china.

He couldn't waste time worrying about that. He had to get them both off the plane. Only seconds had actually passed since the Lear had shuddered to its final resting place; it felt like a lifetime.

Suddenly she awakened. Thick golden lashes flew wide open to reveal alarmed, widely dilated topaz eyes. Cat eyes, he thought fleetingly. Ever so slightly tilted at the corners.

She took one look at him and let loose a piercing scream.

Balancing her weight quickly, he slapped her sharply and full across the face, fearful her struggles would kill them both.

"Stop!" he grated harshly. "The plane could explode!"

Instantly a clarity replaced the dazed panic in her stare

and her flailing ceased. "Put me down!" she demanded arrogantly. "I'm fine."

"As you say, lady." Kyle dumped her on her spike-heeled feet and immediately applied his sure hands and ample shoulders to the door. Jammed by the landing, it refused to give. Kyle wasted no time on futile effort, but turned to the emergency exit over the wing, annoyed beyond irritation to see his elegant passenger fumbling around her seat.

"What the hell are you doing?" he demanded, amazed that, threatened by death, she could be scrambling for personal items.

"My bag," she told him, looping a long strap over a beige cambric clad shoulder.

"Leave it to a woman," he uttered with distaste, now pitting his strength against the emergency exit. It gave, and he crawled out to the wing and leaped to the ground.

"I've already gotten the thing," she hissed, her topaz eyes amazingly daggerlike for the delicate creature she appeared as she stood on the wing. "In less time than it took you to bitch, I might add!"

"Shut up and jump!" Kyle commanded, catching her slender body as she saw fit to obey him. He gripped her wrist. "And now, lady, I suggest we run like hell."

They started off down the beach, hand in hand in the simple pursuit of survival. Suddenly she let out an anguished cry and fell to the sand, jerking Kyle back. He glanced down to see that her ankle had twisted.

"Damned idiot!" he muttered, knowing he could not spare a second on venting his anger. "Stinking heels." A spatter of crisp curses on his lips, he once more hefted her slim frame—and the offending bag—into his arms.

"Sorry!" she retorted bitterly, forced to loop her arms around his neck. Her cat gaze, the pain shrouded by indignity, met his briefly. "I didn't dress for a plane crash."

He started to run again. Her hat blew from her head; a cascade of honey-blond hair tangled around his shoulders and arms and frothed a silken fragrance against his cheeks.

"This damn bag of yours weighs a ton!" he informed her, realizing his words were a waste of breath, but issuing them anyway. Her hair was blinding him, seducing him from his purpose with its fragrance; the bag she was so determined to keep was heavy; his lungs ached with the effort, his legs were heavy. Thank God, she hadn't decided to salvage the rest of her luggage.

She didn't reply, and he wisely chose to waste no more breath, striving to put distance between them and the promised explosion instead. He knew the plane was going to blow. It was almost a sixth sense—he knew from the air, just as he had known that speed was of the essence.

And when it went, it was as if the ground had been split asunder. Fire raked the sky with blinding brilliance; the boom was deafening. Acrid smoke shut out the day.

Kyle hadn't gotten far enough. A wave of hot air assailed his back, reaching down like a massive hand out of the heavens to lift him effortlessly.

They sailed through the air; the canvas bag wrenched free from them and hurtled ahead on its own.

Kyle's reaction was simply instinct. What he held in his arms was light, soft, fragile, and feminine—a woman. He twisted his body with every ounce of effort to protect her.

Consequently it was he who landed hard against the sand, his head striking the tip of a beached log.

Her fall was softened by the cushion of his body, yet still the impact robbed her of breath.

For each of them the world went black.

And then the earth began her own healing process to cleanse away the smoke and fire.

It began to rain.

One

Skye Delaney moaned as the first drops of rain trickled from her hair to trail down her forehead. She lifted her head groggily, blinking to clear her dazed mind. Then the events of the last few minutes—God, it had all happened in less than five!—crowded her mind with panic and a severe trembling shook her body in convulsive spasms.

The plane had crashed, but oh, sweet God, she was still alive!

Skye suddenly realized that her fingers were tensely curled into cloth. She blinked again and looked down— into the double-breasted navy blazer of the man who had saved her. He was rude and domineering, but she was thankful he was strong, agile, and quick thinking. She swallowed and winced, biting into her bottom lip to fight against tears that would vie with the rain to blind her. What was the matter with her? It was thanks to him that she was alive, and her first memory was that of his chauvinism!

Real panic hit her hard again as she made another realization. She was not only alive, but in sound and functioning shape because he had used his own body to shield hers. His limp arms were still twined around the small of her back and she was sprawled over him. Part of him at least. His length and breadth completely dwarfed hers.

His eyes were closed. His hair, a burnished copper color, was disheveled over a bronzed forehead gone disturbingly ashen. Ridiculously, Skye registered several aspects of his face without really thinking about them. Somewhere in her mind she stored a memory of high, wide cheekbones, dark, arched, cleanly spaced brows. A long, arrogantly straight nose. Lips that in repose were full and well shaped were clearly outlined in a jaw that even now was ruggedly squared, as if cast in iron—a recently shaved jaw. Of all the infinitesimal things to note, she stared into the face just inches from hers, studying the tiny laugh lines ingrained on the sides of his closed eyes and the full, sensual mouth.

She shook herself, wondering once again what the hell she was doing. Had she gone into shock to stare into a man's face when he might be . . .

"No!" She said the word aloud. "Oh, God," she prayed, lifting her face, drenched and hair plastered against it, to the sky in supplication. "Please! Please, let him be okay!"

Skye rolled from his chest, tears seeping now down her cheeks, unnoticed along with the raindrops. Drawing her feet beneath her in the sand, she slipped her fingers through the blazer opening and felt his chest tentatively, holding her own breath as her prayers continued silently. She exhaled, trembling again with relief as she felt movement through the thin material of his shirt.

He was breathing. Frantically she felt his wrist for a pulse, fumbling to find the vein. Again she exhaled tremulously, unaware that she had held her breath again until dizzy relief caused automatic expulsion. His lifeblood was pounding with sound regularity.

But what did she do now? Her first-aid knowledge was pathetically weak, but if he had blacked out from the force of the blast, why wasn't the rain awakening him as it had her? Maybe it wasn't enough. She touched his cheek gingerly but received no reaction and cursed herself as a fool. It was agony to be so frustratingly helpless!

Get a hold of yourself, she commanded silently. The bag she had been determined to get off the plane lay a few feet away. She stretched for it and gently lifted his head, only then noticing the ragged edges of the log beside them. As her fingers gently wound into the nape of his neck, she felt the stickiness of blood.

Skye groaned aloud, the sound a wail that was lost to the wind and still-spattering rain. Why wasn't she one of those people who was just great in emergencies?

The rain stopped abruptly. It was as if the air had been washed, and that accomplished, a faucet had been turned off. In the not-too-great distance, twisted fragments that were once the sleek Lear still burned, but the fire no longer reached to the sky. The flames were low, as if sated and content with the destruction.

Skye gave herself a good mental shake and locked her eye teeth into a corner of her mouth to brace herself. Very carefully she turned the dark auburn head now resting on the bag. She burrowed through a thick wealth of hair until she found the wound, drawing a spot of blood from her own mouth as she bit even harder with another spasm of relief. Although there was a good size bump on his head, the blood came from a comparatively small cut.

Ice.

How ridiculous! Where was she going to get ice? All she could see was beach, sand, high grass, and multi-rooted trees. Don't be such a damned idiot, she chastised herself harshly. Do something!

Common sense finally won out over the shock of the situation. Skye leaped to her feet and wriggled out of her shoes and slip. She started a quick rush to the shoreline, then groaned as a wave of burning pain shot up from her twisted ankle. Gritting her teeth, she limped to the water, glad to find it cool and refreshing from the rain. She hobbled back to the stricken pilot, then methodically worked on cleansing the wound. Honestly, she told herself with disgust, after all the time she had spent bringing emotional support to Steven in the hospital, she should have assimilated something of the practical work done in a medical emergency.

But then, in Steven's case, there had been little practical left to do. She could only hold the hand of one destined to die . . .

She shivered and tears trickled down her cheeks in silent rivulets. That tragedy was in the past, but suddenly made acutely aware of life, Skye grieved afresh for the brother who had lost the precious gift.

But her tears were more than pain; they were an incredible joy, and a tinge of guilt at the incredible joy and gratitude of merely being alive. This morning in Sydney she hadn't even given life itself a thought. She existed in a whirlwind, always a bevy of activity surrounding her.

One business trip to another, never realizing to this moment that all else had been secondary, she had been living for and through Delaney Designs. She couldn't remember a time when she had looked into the blue of the sky for the sheer joy of the experience, walked in the rain to revel in its delightful patter, taken time to glory in the feel of a breeze against her cheeks . . .

"But I didn't realize!" she whispered in a moan of self-excuse. Steven had been sick, and then Steven had died, and the business that had belonged to them both had floundered minus its cofounder. The fight to keep it alive, to make it prosper, had been a panacea, a shield to hold against pain, a shield to hold against the world.

Leaning the pilot's head back against her canvas bag, Skye hobbled back to the surf and resoaked her makeshift cloth. She took a moment to survey her surroundings. Sand, high grass, water, and tall trees. Were you expecting something to change? she asked herself in wry silence. But surely she was in the known world. Help would come. When the Lear didn't arrive in Tahiti to refuel, search parties would begin to comb the area. Perhaps rescue was already on the way. The pilot had probably radioed a May Day . . .

The pilot! Even if he seemed to be a rude and chauvinistic SOB—the type of man she fought against every business day—he had certainly saved her skin! And good Lord, they were *people!*

Skye limped quickly back to the pilot and carefully began to bathe his face with the cool seawater, her fingers absurdly slender and elegant against the rugged planes and chiseled angles of his features, "Live, please, will you?" she whispered desperately. "Please! Come to!"

Her fervent prayers were answered by a groan; the ashen color was leaving his skin, the natural bronze replacing it. Skye watched as facial muscles twitched; his eyelids flickered, but didn't quite make it open.

"Hey!" Skye pleaded, tapping his chin with light strokes. She slipped a hand around his sinewy neck to slide his head as easily as possible back to the sand so that she might rummage through the bag she had been determined to save. The weight he had complained about was mainly that of the bottles she carried among other things. Two quarts of an associate's homemade rum; several small bottles of Burgundy that were a part of cheese and cracker gift sets. Brandy was supposed to be good in a situation like this—wouldn't rum serve just as well? Or perhaps the Burgundy. Or was a sip of liquor just for fainting spells? Would she choke him to death rather than save him?

Rum or Burgundy?

"Oh, the hell with it!" she muttered. She was an executive who made split-second decisions and she was going into mental trauma over a swallow of rum . . . or Burgundy. It would be the rum, and he would take a swallow.

Cradling his head in her arms, she was glad that she hadn't decided to try to move him. If muscle weighed

more than fat, as she had heard, he must be composed
of one muscle after another—down to his toes. Carefully
straining to hold his head so that there was a clear path
down his throat, she fumbled with the screw cap and finally discarded it with her teeth. Sliding the mouth of
the bottle against his lips, she angled it so that a slender
stream of the potent liquor trickled partially into his
mouth and partially onto his chin.

He coughed, sputtered, and gasped. The muscles in
his eyelids twitched briefly and then his eyes flew wide
open. Cool, riveting lime-green eyes surveyed her accus-
ingly.

"You!" he grated in a harsh whisper.

Skye compressed her lips tightly and blinked, fighting a
wave of defensive anger. Of all the nerve! Here she was—
solicitous of his needs, after *he* had crashed the damn
plane!—and he was staring at her as if he had been marooned with the beast with two heads.

"Who were you expecting?" she demanded irritably. "I
would have called the Red Cross, but I'm sorry, I didn't
have change for the phone!"

His quick raking gaze seemed to sear her with a cold
scornful reproach. His head was still in her lap; a tendril
of sodden blond hair grazed his cheek as she returned
his scrutiny with defiance.

His gaze left her and he abruptly rose to sit, half knocking her out of the way in the process. He groaned deeply
at the movement, clutching his head with both hands and
bowing it. Skye saw furrows work their way tensely into
his brow. "Who *was* I expecting?" he muttered, more to
himself than to her, his voice strangely puzzled.

"What do you mean?" Skye demanded, her voice rising
with bewildered alarm at his confusion.

He shook his head without glancing her way and very
gingerly attempted to stand, pausing for balance on the
balls of his feet in a crouch, then rising slowly, one hand

assiduously rubbing his temple. He was silent for a long time. His eyes were sharp and piercing as they lit first upon the surf lapping the beach shoreline, then scanned the trees, the high grass field, the distant horizon, and, way down an interminable length of sand, the burning scattered remains of the Lear.

"We made it," he murmured thickly, his features tense with the abrupt return of memory. "We made it . . ." he repeated.

Skye watched with a certain annoyance as he began to pace the bleached white sand. She started when his sharp gaze came to rest once more upon her and he barked, "How long was I out?"

Taken aback by his crisp demand, Skye fumbled for an answer. "I—I'm not sure—"

"An estimation," he snapped impatiently. "An hour? Ten minutes? Ten seconds, what?"

"About ten minutes," Skye replied acidly, her eyes narrowing with anger. Damn, he was hostile!

He started walking the beach again. "I *am* a pilot," he murmured with a wondering pride that deeply rankled Skye. He vas acting as if he had just performed at an air show when he had brought them to this desolation.

Hardly cruel by nature, but caught at the limits of her patience, she plunged in with a dry, "That *is* debatable."

Now his gaze seemed to slice cleanly through her. "I must be a halfway decent pilot, lady, or else that spot of sand where your pretty little derriere rests would be your final resting place."

Blood suffused Skye's face hotly and new anger washed through her, but she refrained from a reply. It had been hitting well below the belt to hint that he was responsible for the crash, and he was probably right. Thinking back to those few terrible moments when she realized they had lost power—before mercifully blacking out—Skye bit into her lip. She was well aware—despite her limited knowledge of aeronautics—that the landing on the tiny island had been a tricky maneuver indeed, combining incredible luck with incredible skill. A hair in too far and the trees would have caused an explosion before impact, but the flying had been just right, the high grass clearing had buffered the descent of the craft before its landing on the sand.

Several moments passed with no exchanges between the two. The frosty-eyed pilot sank to the very log that had caused his injury, resting his elbows on his knees, his head in cupped hands. Skye lifted her own vision from the ground to the sky, alarmed to note that the brilliance of the after-rain daylight was fading.

At best they had another three hours of any kind of daylight left at all.

She glanced back to her companion. He was still contemplating the sand in deep thought.

"What happened?" she suddenly demanded, her own voice startling her as it slashed through the air. Aware that her panic, rising again like a ghost within her soul, was putting a high, ragged edge on her tone, she cleared her voice and started over more softly. "What happened?"

She finally had his attention. The frosty green eyes met hers with sheer annoyance. "What happened? We made an emergency landing. The plane exploded. If you want further specifics, we were caught between cross currents and a freak wind storm. Then the hydraulic system failed. I was lucky to grind out the landing gear manually." His gaze flashed with a sizzle of contempt. "After that you tripped on those stinking heels, cost us time, and became a wise ass to boot."

Totally irritated, Skye wished she could shake him, scream at him like a banshee. Recognizing the futility of such an action—and seriously doubting that she was capable of shaking him—she ground her teeth together and opted for renewing a line of questioning, as calmly as possible.

"Did you radio an SOS?"

"No," he replied with a rueful twist of a brow. "I wasn't able to. Static was clogging the air waves."

"Oh, Lord," Skye murmured with dismay. She closed her eyes tightly against a rush of fear. "Surely someone will come anyway. When the flight doesn't arrive . . ."

He shrugged again, and a new silence sprang up between them. Skye watched him, amazed that he merely sat upon the log and stared dismally in the direction of the wreckage.

"Don't do this to me!" she suddenly exploded.

His glance swung to her with surprise and he suddenly laughed with true amusement. She was startled to see just how attractive his eyes could be when lit with the warmth of humor.

"Do what to you?" he inquired.

"Just sit there, as if you were still out cold, when night is falling!"

His brows rose with mockingly polite inquiry. "I take it I'm supposed to be doing something?"

"Of course!" Skye sputtered.

He smiled, very lazily, and leaned back on the log and crossed his arms over his chest. "Don't let me stop you."

It was Skye's turn to cross-query irritably. "Stop me from what?"

"From whatever it is you think I should be doing."

Skye stared at him, at first stunned, and then so mad she was ready to throw handfuls of sand into his absurdly smug face.

"I'd watch that temper, if I were you," he warned with amusement as he watched her hands ball into fists at her side. "Just like a woman." There was a touch of real disgust in his tone. "Stands in a boardroom and proclaims herself the equal or superior of any man. Then get her on an island and Miss Macho is back to thinking the man should be doing it all."

Skye rose then, rage constricting her throat. "Listen!" she snapped heatedly. "It's certainly plain as hell that you're not fond of the female gender. In a boardroom or beyond. But frankly you have no right to take it out on me. All I ever did to you was make the mistake of bringing you back to consciousness. I'll find my own little spot on the island and happily relieve you of any and all masculine responsibility. Just be so kind, should you be discovered, to mention the fact that there is someone else stranded on the island! Surely, that wouldn't be bending too far!"

In her hurry to get away before frustrated tears fell, Skye forgot all about her ankle. Consequently, she managed only one step before tripping and landing ignominiously back into the sand.

The air was suddenly filled with honest laughter, and before she could gather herself back to her feet, he was beside her, helping her up despite her furiously flailing protests.

"Hey!" He chuckled. "Calm down!"

Skye continued to struggle against him, but her only accomplishment was to find herself gathered to his chest, held imprisoned by seemingly ironclad arms. The tip of her head just reached his chin and she found herself staring into long collarbones—as bronze as his face and fringed by the curling hint of a mat of burnished copper chest hair. Apparently he had seen fit to make himself comfortable when flying. He wore no tie and the first two buttons of the white shirt he wore beneath his blazer were open.

"I'm sorry, really sorry," he soothed as the fire drained out of her and she went limp in his hold. What would she have done if he had let her go anyway, she wondered bleakly. Would her survival have been a simple matter of common sense?

She felt his hand rubbing the back of her neck—an automatic gesture, one he had performed perhaps countless times before for countless women. "It's just that you were sitting there shrilling like a harpy and I'm not any happier about our situation than you are."

"I never shrill like a harpy!" Skye announced crisply, finally managing to push herself away from his chest and retain her dignity. His touch had been soothing, she thought fleetingly, but she wanted no part of it or him. For a very weak moment she thought it would have been nice to admit herself the weaker sex, beg his mercy, and rest the entire burden of the nightmare on his ample shoulders. No, no, never with such a cynic! Nor was she weak . . . nor had she ever felt the overwhelming urge to cling before.

"All right, Kyle—"

"How do you know my name?" he demanded sharply, eyes narrowing with a curious and instant suspicion.

"No great mystery, Sherlock," Skye murmured dryly. She indicated the gold wings attached to the pocket of his blazer which had scraped her cheek lightly in her struggle. "I do know how to read." She couldn't resist the temptation to feign bland feminine innocence.

He grimaced as he glanced down to the wings and back to Skye. "So you do."

His tone wasn't harsh. It was almost teasing. It was curious, Skye thought, that he should be so suspicious over her knowledge of his name. She shrugged away the thought. His entire manner was curious—one minute he was treating her as gently as a child, the next as if she were Mata Hari. She really wasn't much concerned with the problems of his past life— she wasn't concerned with him at all, except that they were definitely in a mess.

"Well," he murmured, abruptly tapping her chin with

a sudden return to good humor. "Let's see what we've got." He began to comb through his pockets, producing a pocket knife, assorted change from assorted countries, a disposable lighter, and a pack of Marlboros. He idly wandered back to the log to take a seat, pensively lighting up a cigarette. He watched as the smoke drifted away, then shifted his gaze to the cigarette package in his hand. "It's going to hurt when these run out," he said with a little-boy desolation that made Skye ready to laugh despite all else. The sound of her laughter seemed to realert him to her presence and he offered her the pack. "Sorry, I guess you're not stranded with Sir Galahad."

Skye pursed her lips and shook her head. "No, thanks, you'll be glad to hear that I don't smoke. And I probably shouldn't tell you this—you were so nasty over my bag as well as other things—but I've got a carton of some type of English cigarettes in it."

"You just said you didn't smoke."

"I don't."

His gaze lit on the handsome and intricate emerald that she wore on her left-hand ring finger. It was a stunning piece of jewelry, but whether an indication of marriage or not he couldn't tell. It was small and tasteful—possibly a wedding band.

"Hubby?" he inquired.

Skye shook her head, unwilling to discuss her personal life. "For a friend."

He shrugged. "Thanks. What else have you got in that wonder bag?"

"A couple of gift boxes with Burgundy, cheese and crackers. Two more bottles of that homemade rum, and— absurd of me to think such things might be useful—a sewing kit with good scissors, several yards of wool, mineral water, and another little kit with small pliers and a screwdriver." At his lifted brows she added, "I design jewelry."

He chuckled at her sarcasm. "Boy, you don't let things drop, do you?" he demanded with wry amusement. Skye remained silent. She was already constantly on guard with him. "All right," he continued, "I'm sorry I gave you grief over the bag, and I'm sorry I gave you grief over those ridiculous shoes. I applaud you for managing to carry that bag with that kind of weight in it! Can we cut the bickering now?"

"I can," Skye responded sweetly, "but I'm afraid I can't change my gender."

He shrugged indifferently. "Just don't let it get in the way."

The mention of the word "gender" reminded her of something else, and she was suddenly stretching across the sand to drag the bag over to her. At his questioning glance she informed him, "I have my purse in here—"

"Oh, Christ, of course!" he moaned. "I should have known that since we didn't stop to retrieve that too, you must have had it stashed somewhere. God forbid we begin this survival party without the lady's handbag!"

Skye gave him an acid stare. "My purse is small. I stash it in the larger bag so there's less to carry—"

"But you need a damn pack mule for the rest!"

"Oh, shut up!" Skye murmured in exasperation. "There just might be something in my purse that can help us."

"Maybe," he was quick to grant, reaching for her small leather bag as she extracted it from the larger one.

"Hey!" she protested. "It is *my* purse!"

He dropped his hand but ordered, "Open it."

Why did she feel as if he had blandly demanded she strip? There was nothing in her purse that he surely hadn't seen before, but her items were personal, things that belonged to the intimacy of her day-to-day life.

He would never understand her feelings. He would be merely impatient with more "feminine" sentiment.

With a sigh she dumped the items over the canvas of the other bag. He began to thread through them one by one.

"Wallet, address book, handkerchief—monogrammed, my, my—compact, lipstick—what's this?"

"Mascara," Skye supplied with great patience.

"Great, it's going to do us a world of good."

"You didn't have too much to offer yourself."

"Passport, more makeup stuff, pen, more makeup stuff, comb, keys, memo pad, more makeup stuff—"

"Will you stop!" Skye demanded with annoyance. "Eyeshadow, a blush, and a liner. That's it."

She didn't like the amusement in his arched brow, but said no more as he continued, "Another pen, a pencil, postage stamps, tampon—ahhh, that time of the month, huh? Explains why you're such a witch."

"I'm not a witch!" Skye snapped, hastily retrieving her items. "And it isn't my time of month." She didn't know why she had added a statement that was clearly none of his business, except that his attitude—it seemed that every time a woman had an opinion, a man was blaming it on her hormones—highly irritated her. "I think you've made a concise assessment!" she added briskly, snatching things right and left.

"Wait!" He brushed her hand aside. "Now this is useful." He picked out her nail file.

"Sure," Skye murmured, "we can file through our prison bars."

The glance he gave her was pure impatience. "I'm not sure yet what we'll be gouging, but any sharp tool is going to be useful."

Funny, Skye thought with a little chill, when was it—maybe an hour ago?—she had been idly repairing a chipped nail. The thing in his hand had been a nail file—just that and nothing more. Now it had become a "tool."

That her nail file might have something to do with their survival was frightening.

Kyle kept the file, fingering it idly in his palm, then pocketing it. Skye snapped her purse shut and returned it to the canvas bag, watching him from the shade of her lashes as she did so. She realized suddenly that despite his insistence on sticking to the role of semicallous male, many of his charges and innuendos were made with a certain grain of salt. Did he believe himself, she wondered?

She cleared her throat and broke the silence between them. "You don't by any wild chance happen to know where we are?" she asked hopefully.

"As a matter of fact, I do."

"Oh?" Her hope increased although she raised a skeptical brow.

He laughed easily at her expression, impatience gone. "Stop scoffing and I'll give you my educated guess. We're in the Pacific—"

"Oh, that narrows it down!"

"Eh! Listen up!" He was capable of being friendly . . . and of possessing a devastating smile. It was amazing to think that any woman might have given him a hard time.

"Please," she murmured, waving a hand. "I stand admonished."

"I believe we're due east of Pitcairn Island and due south of Tahiti."

Skye waited for him to continue. When he didn't, she persisted. "That's all?"

"What do you mean, that's all? You asked if I knew where we were."

"I mean, what island is this? Where are we?"

"Lady," he muttered, impatient again, "I doubt if this island has a name, or if it has ever been charted on a map. We're on a small atoll—an island created by volcanic action along the ridges on the floor of the Pacific. There

are thousands of these little islands scattering the South
Pacific. And you have to bear in mind that the Pacific
covers a third of the earth's surface—"

"Oh, my God!" Skye interrupted, "You mean—"

"No, I don't mean that we'll never be found. It's unlikely that the explosion was seen, though, so it might
take some time. The storm veered us off course, and then
as I said, a search will be difficult because there are thousands and thousands of miles to cover."

Sick with desolation, Skye lashed out at him. "Damn
you! You're the pilot! And Executive World Charters is
supposed to be such a reliable, dependable service!
Shouldn't you be able to do something? Why don't you
have emergency flares? Why not a procedure? Why not
something?" Her impetus had grown so that she charged
him, wishing she could do him physical harm. Then she
realized he was right—she was capable of sounding like
a harpy. And trying to cast blame was an exercise in cruel
futility. She wound up sliding hopelessly to her knees in
the sand before him, her clenched fists falling weakly to
his kneecaps, her head bowed. "I'm sorry."

His hand came to rest on her head. "I'm sorry too,"
he said softly. She hadn't cried, but he couldn't risk gen-
tleness too long. Anger was the best emotion to retain
for survival. "I should have gotten the flares," he announced briskly, not bothering to tell her they would
probably be useless anyway—little traffic would come
their way. He carefully placed her hands at her sides and
drew her to her feet by her shoulders. "I'm afraid I knew
the plane was going to blow and all I could think of was
getting us off." Leaving her standing by the log on the
beach, he brushed past her and started off for the high
grass that began in clumps off the sand, whistling. Skye
stared after him incredulously.

"Where are you going?"

"To do something!" he called back. "Can't you see? It's going to be dark soon!"

It was going to be dark soon—she could see it all too easily. It might have been a beautiful dusk at any playground beach—the sky turning pink and crimson, the water taking on the hues of deepest, mysterious indigo as the surf gently lapped the shore.

Except it wasn't a playground. There was no luxury suite in a hotel to return to; there would be no light to turn on when the night became black.

"Wait a minute!" Skye called after him. "I'm coming with you!"

He halted and turned around. She was suddenly aware that despite his disheveled clothing and mussed auburn hair, he could be very attractive when his thick lashes hid a teasing, lazy light in the lime-green eyes. "Well, I certainly hope you do plan on being useful!" He chuckled. His teeth were amazingly straight and white. "No offense, but at the moment, I'm afraid you can't get by on ornamentation alone."

"Thanks," Skye muttered briefly, realizing he was all too right. The crisp beige business suit in which she had begun the day was sadly soaked and drying badly. The natural waves in her blond hair were nonexistent as it was still plastered around her face. She also felt literally covered by sand. "You don't look much like Casanova yourself, you know," she retorted, starting after him.

She didn't get very far. Even half hopping and half stepping gingerly, her ankle buckled after the third step. She heard his chuckle.

"Never mind!" he told her. "You stay there. I'll find something for you to do."

"No!" Skye protested. "Just slow down and I'll be able to make it."

He was silent for a moment and then smiled slowly. "You don't want to be left alone, do you?"

"Don't be ridiculous!" Skye huffed indignantly. "I simply intend to prove that I can—"

"That you can what?" he demanded. "Slow me down?" He started walking back to her, pausing just feet away.

"No!" Skye began, but before she could continue, he had none too graciously pushed her onto the log. As she gasped for breath to sputter a furious and stunned protest, he knelt before her on one knee and gently probed her injured ankle, carefully persistent despite the moan that escaped her. "At least it is only a sprain," he murmured, setting her foot down and rising. His eyes lit upon her heels, cast in the sand a few feet away. Skye was surprised at the vehemence with which he suddenly attacked the shoes. "Stinking heels!" he hissed disgustedly, hurtling both out to the surf.

"What the hell did you do that for?" Skye protested. "Now I have nothing."

"Nothing is better than those ridiculous shoes," he told her. "All I need is your other ankle going—then you will be utterly useless.

"So far," Skye said, her eyes narrowing and her tone dangerously level, "I think we've both proved ourselves to be equally useless."

He ignored her comment and stood. "I'll be back shortly."

"I told you," Skye said stubbornly, "I'm going with you."

The glimmer of a smile sparkled again in his eyes. "Lady, I believe you must be afraid of the dark."

"Don't be absurd," Skye reassured him acidly. "I haven't been afraid of the dark since I was two! And," she informed him, rising carefully to prove that she could stand and hobble, "I do wish you'd quit addressing me that way in that tone of voice. I happen to have a name and I do far prefer that I be addressed by it."

"So sorry!" he mocked lightly. "What is your name then?"

"Skye. Skye Delaney."

Kyle stretched out a large sun-browned hand. "So very glad to meet you, Ms. Delaney."

Accepting his hand, even slowly with reservation, turned out to be a mistake. As soon as he had her slender fingers entrapped in his larger ones, he stooped, butted her midriff with his shoulder, and used his grip on her hand for leverage to cast her like a burlap bag of potatoes over his shoulder. "What the—" The rest of her words were cut off as her chin smacked into his back with his first long stride. Enraged, Skye balanced herself with her elbows against his back before trying to demand an explanation again. "What do you think you're doing now?" she grated.

"You insist upon coming with me. If you walk, it will be tomorrow morning before we get anywhere, so if you're coming, you're coming my way."

It made a little sense, she admitted grudgingly, her chin cupped in her hands and her elbows still braced to ease some of the jouncing of her torso with each of his distance-eating strides. "Marvelous!" she grated through clenched teeth. "What a wonderful day. Not only am I stranded God knows where after a plane crash that almost kills me, I get to be stranded with a damned Neanderthal!"

"A Neanderthal!" Kyle protested, laughing. The sound rumbled pleasantly—too pleasantly—from his chest. "Then watch your step, lady, or I'll handle all our disputes with the old Neanderthal standby—a club!"

"Oh, do shut up!" Skye snapped. She gouged her elbows into his back, which only served to start him chuckling again, and a second later he leaped over some unseen obstruction, smacking her chin back into his muscles.

"Hey!"

"Oh, I am so sorry!"

"Like hell!" Skye muttered. "Where are we going, anyway?"

"To see what we can find to rig up some kind of a structure. I like the rain just fine but not to sleep in. And some type of material to plan for a distress signal, and"— he paused, his tone going quietly serious—"water. Our biggest worry if we're here for any amount of time is going to be fresh water. We really need to hope that a fair supply of that rain has been contained in something somewhere because I don't think we're going to find any lakes or streams. Your cheese and crackers will make a nice snack for tonight—and thanks to the rum we can get nice and plastered if we wish—but we also need to see what might be edible . . ."

He kept on talking, but Skye stopped really listening to his quiet murmurings. Just hours ago her biggest worry had been her meeting in Buenos Aires. She never gave any thought to creature comforts. A glass of water was something you asked a waiter to pour when you'd had enough wine. Rain was just something that happened like sunshine, snow, or sleet . . .

It was amazing how fast and how completely life could change.

Two

The fire burned cheerily, a single glow of orange warmth against an eternity of black. Not even the stars were out.

"Not bad," Skye commented.

Kyle shrugged, still watching the flames. "I was a Boy Scout once," he said dryly. His gaze turned to the rather shabby-looking structure he had concocted of shorn upper tree trunks and fronds from the numerous palms abounding on the island. The work of building, with only his pocket knife and her scissors for cutting utensils and vines and fronds for binding the notched inserts, had been rough, but the structure was now sturdy, set into the sand a fair distance from the water to allow plenty of room for rising tides.

"It won't make *Better Homes and Gardens*," Skye said, and chuckled softly, "but we will stay dry."

"Glad you approve, woman," Kyle retorted amiably. He finally turned his gaze to Skye, who was seated Indian fashion by the fire. A smile quirked his lips. A pin-up queen? No, she wasn't tall enough, but dry now, with waves of that rich honey-blond hair spilling around her face, those enticing, almond-shaped topaz eyes alight in the blaze, she wasn't a bit less appealing. She might be small, but her tiny frame packed a wallop. Although he hadn't pondered it at the time, from carrying her around he had become aware that she was exceedingly well-shaped, with fullness just where it was desirable.

"What are you smirking at?" she demanded.

"Nothing," he said quickly, his smile fading. He had suddenly felt the shaft of pure desire riddling him. A primitive desire—there was nothing but the night and them. He clenched his jaw with a twinge of pain and also a wry, inward grimace. The locale was getting to him. It was wild, exotic, and heathen—making him feel wild, exotic, and heathen. They could have been alone at the end of the earth and the one-on-one situation would have been no stronger. He wondered what his luscious cosurvivor would think of his chauvinism if he responded to instinct and pulled her into his arms . . .

Not much. She didn't seem highly enamored of him to begin with. And yet she was due for a few cruel surprises if they were to survive. As curt as he had been with her so far for inexplicable reasons, he was, in his way, still trying to shield her.

And he wasn't a barbarian. They hadn't left civilization that far behind. One didn't accost a woman simply because she had the ill fate to be stranded with you. He still didn't know her marital status, and yet her name sounded familiar. He should have checked up on his passenger when he decided to take the flight himself, he reminded himself. But then he had been too obsessed with his own thoughts, his own desire to reach home and the freedom he was finally receiving. He wondered vaguely what she would think of his marital status.

He turned then to the girl with a grin covering his thoughts. Woman, he corrected himself. She was far too assured and quick witted to be considered anything less, even if the tip of her head did barely reach his chin.

"Hey, duchess," he teased briskly, a dry note adding a trace of seriousness. "I did the macho bit with the fire and the building. How about getting dinner together?"

Skye leveled a narrow eye in his direction and compressed her lips but struggled to her feet. Her ankle was beginning to feel better, but she still favored her left foot carefully. "If you'll recall," she reminded him coolly, "I did weave the fronds!"

"Mmmmm, I recall. And after you drum up the food, I'll put my own cheese on the crackers. And if you're real nice, I'll crack a coconut for you."

The look she gave him just might have frozen water. He could well imagine that she could be a little demon in a business deal . . . He lowered his head as he felt a full smile creeping into his lips. Despite the gravity of their situation, he couldn't help but appreciate a little of the humor. A person as independent as she probably never asked advice, but plunged right in with her own decisions. She was obviously wealthy enough to have anything done rather than ask for help, but here she was now, at his mercy, so to speak.

He would have been less than male not to enjoy the roles they were being forced to play. Chalk one up to men's lib! he thought with a chuckle that turned to a frown. He couldn't understand his relentless teasing of her—he didn't have a thing against her personally. And he was actually all for females carrying their intelligence and skill as far as they could take it in the business world.

Pensively, Kyle took her place by the fire. Did she know who he was? he wondered. Either she didn't, or she didn't care, or she was one fine actress. It wasn't that he lacked personal confidence, he had a bundle of assurance, but he was a practical man and the number of women who managed to seek him out had often amazed him— even when the women were fully aware that there would be limits to what he could give.

He was a bit of a cynic—his associations had made him so. Yet he still wasn't prone to judge or condemn on short acquaintanceship.

A box of crackers suddenly landed in his lap. "Think you can manage to spread your own cheese?" Skye asked dryly, sinking back down beside him. "What are we drinking?"

"I don't know about you, but I could use a good belt of that rum."

Skye handed him the bottle she had opened earlier. He smiled. "You forgot the cups, my dear."

"Sorry, lost my head," Skye returned acidly, scrambling to her feet to return to their makeshift hut and retrieve the "cups"— gourds Kyle had fashioned from a split coconut. "Anything else, *dear?*"

"Yeah, a steak, about two inches thick and medium rare."

"I guess you'll just have to hit the bananas or coconuts."

"Yeah, for tonight, I suppose," Kyle replied, stuffing his mouth with a cracker. "You don't happen to be an ace fisherman, do you?"

"Afraid not," Skye answered. "Do you?"

"I guess I'll be finding out," he replied lightly. "Tell me about your business, Ms. Delaney."

Skye shrugged. "There isn't much to tell. I'm a jewelry designer. I started with clothing, and I still work some in that field, mostly evening wear. But my main line now is jewelry."

Kyle was suddenly aware of who she was, of why the name had been familiar. She had been written up in at least a dozen articles. She wasn't just a designer, but the queen of contemporary fashion. Some of her jewelry was designed specifically for some of her glamorous outfits.

And he knew now that she wasn't married. She had also been unlucky enough to hit the covers of a number of the gossip rags. If memory served him correctly, a tabloid cover had announced her four-year romance with a Broadway producer as still one of the hottest items in a jet-set society where long-term relationships were almost nonexistent.

"So," Kyle said, crunching into another cracker, "were you in Sydney on business?"

"Yes—and no," Skye replied, wondering why she had supplied the last as she was assailed by a stab of pain. "My sister-in-law lives in Sydney," she explained hastily, hoping that would end his questioning.

"What about your brother?"

"My brother is dead," Skye said quickly, almost negligently. What was the matter with her, she wondered. It was just still so hard. She couldn't say those words yet in a calm, controlled voice without a catch constricting her voice, without tears forming in her eyes. She wasn't about to cry in front of this stranger. I sound flip, she thought with a wince, but when she continued, the sound was still flip to her own ears. "I travel to Sydney frequently to buy gold, so I'm able to see Virginia often while I'm on business."

Kyle was silent for several seconds, his expression completely bland. Then he spoke, his tone condemning. "Truckload of empathy, aren't you?"

Skye stared at him blankly, stunned that anyone so hostile and callous could actually exist. Empathy! Surely anyone human would have understood that she brushed off the subject because it was just too painful. Suddenly she was so furious that she forced herself to a great calm to prevent herself from doing damage to one or the other of them. With infinite precision she set her gourd in the sand and rose. "I sincerely doubt that you know or understand the meaning of the word 'empathy,' Kyle. At any rate you may take your opinion of me and my emotions and go to hell. I didn't ask to be here, and I'll be damned if I'll sit and listen to abuse from a man I don't know, *who* doesn't know a single thing about me."

Her tone had been level, quiet. When she finished

speaking, she turned and walked to the shore and sat so that the warm surf just trickled over the torn nylon on her toes.

She was shaking, but her emotion was that of impotent rage. At least I won't sink into self-pity at this rate! she told herself. Never in her existence had she come across anyone as strange and blatantly brutal. Of course, she reflected, had she ever met anyone like him in a social or business situation, she wouldn't have endured him this far. She would have closed a door in his damned face.

Trying to calm down, she tried to assuage herself with the reminder that he was extremely competent, intelligent, and amazingly resourceful. Not only had he managed the hut and the fire, secured an ample supply of fresh fruits, and created a cistern out of a hollowed log to collect the remaining caches of rain water, he had also arranged an SOS pattern on the beach—visible, one hoped, to any low-flying pilots—which could be lighted as long as it stayed dry.

Skye gritted her teeth and muttered to the sea, "I suppose under the circumstances, it's better to be stranded with a knowledgeable bastard than an incompetent charmer!"

But damn, he seemed to have a talent for zeroing in and drawing blood from her scars.

Kyle swallowed a deep draught of the rum, wincing as it burned down his throat. The stuff was one-oh-one proof, liquid fire, but he was glad of the searing sensation. He needed the jolt, he thought with self-disgust. Why the hell was he being so cruel? Skye was doing damned well—she didn't complain, she didn't become hysterical, she followed his directions with quick-witted compliance. He liked her, he realized, and he admired her. Why then the cutting comments?

He turned to watch the rigid set of her spine as she sat by the dark water and became doubly ashamed. She was small, but strong. There was some saying . . . it wasn't the size of the man in the fight, but the size of the fight in the man? Well, she was a woman, but the saying seemed to fit. Skye had fight, and he was sure drawing it out of her.

He started to rise, then decided against it. In the morning she would probably be in a better frame of mind to accept an apology. He stared back into the fire, sipping the rum and allowing the potent brew to work its relaxing magic over frayed nerves and tired muscles.

Skye stared at the water awhile longer, then withdrew her toes as the slight chill in the night air made her shiver. She took a brief moment to be thankful that their crash landing had taken place in a warm climate, then stood and walked to the shelter of the hut, ignoring the bowed auburn head of her companion as she walked by the fire. She hoped she would be so exhausted that she would sleep.

Her sand bed left a lot to be desired, but she determinedly curled into a little ball in the far side of the shelter, crumpling the now empty canvas bag into a pseudo-pillow. She felt as if she stayed awake for a miserable eternity, staring out at nothing. Occasionally she heard the crackle of the fire, or a rustle as the breeze drifted lightly through the nearby foliage. But she didn't hear a single movement by Kyle. Eventually the monotonous and constant wash of the surf lulled her into an uneasy sleep.

She should have expected to dream. In fact, in the absurd way that dreams went, she knew in the dream that she was dreaming.

She *was* afraid of the dark.

Oh, the childhood fear she had outgrown. This had come when she was an adult, and it wasn't so much a fear of the dark, but a fear of the memory nightmare that the dark brought like a diabolical, lunging shadow land.

Steven. Steven with his quiet ways and easy, accepting manner. Steven who never raised his voice, and handled the worst with brave serenity.

Only once had he ever broken, toward the end, delirious after a treatment. She had been with him while Virginia slept. He had cried out loud to her in agony, and she had not been able to do anything. He didn't feel her hand in his; he couldn't hear her voice. He just kept calling her. "Skye . . . it's so dark, so dark, so dark and cold. Skye, oh, please, Skye, where are you? It's so horribly dark and cold . . . please, please, make the darkness go away . . . please, Skye . . ."

In the morning he had been lucid again. He had placed his hands in those of the wife and sister he loved to say there would be no more treatments.

"Skye!"

She snapped awake to realize she was really being called and her shoulders were being lightly shaken by strong, firm hands. Disoriented, she blinked, finally becoming aware in the near total darkness that a pair of cool green eyes, reflecting the very faint light, were staring into hers. "Skye!" His tone was surprisingly gentle, his face drawn with what appeared to be honest concern. "Skye!" He repeated her name softly, giving her another slight shake. "Are you all right?"

She sprang to a sitting position, jerking from his grasp. Here she was with machismo personified and she had done something ridiculously—weakly—feminine in her sleep. "I'm sorry. Did I disturb you? Did I scream? I'll try not to let it happen again."

He shook his head slowly, his expression indiscernible

in the dark, his tone peculiar when he finally replied. "No, you didn't scream." He didn't tell her what she had done. "Are you sure you're all right? Would you like to talk about it?"

"No!" she exclaimed, horrified

"You know," he offered gently, "you are here with another human being."

"Am I?" Her question was toneless, a vaguely interested query. She was too tired and worn out to attempt anything cynically witty.

For once he made no abrasive comeback. She didn't see his movement and flinched as his knuckles grazed her cheek gently. "Yes," he said quietly, following her high cheekbones slowly down to her chin with his gentle grazing. His knuckles lingered for a moment, then a callused thumb lightly tapped her lower lip. "Yes, Skye, I am human."

Skye was mesmerized momentarily by his hypnotically tender touch; seconds ticked by as she stared spellbound at the reflected glimmer in his eyes. Then she drew a shaky breath and pulled away, having no desire to trust in this new side of a hostile stranger, nor to unburden her secret nightmares to him. They were less than ships that passed in the night; they were, at best, ships that had crashed together by some cruel trick of fate. "I'm fine, really," she said firmly. "I'll try not to disturb you again."

"I wasn't disturbed," he said, but he didn't push her, and he didn't touch her again. She heard his lithe movement in the darkness and realized he had gotten up. She couldn't see him as he left her, nor hear the silent pad of his feet across the sand. Curious, she waited, still startled when he loomed before her again, offering her something in the coconut shell.

"Shot of rum," he told her briskly. "You're still shaking. This will help you sleep."

"I can't drink that straight!" Skye protested.

He laughed, and the sound was easy. "Sorry—bar's out of Coke, soda, and tonic! Just swallow—guaranteed to kill what ails you."

Eyeing his form dubiously in the dark, Skye accepted the liquor. Tossing her head back, she swallowed it down, gasping as her throat burned and her eyes watered. She choked and coughed, and he patted her back, still chuckling softly.

"Better?" he inquired.

"I suppose," she acquiesced, still doubtful.

"Think you can sleep? Or do you think you would like to talk now? I'd like to do *something* for you."

"Really," Skye stressed. "I'm fine!" To press her point, she curled back into the sand and closed her eyes. "I'm sure I can sleep."

She wasn't sure why, but as she kept her eyes closed and breathed evenly, she knew he still hovered over her. For several seconds she hesitated, but he didn't leave, he maintained his vigil. Finally she spoke, her back still to him.

"If you must do something," she said, inadvertently husky, "I'd really appreciate another fire."

He didn't reply, but again she sensed his movement. Apparently he had no problems with the dark. This time she could hear him as he gathered fresh sticks. Moments later another fire blazed.

The total darkness was gone. Warmed by the pale orange glow, Skye slipped into a restful sleep even before he returned to the hut.

Kyle returned from the jumping flames to gaze down at the honey-haired woman curled so defiantly against him. Another inch, he thought wryly, and she would be outside the shelter of the makeshift roof. Now she lay quiet, beautifully formed lips slightly parted and curved just a shade in a smile. Her topaz eyes were closed to him, but he could still see the hint of their subtle, intriguing tilt. She was not beautiful in the classic sense, but in a way far more unique and arresting. Her nose was fine and straight, her lips full, very sensuous looking as they were now with that slight parting, the tips of small pearl-white teeth just visible.

He frowned, thinking of how her restless, pained murmurings had awakened him. Her features had been terribly strained, and although he hadn't been able to make out her words in their entirety, it had sounded as if she were trying to reassure someone. "It will be all right, it will be warm, the light will come . . .

Was that what she gasped in half sobs that subjected her body to fitful tossing?

He would have liked to kick himself. He was sure she'd dreamed of the brother she had lost; the dream was probably caused by his offhand comment. An unnecessary comment. But he had spoken because she had made it sound as if she deigned to visit her sister-in-law merely because her business made it convenient to do so. Business first. And he was sick of business taking precedence over domesticity. It wasn't merely a chauvinistic pose. He had firsthand experience. He had learned to make his son come first, and his business had still thrived. Lisa had made business everything; she had never been there for Chris.

That was so long ago.

It should have been over.

It should have been finished. The twenty-year debacle that was his marriage should have finally ended, he thought bitterly. Odd priorities, he told himself next. He should be worrying about survival, not grieving an upset in his plans. He knew the truth of their situation; rescue could be a long time coming, if ever. The tiny scattered islands of the Pacific numbered in the thousands; the ocean stretched eleven thousand miles at its greatest width. Even knowing approximately where they had gone down, it could take searchers forever.

And yet he wasn't bitter that his life as he had known it—high powered and high level—might be a thing of the past.

He was bitter because the end of a twenty-year battle had been in sight—triumph an obtainable goal within days.

And he was bitter because of Chris, his son. The boy who had made the wasted years worthwhile, a man now, able to face both his parents with a level head, make his own judgments, accept all the truths and faults and still love. . . .

Skye shifted suddenly beside him and his attention returned to her. He had wanted so much to help her. He had been seized by a fervent desire to envelop her in his arms and comfort and protect her, but he knew—and not without sound reason—that she would be horrified by such an overture on his part.

Frowning, he stretched his length a few feet from hers, cradling his head in the crook of an elbow as he stared at the frond roof. He was truly baffled by his reaction to her. Although he was legally wed according to a piece of paper, his marriage had been over before it started. He had been legally separated for the last ten years, and in that time he had become hard. He hadn't pressed for a divorce at first; he had no intention of marrying again. The very term had soured for him. But neither had he been cut out for a life of celibacy, and so the years had been filled with various women—sharp women, willing to accept him on his own terms. He always made certain they understood the circumstances, and he respected those who knew the score. With all cards laid on the table, he was usually gallant, kind, and enjoyable to the opposite sex.

Skye was wrong, he thought fleetingly. He had never

been bested in a boardroom by a woman. Would that it had been a boardroom. He could have said the best of luck and moved on. As it was, he had been bested by a different kind of scheming, a different kind of wile, and his heart had been indelibly scarred forever . . .

His heart, he decided dryly, but not his senses. He was reminded of the raw desire that had overcome him earlier. He wanted her more strongly than he had ever wanted a woman before. Probably the circumstances, old man, he told himself. Despite everything, all that he had wanted over the past years had been his all too easily.

And yet it was strange. Skye might not be married, but from all he had read, she did belong to another man. But she had yet to mention his name; her dreams, her pain, had been for a brother already lost. Consciously, she hadn't given him a clue to any personal feelings.

But then he hadn't exactly poured out his life story either. It seemed unbelievable after the day they had spent, but in reality, he was sleeping beside a perfect stranger.

A perfect stranger who had become the focal point of his life. A stranger who had an effect upon him as no other.

A woman who drove his senses mad.

His eyes tightened as if he could force himself to sleep by such a measure. He could handle desire. It was the other feelings he was having difficulty dealing with. He didn't want to lash out at her. He was hard, but unaccustomed to cruelty. And he didn't like his strange urge to protect . . . to comfort.

What you usually wanted to protect, you usually wanted to possess. He vaguely understood a little of his irrational anger. She belonged to someone else, and that angered him. And that was absolutely ridiculous.

With a disgusted grunt he turned his back on her. In time he finally slept.

* * *

Poised upon a level stretch of coral, Kyle stood tensed, ready to spring into action. His back and shoulders were beginning to ache, the arm that held his best effort at a spear—a branch with a spiked point he had spent a good hour whittling to a deadly sharpness—was beginning to feel as if it might fall off.

It was hard to keep his grip on the branch in the water, and he ruefully and belatedly berated himself for having tossed Skye's high-heeled sandals into the surf. The long leather straps would have been perfect for a binding to give his hand a better grasp. We live and learn, he told himself dryly. Yesterday he had been so aggravated by those damn shoes, he would have tossed them away if they had been diamond studded. Oh, well, that water was over the dam. But in the future he would learn to think before acting on impulse—even aggravated impulse.

He tightened stiffening fingers around his spear with a sigh of determination. He had already made at least two dozen plunges after fish that appeared to be standing still in the clear water, probably laughing—he could swear the fish did laugh—at his clumsy efforts. He had seen the natives of at least a score of islands manage this task easily. Of course they had been at it since birth . . . No excuses, buddy, stick to it, he warned himself.

At least no one was around to see his fumbling attempts. He would never take the talents of a Polynesian fisherman for granted again.

A little yellowtail ambled lazily by his bare legs, actually brushing his flesh. The fish moved out a few feet right before him, unblinking black eyes staring straight at him. Kyle lunged. The fish calmly moved a foot, not even swimming away in the mad fear a fish was supposed to feel.

Damn! Kyle thought with wry disgust. Some menace I am! Sheepishly he sighed, but raised his spear once more with perseverance, waiting for the spinning circles he had created in the water to cease. The haughty yellowtail watched him still with those blank, unwavering eyes. Its gills moved in and out. Kyle plunged again.

And this time he caught his prey. Wriggling madly, the fish appeared at the end of his stick as he lifted it from the water. Kyle laughed jubilantly. "This is one fish story no one is ever going to hear about!" he assured the flapping yellowtail. Walking to the shore with his prize, he found Skye still sleeping soundly. He filleted his fish with deft strokes of his pocket knife and created a brazier of sticks from the fire to cook the meat slowly. Feeling absurdly pleased for a man who had personally destroyed the first craft ever of his fleet and was now marooned, away from family, friends, and his corporate empire, he returned to the coral-strewn water for a brisk swim.

Skye woke slowly. Nothing had happened to make her open her eyes, rather the enduring heat of the rising sun warmed her until she languorously lifted heavy lids. She wasn't startled to realize she was on the island after sleep had blacked out yesterday's disaster; the discomfort of feeling like a sand dune had jarred her memory before she was fully awake. Surprisingly, once she had choked down the rum and the fire had burned brilliantly again, she had slept fairly well.

Pushing up on an elbow, she saw that a fire still burned—and more. Something with a tantalizing aroma was cooking above it, strung on a crude rotisserie set between two branches. Skye wondered what Kyle had found to cook and warned herself that anything was going to smell wonderful since she had barely touched the crackers last night. She didn't want her stomach getting too excited until *she* believed that what was being barbecued was edible.

Fleetingly, Skye glanced around the visible portion of the island. If there were only a private villa or beach club around the corner, the place would be a paradise. She had never seen whiter sand. The high grass and tropical forest were an incredibly deep green, and rising in the center of the island, the crest that had once been a spouting volcano seemed to kiss a blue heaven softened by lazy, puffy white clouds. But she wasn't in paradise, she had been fated to hell . . .

Stop it, she warned herself. Someone would come. They would be rescued. Stretching to sit with crossed legs, she glanced more closely around her. Odd, she thought, the fire was going with food cooking and her cohabitant of the island was nowhere to be seen. She absently twisted to scratch her back, wincing at the feel of sand filtering through her clothing. What she wouldn't give at the moment for a giant tube of toothpaste and a bar of soap. And oh . . . to soak her head in a bucket full of shampoo and lather away the scratchy sand!

Movement following thought, she threaded her fingers through her hair, a rather pathetic attempt to loosen any tangles that had formed during the night. She yawned, wondering idly if she should be doing something to whatever it was that was cooking. Then Kyle ambled into sight.

Her mouth remaining open, she sat perfectly still. Arms swinging easily, whistling cheerily—and naked as a jaybird—he was rising from the surf and returning to their little camp. Forcing her mouth shut, Skye felt her temper begin to boil even as she averted her gaze and noticed what she should have noticed before—his clothing in a neat pile by the fire.

"Dammit!" she hissed, drawing his startled gaze instantly, "Haven't you a shred of common decency in you?"

His whistling ceased and since Skye was carefully staring into his eyes, she was easily able to see the cheerful light leave them as they went hard. "I suppose I have a shred—

somewhere," he replied, hands on hips as he stared her down.

"I happen to be a woman, if you haven't noticed!" Skye reminded him, her color growing as he made no move to oblige her by reaching for his clothes.

"I warned you not to let gender get in the way."

"Would you please put something on?" she demanded, exasperated.

A brow was raised high in mockery; one corner of his mouth twitched in cynical amusement. "What's the matter, Ms. Delaney? Don't you like what you see? Or perhaps you like it a bit too much?"

Thus challenged, Skye prayed that she wouldn't give way to a blush. Her expression immobile, she kept her eyes steadily on his while she shrugged. Then she carefully allowed her gaze slowly to run down his body to his toes—pausing just a fraction of a second at three strategic points: chest, hips, and thighs. To make her scrutiny truly deadening, she thought fleetingly, she should be posed on a bar stool with the smoke of a cigarette in a long, elegant holder swirling before her eyes. Lacking the proper props, she brazened it out as best she could, her arms wrapped around her knees in what only she knew to be a frozen lock.

Only the scrutiny didn't quell his audacity as thoroughly as it should have. He smiled nicely. "Should I turn around?"

She managed a slight, indifferent gesture with a hand and replied with perfect, condescending boredom, "Oh, please do."

He turned slowly, playing her game with amused interest.

"Well?"

Their eyes met again. Skye was amazed that she was carrying out her bluff so well and determined not to falter for a second. Once more she shrugged, pretending to stifle a yawn politely.

"Just the usual. Nice backside though."

He tossed back his head and roared with laughter, then congenially reached for his briefs and pants. "You are a cool one, lady," he granted her, husky and admiring, the "lady" soft, nearer an endearment than a casual title. "Just the usual, eh? Well, at any rate, I'm willing to bet my 'usual' is feeling a whole lot better than your 'usual' at the moment. Being a little salt sticky feels ten times better than yesterday's grime and sand. You should try it."

"I plan to—when I'm by myself."

"You'll feel better."

That would be logical, she thought, because she couldn't feel much worse, but she had no intention of telling him so. And if there was anything that she was feeling, it certainly wasn't very "cool." It had taken every bit of willpower that she possessed to manage her seemingly aloof assessment, and she was now shatteringly aware that his second assumption had been correct—she had liked what she had seen a bit too much. Whoever the hell Kyle the pilot was, it seemed highly possible that he worked out in the same gym as Sylvester Stallone. If he had wanted an assessment of himself at the moment, she could have quickly told him that he was in superb shape—taut and sinewed, broad and tapered. She could have informed him that he spent a lot of time in the sun because he was very darkly tanned except for an area that stretched from high on his hips, over the spot that proved him very amply male, down over the top of his thighs, which probably meant he preferred cutoffs to a bathing suit. Yes, she had liked what she had seen, and it was very disturbing because she was forced to realize that although she had thought of her family and business since the quirk of fate had brought her alive to the island, she hadn't given a single thought to Ted.

I'm supposed to be in love with him, she told herself, summoning up a picture of the man she had always told herself she would eventually marry, when circumstances were right, tragedy behind her, her business flourishing.

Ted. Warm brown eyes, tawny hair, aura of hectic suavity. The vision dissolved, and she couldn't bring it back. How ridiculous, she thought with dismay, because Ted was charming . . . handsome . . . strong . . . They had so much in common, they respected one another, they admired one another . . .

The picture wouldn't return. When Kyle was gone, she assured herself, she would pull out her wallet, she would find the photo of herself with Ted at his last opening, she would remember all the little things, all the endearing nuances of his face.

But she was annoyed that her mental vision had so quickly faded, and she was even more annoyed with herself because she hadn't even given a thought to the man. She should have. Her very first thought should have been of him, knowing he would have to be going crazy when she didn't call.

No, Ted didn't go crazy. He would be strong and silent. Suddenly she found herself growing angry. He should go crazy; he should cry for her.

I'm the crazy one thinking he should be crying when I haven't even thought about him, worried about him.

It's because it has been two months since I've seen him; I've been with Virginia. And she and I have been talking about Steven.

And besides she dragged herself back to present reality and the vision that had sent her into this spiral of shock and thought and defense—it was frankly impossible to picture another body with one very blatantly in front of her.

Skye suddenly realized she was staring.

Alarmed that her afterthoughts could be her undoing

after she had handled the initial situation with such aplomb, Skye hastily pretended to busy herself brushing sand off her clothes.

"Actually," he continued pleasantly, "I didn't intend to assault your sense of decency. You were very soundly sleeping when I set off skinny dipping—snoring like a small dragon—and I didn't think . . ."

"I do not snore!" Skye interrupted with outraged dignity.

He shrugged with a wry smile, neither pushing his point nor acquiescing to hers. "You were definitely soundly out—I didn't think you'd wake up for some time."

Skye grimaced indifferently and rose, carefully checking her ankle as she did so. Although still sore, it accepted its share of weight.

"Go easy on that today," Kyle warned. He was dressed now—or at least he had his pants on. His feet were bare, as was his slick chest, glistening with the saltwater on taut muscles. His dark hair was also very wet and it formed curling waves over his forehead, giving him a much younger look than the austere combing of yesterday. When he grinned now, it was with an almost boyish charm—a far cry from the hard man who had such a talent for slicing into her. Still, she was no fool; the hard man did exist as well as the pleasant one. If she found his physique appealing, it was surely nothing more than an aesthetic appreciation for a fine male specimen.

"I should be able to go nice and easy on my ankle," Skye said dryly. "No marathons to run around here, no place to get in a hurry." Shedding the lightweight jacket of her suit as she moved, Skye walked closer to the fire to inspect the cooking meat. "What is it?" she quizzed him, puzzled.

" 'What is it,' she asks!" He groaned. "What would you expect? Fish."

"I know it's fish," Skye replied with condescending patience, even though she hadn't been at all sure it *was* fish. "What kind of fish?"

"A little yellowtail."

"You caught it?" she queried dubiously, kneeling by the fire and rolling up the sleeves of her blouse as the morning sun was intensely hot. "With what?"

"I speared it," he replied with rueful pride, careful not to tell the number of attempts it had taken. "I'm not sure who was more surprised—me or my victim."

"Well, congratulations," Skye murmured. "Shouldn't we be turning it or something?"

"Yeah." He turned the stick that was poked through the fillet. "I've kept it high to try to smoke it."

"Oh," Skye said simply. She could sew like a dream, but gourmet cooking was not at the top of her talents. She could manage passably with beef and chicken but wisely stuck with specialty restaurants when the desire for seafood hit her. She grinned at him suddenly with grudging admiration. "You certainly do seem to have a knack for some useful things."

"Why thanks, Ms. Delaney." He sank down beside her and returned her grin. "You're going to use a few of your talents today too, ma am!"

"My talents?" Skye frowned. "Like what?" She arched a doubtful brow and scanned their visible world. "Casual wear for those who wish to crash-land on uninhabited tropical islands?"

Kyle laughed good-naturedly and shook his head. "I'm sure you have other talents than design, but actually that is the one I have in mind. As you will have noted, it's hot as the blazes here during the day and a little cool at night. I'm going to cut these pants off—since you've already seen the whole and been totally unimpressed I'm sure bare kneecaps aren't going to offend you—and I suggest you turn that skirt into something more practical. Cut down that blouse. Then use all the scraps and both our jackets to whip up some kind of sheets for bedding with that trusty little sewing kit of yours."

Skye had been frowning as he spoke and when he finished, she tried to keep her voice from quavering. "It sounds as if you think we're going to be here for a long time."

Kyle weighed his answer quickly. He didn't want to depress her, but he didn't want to offer empty promises. Not a single plane had passed them by since yesterday; he had yet to see even a dinghy on the far distant horizon. It must be obvious by now that the Lear had not reached its intended destination. Search parties should have already been out. Of course it was daylight again . . .

"I don't expect we'll be here forever," he said with a casual shrug. "But we might as well get as comfortable as we can while we are here. And we'll remain a great deal saner by keeping busy. Boredom leads to depression. And to nit-picking arguments."

Skye nodded slowly, remembering how quickly last afternoon and evening had gone by once they had started on survival tasks. They had been too involved with work to talk, much less to think up witty sarcasms.

"Is this fish done yet?" she asked. "I'm starving."

"Umm . . . he should be good and done." Kyle removed the crude fillet from the fire, issuing an "ouch" as his finger sizzled in the effort to spit the food on sticks. Skye chuckled, surprising herself with the sound. Even with the odds, it was good to be alive. Laughter was proving to be as irrepressible a human expression as tears.

Kyle half scowled, half smiled. "Okay, duchess, laugh. But hop to. No skimping labor on my island. How about some morning brew."

Skye wrinkled her nose with distaste but collected coconuts. The taste of the juice, or coconut milk as it was called, was something she was going to have to acquire a liking for. But her mouth was parched from the night and her stomach was rumbling, and once Kyle had gouged holes in the coconut with his pocket knife and handed her a piece of fish on a stick, she lit into both greedily.

"How is it?" Kyle inquired.

"Lacking bacon and eggs," Skye acknowledged after swallowing, "it tastes just fine." Her brow knit curiously. "I've always heard that snapper and grouper were the most common fish around reefs. How did you happen to trap a yellowtail?"

His eyes lit with that pleasant sparkle of amusement and he pursed his lips to hold back a chuckle. "A yellowtail is a snapper," he told her.

"Oh." Annoyed at his very ill-concealed humor over her ignorance, she snapped, "I told you I didn't know a damned thing about fishing."

"Did I say anything?" he inquired innocently.

"You don't have to say anything. You're smirking."

"Sorry, I can control my words but not my smirks."

On the verge of anger, Skye suddenly found herself laughing along with him instead. He did seem to be doing his best—except for his taunting over his nudity—to make life pleasant between them. He had rekindled the fire for her during the night; the least she could do was make an effort herself.

"Okay, so now I know that a yellowtail is a snapper," she said easily. "Actually, I'm just glad that you know. I'm sure there must be a pack of inedible fish out there and I surely wouldn't know which were which." She smiled. "And I haven't hit a single bone. I'm glad you have such a talent for cutting a nice fillet."

Kyle shrugged. "I'm sure we'll both be discovering numerous talents."

Skye glanced at him uneasily. "Maybe we won't have to discover many more. It's daylight now; search planes could be out."

"Sure," Kyle agreed, concentrating on his fish and not meeting her eyes.

She didn't like the tone of his voice.

"We will be found—and soon," Skye said stubbornly.

His eyes came to hers with something like malice, taking Skye aback. "Oh, there will be planes out. I'm sure that boyfriend of yours will be searching heaven and earth to retrieve you."

Skye stiffened instantly. "You're right," she said curtly, aware for the first time that he had obviously read articles in which her name appeared. Her relationship with Ted was one of her own choosing, but she still resented being judged because her private life had been exploited in tabloids.

"Why haven't you ever married him?" Kyle demanded abruptly.

"I don't think that's any of your business," Skye informed him coldly.

Kyle shrugged indifferently. "If what I've read is true, you've been seeing Ted Trainor for four years. That's a long time to make up your mind, lady. Something must be wrong there."

"I repeat"—Skye was icy—"it's none of your business." He shrugged again and Skye was startled by the depth of annoyance he had managed to bring out in her. "There is absolutely nothing wrong,"—she heard herself saying, explaining where no explanation was needed. "Ted is a wonderful human being, he's—"

"Oh, Lord!" Kyle chuckled, undaunted by her cool vehemence. "A wonderful human being? Oh, honey, there is something wrong!"

"How the hell would you know?" Skye demanded, fully irritated with herself and him. She should be the one shrugging; she was confident in her relationship. And what difference did this stranger's opinion make anyway? Still, she heard herself answering. He was baiting her and she knew it but she was going for the bait. "For your information, just in case you lose your flying job and look for employment among the less reputable newspapers, Ted Trainor is everything any woman could want. He's sharp as a whip, industrious, talented—"

"Good-looking?" Kyle supplied with a grin.

"Very," Skye replied coolly, continuing with, "Extremely gallant, strong, charming . . .

"Rugged and yet sensitive," Kyle added with a brow raised mockingly as her voice trailed off.

"That's right." Ted was all those things, Skye thought, so why was she defending him when it wasn't at all necessary. Because she was on the defensive; he seemed to know quite a bit about her, even though he had made no allusions to his knowledge until now. Yet she still knew nothing about him.

"Actually"—Skye smiled with sweet sarcasm—"Ted is quite similar to you in looks. You're about the same height, same build, but there the similarity ends. Ted would never be so rude as to quiz a mere acquaintance on her personal life. Nor would he have any problem adapting to simple, restrained civility were he in your position!"

"Ahhh . . . strong, silent type."

Skye saw that beyond his serious and humble comment he was laughing at her, egging her on. She regained her cool and smiled again—this time with guileless innocence.

"That's right."

"He does sound perfect," Kyle agreed. He finished his last morsel of fish and said blandly, "Is the problem in bed?"

Skye hadn't finished her fish, and her last morsel caught in her throat, causing her to gasp with great indignity. She was thoroughly chagrined to see the laughter in his satyric green gaze.

"That is definitely none of your business."

"Oh, so the problem is in bed."

"Don't be ridiculous!" Skye denied hotly. "We have no pro—" She broke off, realizing her denial was just what he had searched for. "I really don't care to discuss my life with you."

"Fine."

He fell silent, lighting up a cigarette and gazing out to sea. Skye should have left things alone, but for unknown reasons she couldn't. She couldn't understand why he had irritated her so, and she simply wanted to turn the tables.

"I'm sure all your relationships are perfect."

"Far from it."

"I don't see why," she murmured sarcastically. "You must be charming. An island-hopping pilot spending all his free time running around in cutoffs—"

"Cutoffs?" He picked up on the word and raised an amused, questioning brow as he leaned toward her. "That was an astute observation. You do take in all that you see, don't you." He laughed insinuatingly.

She hadn't blushed at the sight of him, she hadn't blushed during his irreverent probing, but now, with his face so close to hers, his bronzed chest near, broad and admirably muscled, matted with hair, she felt the heat rise to her cheeks.

She had been very observant . . . too observant.

What is the matter with me, she wondered. She hadn't been with him a full day, but she was sure she disliked him.

And still he held a strange influence over her. He could anger her, infuriate her . . . and yet she felt dizzy around him. Her heart pounded to a strange new beat . . . her blood surged.

It was the tropics, she thought, the heat of the tropics. Everything was coming home to her, memories of Steven.

And of her own fears where Ted was concerned.

Why hadn't she married him?

She did love Ted, and it was a good love, a quiet love, born of countless hours together, of companionship . . .

Then why hadn't she been able to make a commitment, and why was she now sitting within touching distance of this rude stranger, wishing she had the nerve to reach out that short distance and actually touch him?

"I'm not particularly observant!" Skye snapped, withdrawing. "I'm simply not blind."

He laughed suddenly, and it was a pleasant sound. It made Skye think that they were strangers, and yet not strangers.

In all this time Ted had never once concerned himself with her fear of the dark; he had never talked to her about Steven; he had held her, but she had lost her twin, and he hadn't understood how terrible it had been. He hadn't been there.

"I'm glad to hear it!" Kyle said, brushing her cheek with a light, oddly sensuous finger. "You're going to need your eyesight, woman, because we've got work to do."

"Twenty questions is over?" Skye asked dryly.

"For the moment."

"Saved by the need for manual labor!"

"Ummmm," Kyle murmured dryly, rising and dusting sand from his pants. "Let's get started. Hit those scissors of yours, woman."

"Would you stop that!" Skye objected.

"Stop what?"

"Referring to me as 'woman'!"

He grinned, a brilliant, teasing glimmer in his eyes. "Too macho, eh? Sorry, maybe it's a hard habit to break. Besides, a man needs some form of amusement, and as sad as this may sound, it's fun to irritate you. You hold your own quite nicely, and since I've so far been builder, provider, and cook, you need to get your fanny going so I'm entitled to address you as I please."

Unable to dispute the fact that he had carried the bulk

of work, Skye silently procured her scissors. Ignoring his statement, she asked curtly, "What do you want cut?"

"My pants."

"While they are on you?"

"I'll be happy to take them off," he supplied with an evil amiability.

"No thanks!" Skye retorted, kneeling to plunge her shears into the material on his muscled thighs. She was keenly aware of his body heat as she surveyed the project. "How short do you want them?"

"Pretty short!" He chuckled, seeming to sense her discomfort.

He didn't see the uneasy flush she quickly covered with a scowl. "Careful then that you don't move, Kyle. I'd hate to wound . . . your pride."

She heard his chuckle, low and throaty, and his swift rejoinder. "You may be a brave young woman, Ms. Delaney, but I don't think you're quite that brave. Or stupid."

Compressing her lips, Skye set to snipping material, shocked and dismayed again to find that the task was giving her a certain pleasure. Her fingertips were achingly responsive to each brush with his flesh; sensitized nerves seemed to be sending warning signals that both chilled and burned her. Each snip of fabric was making her keenly aware that she was stranded with a very sensual man. And worse, much worse, he was very easily creating very sensual feelings within herself.

She still wasn't sure she even liked him; she *was* sure that *he* was a man who barely tolerated women. Cute playthings for occasional amusement and comfort seemed to be his estimation of the female of the species.

She had no intention of being a sexually obliging companion for such a man simply because they happened to be stuck together. Especially when she still didn't know a thing about *him*.

It was a pity, because like it or not, if she were honest

with herself, she would have to admit that, despite herself, despite her loyalties, she was being subtly but completely stimulated. She was enjoying each touch, enjoying his towering nearness, his deep masculine laughter.

"God I hope we get off this island quickly!" she muttered heatedly.

She was treated to more of his throaty male laughter. His pleasure brought fear. There was mockery in that laughter, as if he had read her thoughts with embarrassing ease and did indeed find great humor in her discomfort.

"Quit laughing and stand still!" she hissed, snapping her sheers in an ominous warning as she rounded one strong thigh.

"Yes, ma'am, whatever you say," he replied with husky gravity.

But although she couldn't see his face, she knew the leaf-green eyes were still flecked with brilliant, taunting merriment.

"But," he added, a very slight warning note in his tone, "I think we both know that you'll be very careful, don't we?"

Skye took a deep breath and replied through clenched teeth.

"I'm always very careful."

"How nice for you. That is something we'll see about it, isn't it?"

"Oh, God! Are you exasperating!" Skye groaned.

"I think I'm a lot more than that, lady," he replied, gone curiously sincere.

They both fell silent. Skye thought he was right. He had to be a whole lot more than she had acknowledged at first.

He was probably much, much more than she dared take a chance to discover.

Three

"Thanks," Kyle said, stepping out from the shorn pants legs. He started off down the beach. "Try to have something done by the time I get back, okay?"

Skye twitched her lips into a smile over bared teeth. "Sure. I'll scrub the floors and Lysol the bath. Where are you going?"

He half turned around but continued walking. "To scrounge through the wreckage. Maybe find something useful—or the log."

"The log?"

"Captain's log. It should have survived the explosion."

Skye watched uneasily as he jogged down the sand, a rugged figure in the lopped-off pants with muscles glistening in bronze play as he ran. What an enigma. She felt as if she were befriending a Doberman. Sturdy, sleek, confident—sometimes affectionate, growling in an instant, and possibly ready to bite with a paw still in your hand.

Ah, well, you could choose your friends, but not your relatives or those who happened to crash with you on remote islands.

Collecting the remnants of his pants, Skye took them back to the hut, where she gathered both their jackets and tossed all the articles together. With all good intentions she began to rip the lining out of her own jacket, but her hands paused in the action. She set the material aside instead and delved into the canvas bag for her purse. Opening it, she stupidly felt tears sting her eyes.

Makeup. By this time of the morning she should have had herself together. Simple routine. Fifteen minutes of carefully applying powders and creams to her face. Carefully, just so that she would look natural, as if she hadn't spent fifteen minutes putting powders and creams on her face. But it was time well spent. Time that let you feel your best if you hadn't slept quite so well, if you weren't quite pleased with your coloring, if you needed just a touch of shadow to bring out a good point.

Her fingers tightened over a plastic snap case of shadows. The stinging tears beneath her lids threatened to fall, and she choked back a sob. Rising, she stepped from the cover of the hut and hurled the case toward the haphazard growth of the inner island, her tenaciously contained sob becoming a wailed curse.

The small plastic case wouldn't even go far. She watched, clenching down hard on her jaw, feeling her teeth grate, as it fell into the sand not far from her.

She spun on her heels and returned to the hut, sinking forlornly to sit with crossed legs before the pile of fabric that had once been clothing for a normal day.

Her makeup, such a little thing, such a small part of life. None of it mattered here. She could imagine Kyle's laughter if she were to pull out a tube of lipstick after a meal of coconuts.

Her tears of self-pity threatened and threatened, but it became a game of self-torture to hold them back. Knowing it was foolish to do so, she pulled out her wallet. Money, she thought, wryly. How worthless. But she hadn't pulled out her wallet to glance at the paper and coin that now meant nothing; she wanted to see the pictures she kept neatly tucked in clear vinyl. Pictures that could remind her there was a real world.

Pictures to remind her of Ted. And there he was. Ted

with his wonderful warm eyes, smiling candidly for the camera. Was his nose really that long, she wondered silently. Funny, she couldn't have possibly forgotten how he looked.

She flipped to the next photograph, Ted and her together, a picture of elegance at his last opening. He was a handsome man; they were a truly handsome couple.

Why couldn't she reach him? The picture refused to become real for her. The image of the man wouldn't come alive to her mind.

Skye closed her eyes. She concentrated. But the only thing she could remember was the day, over a year ago, when she had asked him to accompany her to Australia. The day when Virginia had called to tell her to come quickly, that she was worried.

"Oh, hon, I can't come," Ted had apologized. "That English import is due to open next week. I have to be here, that is, unless it's an absolute emergency."

She should have told him. She should have said it. Yes, it's an emergency. It's the end of a part of my life, it's the gravest emergency I'll probably ever have in my life . . . Don't you understand, it's Steven, and we're twins, Ted. Can you imagine what that means?

But she hadn't said any of that. He knew. He knew Steven was terribly ill. It was an emergency, her emergency.

She had smiled. She couldn't let him in, not when he refused to see. He didn't want to see. "No," she said aloud. "I understand. You need to be here . . ."

"Steven will hold his own," Ted had assured her. "I'm positive everything will be okay."

"Sure," Skye had told him. But she hadn't felt the optimism she had tried to portray; it was as if she knew. And everything hadn't been okay . . . chemotherapy, radiation . . . nothing could have helped him any longer.

Steven had died.

And then she hadn't wanted Ted for the funeral; she hadn't been able to accept the awkward comfort he had tried to give . . .

Skye flipped to another photo. She knew the picture. Steven and Virginia and her, sipping wine before the fire in Sydney, celebrating the day Delaney Designs had come out of the red—a victory accomplished before a year of existence.

Skye snapped the photo section of her wallet closed. She dropped it to her lap and pressed hard on her temples with both hands. It was the past; she wasn't going to cry, she wasn't . . . she was going to concentrate on the present.

Which was just as depressing, she thought, biting her lip. No! They would get off the island, rescue would come; it had to.

Skye put everything back in her purse and her purse back into the canvas bag. She would try not to look at her things again. They were too incongruous, too ironic, with only sea and sand and wild growth around her.

Keep busy, Kyle had said. She sighed. He was right. Dwelling on the fact that she was on the island with only his holiness for company could quickly drive her up a wall of frustrated self-pity and . . . anger and fear.

Because she was afraid of him, very afraid of the way he made her think and feel.

She picked up her jacket again and started ripping once more. She looked at the bits and pieces of fabric around her. Sheets out of this. A giggle—slightly hysterical, but a giggle still—escaped her. She could just see the trade papers. DELANEY ENTERPRISES TAKES ON NEW LINE: DESIGNER BED CLOTHING IN UNIQUE NEW REMNANT GUISE.

Perhaps she should start with herself, she thought ruefully. Her clothing had been just perfect for air-conditioned rooms; here, with the coming of the sun, it was sheer murder. Casting a wary eye down the beach to assure herself of privacy, she slipped out of her long-sleeved blouse and skirt, frowned, and started cutting.

Forty-five minutes later she was able to look at her new creations with a bit of surprised wonder. She had never doubted her design ability under normal circumstances, but it was somewhat astounding that what she had produced from the business suit with her "trusty little sewing kit" actually looked as if it had been planned as a shorts set all along.

Skye peeled down the tattered remains of her stockings and almost cast them into the remains of the fire, then stopped herself. They might become useful as something later. Glancing at the sky, she saw that the sun was directly overhead, its billowing heat visible. She was grateful Kyle had suggested they curtail their clothing as much as possible. Although the hut was affording her shade, it was swelteringly hot.

"Too hot to make sheets!" she complained aloud to a slender palm encroaching on the sand. But she remembered his jibe that she get something done and wrinkled her nose at the absurd combinations of fabric nearby. Sighing, she began to rip and piece, tearing out linings from every square inch of material. They were going to be very short sheets!

And it was going to take more than a morning to sew them. Her fingers began to tire, and she swiped a slight beading of perspiration from her forehead with the back of an arm. Gazing out to the miraculously clear ocean, she suddenly realized that she hadn't taken time for her bath—and that it was probably now or never with Kyle nowhere in sight. Clutching her new short pants and sleeveless shirt, Skye deposited them by the fire along with her underthings. Tentatively glancing along the shore, she satisfied herself that she was still alone and plunged into the water.

Skye wasn't big on beaches, she far preferred to swim in a pool, but she had to admit that the water of their little lost paradise was exquisite. Standing breast high, she could still see the sandy floor and her feet. No beer cans, she thought. But what was good for the ecology was bad for her. No garbage meant no people! She felt a chilling depression despite the warmth of the water and the day. Kyle had warned her to attempt to light their SOS signal only when there was something to attract—a ship or boat on the horizon or a plane in the sky.

There still hadn't been a single thing to attract! Surely rescue planes, knowing they were lost, should have flown over by now! They had been missing almost an entire day.

Something fluttered by her leg and she glanced down to see a school of tiny brilliant fish flash by in startling yellow. They were beautiful, and at any other time they might have cheered her. Now they only proved to press home the point that she was far from her known world of skyscrapers and busy streets, the blare of horns, the plush comfort of executive offices.

Dejected, her head hung low as she slowly began to walk from the water, only to freeze at the sound of a mocking voice.

"Really, Ms. Delaney! Haven't you a shred of decency in you?"

Startled, Skye looked up to see that Kyle had returned while her mind had been wandering. She felt herself flush from her toes to the roots of her hair—though she wasn't quite sure whether she was more angry or embarrassed. Legs slightly apart and feet firmly planted in the sand, arms crossed over his chest, alight with the pleasure of a satisfying revenge, he watched her expectantly—no sign of mercy whatsoever in the strongly chiseled features.

Skye automatically crossed her arms over her chest. She wondered fleetingly if she might appeal to his better nature, then cast aside the notion as futile. He didn't appear to have a better nature at the moment.

"I don't suppose I could get you to walk nicely back to where you came from?" she tried irritably.

"No." He grinned with a pleasant little shake of the head. "I don't suppose that you could."

"Do you know," Skye began, her voice low and calm, conversational, "it might be to your advantage to humor me now and then. When we get to civilization, what I have to say about your handling of crisis situations just might have some effect on your future job security."

"Oh?" he inquired with smiling interest. "Are you that influential?"

Skye shrugged. "I frequently fly Executive Charters."

"How nice."

Despite his pleasant tone, Skye suddenly realized she had made a mistake. "Since you've seen fit so kindly to offer me fair warning," he continued, a chilling razor's edge to his amiable tone, "I suppose I should do the same. Don't threaten me, Ms. Delaney. It can do nothing but create an adverse reaction."

Knowing she had failed completely, Skye exploded with a single expletive and defiantly marched from the water, allowing her arms to swing proudly at her sides as she passed him.

He caught her upper arm with an easy grip that jerked her back. She met his eyes, fury kindled in her own. He was once again amused.

"Aren't you going to offer to turn around?"

"Take another hike, will you!" she snapped, wrenching free her arm and continuing her determined march. Her exit from his reach might have been dignified except that his throaty laughter followed her, and she was sure he could see pink, red, and crimson coloring her body from head to toe. Unwilling to dress before unrelentless, mirthful eyes, she snatched up her clothing and kept walking until she was swallowed up by the high grass and trees. In the shelter of a little banana cluster she fumbled into her clothing, cursing him all the while. Still unwilling to face him, she decided a little island exploration on her own just might be a good idea.

She knew there wasn't too much on the island that could hurt her. Kyle had told her yesterday that the worst she could come across would be a wild boar—mean and dangerous, yes, possibly, but most usually more than ready to leave you alone if you left it alone.

The island was small. Kyle had also mentioned that it was barely two miles square. Even stepping gingerly with bare feet and occasionally squeezing through close trees, it didn't seem to take long to reach the other side. Once there though, she realized that her walk had tired her and her feet were sore—scratched from the rough ground after usually being pampered. It would be nice, she thought, if she could just return by the sand, but the area fringing their hut was not sand. It was thick mangrove root reaching far out into the water. She wasn't sure she could swim far enough to make it around the trees. Sighing, she stared out into the water—another stretch of apparent nothingness—then started back the way she had come.

Skye gave her full attention to the terrain. It was not until she had scrambled her way through the low underbrush and neared the grass plain that she took notice of the sky and the fact that the sun was no longer shining brilliantly. It had grown muggy, the sky had become a dull billowy gray, and although the atmosphere seemed dead still, she could see the rapid movement of angry clouds across the sky.

Forgetting her wrath at Kyle, Skye began to hurry, much more concerned for her comfort and well-being if a storm broke. She almost missed the glass dimly reflecting the haze—she did, in fact, walk right past it, pause curiously, turn back, and search the high grass.

It was with jubilation that her hands closed over the sure sign that some modern man somewhere did know that the island existed—a funny, beautiful green-toned bottle with Coca-Cola in script around it. Thrilled with her discovery, Skye forgot entirely the anger that had sent her walking off and almost ran back to the hut, her face illuminated radiantly.

Kyle was pacing up and down a square of shoreline, his expression nearly as thunderous as the sky. She never had a chance to shout out her good news; at the first sight of her, he stalked to her, flapping her shoulders hard and shaking her as he demanded, "Where the hell have you been?"

Confused and stunned by his rough attitude, she shouted back, "I went for a walk—if it's any of your business! I don't remember appointing you my keeper!"

"Well I am your keeper, you little nitwit, while we're on this island! Your hours aren't your own anymore. You have me to report to!"

"Of all the audacity—" Skye protested furiously.

"Yes, of all the audacity. I'm trying to keep you from killing yourself like a fool. Haven't you seen the sky?"

Skye stiffened in his grip and pulled back. She didn't like his punishing hands on her shoulders; she didn't like his eyes boring into hers as if he were an avenging Saint Peter and she an errant sinner. She did not like the indignity of being shaken—it had been years, years since anyone had done such a thing to her, and that anyone had been her father when she was a very small child.

"Of course I've seen the sky. It's going to rain." she replied coldly.

"Rain! Oh, honey, it's going to do a hell of a lot more than rain!" he exploded. "You little idiot, you've had me half sick with worry. That isn't a little squall working up out there—it's a full-scale tropical storm!"

Skye felt the color draining from her face. "I don't think the winds will be stronger than seventy-five miles an hour, but believe me, Ms. Executive, seventy-five miles an hour can kill! At best we have a few hours to batten down before that weather breaks and you're off for a walk!"

"Well, how the hell was I supposed to know a storm would brew up?" Skye raged, dangerously close to tears but determined never, never to cry in front of such a monstrously hard person. "It was brilliant blue when I left!"

"That's the point, damn you!" he hissed, pushing her from himself. "You don't know! You don't seem to know a damned thing, so don't go running off to sulk!"

"I wasn't sulking!" Skye raged, hands clenching into tense fists at her side. Damn, he was abominable! "And save yourself some grief—don't worry about me. You are not my keeper so if I kill my stupid little self it won't have to be on your conscience."

She spun around as if she were about to leave again, although all she intended was to escape with dignity the battle she couldn't expect to win. His arm lit on hers again and she was swung back into his grip. "Not this time, Ms. Delaney. You take one step outside of my vision and you sure as hell won't be *sitting* the storm out—if you catch my meaning. I'm not Joe the handyman or Billy butler. You can get busy with me right now."

She was good at controlling her temper; she really was. Still, controlling it around him was like asking a volcano not to blow. Never, never, never in her life had she ever come across such an irritating and abusive human being. And she had to be stuck with this one! Infuriatingly dependent on him. She stared at him so long with dagger-like malice in her eyes that the shift of the wind changed and a salt breeze began to fan her face. She had counted to one hundred. Now she brought her stare from his eyes to the large brown hand clenching the soft flesh of her upper arm and back to his eyes with pointed contempt. "If you will let go of me, I'll be happy to follow your work instructions. Just for casual information, I was not planning to walk off anywhere. I merely hoped that the urge to prefer the storm to you might pass if I alleviated myself of the aggravation of listening to you and watching you shout!"

Once more he released her with a small shove. "Start collecting things. We're going to have to brace and bury what we've got in the strongest tree shelters." His gaze drifted to her hand. "What's that?"

Skye followed his eyes with hers to the forgotten Coca-Cola bottle. "It's encouragement and hope, Kyle," she spat. "There have been people on this island before. They left it behind."

"Save it," he barked. "We can use any kind of container."

They barely spoke to one another as they gathered the few things they possessed. With every passing second, it became more and more apparent that they were going to be hit by one bad storm. Kyle made a deep shelter for their few utensils in the harbor of a deeply rooted mangrove and finally turned to her, giving her his full attention.

"We have to lash to the tree!" he shouted. Skye wasn't sure what he meant, but the mood to argue with him had passed, blown clearly away by the wind that increased with ferocity each time she drew a breath. It howled and moaned around her, chilling her with the smell of rain it carried. The sky was no longer gray, but increasingly black.

And then the rain did start. Not in gentle pelts like yesterday, but in saturating, stinging buckets. Skye opened her mouth to reply to him, but it was immediately filled by wind and water. Choking, she reached out to him.

A strong, steady hand gripped hers and pulled her along. With firm, pressure he pushed her down to the sturdy root trunk of a tree, one that she could wrap her arms around, and before she knew what he was doing, she found herself secured there, tied by a swatch made from the half-sewn material remnants she had left earlier.

And she was scared. Through the screeching wind and blinding rain, she could see the high grass laid flat; the tips of palms bent low to the ground, kneeling in supplication to the storm. Soaked, trembling, freezing, and miserable, she realized she had never been more scared in her life, not even when she knew the plane was going down. Blackness had claimed her quickly then—this she was having to endure. Her tears were once more mingling with the rain.

Skye strained around to search for Kyle but soaked strands of her hair clung to her face and obscured her vision. But he was there. A second later she felt him, the wide breadth of his chest against her back, his face near her ear as he struggled tensely to secure another of his makeshift ropes around the tree. Giddy with relief yet terrified he might see her tears, she snapped, "Can't find your own tree, huh?"

"Shut up," he hissed.

She complied, grateful to feel the taut pull of his muscles against her as he strained with another knot. Finished with the task, his arms came around her. They both hugged the tree like a pair of doubled-up koala bears.

So far they had only tasted the beginning of the storm. It raged on and on, increasing to a frenzied pitch, wailing like a fleet of vengeful banshees, destroying like the hand of Almighty God sent down from the heavens to heave and toss indiscriminately. Trees bent and soared, massive branches snapped like twigs, and somewhere, not far from them, the ocean swirled and foamed in white-tipped fury. Its sound was part of that banshee wail that screeched with the wind, a thousand demons in a ravaging orgy.

Skye clung to the tree as if its bark was life itself. Branches snapped and swirled around her, but Kyle had chosen well. Their angle and that of the nearby old, sturdy trunks kept them from being bombarded by the flying missiles that whistled clearly by their ears.

The fury of the storm seemed endless. Her arms were stiff and seemed frozen around the tree; every breath she took was a great effort as she fought for air against the power of the assault of wind and water.

Yet still in her misery there was warmth, supplied by Kyle's protecting form around her. It was the only warmth, and against all else she was barely aware of it. Only when the wind would die to renew itself to die to shriek again, would she feel the expansion of his chest and hear the barely audible whisper of his breath. There were times when she felt as if they were one, and in the endless flurry of thoughts that riddled her mind through the holocaust, she was fervently grateful for him, for the heat he supplied, for the endurance his powerful embrace brought to her.

The storm left them as it had come, slowly, at first imperceptibly. But bit by bit, through the chattering, semilucid state of Skye's consciousness, she realized the winds were abating. The deluge became a gentle patter. Skye shifted against her human shelter.

"Not yet," he whispered hoarsely to her.

Her flesh was as cold as ice; her muscles and limbs as stiff. "I can't stay here anymore," she moaned, "I can't . . ."

"You have to. This may just be the eye passing."

And so they waited. Skye couldn't control her shivering, even as he wrapped more tightly about her. Then finally, when Skye was sure she could hold her wet and frigid position no longer, Kyle began tearing at their bonds. A moment later he moved laboriously to his feet. Skye attempted to do the same, but her numbed limbs simply wouldn't obey her. She would have fallen had he not been there to grab her.

"I—I'm all right," she protested as he swung her into his arms.

"Yes," he said, a faint grin twisting his lips. "Yes, I think that you are." But he didn't set her down.

The rain ceased entirely as he picked his way through the tangle of destruction that was the island. When they reached the beach—the sand only partially visible, its surface literally dotted with the palm debris from the inland—Skye saw with utter amazement that it was still daylight. Pink was streaking through the gray—the storm was going to leave in its wake a glorious sunset.

"I don't believe it," Kyle said incredulously.

"What?" Skye demanded.

"The posts stood!" Kyle dumped her to her feet and rushed to the remains of their hut, staring at the four corners that still stood. "I'm a better builder than I thought!"

Skye watched him, partially amazed that he seemed so oblivious to discomfort after the storm, partially amused at his boyish pride.

She cleared her throat, hoping her wet and cold state wasn't going to lead to pneumonia. "What do we do now?" she asked.

He looked back to her, his eyes surprisingly gentle. "We start over," he told her softly. "Shouldn't be too hard—we didn't have that much to begin with." He walked back to her and set his hands upon her shoulders. "You okay?"

Skye nodded slowly, aware there was a lump in her throat. "Yeah," she said huskily. "Except that I'm freezing and everything is sopped."

"We'll get a fire going."

"How? Nothing will be dry?"

"First," he said, tapping her chin, "we'll go see if our little cache survived. We'll find enough kindling that isn't saturated and get it going with some of the alcohol." Suddenly he was off again across the foliage-strewn beach. "Coming?"

Skye blinked, wondering at his easy ability to get on without crying over spilt milk. "Might as well," she returned briskly, adding dryly, "I certainly don't have any other pressing appointments."

An hour later, just as the sky cleared entirely and the sun made a belated attempt to reign through clouds, Skye and Kyle returned to the beach with the last of their supplies. Kyle set determinedly to creating a fire while Skye studiously attempted to release the knots in the material ropes Kyle had made earlier.

"Boy Scout, hell!" She heard Kyle chuckle exuberantly. "I am a damn Eagle Scout!"

Skye glanced at the fire, which was picking up a cheerful blaze. She was very pleased at the idea of some warmth, but couldn't help feeling a tinge of resentment. Wasn't there anything he didn't handle capably?

"Eagle Scout all the way," she muttered, taking her task to the fire.

He scowled at her. "Hey, you could have done worse."

"Yes," she admitted quietly, "I could have done worse." She clenched her teeth together and strained against a knot that wouldn't give. "Damn," she murmured irritably. Her eyes rose to meet his. "I guess *you* could have done a bit better," she half apologized.

Kyle bent low beside her on one knee. He reached out with his thumb and very gently drew a soft pattern from her cheekbone to her lips, pausing just momentarily to rub her lower lip. "I don't think I did badly at all," he told her. His hand dropped to his side and the extremely husky timbre left his voice. "You never did give me a chance to make a return assessment," he teased.

"Pardon?" Skye demanded, bewildered both by his words and the strange, chemical emotion that seemed to fill her with warmth at his tender touch.

His grin went rakishly wicked. "Very nice backside!" He chuckled. "Very nice, ah, everything!"

"Ohhh!" Skye murmured, creating her own warmth as a wealth of heat flushed her face. Further confused, she turned her attention back to the knots that stubbornly resisted the efforts of her fingers. She couldn't be insulted; in fact, it pleased her very much that *he* found her *pleasing*. But she had to tread warily. They were alone in a perilous situation, and he was proving to be very much a man—wasn't that something that automatically called out to feminine instincts? Skye didn't want to come too close. They seemed to be veritable opposites prone to easy argument. If they had met under other circumstances, would they have even given one another a second glance?

But why did his touch thrill her so, send the ache of fire burning sensuously through her bloodstream. Now that the crisis was over and the wind no longer pounded against reason, she could remember the feel of his powerful body harboring hers so clearly. Half the time she was ready to hit him, but she was slowly finding that the intrigue to touch him, to press herself against the auburn mat of his bronze, gleaming chest, was becoming almost a mystical compulsion. Of all the men she had met in her lifetime, he was unique: sometimes brash, sometimes tender. She didn't know who he was, and yet she had never met a man more confident of *what* he was.

Skye decided her best course of action at the moment would be to change the subject—and not discuss any of the confusion she was feeling. "I thought you said it wasn't going to be a typhoon?" she accused.

"That was hardly a typhoon!" he assured her, withdrawing slightly. Had he expected her to make a comment on his favorable assessment of her physical attributes? Was he disappointed that she had neither sprung to anger nor floundered with embarrassment?

"Those winds were nothing," he continued. "I've seen them when they've destroyed entire villages, when the tidal wash created has shifted entire coastlines."

Skye shivered slightly; a chill she hoped was not apparent creeped along her spine. She didn't want to ever see another storm in the South Pacific, and yet here they were marooned. What if another storm blew in, a storm with winds more vicious . . .

She cleared her throat, not about to let him sense her fear. "How long have you been flying, Kyle?"

She should have noticed that his smile held a wry trace of amusement as he slowly replied, "Awhile. About twenty-four years."

Her eyes widened a hair. He appeared to be in his early thirties, but she suddenly realized that couldn't possibly be. Not if he had been flying that long. Her curiosity satisfied, she noted inwardly with surprise that she really hadn't asked him a thing about himself. She didn't even know his last name.

"I lied about my age and joined the Air Force at sixteen," he explained without further questioning.

"How do you like flying for Executive Charters?" Skye asked.

There seemed to be another devilish glint to his smile, but it was quickly masked. "Why do you ask like that?" he said softly.

Skye shrugged. "Just because I hear that it's a perfectionist operation. That the owner of the company is great on pay and benefits, but one hell of a tyrant."

"Oh?" Kyle's brows rose. "What else have you heard?"

Again Skye shrugged. "Oh, not too much. Your boss is never photographed, you know. I read one small article on him that compared him to a present-day Howard Hughes. A bit of recluse, you know?"

"Eccentric, eh?" Kyle murmured dryly.

Skye laughed. "You tell me! All I know is what I've read. You work for the man."

"No," Kyle interjected, "you tell me what you've read and think and then I'll tell you how it compares to what I know!"

"Okay," Skye agreed, glad to have her mind distracted from reminders of the storm. "K. A. Jagger—self-made millionaire, surely ruthless and relentless. Started off with nothing and created an empire—the largest fleet of private Lears anywhere in the world. Fame and fortune, however, made him a tyrannical despot. About ten years ago he threw out his wife of a decade, and since then he has been linked with names of stage and screen, all sorts of international beauties. Which just goes to prove that money can buy anything," she added with a small, wry smile. "He has never been divorced, so all these lovelies are content to bask in his aura of power and accept whatever he magnanimously gives." If she hadn't been caught up in her storytelling, Skye might have noticed that Kyle didn't appear to be quite so amused. His gaze had become distant and cool again; his eyes were narrowed in a way that might be construed as dangerous by an astute observer.

"He sounds like a monster," Kyle said.

"I would imagine," Skye agreed.

"So why do you fly the lines?"

"What do I care about the owner?" Skye laughed. "I fly to Australia frequently. I buy my gold straight out of the mines, and, of course, Virginia is there . . ." Her voice trailed away for a second, and then she continued. "Executive Charters gets me where I want to go when I need to be there. Usually," she amended with a wince.

Skye hesitated uneasily for a second before adding, "And they've never had a crash before, you know."

"Yes, I know," Kyle answered bitterly.

Fervently wishing she had kept her mouth tactfully closed, Skye fell silent for a moment. There had been many a time when she had wished to wound him, but now wasn't one of them, nor did she wish to cause him the pain her simple words had brought. She opened her mouth to say something, then let it fall shut. What could she say? They had crashed. He wasn't the type of man who would appreciate her sympathy. Was he worried about his job, if and when rescue came? Perhaps she could assure him on that count without sounding as if she were patronizing him or offering pity.

"Don't worry about your employer," she finally told him, opting for a teasing vein. "I'll be happy to inform him that only your skill landed us alive. And," she added impishly, "keep up the good work around the island and I'll even stretch the truth a bit and tell him you were charming—a perfect representative of his airline!"

Kyle raised a brow with wry skepticism. "Is that bribery?"

There was a subtle change in his eyes, something akin to challenge, that made Skye wary. She was suddenly sorry she had tried to be nice. Sympathy was wasted on him. An interlude of civility with him was just that—an interlude and nothing more. She knew by his cool, mocking expression that any moment he would return to his assumption of autocratic command again.

"Yes, it is bribery," she snapped with annoyance. She smiled with a warning sarcasm. "Toe the line, Kyle," she informed him, allowing her tone to leave doubt as to whether she was serious or teasing, "or I'll happily inform your boss that you're a bit of a monster yourself!"

"Really?" His voice was soft, his brow still slightly raised. "That's not bribery," he said, kneeling beside her and tugging the fabric she still struggled with from her hands. "That sounds just like blackmail."

Fascinated as the stubborn knots gave way instantly beneath the power of Kyle's hands, Skye felt herself growing more defensive. "Maybe it is," she replied, trying for a light tone. What was the matter with her? she wondered fleetingly. She couldn't seem to find middle ground with this man. He could raise her temper with a look, send unwanted shivers racing along her spine with mere proximity. He frightened her, he infuriated her, he compelled her.

"I told you I don't like threats," he said, his lips set in a tight but apparently pleasant smile as he brought a finger to lift her chin. Skye was tempted to tear away from him in panic, while at the same time she felt mesmerized by his eyes. They seemed to root her to the spot.

What happened? she wondered desperately. A moment ago they had been engaged in idle conversation. She had simply been talking, he had been polite, they had been putting the storm behind them.

And now there was suddenly a tension between them, tangible, explosive. She was drawn to the power that emanated from him, yet she felt the need to fight it, to assert herself, to set up a barrier before she found herself running with no more chance of escape than a mouse cornered by a cat.

She raised her chin above the pressure of his finger. A soft, cynical chuckle escaped her. "You don't like threats? I'm so sorry. I don't care for being pushed around—and you're quite adept at pushing." She sighed with mock resignation. "I'm afraid I have a talent for threats."

"That's too bad for you, Ms. Delaney," he said, that quiet tone still with him, his tight but amiable smile still in place.

Then the smile disappeared. Skye was made aware that she had been a cornered mouse all along—the cat pounced. With mercurial swiftness, she found herself brought flat to the sand, her shoulders pressed down effortlessly by his hands. He hovered above her, his volatile energy still leashed, but all the more frightening because it was so obviously under control. Stunned as she stared at him, Skye was tempted to howl with frustration. At the moment she wanted nothing more than to be able to tear him to shreds. He was in a position to do exactly as he pleased, and she hated him for it.

"Get off of me!" she hissed but she was rudely interrupted by a cutting laugh.

"Or what?"

"What do you mean?"

"Or what? You just informed me you had a talent for threats. Go ahead. Threaten me. What are you going to do?"

Skye had never felt such a pure blinding rage before. Tears formed in her eyes and she closed them, trying to wrench free of his grasp. He calmly straddled her, holding his weight off of her, pinioning her down. She was growing incensed and panicked, and despite all logic and reason, she began to flail madly against him. So much for civilization! Away from law and structure for a day and they were reverting to caveman and his captured prey.

No! I'm *not*, she told herself. He is . . . he's stronger and he's taking full advantage of that simple fact. But that wasn't it. She had the sudden feeling that Kyle would disregard any but his own moral law wherever he was. She struggled madly just to strike him.

And he was finding all her efforts nothing less than amusing. Nonchalantly, with less effort than he would probably need to swat a bothersome fly, he captured both her wrists, and held them calmly, securing them with the long, powerful fingers of one hand. Seething and shivering with her frustrated rage, Skye finally lay still, watching him, the will to commit murder shining in her eyes.

"I'm waiting," he said softly.

"For what?" she demanded, panting with hostility.

"Your threat."

"All right, you want a threat?" she hissed, her slender frame shuddering with the impact of emotion. "We can't be on this island forever. And when we get off, you will rue this day!" Growing icy now, Skye couldn't seem to shut herself up. She was too humiliated by the entire debacle. She had never before been in a position where she wasn't the one in control, and it was galling. "If I don't manage to get you behind bars, I will make damn sure you are fired! I'm a wealthy woman, Mr. Pilot, and not without a certain prestige."

"Aren't you going to threaten to have your lover beat me up?"

"Don't be ridiculous!" Skye snapped.

"That's very reasonable of you," Kyle said dryly, and Skye winced. At the moment her own behavior could be classified as anything but reasonable. But what about Kyle? He had pounced upon her, but he hadn't hurt her. He had merely prevented her from hurting him, and he hadn't made a single threat.

Her words had spurred him on—words issued because she was afraid of him, afraid of herself, afraid of her reactions to him. She couldn't handle the situation. The need to lean on him was overwhelming, and she had never felt such a need. He was destroying the confidence it had taken a lifetime to acquire.

He, not the crash, had single-handedly destroyed her entire vision of her pleasant life. He had shaken her belief in her love for a perfectly fine man . . . a good man.

He had taken over her senses.

He released her suddenly with impatient disgust, rising and towering over her as he stared down at the sand, his eyes holding her prisoner still.

"If you have anything to say to Mr. Jagger," he told her coldly, "do so now."

"What?" Skye demanded with confusion.

"I am K. A. Jagger. I'm sure you find me quite in keeping with the tyrannical monster you've imagined."

As Skye stared at him with shocked dismay, he turned abruptly and disappeared down the beach.

Four

Skye lay in the sand for a long time after he left her, trying to assimilate the fact that her cosurvivor was none other than *the* K. A. Jagger. It made sense, she thought stupidly. Kyle. Of course. Why hadn't she asked him about his name earlier? It would have been a normal, civil question . . .

She had been too caught up in herself, Skye decided with a sinking feeling. Too worried about her own survival, too concerned with her own emotions. Too unnerved by him . . .

And now she was stuck wondering, trying to remember all that she had said about Jagger. It didn't really matter. She had surely damned herself. What did it matter how far?

And what did she care, she thought, trying to dispel her dismay with anger? She owed the man nothing, and nine out of ten she despised him—whoever he was! And what had he been doing flying his own plane anyway? He deserved anything that she had said.

Skye still felt a little ill. She thought about the overpowering attraction she felt for him despite everything, and even lying down, she was swamped by a jittery feeling. She had always felt that surely only idiots allowed themselves to feel anything for a married man—separated or not. She had felt only contempt and pity for the women who, she had read, bounded to the side of Jagger with no questions asked.

"Well, I'm not an idiot," she said aloud to herself, trying to convince herself that no attraction existed. "And I hate the man. He's using this situation to take all his frustrations out on me because I'm in no position to fight back." She was alarmed to find herself fighting a mental battle of her own, attempting to inform herself that he was, yes, a handsome man, but nothing more. She felt nothing for him. She had crashed, she had gone through a storm. Any kindred feelings were merely a result of the environment.

Ted was every bit as striking in looks as Kyle. He was dynamic, he was personable. He was wonderful, kind, and a sensitive lover.

And his image weaved elusively in and out of her mind, it wouldn't stay . . .

But it will! she assured herself. It will, It's just that it has been weeks and weeks now since I've seen Ted, days since I've spoken to him, and that across an ocean.

Skye began to shiver uncontrollably. Her clothing was still damp from the drenching. Pulling herself up as if she had suddenly become an old, old woman, Skye moved back to the fire and rubbed her hands together. She continued to shiver. The fire was burning low. Grabbing a stick, she tried to poke it back into action. She managed only to scatter the kindling and reduce what little warmth remained.

I do hate Kyle Jagger, she told herself, tightly closing her eyes. He had done nothing but bully her and push her around . . . and shelter her from the explosion of the aircraft, and from the wrath of the storm.

She didn't really hate him because of the bullying, she knew. She hated him because of the reactions he could draw from her. She was so defensive! She simply wasn't behaving like herself. She didn't run around threatening people. And she never gave away her personal life. No one knew she was afraid of the dark; no one knew how badly Steven's death had desolated her, not even her brother's widow, not even Ted.

She hated Kyle because he was so much stronger than she was. Because she wanted to lean on him so badly. Because she had always scorned women who couldn't control their emotions.

Kyle was K. A. Jagger. Just knowing who he was unnerved her. Jagger, she had always thought, was a legend—not a real human being. And if a reality existed, he should have been an old, graying despot, not a powerful, well-toned flesh-and-warm-blood, sensual, and virile man . . .

Not alive and vibrant, and alone with her on an island.

So what? she demanded of herself with annoyance. They had definite difficulties getting along. Rescue would come; it would surely come soon. A multimillionaire couldn't be allowed simply to disappear. And then they would both be off the island; they would return to their lives. She would be safe.

"I am safe!" Skye hissed aloud to herself. She was no fool. She would control her emotions. She was an entity herself; she would not be used by a man like Jagger, no matter what the circumstances. A tiny shiver of heat rose up her spine despite her still damp cold, and she tightened her jaw with misery. She was terribly afraid that she was going to learn that she was a fool. In spite of her self-disgust, an uncanny fear assailed her. She had never known the feeling of wanting someone the way she was beginning to want Jagger. And the pity was, if only he weren't Jagger, she would probably not be half so critical of her own appalling confusion.

He returned as she still hovered nervously by the fire. For several moments he held his distance, arms crossed over his chest as he watched Skye, who continued to gaze into the fire even though she was well aware that he had returned.

"I'm sorry."

Skye shrugged, and kept her vision on the dying flames.

Kyle emitted an impatient oath and moved to the fire himself, adding twigs and kindling to stoke the flames expertly. He was annoyed with himself—he hadn't intended on hiding his identity, belatedly he had realized he had liked her not knowing who he was. It had been the first time in years he had had the simple comfort of being nothing but a man.

Not that she seemed overly impressed by his name. In fact, she was less than impressed. Oh, well, he thought bitterly, she had already decreed Jagger a monster. He knew she found him autocratic and less than liberated when it came to women. She was probably thinking— smugly, at that—that he fit the monster image of K. A. Jagger perfectly.

So what did it matter anyway? he asked himself with irritation. They weren't cohabiting the island by choice. She was a woman happily attached to another man, and he didn't think much of the attachment. Kyle had a dry feeling that she was the one who scorned marriage. Her business was a good one and she traveled like butterfly.

The fire sparked back to life and he looked at her to find that her eyes were finally on him, enigmatically. He stared into their beautiful topaz depths for a moment. They were femininely feline, with the light of the fire giving them a glimmer of deep, enchanting mystery. Even with the still damp tendrils of her honey hair tangled about the fine bones of her face, he was suddenly sure he had never seen a more beguiling woman. Women more beautiful existed, but there was an essence about her that was the most arresting he had ever come across. She was tiny, but along with a rare combination of traits he admired—spirit, pride, and independence—she possessed an innate sensuality that was a part of her every movement. It was in her walk, in the cast of her eyes, in the tilt of her head. It was in the touch of her fine, long fingers . . . it was in every gesture of her slender body.

And the amazing thing, he decided, was that she was totally unaware of the sensuality, which was all the more seductive because it was still innocent and subdued. In self-assessment, she would surely grant herself confidence and pride. But knowing that she tantalized and intrigued would most probably be quite a surprise.

And he had to crash with her—a woman he clashed with instantly; a woman who drove him half crazy. He couldn't comprehend the stark desire she elicited within him, a desire that went beyond the known and ordinary . . . that tortured his moments, waking . . . sleeping.

The island wasn't helping any. He craved rescue on the one hand. He had created his business over years in which it had become the center of his heart, of the love he had learned to withhold from women. Two things had come to matter to Kyle—his business and his son. Rescue would be a return to both.

But on the other hand he was finding a certain pleasure in the island—until just moments ago, when Skye had learned his identity. Until then he had had the rare opportunity to be just a man with nature in an environment that offered a survival simply. So he craved rescue, and yet he wouldn't mind if it took a little time in coming. His fear was that it might never come. The Pacific had already claimed and stranded many in her vastness.

But still, he wasn't a pessimist. He believed they would be found, and perhaps that was why he could accept his situation. He was aware that Skye believed they would be off the island within days, and no matter how angry he grew, he didn't have the heart to tell her that might not be so.

But if the tension between them escalated, he knew he would blow and give her the facts in no uncertain terms.

She would then learn that life was going to be a bit rough for an indefinite period.

Except that it was going to be far rougher for him. Each hour that passed was taking him farther and farther away from the laws of society. He didn't give a damn what was back in the States. The here and now was overpowering. In this enforced Eden it was taking all his concentration to remember that he could not revert to simple laws of nature and demand that she accept the role of female to his male.

Kyle moved away from the fire, annoyed to find that she was watching him, a wary cast to her almond eyes. He smiled, amused his own wanderings. He was tempted to tell her to relax, that he wasn't a rapist, but he wasn't entirely certain that he wasn't. That thought made him even more amused. Despite his marital situation, he had never, never lacked for feminine companionship, and the idea of forcing a woman, any woman, was so alien to his character that it was ridiculous. And if he was composed of any one thing, that one thing would be control. She might not know it, but if it was her choice, she was as safe with him as she would be with a cloistered monk.

His smile became very warm with his thoughts. Her eyes, even when wary, looked upon him with a gaze that made him feel special. He was sure she gave that impression to everyone—and that the successes of her life were partially due to that endearing quality. Her vibrant topaz gaze had the ability to create a world. When one gazed back, she became the most beautiful woman in the world. The effect was strange, Kyle thought, something he had never felt before.

"Are you any warmer?" he asked her.

She nodded.

"Don't worry too much about being cold," Kyle offered. "I'm sure the temperature never goes below seventy."

Again Skye nodded, but this time she lifted her head and gave him a tentative smile. A momentary truce was being offered.

"Kyle?"

"Yes?"

"If you're . . . if you're K. A. Jagger, shouldn't a host of people be searching for you with a fine-tooth comb?"

"Yes," he said slowly, wondering what she was getting at.

"Shouldn't they have found us by now? Won't they wind up believing us dead if they don't find us soon?"

"It hasn't been that long," Kyle said reassuringly. "It just seems like forever because of all we've been through. Don't worry—they won't give up until they do find us. And don't forget that Coke bottle! Someone has reached this island before."

"Yes, I suppose so." Skye saw that Kyle had unknotted all their fabric pieces and was spreading the lot out to dry. She was still hunched by the fire, numb and spiritless. He was always practical, she thought, her feelings resentful, but also grudgingly admiring, always moving, always working. She finally stood herself. "What would you like for dinner? I'm afraid the menu isn't vast. Coconuts, bananas, or figs. Or a few crackers and cheese, I think."

Kyle laughed at her distasteful grimace. "I'll take some of each, and if you take that imperious little twitch off your face, I'll make you a piña colada to go with dinner."

"A piña colada?"

"Minus the pineapple, I'm afraid, and certainly not what they'd serve at the Plaza, but better than nothing."

"Maybe it wouldn't be a bad idea," Skye agreed. "I've still got chills."

"Well, it won't take you long to cook," Kyle said dryly. "Fetch dinner, my lady, and seat yourself back by the fire."

"Aye, aye, captain, I won't argue with you there!" Skye

left the fire only long enough to rustle in their cache of things for the food and then returned. She glanced uneasily at their roofless shelter while handing coconuts to Kyle. "What do we do if it rains tonight?"

"Get wet."

"Thanks."

"It's not going to rain again."

"How do you know?" Skye demanded, annoyed by his positive assurance.

"I don't know how I know, but I do. Maybe I always wanted to be Weaver the Weatherman."

"I'm beginning to think you believe you're a stand-up comic."

"No, you're stuck with a levelheaded businessman, Ms. Delaney." Skye saw his eyes glaze slightly. "Never a comedian. Where's the rum?" He looked back to her abruptly.

"I forgot it."

"Well, go get it."

Skye automatically felt herself stiffen at his tone. There were times when he teased that she could tolerate his autocratic tone, but blunt orders had always set poorly with her. She wasn't accustomed to being told what to do, and although she wasn't ordinarily argumentative or petty, he happened to push the wrong button at the wrong time.

"Go get it yourself!" she snapped.

He glanced over at her slowly, hands crawling to his hips, eyes returning to the mint frost she was coming to know so well. "You're not much on cooperation, are you?" he demanded icily.

Skye took a slow, deep breath, returning his chilling stare. "I'm a great believer in cooperation. I also believe in 'please' and 'thank you' and requesting instead of demanding."

It was such a small thing, and she was right. He could have said please. He could have changed his tone. He could have gotten the rum himself. He was used to having orders obeyed without question. What did it matter? he asked himself, his temper rising. They weren't at a damn tea party. He really didn't mind carrying the bulk of the work, but he'd be damned if he'd treat her like a snow queen while he did it. He knew he was tired and disgusted, but he couldn't help it, his temper flared.

Suddenly, before he was aware of what he was doing, he was crouched like a tiger beside her at the fire, his hand snaked out to cup her chin. "Listen, duchess," he told her, shocked by the harsh coldness of his own voice, but momentarily unable to control it or the tension that spread through his muscular frame. "I really do hate to put you out of your way, but you weren't stranded on this island with a personal servant. Now I'm not sure if you've noticed or not, I've put myself on a few lines to keep that fair skin of yours in nice shape. I haven't received a bucketful of thank yous for my efforts either. You want requests? All right, here's a request. Would you mind, would it break your sweet little derriere, to get up and get the rum?"

"Yes, I would mind terribly!" Skye hissed. She was shaking from his assault, yet mesmerized by his eyes blazing into hers. He was hateful, but she was suddenly aware that his grip upon her was firm but not cruel or painful, and as they stared at one another, his fingers began to graze her cheek caressingly. Again, although she half wanted to shoot him, she felt a startling desire to grip his hand and hold it to her, to crawl into his arms and forget the dignity she struggled to maintain. "Get your hand off me," she managed weakly, "and I'll bring the damn rum."

He didn't let go of her, but the fire died out of his eyes and he winced. "I'm sorry. Christ, this is stupid!"

His remorse was sincere, but it didn't make Skye feel any better. With him hovering over her in his leashed pounce, exuding tense energy and vitality, she was far too keenly aware of his physical presence. Clad only in the cutoff shorts, he was frighteningly male. Skye was aware of the thick abundance of the auburn hair on his wide, taut chest, on long corded legs. She was aware of his tight, stretched belly, of the smooth, glistening bronze of his skin. Acutely, achingly aware of the strength behind the callused fingers that feathered along her cheek . . .

"Please," she whispered uneasily, "just let go of me. I'll get the rum. I'm sorry, too. I guess we're both just jumping at each other's throats . . .

Her words were swallowed up by his lips. They descended upon hers completely, hungrily seeming to demand and consume. There was no "request" to his kiss, no subtle, seductive, persuasion, just an assumption of mastery, of a need that compulsion dictated be fulfilled. The hand that had cradled her chin moved to thread through the hair at the nape of her neck, holding her steady as his lips moved savoringly with that assurance, assuming her stunned stillness to mean a simple acquiescence. Or did he care? Did he need her agreement?

Or could she deny it? Sensation flooded through her, blind sensation. And the feeling was good. He had easy access to the recesses of her mouth as her lips had been parted in speech; his probing tongue seemed to bring a surge of warmth that spewed forth from within her. While she still fought to ponder the sensation, he shifted, bringing his weight atop hers and both of them down to the sand, never breaking the kiss. His tongue slid to glide and taste her teeth, then plunged again, stirring another wave of erotically surging pleasure in her racing bloodstream. And his hands began to move. They cupped her face, touched upon her throat, caressed her shoulders. A finger moved slowly down the tender flesh of her inner arm, and all the while she was disparagingly aware of the warmth and strength of his body, pressed to hers, feeling so right, so shatteringly good. If she moved a hand, she could feel the ripple of a shoulder . . . marvel at the smooth texture of bronze, taut skin . . .

Skye moved more than a hand. As compelled as he, she touched him, gripping her delicate fingers into his back, making an entire sensual adjustment to make her body more accommodating to his. The firm softness of her breasts were crushed against the wall of his chest, tingling with the contact; she felt the grind of hips against hips and, despite the material that separated them, the male arousal she had known would be so potent. And she wanted it all. The sky, the sand, the sea—all seemed to fade. Her past, the life that had been hers until just yesterday, seemed to evaporate to nonimportance. She felt as if her flesh had merely survived for all that time, waiting.

Only coming alive now, with his touch. His lips left hers to rake a line down her cheek to her throat. Skye opened her eyes, but remained spellbound. Up above the night was becoming black, hazing out the few remains of the blood-red sunset. Tonight there were stars, the pale sliver of a moon. She was damp and sandy, a scraggly mess, but the sky had never been more beautiful, she had never felt better, more feminine.

More alive. More sensual. More complete. More uniquely a part of a whole. She shivered deliciously as his wandering, fiery lips continued their trail, his tongue tracing her collarbone, nuzzling aside the fabric of her shirt. A day's growth of beard furred his cheeks and chin, but the abrasive quality only served to heighten the sensitized awareness that assailed her. He shifted again, allowing a hand to fondle her curves firmly from breast to hip in exploration, then move back to cradle her breast and massage the nipple. Through bra and shirt it hardened satisfyingly for his touch. Skye moaned beneath him. Her fingers feathered over his ear, sank into auburn hair that was still heavy and wet. The top button of her blouse slipped open, abetting his forays of moist exploration with lips and tongue. Again Skye felt herself possessed by compulsive trembling, shot through with the white lightning of raw, explosive desire.

And she was still in wonder that her rampaging craving for him could have been so easy to create, so undeniable and immediate—still too stunned to protest, too spellbound to halt.

In the back of her mind she knew it was wrong. Physical attraction in the heat of an explosive situation. There were a dozen reasons why it was wrong, and she could never tell herself that she had been too mindless to resist. She wasn't mindless at all. Every beautiful sensation was being tenderly registered and ingrained, as if catalogued for blissful memory. She needed the heat; she needed the explosion. In the calm that followed the storm, her own winds, dormant for so long, had grown to twist and whirl at ferocious speed. It was the island, it was the sea, the sun—the man. They had taken from her, they had given to her. They had brought her back to life.

She had to stop. But when she protested, his lips would stop tasting her skin, his mouth would stop its sensuous movement. The firm glide of his hands would cease; they would leave her, she would feel the cold again. And so she waited, fingers entwined into his hair, grazing the sinewed neck. She fought back tears. And when he slipped hands beneath her shirt and around her back to loosen the hook of her bra, she finally shuddered, drawing breath for strength, and issued a firm if wavering, "No, Kyle, no, please. No further."

She had expected anger. She hadn't thought there would be any way to explain that she wanted him but could allow him to go only so far, and still control her own mind, her own desires.

Yet when his eyes met hers, they remained warm. They

narrowed, but with concern and puzzlement rather than disdain. He very carefully rebuttoned the top of her shirt, keeping his gaze steady with hers, his hands caressing. She could still feel the heat of him against her, the extent of his desire, and guilt brought her further misery. He had taken her unawares, but his assault had been entirely open. She had only herself to blame for allowing his arousal to grow keenly with anticipation.

His anger she had been prepared for; his tenderness hurt.

"What is it?" he queried softly.

Skye's eyes widened in surprise. "What is it?" she repeated with disbelief. He was married. She was committed elsewhere; she had merely lost her head because of their situation—this damned island. Surely he knew that without question.

Skye watched Kyle's high brow furrow in confusion. "I don't think I understand you. We've both known this was coming. I don't think I've ever wanted anything, or anyone, as I want you. And I know that you want me. Bodies don't lie. They can respond only with truth."

Skye bit into her bottom lip and lowered her lashes. "I'm not denying that I want you. Please"—she lifted her eyes back to his in open entreaty—"please move away from me." Skye smiled apologetically, straining to take the fear of her request from her voice. "I don't want you listening to my body when my mind is going to try to make sense."

Obligingly, he moved, sitting Indian fashion again, elbows on his knees, chin rested on his knuckles as he surveyed her, waiting. Skye breathed deeply and blinked—imprinting on her memory the look of compassion that could soften the harshness of his features, the slight beading of moisture that made his broad shoulders copper in the night. He was capable of being the world's worst chauvinist, she thought suddenly, then turned around with the patience for understanding when other men would go berserk.

"I'm really not a tease," she began lamely. His face was completely unfathomable; he waited patiently to listen, but apparently not to help. "Kyle," she tried again, "I know what you're feeling, because I've felt it. But don't you realize why? We're alone out here. We're experiencing nothing but a very base desire, and I really don't like it. We fight every other second, Kyle. I'm not sure we even like one another. Besides that, you're a married man. And I—"

"You are not married," Kyle interrupted, and Skye was surprised to see that the compassion and tenderness he had previously shown her had entirely disappeared. He was angry, really angry. Why now, she wondered? What had he expected her reasons to be?

"No, I'm not married, but I—I—"

"You have someone else you sleep with?" he inquired sardonically.

"What I do is none of your business," Skye snapped, annoyed that he could make her one affair of a lifetime sound like an illicit liaison. And she and Ted were both free adults . . . "If I'd never been on a date in my life, Mr. Jagger," she said icily, "I would just as soon not start with you."

"Why?"

Skye stared at him in highly irritated exasperation. "Because you're a married man—and a user!" she exclaimed.

"A user?" His eyes narrowed to a dangerous glitter that almost made her wish she hadn't spoken. She lowered her eyes. "You do have a wife," she said quietly, "and yet you still change women as you do coats. You—you use them. I don't care for being used."

"I'm amazed, Ms. Delaney, that you see fit to judge me on the basis of a few magazine articles," he said harshly, not denying a thing. "So I'm a user. It seems likely to me that, being as well read as you claim to be, you would also be aware that I've been separated for ten years. That's a long time, my dear Ms. Morality. And you don't know a damned thing about my marriage. Except that I would say that I at least had the guts to make a commitment—a real try at a relationship. You're too much of a coward to do that. But that's all beside the point. I'm beginning to really wonder about you and this stagnant affair you're having. Is anything ever real with you? Or is it just convenience you crave? You don't want marriage, but you don't want to take any chances. Sex is something that is properly scheduled into your neat corporate life—something you indulge in when you have a weekend, or an evening to spare. Well, Ms. Delaney, in my opinion your values are more off base than mine. I may not be able to make the promises, but I do what I do because of what I feel. Anything that I give is honest—"

"You don't have anything to give!" Skye interrupted furiously.

"That's right," he continued coldly, "I'm a user. Except that using usually entails taking something only. I've just discovered that I've been rather lucky. The women I've known haven't felt so terribly used. I've taken pleasure from them, but I've given it in return. And I've never met a woman more dishonest than yourself. I sure as hell wasn't 'using' you. You were taking, you were receiving. If you want to get down to brass tacks, I was being used. Like an idiot. Go just as far as Skye deems okay. Then she smiles and asks that you turn yourself off like a faucet."

"I didn't start it!"

"I know," he replied disdainfully. "You wouldn't have had the nerve to just go for something you wanted. You're all tied up in some little code of absurd self-ethics. You know I have no loving wife awaiting me, and I don't think you're terribly concerned about betraying your lover.

You've just decided that come hell or high water, you're going to be the woman who said no to K. A. Jagger."

"Your ego is incredible!"

"Un-unh, duchess, I just see things the way they are."

"You see things the way you wish!"

"Do I?" His dry smile was hauntingly sardonic, and he moved in close to her, his eyes pinioning hers although he didn't touch her in any way. His voice was a razor's edge, but low and husky; it condemned, but it also shot fever into her blood. "You verbally and physically admitted you wanted me."

Skye's eyes fell. "I don't believe this," she murmured. "We're stranded on an island and arguing over morals. I don't want anything to do with you. Isn't that enough?"

"Not when I don't believe it," he replied tensely.

Skye looked down and drew a pattern with her finger in the sand. He was totally infuriating—a combination of every male characteristic she had always been sure she despised. Yet instead of the righteous anger she should have been exploding with, she was busy willing away tears that burned her eyes. She closed her eyes for a second. Why was she beset with such confusion? The situation was cut and dried. He had a wife, no matter how estranged . . .

Kyle moved away from her. She heard and sensed his actions as he searched out a cigarette and lit it in the fire's flame. She felt his astute gaze continue to blaze into her and she snapped out to ease her confusion.

"I may owe you a few 'thank yous,' but I don't owe you any explanations—or excuses—for anything I choose to do or not do."

"And what do I owe you?" Kyle asked sardonically.

"A lot, Mr. Jagger," Skye retorted. "It was your airplane that crashed." Skye saw his jaw tighten, although it was the only sign of emotion he displayed.

He smiled dryly and lifted a brow. "So sue me."

"I just might," Skye muttered uneasily. She suddenly

found herself walking idly around the fire, more agitated
than she cared to admit. And then, to her annoyance,
she found herself half trying to explain and apologize
anyway.

"This just isn't a good situation," she murmured. "I
mean, I have to think about myself. But it isn't all myself . . . it's you, it's complications . . ."

"Ahhh . . ." That dark, single brow rose even higher,
his voice maintained an almost casual air. "I thought
there was more here than met the eye."

Skye glanced at him with surprise. Her unease hadn't
fully formed in her own mind, but she knew as he
watched her that he had an uncanny perception of her
thoughts.

"I do believe you're afraid of an unwanted pregnancy
from an island affair, aren't you?" he asked bluntly.

"Well, it's not an unheard of possibility!" she retorted
instantly, wincing as she did so. She hadn't meant to admit such a thing—it made it seem as if all else had been
lies, which wasn't true. It also made her accept the fact
that she was afraid of him, that she might come to care
when he . . . when he what? Could never be serious?

There was a strange glitter to Kyle's cool eyes. "You're
not on the pill?"

Skye felt herself blush beet red. She had never imagined herself discussing contraceptives with a man she
hardly knew. And she certainly wasn't going to discuss
her reasons for choosing to use a diaphragm. And yet
she had never imagined herself pulled into the arms of
such a man . . . she had never imagined herself in such
a situation.

"No, I'm not," she replied, further irritated by her own
embarrassment. Really, he was intolerable. He thought he
could say or do anything. The fact was that she now had
to realize the character of the man was the power, not
just the name. Skye strove to be as tough and crudely

blunt as he. "This is merely another point—a serious one, I'm sure you'll agree. But besides all the issues that should keep us apart, this is definitely a major point. The possibility of our . . . of our . . ."

"Conceiving a child?" Kyle offered with vast amusement at her difficulty, his features so cool and sardonic Skye was once again tempted to bury him in handfuls of sand.

"Yes," she murmured icily. "It would be a disaster."

Did he know how he pricked beneath her skin, she wondered. His grin suddenly split his bronze features with a handsome slash. "Skye," he said simply, "it seems I've been elected to take care of you now. Surely you must realize I would always do so!"

For some reason she couldn't prevent the bitter laughter that exploded from her. "Take care of me! How archaic. I can take care of myself, very well, thank you. My income is quite sufficient!"

"Do excuse me." His voice remained level, he dragged upon his cigarette, but there was an edge of steel in the tone, subtle mockery.

Skye felt heat flush her face. "You don't understand," she accused curtly, annoyed that he had made her feel so guilty when she owed him no reasons. "Children should only be born to happily married couples who both—father and mother—wish to have and raise a child."

"Very moral," he returned pleasantly, with just the hint of sarcasm.

"Oh, go to the devil!" Skye ejaculated, torn herself and infuriated that he could twist knives into her so easily with a variance in tone or flick of an eye. "There's no reason we should be acting like a pair of animals just because we're on an island together!"

"I hadn't thought that was the reason," he said politely. "Nor have I ever thought of making love as acting like an animal."

They stared at one another for several seconds, like puzzle pieces that simply didn't fit together. "I don't think I'm hungry," Skye finally said. "If you'll excuse me, I'm going to sleep."

"Just a minute, if you don't mind." Kyle rose with lithe agility and stood before her, now towering over her small frame. "You do need to be taken care of, Skye Delaney. Everyone does. But I'll play by your rules; I'll play the handyman. As long as I can. But watch your step. On this island you aren't the reigning queen. I don't give a damn how much money you make. This is a primitive place, honey. I see to your well-being—you see to mine. That means that we both put in. And"—his hands rose, he gently lifted the hair from her neck and lightly grazed an erratic pulse with a moist kiss, then moved back and dropped her hair—"you start thinking I'm a toy to play with only so far as it keeps you amused again—or falls in line with your moral values—and I'm afraid I won't make any promises about not falling into the role of me Tarzan you Jane." He fell silent for a moment, watching her. "Understand?"

"Oh, I think I understand," Skye said acidly, hating the fact that his lips against her bare skin had started her shivering again and praying that he hadn't seen the instant reaction. "I believe you're threatening me."

He shrugged. "Not really. I don't like threats—not to give, not to receive. I'm simply telling you what is, and what will be."

"Is that all?" she lifted her chin and demanded.

"That's it. Sweet and clear, I believe."

"Quite clear," Skye said crisply. "So I'll remind you that you started that little fiasco that I played a little too far! You keep your distance, and I'll keep mine." This time she watched him for a reaction, then smiled stiffly. "Good night, Kyle."

He gestured toward the remains of the shelter, inclined

his head slightly, and smiled as coldly in return. "Good night, Ms. Delaney."

It was probably ridiculous to crawl into the roofless shelter, but Skye thought with a sigh that human beings were creatures of habit, and in a single night they had formed the habit of that being the place to sleep. Skye curled up with her back to Kyle, miserably aware that sleep would be a long time coming in her state of tumult and confusion. Everything she had said to Kyle was reasonable; he should have granted her the truth of the situation! And yet he had his point. Maybe it was the primitive circumstance of the island where all that was essential was elemental. She had never felt more of a purely physical need in her life, had never been so stimulated, so set afire with sensual longing. Even now she could feel the burning deep within her . . . And although he had instigated the kiss, she had not protested. She could still feel the surging warmth of his arousal. She had allowed him to believe that their lovemaking would continue in a natural course . . . because she had wanted it to go as far as possible before turning back.

Her fingers clenched into the sand as she teetered mentally between shame and indignant defiance.

Hours later, although her eyes were tightly shut, she remained awake. She felt Kyle's presence as he stared down at her and she could see him fully in her mind—long, muscular legs spread firmly in the sand, powerful hands on his hips, so much bronzed and sinewed flesh visible with only his cutoffs for covering, his roughly hewn face, more rugged than ever with the scratchy growth of beard, a thick wealth of auburn hair on both head and broad chest . . .

Icy eyes, arrogant, hard, occasionally tender . . .

Skye began to pray that a plane or boat would make it the next day. She needed rescue from more than the island.

She heard a grunt from him, then a rustle as he turned.

Moments later she realized what he had done. Before curling his length into the sand for sleep, he made sure that the fire would blaze brightly until dawn brought new illumination. Skye carefully opened her eyes. A glow of orange warmth was all around her.

She finally slept, aware of his easy breathing just feet away.

Five

A rescue boat or plane did not appear the next day. Or the next or the next or the next or the next.

Skye and Kyle worked into an uneasy pattern of keeping a polite distance. Uncomfortable in his cold, remote, and aloof presence, Skye took to roaming the island daily—after curtly checking with Kyle on weather conditions. The skies, however, remained clear, and she was free to stay away from their encampment.

The island, despite all, did hold a spell of enchantment over her. Her life, even when she traveled, tended to revolve around pavement and concrete. The profusion of plants and birds, earth, sea, and sky, fascinated her. She was amazed by the teeming life on the small island, at the richness of the inner soil—rich, as Kyle had told her, because the lava of a onetime active volcano had made it so, thousands and thousands of years ago. Figs, bananas, and coconuts abounded, and huge fronds that still dipped low with water from the storm.

There was a deep gully filled with rainwater now, too. Kyle had told her that at one time it might have actually been a freshwater stream. It was well shaded, and it seemed the water would remain. As long as the rains came, they would be okay. It was ironic, but the storm she had feared might take her life had provided instead substance to maintain it.

Skye had learned after the first day that Kyle kept busy

in her absence. He mumbled many mornings that he was off to search for the elusive captain's log, but he still spent plenty of time around camp. As the week passed, the hut was repaired and enlarged and thatch walls added. A terrible-looking but sturdy table greeted her return one day, tree trunk stools the next. He had made a curious-looking hatchet out of driftwood and metal debris from the plane, and with that primitive tool, his pocket knife, and her nail file he seemed to be able to fashion all kinds of crude things by whittling and notching.

He had also perfected his tree-branch fishing spear. There were also crabs and scallops from the shell-strewn beach to supplement their diet. A night didn't pass when they weren't satisfactorily filled. Still, conversation between them was practically nonexistent. Guiltily aware that he was carrying the bulk of their survival, Skye could still not offer verbal assistance. Instead, she silently began taking on the task of collecting fruit daily on her rambling excursions and collecting water from the gully in huge palm husks to keep filled the hollowed log they had dragged to their encampment. It was heavy work, but it was good; it forced her to keep her muscles working and her mind at least partially occupied. It tired her for the long nights, for the disturbing time she was forced to spend with Kyle.

Theirs was indeed a strange partnership, one that did little to alleviate the terrible depression as the days passed with no sign of help on the horizon. Skye was learning to close her eyes to many miseries—such as wondering what microscopic creatures might be swimming in the water she drank and what might be flying in the trees when the darkness shielded them. She learned to ignore the small crabs on the beach, the jellyfish that occasionally washed up. Or to try to ignore them. Her nerves were fraying badly, especially when she tried to brush her teeth with bark. About other things she came slowly not to care. Her hair was filthy and tangled. Saltwater left it a mass of mats, freshwater alone couldn't help. Three nights ago she had become so frustrated trying to untangle it with her small plastic comb that she had broken several teeth out of it. Absurdly furious with the comb, she had broken that. Her nose to spite her face, she mourned belatedly. Kyle's look had signified just that, but his expression had also strangely denoted compassion. He had started to speak, but then said nothing . . .

If Kyle were ever to know how she spent the majority of her time away, his reaction would be a condemning frown. Basically she sat on the other side of the island and clenched her eyes against the tears of reality. Skye Delaney, bright, fashionable, intellectual, cool lady exec of the fashion industry, reduced to a barefoot waif who crawled around mangroves and coconuts with tattered hair.

Damn, what she wouldn't give for a cup of coffee, a toothbrush, and the excitement of looking out her penthouse window to the streets of New York far below.

Times Square in five-o'clock traffic would be heaven.

Increasingly, though, she thought of Kyle. Perhaps the island would be more bearable if the tension between them could ease, but she knew intuitively that it could never ease. It was a sexual tension, more apparent each time they accidentally brushed a hand, each time they actually looked at one another.

But Skye knew she was right. She clung to the hope that they would soon be off the island, their paths parting forever. No matter how comfortable it might seem in the heat of passion beneath the stars, a relationship between them could only lead to unhappiness and disaster. She didn't like to admit her fear, but she was afraid. He was a little too much to handle, on top of everything else. Too male, too strong, too competent . . .

And it was too easy to lean on him, too easy to depend on him. Too easy to want him, too easy to need him.

Sighing, and afraid to let her thoughts wander any farther, Skye was plagued by visions of his virile naked body rising from the sea. She left her perch on the far side of the island and began to make her way back across, a clutch of figs bundled into the crook of her elbow. If she kept up her self-inflicted mind torture, she told herself sternly, bracing herself for the evening ahead, she would have to move herself to her own side of the island.

But she didn't think she could do that. As bad as things were, he was there. She could watch him, feel his strength near her.

Skye had just scrambled through the trees to reach the stretch of high grass that fringed the beach when she froze and blinked hastily, wondering desperately if the heat of the sun was causing her to hallucinate. But opening her eyes a second time, she fell to the earth with the delirious joy.

Not one, but two boats lurked beneath the dazzling glimmer of the sun on the horizon. Skye dropped the figs and scrambled to her feet, ready to race across the high grass and scream from the beach. Where the hell was Kyle? she wondered bitterly. He should have already seen the boats; he should be waving madly, lighting a high fire. She began to run.

Kyle had already seen the boats. Ducked low beneath a dune that afforded a shield of scruffy grass, he watched the proceedings with dismay.

Humanity had found their island, but he didn't dare reach out. His first sight of the crane on the larger of the two ships had made him tense, creating an uncanny sense of danger. Now, as he watched, he railed against his helplessness and sickly prayed that the gun-wielding men aboard the drug-running boats would not see fit to investigate curiously the debris and thatch workings on the beach.

A thumping sound, a fleet padding that sent vibrations through the sand, worked its way into his consciousness. With blinding dismay Kyle realized that Skye had seen the boats and was racing for the beach to alert the ships to inhabitants on the island.

"God!" he groaned aloud through clenched teeth, his facial muscles stretched taut with the danger. Tensing into a crouch, he dug his toes hard into the sand and waited, waited until her fleetly flying form was just a foot away. In that second she glanced at him, her face playing a spectrum of split-second emotions. What the hell was the matter with him? her glance asked, before it dismissed him for a fool. Help was out there, and she was going to get it.

He unleashed the tension and energy that was wound in him as tightly as a coil and pounced, hurling himself over her, bringing them both rolling behind the dune. Skye fought against him frantically, gasping to draw breath from the fall. Her eyes, glitteringly feline and furious, accused him of insanity before she could speak. "What are you doing?" she shouted. It was all she could get out. His weight secured her against the sand as his broad hand effectively silenced her mouth.

"Shut up!" Kyle hissed. "Those men would just as soon kill you as look at you."

Tears sprang into Skye's eyes. She had no earthly idea of what was going on, and she was ragingly, frustratingly helpless. Help drifted out on the ocean within shouting distance and here she was, powerless against the sinewed strength of a chauvinistic, muscleibound autocrat turned maniac. Twisting desperately, she managed to sink her teeth into the flesh of a long, callused finger.

"Damn you!" he hissed. His head came beside hers, his ragged, commanding whisper seared her ear. "Listen to me, duchess, listen good, because I don't want to have to knock you into silence. Those people are drug runners. A nice quick look will assure you they are toting a fair amount of hardware. I'd like to stay alive myself, Ms. Delaney, and even if I shielded your body from a bullet for you, they'd have another one waiting. So just sit tight and shut your trap."

Skye still didn't understand what was going on, but she had little choice to do other than he said. His arms were still around her; his weight still held her prone. Seemingly assured that she was no longer going to shout out, he released her mouth, then finally gestured that she might twist and watch the proceedings as he did.

The men aboard the boats did indeed seem to be heavily armed. Skye watched as the crane lifted bale after bale from the larger boat to the smaller one, where they disappeared below the decks. A trickle of unease filtered through her as she realized that if she could see them, they could see the beach. Inadvertently she edged closer to Kyle, torn between fear and fascination. She wouldn't have had any idea of what was being transferred from boat to boat. How did he know it was drugs?

She didn't ponder the question any longer; her breath suddenly seemed to leave her body in a gush.

Two of the ten or so men aboard the two vessels were suddenly pointing at the beach. They appeared to argue for a few moments, then one, a heavyset, florid man, stalked angrily away. The other continued to stare at the beach. Finally he shrugged and went back to work.

Skye had no idea of how much time passed, but eventually the rendezvous between the two boats ended. Kyle held her tensely still until both boats disappeared over the navy line of their visible horizon.

He stood, looking off into the distance, then down to where Skye lay on the sand, back braced by her elbows.

"I don't think I really understand what just happened," Skye charged him, miserably aware that they were completely alone again. "Why couldn't we have asked for help? We could have explained that we didn't care what they were doing . . ."

Kyle glared down at her incredulously. "Don't you listen to me? Or don't you understand what I'm saying? Those were drug runners."

"So! I don't give a damn—"

"Oh, Lord, give me strength!" Kyle exclaimed in exasperation, looking heavenward as if he expected a sign. Shaking his head with impatient exasperation, he looked back down at her. "That wasn't a little pot party, Skye. There were tons in that black-market transfer—probably a nice shipment of cocaine, too. People caught doing that go to jail for half a century. And you want to run up to them and say you promise you won't speak if they'll just deposit you in some small, friendly port?"

"Quit patronizing me!" Skye stormed. "If you take the time to explain something, I understand it. I'm sorry. We have muggings in New York, a murder here and there, and a lot of embezzlement. But I've never seen a high-seas drug ring in action before! If I didn't recognize it right off, you'll have to forgive me!"

Suddenly the disappointment of the situation hit her. For seconds there she had believed that she would be off the island within the hour.

They were right back to square one.

No, below square one. The Coke bottle had meant hope before. Now it only meant that their island was known by twentieth-century pirates.

"We're never going to get out of here, are we?" she demanded desolately. "And now we're always going to have to be watching . . ."

"Don't be absurd." Kyle sighed, his eyes gentling at the bleak awareness in her delicate face. He reached a hand to her and pulled her up, smiling. "We *will* get out of here, we are in the known world! You have friends who will search forever."

Yes, surely Ted would search forever. And she had friends, close friends. Lucy Grant, her personal assistant and secretary, would move heaven and earth before she would accept the fact that Skye was gone for good. Harry Dunbart, the corporate lawyer who had stuck by her during everything, would also keep planes flying in search until hell froze over.

And Kyle also had people who would never accept his loss. Then there was the fact that Executive Charters had never lost a flight. Skye finally, slowly, returned Kyle's smile. "Yes, I guess eventually we will be found. I can't imagine Executive Charters allowing their eccentric employer to simply disappear." Trying harder, Skye made her smile ruefully cheerful. "I got excited and dropped the figs. I guess I'll go back and find them." She was rubbing the back of her neck absently. "I wish you could learn to just tap me on the shoulder if something is wrong," she teased him. "I think I have bruises from head to toe."

Pleased and achingly relieved that Skye seemed to have fully grasped the situation and taken it in stride—and equally pleased that she seemed willing again to form a bond of bantering friendship between them—Kyle reached out and kneaded her neck between his thumbs and forefingers, quelling tension with a strong and firm touch. "Forget the figs. We have enough fruit by the hut to last a week. Let's head on down. I have a present for you."

"A present?" Skye couldn't prevent the wistful curl to her lips—an action that amazed her. They were following Murphy's Law—everything that could possibly go wrong seemed to be doing so, yet at the moment she didn't seem to care. She had narrowly escaped death in the crash, flirted with pneumonia during the storm, almost embraced a host of cutthroat criminals.

And it just didn't matter because Kyle was smiling tenderly and he must care for her very much, no matter how blunt his behavior was at times, because at every turn he had sheltered her.

And now he was offering her a present. Such a little thing in ordinary life—gift giving was a common practice. But here, with the sea, sky, sand, and just the two of them, it was everything.

"What is it?" Skye asked, feeling like a child with a large box that must not be opened before Christmas.

"A surprise," he returned with a subtle grin. Maybe relief was making her giddy, perhaps that combined with the end of their cold stalemate, but suddenly she clutched her stomach and half doubled over, overcome with laughter.

"What on earth amuses you, lady?" he growled, his brows joining suspiciously.

"Oh, Lord, I am sorry!" Skye managed through chuckles. "I was just looking at you and thinking . . . I mean, the owner of a multimillion-dollar corporation in those truly ragged cutoffs and growing a beard that would put a hippie to shame."

Kyle's hand left its comfortable grip on her neck with a teasingly punishing squeeze to move self-consciously to his own chin, where he ruefully rubbed a thick growth of auburn stubble.

"Sorry about that," he murmured, his eyes catching hers with a twinkle. "I wonder how all the heroes in the movies about lost islands and jungles managed to keep clean-shaven faces?"

Skye chuckled and shook her head. "I don't know. I guess I never thought about it before."

"Oh, well, sorry if I'm not making the grade." He rested his arm on her shoulder as they headed down the slope to the beach.

"You make the grade okay," Skye assured him automatically, unaware at first that she was voicing thoughts best kept hidden. "The face may be a bit scratchy, but the body certainly lives up to the very best matinee hero—" She broke off abruptly, dismayed as she kept her eyes on their sand path below. She was the one who had insisted their relationship remain totally asexual, and here she was making innuendos.

"Whoa!" Kyle chuckled with surprise. His fingers trailed down her back, the nails sending shivering excitement down her spine as they lightly scratched—a simple, affectionate gesture. "A compliment, Skye? Thanks, I'll take it."

"Well, now," Skye put in dryly, fighting to keep the conversation entirely nonchalant, "don't go letting it get to your head. I don't think heroes are supposed to have overinflated egos either."

"Hmmm," Kyle mused, sending whiplashes of sensation through her as he teasingly kneaded her back again. "Maybe heroes are usually younger."

"Maybe," Skye agreed simply.

"I'll let you in on a secret."

"Oh? What's that?"

"You're legs are much nicer than the run-of-the-mill movie heroine's."

"Thanks." Why did she have to struggle to get the word out? He was teasing, of course. No! she thought with sudden clarity. They were flirting! Actually flirting as if they were out on a date.

"And . . ."

"And what?" He was leading her into something, but she couldn't resist the wicked insinuation of his tone.

"Like I said before—nice, nice derriere!"

"Oh, quit!" Skye laughed, dismayed that her face was very visibly flooding with color. "Where's this present you're boasting about?"

"On the table by the hut. Go get it, but bear in mind that I get to help you use it!"

Giving him a last suspicious glance, Skye raced ahead of him to the crude notched-together table. Her present brought startling tears to her eyes; she knew it had taken him hours to make.

It was a comb. The prongs were rough and far apart, but very sturdy and all of one piece with the handle. Trying to keep her fingers from trembling, she reached for it wonderingly, curious as to what it was carved from.

"Tortoiseshell," he supplied. "It was washed up on the beach—minus the tortoise."

Skye glanced quickly to Kyle, standing a few feet from her, bearded face unreadable, hands planted on trim hips.

"It's beautiful," she murmured, glazed eyes turning back to the comb. "Thank you." It was more than beautiful; carved with a pocket knife, it was an incredible feat—a feat of compassion, a feat of caring.

He moved a step nearer and his eyes focused on the wealth of tangled honey hair that his hand moved into. "I'd hate to have to see you cut it all off when we get out of here," he murmured. Stepping back, he smiled into her eyes again. "The storm left us plenty of water. Tomorrow we can try to wash it with coconut oil and a little juice from those key limes."

Skye nodded slowly, allowing her gaze to fall quickly from his and back to the comb. They were coming close, and she wanted the closeness badly, but it still scared her terribly. It was dangerous for them to touch. She wanted too badly to fall into his arms, to taste his lips.

Be honest, she chastised herself harshly, you want a whole lot more than that . . .

And she did, but her emotions and values were too confused. She had always believed she loved Ted and, although she accepted the fact that a sexual relationship didn't have to be based on deep-rooted love, it was hard for her to equate making love with any emotion other than love. But now she was being forced to wonder if she did really love Ted.

Her feelings for Kyle bewildered her. She admired him, she respected him. Even when she was ready to hog-tie him and close his wise mouth with an apple between his teeth, she did need him.

She was also coming to know that she did like him very much. But love? Was it possible to love a stranger? Even a very intimate stranger who for the time was the most important person in the world?

Or was she afraid that she was falling in love? Would it be all right to reach for comfort that could be easily cast aside—returned to someone else—when their days together ended? Surely a loved one—husband, wife, lover—would understand and forgive an affair under circumstances such as theirs.

Skye thought of the long days she had spent with Steven and Virginia before her twin's death. They would often go for long walks, and Steven would quiz her relentlessly about Ted. He would never judge, he would never advise, and yet Skye had known he wasn't pleased with her relationship. If Skye were to ask her brother's opinion bluntly, Steven would shake his head with a small smile. "Just never let real happiness pass, sis," he would say, hugging her shoulders. "When it comes, you'll know, and then grab it."

"I am happy with Ted," she would always reply. And Steven would say nothing more, but the questions would be in his eyes. Then why isn't Ted with you, and why do you two never take the chance and marry . . .

And she had to wonder herself. Why hadn't she made Ted be with her at a point in her life when she so badly needed comfort?

And yet Ted did offer security. He was always there when she returned. And she knew that she was the only woman in the world to him, which only intensified her guilt. But in all honesty, although she didn't like her feelings, she had to admit that in thinking of Kyle she was afraid. She didn't believe she could ever be the only woman in the world to him. She didn't want to be the protected pet of a more powerful man.

And Kyle was very much a physical man. There were women in his life, but they held second place to his other pursuits. He obviously won love easily; he was obviously kind in return, while still legally married.

God, how she wanted off of the island! Sanctuary from the man who frightened her, compelled her, made her weak. If only time would bring rescue. Once away from Kyle she would forget him, she would be free from his bigger-than-life strength. Retrospection would dull his magnificence.

But it wasn't the magnificence she would miss, nor the heroics that were basic to him. She knew deep within that she would remember the little things—the auburn tufts of hair on long, work-roughened fingers; the gold that made his sleek shoulders shine and glimmer when the sun played down upon them; the way his eyes could be icy one moment and then narrow to warm amusement in just seconds. She would always remember the endearing quality of humor that could soften his squared and bristled chin.

"Well?"

Well what? She suddenly realized and admitted a sad truth. Whereas she had always avoided marriage with Ted, she would want to be Kyle's wife. And Kyle already had a wife. He didn't live with her, he had been long away from her, and yet she was still his wife. Maybe he still carried a torch for her, and simply couldn't bear to divorce her, to leave her free to marry again. All Skye could ever be to Kyle was a mistress.

What an archaic word. Mistress. Fallen woman.

Surely she was going crazy. She didn't love Kyle. She

was merely a victim of her own desire, stranded in a remote paradise. She had to force herself to remember Ted.

Skye realized suddenly that he had been speaking and she hadn't heard a single word. She might have been staring straight through him rather than at him.

"I'm sorry. Well what?"

"Are you game to try?"

Try what, she wondered? How long had she been staring at him blankly?

"Spear fishing," he prompted. "Damn, you really don't hear anything I say to you!" He laughed.

"I guess I was wandering," Skye said hastily. "Uh, sure. I'll try, but no promises!"

A few moments later she was armed with a long stick, honed to a fine point at the end by the pocket knife. Glancing dubiously at Kyle, she followed him into the water. "I forgot to ask," he called to her. "You do swim, don't you?"

"More or less."

"Don't step on or touch anything red. Fire coral."

"Coral!"

"The island is a raised atoll, surrounded by coral reef. That's probably why our visitors decided not to venture in. If they didn't navigate those large ships just right, they'd cut themselves up good."

"Great," Skye muttered beneath her breath. "How far out are we going?"

"Just a little farther," he returned.

"Great," she muttered again. Great for Kyle, who was still standing. Skye had already been swimming for several feet. "How am I going to hit a fish when I can't even balance?" she wailed, gulping as a wave filled her mouth with saltwater. She was already having problems staying afloat and handling the stick.

"Go fast for something big!" he chuckled, stopping abruptly. "See—we've hit coral."

Skye could see the outcropping through the clear water, alive and teeming with life—beautiful, multicolored fans, tiny fish flashing through the underwater fantasy land. "Don't step," he warned her. "Coral can slash feet as well as boats!"

Skye grimaced, treading water furiously. "What now?"

"We wait."

"Wait! How long do you think I can do this?"

"Hold on to my neck," he offered.

Warily, Skye complied. Kyle was tall enough to stand where the last of the smooth sand covering just met the coral. Apparently he wasn't as worried about his feet as he was hers, or perhaps he had more faith in his ability to pad the coral carefully without hitting anything dangerous. "I don't think I'm going to be too terribly good at this," Skye murmured dryly, clinging to him piggyback. She wasn't too terribly sure the whole thing had been a good idea. With arms curled around his neck, legs around his waist, and torso pressed to his back, she was just too aware of every slight ripple of his muscles, of warm, radiating male heat.

"You're going to do fine," he assured her, glad she couldn't see his wide, spreading grin.

She felt his deep chuckle vibrate powerfully across his back.

He was quickly rewarded with a light cuff to his head. "Watch it, Tarzan. I don't want that spear getting stuck where it doesn't belong."

"You watch it!" he laughed in return. "And quit acting out those violent feminine impulses! You'll scare the fish away."

"What am I going after anyway?" Skye said with a disgruntled humph.

"Anything that looks good," Kyle replied. "Don't go for a barracuda or a shark."

"Shark!" Her fingers wound more tightly around him,

he felt the pleasant sensation of her breasts crushed against his back, the wet blouse doing nothing to create a barrier between her nipples and his bare flesh. Kyle dipped his head low, once again grateful that she couldn't see or read his features.

"Umm . . ." he murmured. "Sharks do live in the ocean. But don't worry, I haven't seen any around here yet, and as long as you don't panic and thrash, they'd probably leave you alone anyway. A barracuda won't come for you period unless you go out of your way to aggravate it. What we want is a nice fat grouper if one will venture by."

"Will he stand still so that I can hit him if I ask him?" Skye demanded tartly.

"I'm not really expecting you to hit anything," Kyle responded.

"Thanks for the vote of confidence."

"Just keep your eyes open."

"Yes, sir!" Very aware of the length of collarbone beneath her fingers, Skye was shocked that she was able to notice the large fish cruising their way almost as the words left her mouth. She tensed, and whispered into his ear, "There!"

"Where?"

"Right there!"

It was to their right—kind of an ugly-looking fish, colorless when compared to the brilliant tinier fish that abounded. "That's it, Skye!" Kyle replied excitedly, whispering in kind. "Right on the nail. A grouper!"

She was unprepared for the powerful coiling of muscles beneath her, for the explosion of energy that erupted with lightning power and speed. As Kyle lunged for the fish, he brought her with him. The sudden splurge into the water left her blinded by the sting of the salt, coughing and sputtering as if she had consumed half the Pacific, and clinging to him more fiercely than ever.

Kyle chuckled as he shifted his weight and swung her around with one arm to his chest, balancing his stick, which now successfully carried the grouper, so that he could also pat her on the back.

"Hey, you're the one who saw the fish! You should have been ready."

"Sorry!" she sputtered, feeling the expansion of the broad chest beneath her fingers.

"Don't be—you'll know better next time."

Kyle started walking back toward shore, still carrying both her and the fish. Skye lowered her head without comment. Was there going to be a next time? Had their cold war ended? And if this was a truce, where would it eventually lead?

She broke away as they neared the shore and swam in the last few feet, pausing to duck her head and pull her wet hair back before exiting the water. "I'll go collect twigs to start the fire," she murmured hastily.

"Do that," he replied amiably. "Grab a few larger logs, too. I think we're running a bit low."

Jogging out of the surf, Skye suddenly paused and turned back uneasily. Kyle was already crouched low with the fish, deftly slicing fillets from bone with the pocket knife.

"Kyle?"

"Hmm?"

"Is it safe? Do you think those boats might return and spot the fire?"

He stopped his work and turned to her with an easy smile. "They aren't out to get anyone, Skye, they just can't afford people in their way. They won't be back for some time. That was a major transfer today. Hopefully, if this is a regular rendezvous, we'll be long gone before it ever takes place again. We're safe."

Skye watched him a moment, biting her lip, then knew she could trust his judgment. She turned again and started on her self-appointed task, collecting their gourds and an abundance of fruit and water to go with dinner. Occasionally they sipped on the rum or Burgundy, but Kyle had announced they had better start conserving the alcohol for any medicinal purposes that might arise.

Among his other talents Kyle seemed to have a way with fish, even when crudely cooked over an open fire. Seated at the table on one of his rough-hewn stools, eating off a rough-hewn plate with a rough-hewn two-pronged fork, Skye suddenly realized that she had been very lucky indeed. A slight shiver rippled through her. Had she survived the crash landing alone, she might have been in serious trouble. Feeling much more magnanimous toward Kyle than she had for some time, Skye tentatively instigated a conversation.

"You must be a joy to have around the house," she said lightly. "You must be missed."

Kyle bit into his fish and shrugged. "I should hope I'm missed. My brother, my son, my company . . ."

"Your wife?" Skye didn't mean to ask the question; it just slipped out.

He raised a bemused brow. "My wife? I doubt if she'll shed any tears for me now. Knowing Lisa," he said with indifference, "she's probably working hard on having me declared legally dead. In fact, she probably thinks my disappearance is wonderful."

"Why?" Skye murmured awkwardly.

Kyle hesitated a moment, swirling the water in his gourd. "We were due to sign divorce papers last Tuesday. That's why I was flying your plane. It was a convenient way to get back myself."

Skye felt curiosity spreading through her. They had avoided speaking of such personal details of their lives so far, but she couldn't prevent herself now from wanting to delve further. Was he telling the truth about getting a divorce? Or was it a line he was accustomed to using?

"If you've been separated for ten years," she asked nonchalantly, "why were you going for a divorce now?"

Kyle caught her eyes, amusement lighting his own. "Do you care?"

Skye flushed with annoyance. "We have to talk about something, don't we?"

"I suppose." Smiling, he leaned back in his chair, balancing with his feet crossed over the end of the table, his fingers laced behind his head. "I wanted a divorce twenty years ago. But we stayed together ten years because of our son. Then we separated. Lisa was too attached to money by that time to let me out easily. And then I didn't care. It made my life less complicated to have a wife. Now Lisa has decided a settlement of a lump sum might be preferable to a husband. And I think it's wonderful to finally be freed from her shackles. And Chris has been old enough for a long time now to understand."

"Oh," Skye murmured. "Chris is your son?"

"Yep."

"How old is he?"

"Twenty."

"Oh," Skye murmured again. Kyle laughed.

"I can almost see the wheels spinning in your head, Ms. Delaney. Yes, I married Lisa because she was pregnant. There has never been any great love lost between us. Your turn."

"What?"

"Your turn." Skye found herself flushing again, sure he meant to quiz her on Ted. Her mind raced to formulate some evasive answers.

"Steven," he said softly, his eyes darkly compassionate. "Tell me about your brother."

Skye lowered her head and fiddled with her fork, oddly disturbed by the compelling intensity of his words. "He was my twin," she surprised herself by saying quietly, grimacing slightly as she raised her head. "We were very close.

When my parents died, all we had was one another. Delaney Designs came from the two of us. Virginia was a school friend of mine before she married Steven, so even after the two of them moved to Australia, we were often together."

"How did he die?"

"Cancer."

"He must have been very young."

Skye winced. "Yes, twenty-five. He died just a year ago." She was gazing into Kyle's eyes, and it was as if she were hypnotized. She kept wanting to continue talking, although it made no sense. She had never discussed Steven with Ted, but here she was, talking and talking . . .

She told him about the years of cobalt, chemotherapy, and radiation. About the fear, about the hope. About Steven. His wonderful optimism. His appreciation of life. That one terrible time he had broken . . .

Kyle listened to her, startled by the depth of tenderness she could evoke within him. He wondered at her halted speech, certain that she was sharing emotions with him she had never shared with anyone before. He became more and more certain that she didn't, after all, belong to another man. Not in a real way, the way that mattered most.

He rose slowly from his side of the table as she finished speaking and walked around to wedge himself beside her and lean a thigh against her. With thumb and forefinger he gently tilted her chin, bringing her eyes to meet his, lightly brushing the soft skin of her cheek. Caught by that power in his eyes, Skye watched as his lips descended very slowly over hers, catching them in a soft, gentle caress. His lips moved enticingly against hers, warm and giving. She was ready to accept them, ready to part her mouth with invitation and savor all his masculine sensuality. But his kiss was too brief, too tender. The tip of his tongue flicked sensuously over her lower lip, and then, to her surprise, he released her, a deep heat of fire still in the luminous green eyes. "I won't ever let the fire die out at night," he promised her, a rueful half smile curling his lips beneath the stubble of beard. "Never."

Then he was standing. Mesmerized, Skye watched as he walked away, moving down toward the surf, now dark and ominous with the coming of the night.

"Where are you going?" she finally called out, reminding herself that she really didn't want him near her, but still aware that something had changed between them. She needed to break the hold he had, she was afraid, but she needed him . . .

"I'm going swimming."

"Now?" Skye protested with confusion. "It's dark."

He was whistling, but the sound was rather strained. "I know it's dark. I want to go swimming anyway."

He didn't want to go swimming; he needed to go swimming. He had to do something to work away his tension and his growing desire.

He had sensed the give in her, had known that she would have yielded had he pulled her into his arms.

But it wasn't the time. He wanted two things when he finally claimed her as his own—that she know and accept whom she lay with, and that no ghosts come between them.

He didn't really comprehend his own feelings, but he knew that he wanted her in a way he had never known.

And he knew he would never allow her to return to another man, civilization or not.

Six

Something was crawling on her.

Blinking at the light of dawn, Skye became more and more aware of the creeping sensation. It had begun near her ankle, and now seemed to slither up her leg.

Groggy from having just awakened, she sat up with a frown, knitting and creasing her brow. She blinked again and stared down at her leg.

It was a beetle. Dark brown, a good two inches long, slithering up her leg, its antennae flickering with each of its erratic movements.

Skye curled her face into a mask of sick horror. "Oh, Lord!" she shrieked at the top of her lungs, flying to her feet with a furious movement and striking at the creature at the same time. She missed, then stared with amazement and panic as the creature spread wings and began to fly, lighting upon her elbow, soaring again as she brushed it off.

Very feminine panic-driven shrieks tore from her as she lashed out at the creature. Had Skye been rational, she might have calmed herself for she didn't have a paralyzing fear of insects, but just to waken and to see such a large one crawling over her . . .

Awakened by her ear-splitting screams, Kyle, too, tore to his feet, eyes wide, body tensed as he searched out the danger. "What? What's wrong?" he demanded again, his vision focusing on Skye and the bizarre, ritualistic dance she seemed to be performing.

"Oh, my God!" her voice wailed with cringing disgust and terror. "It's in my hair!" Like a flash Skye was bolting for the beach, her feet barely touching ground. Still bewildered and fearful, Kyle raced after her, reaching her in thigh-high water where she was furiously dunking her head. Firmly grasping her shoulders, he pulled her up and held her a few inches from his chest, trying to make sense of her thrashings and exclamations.

"What, Skye?" he shook her, his eyes still dark with the fear and concern he tried to control. *"What is it?"*

"Is it out? Is it out? Oh, God! I can still feel it!" Pulling from him with amazing strength, she slipped beneath the surface of the water again. Sure she had gone mad and striving for patience, Kyle fished her out again, this time looping his arms around her in a hold she couldn't possibly escape.

"Is what out?" he demanded, taking in her wide, dilated eyes, the wet tendrils of hair that dripped down her face.

"Look!" she repeated anxiously.

Kyle placed both hands on her head with a frown and carefully separated her hair, searching for he knew not what. Finally convinced that there was nothing there but a wealth of hair, he nodded. "What was it?"

"A roach," she told him with a shudder.

"A roach?" he yelled, face hardening with furious exasperation and hands held tightly around her head. "You just cost me ten years of life and a head full of gray hair over *a roach?*"

"It wasn't an ordinary roach!" Skye snapped indignantly. "It flew!"

"A palmetto bug!" he railed. "Dammit, Skye, you scared me half to death over a bug that can't even hurt you!"

"It was in my hair!" she shouted, wondering how he could be so dense. "It was crawly and disgusting!"

Suddenly, looking into her delicate but outraged face, the amber cat eyes ablaze, her hair in scraggly clumps, Kyle burst into laughter. He laughed so hard that he released her and stumbled to the shore, where he sank to the sand, still overcome with laughter.

Skye watched him, then bit down on her lower lip. She walked over to him with great dignity and looked down at his face, eyes alight with a twinkle, pearl-white teeth perfectly displayed as his full lips split wide through the amber beard to grin ear to ear.

"Oh, my God!" he chuckled, staring up at her, "All that over a bug."

"It certainly wasn't funny!" Skye snapped, crossing her arms over her dripping shirt.

Kyle tried to sober himself, but couldn't. "I'm sorry, Skye, it was funny."

She was half tempted to laugh with him. With his lean, sinewed body so dark against the sand, his eyes seeming to sizzle, his hair in a damp wave against his forehead— growing longer every day—he had never seemed so appealing, so boyishly endearing, despite the shaggy growth of beard. His lips, curled full and sensuously in that broad smile, seemed to beckon to her with bold mystery. She should laugh and fall down beside him . . .

But she didn't laugh. She couldn't fall down beside him; she still had too many reservations. And those reservations hurt. Coupled with the perhaps ridiculous horror she had just experienced over the bug, restraint and the entire dismal beginning of the morning weighed down on her like lead. The reality of everything that had happened slapped her in the face.

She suddenly believed she would never, never get off the island. Day after day something new and horrifying would happen. Back at home they had surely given her up for dead. If another storm came and they survived, it wouldn't matter, because drug dealers would return and probably kill them anyway.

Without another word to Kyle she spun on her heels and returned to the hut, where she lay down. She didn't cry; she was just empty. Emptier than she had ever been in her life.

Kyle watched her go, his laughter slowly fading. Her reaction shocked him. She always had a sense of humor and the ability to laugh at herself. Her wit could be piercing, but it was always there.

Frowning, he shrugged off the incident, assuming that she was in a foul temper and would simply just have to work it out. With a little curse he rose. He was damned if he was going to play nursemaid to a fit of the sulks. She was just going to have to snap out of it without an ardent apology on his part.

She remained in the hut while he ate a banana and consumed a coconut—fruit and milk. She was still there when he rinsed his face with fresh water and did his best at scrubbing his teeth. Totally irritated, he finally decided to leave her and scout the foliage again for bits and pieces of plane debris.

Kyle returned hours later, further irritated by a fruitless search beneath the scorching sun. A quick glance told him that Skye had moved; she was no longer sequestered in the hut, but sitting on the beach—staring out at the ocean.

Annoyance surged through him as he saw also that nothing had been done. The water was low, the fruit supply low, and soiled dishes, which he had so painstakingly fashioned, still sat upon the table. He asked so little of her, he thought bitterly, taking all the real burden for survival upon himself, and now, in a fit of temper, she had neglected the few responsibilities that were hers.

Long, swift strides brought him angrily to her side.

"What the hell do you think you're doing?" he demanded bluntly.

She didn't bother to glance up at him; her eyes remained trained on the empty sea. "Does it matter?"

"What?" he exploded.

"Does it matter?" her tone was flat, despairing. "What sense does doing anything make?"

"I don't think I follow you," Kyle said, his eyes narrowing as worry combined with anger.

"It's just not worth it," she said, oblivious to his tenseness. "It's like treatments—it just goes on for nothing."

Thoughts flashed rampantly through Kyle's mind. He realized she wasn't being hostile; she just didn't give a damn. The insect had been nothing, but it had been the catalyst to flay her spirit when crash, storm, and danger had failed. It wasn't a temper tantrum; it wasn't something she could just snap out of.

"I see," he said slowly. "You just don't care about living anymore?"

A bare lift of the shoulders was Skye's shrug. "Death can be preferable to slowly rotting," she said.

It was serious, Kyle decided instantly. Somehow she was relating their experiences to her brother's slow agony, believing that each day was another step toward the inevitable. Why endure anymore when . . .

He had to do something. Whether right or wrong, he had to take a step. Drawing on the anger that had faded with knowledge and then understanding, he reached down and jerked her to her feet, shaking her so that her head fell back.

"Steven is dead, eh, so you might as well be?" Her eyes began to widen, the glimmer of topaz rising with her anger. She opened her mouth to protest, but he refused to allow her a word. "Well, I'm not dead, lady, and neither are you! And things aren't even all that bad. We're in one piece, we have water, food, and shelter. And even if it takes years for someone to come, honey, you're going to survive and you're going to learn to live and put in a full share—to accommodate me, because *I* want to live."

As he spoke, his hands left their grip upon her and his fingers began to work on her blouse, deftly unbuttoning despite her fumbled attempts to stop him.

"What are you doing?" she charged. "I told you I don't want you—"

"I don't give a good goddamn what you do or don't want anymore!" Kyle snapped in command. "We're both going to have a good dunking and then we're going to wash your hair because you're going to care about it to please me!"

Kyle was moving with an agile speed that left all Skye's stunned attempts to counter his actions just a few seconds too late. He spun her around to pull the shirt from her body, straitjacketing her with the material until it was freed and sent flying haphazardly into the sand. Trying to hang on to her bra, she was taken off guard and sent spinning into the sand when his foot tripped her ankles. An attempt to clutch at his arms as he reached for her shorts was futile as he simply jerked harder and sent her torso and head careening backward. Gasping and astounded, still too stunned to grasp what was happening, Skye choked out, "Stop it! Leave me alone! You can't do this!"

"Really?" he inquired curtly. "I don't see anyone around who is going to stop me!"

Frozen with shock as he momentarily released her, Skye stared blankly at him as he slipped out of his cutoffs and briefs. She vaguely noted how very brown he had become against the white of usually covered flesh. Then he was reaching for her again, a grim, determined set to his face that triggered her into action, but again a few seconds too late. He was on her before she had scrambled a foot in the sand, catching her around the midriff and drag-

ging her into the water. When she lashed out furiously
at him, he dunked her, holding her under until the mad
flailing of her arms and legs ceased. Then he pulled her
up, holding her at the small of the back with one hand,
at the nape of the neck with the other. "Are you mad,
Ms. Delaney?" he inquired, eyes glittering.

She spat out wheezed oaths in reply.

"Good," he said simply. He released her, and she made
a choking, scrambling effort for freedom again. He
merely shot out an arm and pulled her back, dousing her
once more in the sea. This time when he let her up, she
stood still, shaking with fury and indignation.

Skye had entirely forgotten the deep and debilitating
depression that had besieged her. She was convinced she
was in the hands of a madman, and her mind ticked in
double time, fighting the daze of disbelief, searching for
a way to elude him. Her breasts heaved with the effort
to draw breath, her hands formed into fists at her sides,
the nails creating crescents in the flesh. She stared at him
as he cupped water in his hands, dropped it over her
shoulders, and followed its dripping trail with his hands,
as if he held soap and bathed her. Skye's ragged breathing ceased with a sharp intake as his fingers worked over
her breasts, caressing and rubbing the nipples with rough
thumbs. All the while his eyes held her, brashly, relentlessly challenging her. He continued to hold her in his
imprisoning gaze while his fingers continued a downward
route, sliding with languorous leisure over her rib cage,
rounding her hips with insinuation, curving inward to
shape with bold expansion over the trembling flesh of
her upper thighs. An outraged, strangled gasp escaped
her as he calmly explored further—drawing nothing
more from him than a smile that was purely sensual. He
laughed as she jerked away again. With that deep, throaty
sound ringing in her ears Skye desperately tried to run
against the pressure of the water, but it was clear why he

was so easily amused. It took him less than two of his much longer strides to recapture her.

Swinging her into his midriff hold again, Kyle walked from the water, undaunted that she once more flailed and kicked. Her energy was failing her, he thought with a smile, glad that her feeble efforts were having no effect upon the iron clamp of his arm. She was small, he decided wryly, but when at full swing, she was a hellion to handle.

"Let—go—of—me!" she panted in a hiss.

"Not yet. We haven't finished your hair," he replied cheerfully, depositing her with a sharp smack of wet flesh upon one of the stools. Before she could raise herself more than one inch, his hand was bracing her down. By stretching, Kyle could reach his coconut mixture and hold her at the same time; seconds later he was working it into her hair while she sat seething beneath him, alternating between raw fury and the impulse to burst into bewildered tears.

"You'd better sleep with one eye open from now on," she hissed. "I can promise you that you will pay very dearly for this—"

"I think that should about do it," Kyle interrupted, his fingers finishing their thorough massage of her scalp. "All we have to do is rinse it. I'll get the water. No"—he paused, then gripped the long trail of her hair—"better yet, you come with me."

Skye yelped as a light jerk brought her trailing rebelliously along with him. At the hollowed sea grape trunk they had adapted to a water trough, he pressed her down, her back braced by the wood as he forcefully arched her neck with the skill of a haute couture hairdresser and saturated her hair with fresh water.

It was difficult to keep his hands on her hair. With spread knees trapping her to the sand, chest and belly pressed to her arched ribs, he was in marvelous view of a long, graceful neck leading with finely chiseled lines and delightfully tanned skin to the firm mounds of high, full breasts. Smoothing her hair back from her head and squeezing away the excess moisture, Kyle finally released her.

She fell fully into his form, grappling for balance in the small space between his body and the log.

"Is—that—all?" she enunciated grindingly, teeth clenched, eyes blazing, entire body chattering with indignant fury. "Are we quite done?"

"Un-unh." Kyle shook his head slowly. "Lady, we've just begun."

"No!"

Her shrieked protest once again went unheeded as he lifted her high in his arms and stalked purposefully toward the hut. Skye was unable to read from the hard contours of his face that his conscience plagued him, which was just as well. He hadn't really meant to carry matters this far, but what the hell, she was ready to kill him already.

Might as well straighten it *all* out now.

"Lady," he told her briskly, "fact of life—life has changed. We are partners. Two—get this now—two working parts of a whole. If we spend the rest of our lives on this island, I plan to make it worthwhile for you—and you are going to damned well reciprocate starting right now."

Inside the hut he dropped her unceremoniously to the sheets of clothing remnants. She rolled frantically to the side but he was down beside her, both arms snaking out to lock her into an embrace. She had a flash vision of his face—lean, hard, determined—before his lips moved over hers to envelop them as his muscled body did hers.

Persistent, demanding, ruthless, his tongue plunged into the sweetness of her mouth, allowing no quarter. And yet there was no bruising, no punishing, just a firm force that subtly turned to persuasion, gentling, drawing out, playing. His teeth nibbled her lips, his tongue traced them, coercing a shivering response. Half of his weight leaned over hers, his left hand tangled into her clean wet hair; his right hand made a bold and possessive sweep of her flesh, trailing with firm assurance from her shoulder over the shapely curves of her back to her buttocks. His right leg was wedged casually between hers, muscled, long, indomitable.

Skye wasn't quite sure when she lost the will or ability to fight him. Something infinitely tender and protective in his touch began to quell thought. He was overwhelming; each point of contact became a separate seduction. The hand that held her head moved and massaged, that on her body was never still, searching out erogenous zones, firm and demanding, then light and taunting, until unwittingly she strained for what was given and then denied.

She had been desolate beyond rationalization, then angry enough to kill. Now neither emotion made any sense. She had been wanting him, needing him, since that very first day. And it had nothing to do with the island. If she had met him in a field of thousands, the chemistry would still have existed, drawing her irrevocably. He was like nothing she had ever known, and yet she had known that coming to him would be this wild, this wonderful. Reality was bringing forth nothing less splendid than what her anticipation and fantasies had decreed.

Her arms slipped around his neck, fingers threading the thick dark hair that curled over them. With fascination she brought a hand against his cheek, reveling in the softening stubble of his beard, sliding again to feel the ripple of sleek, taut shoulders. His lips left hers, coming to rest upon a pulse at the base of her throat that throbbed out the acquiescence he sought.

If he left her now, Skye thought she would truly know desolation.

Kyle had no intention of leaving her. Her delicate hands upon him, the sweet, parting invitation of her lips, were all that was needed to assure him he had not been mistaken—she did want him as fervently as he did her. Thank God, he groaned inwardly, because this time he could not walk away. He was drunk with the wonder of her—full perfect breasts that arched to his touch, tiny waist, curved hips that trembled and undulated with instinctive pleasure, giving response as if attuned only to him. There wasn't a blemish on her skin; not even exposure to the sun and elements had touched its unique, compelling softness. Her legs were long yet enticingly shapely for one so small. He shuddered as they shifted against him, unconscious invitation, allowing him freedom to love.

Skye had never thought it possible to be mindless, and yet she was suddenly mindless. Not mindless, she thought through an engulfing cloud of sensation, surely not mindless. She could feel and excruciatingly savor so much— *that* couldn't be mindless. And yet she felt as if she had left all known dimensions, soared slowly at first, and then with whirlwind impetus, into a swirling heaven where nothing existed except for the passion that had erupted between them. Her actions were totally uncontrolled; they were instant responses, piano keys putting forth melody at a touch, soft and then thunderous, quiet and deafening. Having begun with wild, inescapable speed, Kyle now made his seduction a slow thing, half torturing them both with sure, complete arousal. His teeth tugged gently at a rosy hard-tipped nipple, while his mouth moved with sensuous warmth around it, shooting a vibrant spark of electrical need through Skye that seemed to flash a molten heat through each of her limbs, to the center of the driving coil within her. Her fingers clenched into his shoulders; a shuddering, gasping sigh escaped her.

Kyle slowly repeated the action on her other breast, then brought his head up, his eyes grown dark with passion as they stared into hers, half closed, the catlike almond eyes hazy and deep, never more beautiful, never more intriguing and seductive.

"You're magnificent," he murmured hoarsely, his eyes never leaving hers but his hands continuing their forays, fingers splaying to cup her breasts and ride low over her abdomen. And then his eyes did follow his hands, watching her shiver at his touch, watching the convulsive writhing she couldn't control . . . And then his whispered words, husky as a touch themselves, added fuel to the consuming fire lapping through her as he told her what just the sight of her did to him . . .

"Kyle . . ." she managed, but a convulsive gasp choked her as his sure, probing fingers sought between her thighs.

"I love everything about you," he murmured with his whisper of velvet as he moved over her.

Skye's eyes opened but any reply she might have made was cut off with a quavering cry as he merged with her, filling her with a searing heat that was all-absorbing and shattering, blinding her with a brilliant light as if her body and soul had exploded with the shock of pure sensation.

His was a rough magic, wild, and demanding, yet all the while tender, and strangely gentle despite the relentless, spellbinding assault of the conqueror. His fingers locked above her head, cradling her as he commandeered her lips and elicited all the secrets her mouth could give, all the sweet pleasure. He was totally consuming, a volcano, an earthquake, a sure ascent to an earthly heaven. Nothing else existed as Skye was swept along in his rhythm, beguiled, grasping, clinging, taken to heights and peaks of passion she had never known.

The crescendo was an explosion of sweet release that erupted as shatteringly and brilliantly as a lightning bolt. Long after Skye shivered, drifting very slowly in a daze back to the world, back to the hut, back to their bed of sand. She had never known such exhaustion, such perfect, numbing sensation.

He held her still, a hand tenderly cupping her face. Minutes ticked by as they maintained their embrace. Skye dimly noted that the light of day outside had gone from a brilliant blue to an indigo velvet. The heat of the sun had cooled; new shivers ran through her damp body. Kyle pulled her closer, offering her the protective security of his body heat.

Still dazed, Skye closed her eyes and burrowed against him. A flush filled her to still her shivers as she thought of the things he had whispered to her . . . of the things she had gasped in return . . . of the way she had so eagerly offered everything, lost all inhibitions.

She clenched her eyes more tightly against reality. She felt too wonderful to think about what had happened. All she wanted to do was sleep in the comforting arms of the man who had taken her . . . the man she had wanted all along.

When she opened her eyes again, the blue velvet night was gone. Dawn was coming, filtering pink shadows into the hut. Kyle's arm still lay across her breasts, his leg was cast haphazardly over hers. Very carefully, Skye slid from beneath him, watching the natural adjustment of his lean body.

Walking from the hut, Skye paused to stare at the glimmer of the sun struggling to rise in the east. It was going to be a spectacular day, clear and bright.

There should have been a storm; something as tempestuous as her thoughts.

She was riddled with guilt, a guilt made worse because she had not simply betrayed Ted, she had done so with pleasure . . . She still couldn't hold on to a clear image of his features. Even now she still burned and quivered with the simple memory of Kyle's touch.

Skye drew a deep and ragged breath. Her guilt was compounded by the fact that despite his separation, Kyle was married. He didn't care—he admitted he had taken many other women before her. And that made everything all the worse because she had become just another conquest to a man who made many.

And all these feelings were overridden by an emotion she feared to analyze. She felt better than she ever had in her life. She felt a part of Kyle. He had taken her, and she was still filled with him.

It was terrifying.

Always independent and self-reliant, Skye was forced to realize that all else could cease to matter. He was like a drug; he had not merely seduced her, it had made her an addict. Though she was worried, guilty, frightened, embarrassed, and appalled by her abandonment with him, she was already wanting him again . . .

Walking shakily to the crude table, Skye idly allowed her eyes to alight upon the tortoiseshell comb. Picking it up with wooden fingers, she automatically began to work it through her hair. Amazingly, Kyle's concoction of coconut and lime had left it soft and fairly manageable. And the tortoiseshell was durable. Working away her tension with her fingers, Skye lit into her hair with a purpose. The task took time, but when she finished, her hair curled over her shoulders and breasts in pleasant waves. Skye dropped the comb, wincing as she realized she was behaving as if she were shell-shocked.

But she was shell-shocked. She was not a hypocrite, and she was having to accept the fact that many of the things Kyle said were true. Every step in her relationship with Ted had been precise. And all through it she had kept her distance. She loved Ted, he was a wonderful man, but her love wasn't overwhelming—it was comfortable, companionable. And when they made love, it wasn't overwhelming, it was comfortable . . .

The burning of tears struck her eyelids. Skye knew that going back was going to be hard. She was going to have to tell Ted that what they had was over. She didn't know what would happen to her, or what the future would bring, but she could never return to Ted when her entire being was consumed by another man. She didn't think she'd be able to bear his touch again, nor would she ever be able to shake a yearning for another man who came to her as a thunderous flash fire.

Skye's nails dug into the palms of her hands, but she couldn't feel them. Kyle had said such wonderful things to her, intimate whispers that still brought a flush to her face, that still made her feel uniquely, incredibly feminine.

And yet he was still such a stranger. A power she didn't know how to deal with . . . a man who took and commanded, a man with whom she would have no relationship at all once they were off the island.

She didn't want to belong to him. He was hard; he was demanding. Ted, on the other hand, was always gentle. He was understanding. He held nothing over her and made no demands. He was always willing to do things her way.

So why can't I love him completely? she wondered desperately. Why had she given more, opened more, to Kyle in a single night?

Biting her lip, Skye was jolted by the realization that she was standing in full view of sea and sky stark naked. A frown furrowed her brow as she tried to remember where her clothing was. It had to be in the hut. And it was imperative that she shield herself with clothing before facing Kyle after all that had passed in the night. Hesitantly, tiptoeing, Skye returned to the hut.

Kyle still slept, on his back now; his head rested in the crook of arms crossed beneath it. Glancing down at him, Skye studied his profile—the clear, angular cut of his cheeks, the square of his jaw, the long, straight nose, all very nicely defined despite the growth of beard. The tiny lines around his eyes were faint in relaxation, a deep sweep of dark lashes formed handsome crescents. Skye noted the precise arches of his brows, the way his hair dropped disheveled over his forehead.

It was only natural that her eyes follow the superb length of his body from head to toe, feeling, despite herself, the age-old feminine satisfaction that the broad chest had harbored her, the muscles, tight even in sleep, had clasped her to a very male and very virile strength.

Unable to resist temptation, she bent to brush the hair from his brow. Then a startled cry escaped her. He wasn't sleeping at all. A single brow arched with expectant amusement as his eyes opened and his hand snaked out to capture her ankle.

In an awkward attempt to cross her arms over her breasts with instinctive modesty, Skye was unable to balance when he jerked her ankle. She landed half beside him and half on top of him, struggling ridiculously for dignity.

"What are you doing?" Kyle laughed as Skye tried to roll away from him and into their tattered sheet. Startled topaz eyes met his with a wide luminescence.

"I'm—I'm . . . I was looking for my clothes."

"Oh?" Kyle shifted to an elbow to watch her. "Your clothes are an the beach. You know that."

Of course they were on the beach, she thought with a wince of memory. "I forgot," she murmured, lowering her lashes.

"Oh," he replied, his agreement simply implying that he didn't believe her. Skye would have snapped something back, but she was afraid to look at him again. Facing him was every bit as difficult as she had imagined.

His finger touched her chin. "How are you feeling now?"

It was the first she had thought of the awful, almost suicidal depression that had besieged her the day before. "I'm fine," she said quickly, aware that he was eyeing her with deep concern even though she couldn't see him. "I'm sorry, I really am fine now, I guess I was acting like a bit of a child."

"You weren't acting like a child," he said pleasantly, his finger stroking a downward pattern, leaving her chin to wander in a soft stroke to her collarbone, then to brush aside the fabric she clung to and to draw a circle over nipples that responded instantly to his touch.

"Kyle," Skye said in a strangled voice, grabbing desperately for their patched sheet, "please, don't."

His hand went still; Skye could literally feel the tension within him. "Why?"

"Nothing has changed," Skye murmured awkwardly, keeping her eyes from his.

"Everything has changed. You're mine now, Skye."

"No," she protested weakly, her eyes finally opening to his as she struggled to save herself from her own feelings before being further engulfed by this power she could never hold. "Last night meant nothing, you forced me—"

"Like hell!" Kyle interrupted with a curt expletive. "At first, maybe, but you were with me all the way after that."

"I was merely substituting you for Ted," she shot out as she felt his tug on the sheet that sheltered her.

Again Kyle went rigid. When he moved again, it was an explosion. The sheet was ripped entirely away; they lay unshielded and naked alone on the sand. Skye felt fevered shivers assail her as his eyes alone had the power to create mercurial heat within her.

"Tell me, Skye," he demanded roughly, rubbing his

palm slowly over an aroused nipple. "Does your lost lover do this to you?" He bent over her before she could answer, taking her other breast into his mouth, teasing the hardened nipple mercilessly with his tongue as he gently sucked.

The sweet, unbearable desire that gripped Skye was instant. Heat shot throughout her body. Shuddering with need, she wound her fingers into his hair, pulling with her last strength. "Please . . ."

Kyle had no mercy. His lips trailed moistly to her ribs, to her abdomen. "Does he make you feel like this?" Kyle demanded roughly, his fingers stroking her thighs, his kisses burning lower and lower.

"Please . . ." was all that she could repeat. There were no lies that could be spoken. Skye was sinkingly aware that her responses to him were sadly obvious; he was savoring all that he elicited.

"That's right, Skye," Kyle murmured, "please me." He was bewitched again, torn between the anger her comment had aroused in him and the mysterious seduction that was entirely hers. She was unearthly sensual, her natural responses to him were magic. He had never known the gut-tearing desire to possess that she created within him . . . again . . . and again. He wanted to consume her, to cherish her, to be within her forever. And she couldn't deny him. His hand spanned her hip and he could feel the instinctive undulation that was an answer to his need, an answer like no other. He had to taste her, feel her, have her . . .

But for himself. Tautening all his muscles for control, he allowed himself the freedom to devour her with his hands and lips. And then he shifted away, allowing his gaze to appreciate slowly every inch of his exquisite island lover—the fall of luscious hair over heaving, firm breasts, the writhing of lithe torso, slender midriff, shapely legs . . . And then his eyes met hers, daring her to deny him.

Skye watched him in return, dazed with sensation. Then her eyes fell and she curled to him with a gasped cry. She couldn't deny him, and he knew it. He wanted her as she wanted him; she could feel it in the heartbeat that thundered within his chest, in the hard arousal that brushed her thighs. But as usual he was the one in command. His fingers threaded into her hair, arching her head until she was forced to face him with clenched eyes.

"Open your eyes," he demanded.

Slowly, Skye did so.

"Who am I, Skye?"

"Kyle." It was barely a whisper.

"Who?"

"Kyle," she repeated, "Kyle. Kyle Jagger."

"I don't want you ever to mistake me for another man," he told her softly, his tone gentling. "Touch me, Skye, know me."

With trembling fingers she touched his chest. Tentative at first, she allowed her fingertips merely to breeze against the taut flesh, the coarse hair. And then she felt him shudder, she heard the catching rasps of his breath. Her hands moved with more assurance over the provocative band of his lean belly, teasing, taunting. He moaned deeply, his fingers curled more tightly into her hair, and with an abrupt shift he came over her, cupping her breasts as he straddled her, then lowering his weight and bringing his mouth down upon hers, nipping her lips, plunging his tongue deeply. His kisses trailed over her cheek. "Touch me again, Skye," he murmured, meeting her eyes again.

She hesitated only a second," watching him, feeling her face flush. She had no secrets from him, and yet she was still a little shy, a little afraid that if she let go . . .

"Bring me to you," he urged her, watching all the while for response.

She closed her eyes and swallowed. She wanted him so badly. She could tell him anything, but she would always give herself away. He was a teacher, and she was proving an adept student to his tutelage. She should deny him; it was her only hold . . .

"Skye," he murmured, and his gentle tone was the end. She wanted to know him; his flesh was hers, at least for now.

She touched him; she felt his heat, his life. She brought him to the edge, and his pleasure as he entered her was his reward. Hers was that wonderful, filled ecstasy of again becoming his, of again being swept into a magical storm of endless passion.

Interlude

June 27, San Francisco

"He's dead," Lisa Jagger said flatly, her voice carrying the trace of a despair along with trembling resignation. Her finely manicured fingers were curled around a sherry glass, and she watched the liquid swirl. She shivered and took a deep, convulsive breath before bringing sorrow-filled eyes to meet those of her son. "He's dead, Chris, we have to accept it."

Chris Jagger was a mature twenty; intense brown eyes and well-groomed black hair made his sharp but pleasantly angled profile appear older.

But at the moment he was a boy faced with the loss of a father he adored. He fought tears, but they formed in his eyes anyway.

"He isn't dead!" The hard exclamation came from across the room. Michael Jagger, five years younger than his brother Kyle, didn't leave his position by the huge bay windows in the drawing room of Montfort—the family home on the outskirts of the city—but his determination permeated the air. He drew scathing eyes from Lisa to rest them gently upon his nephew. "Kyle isn't dead," he said more quietly. "He's been missing for two weeks. And the area of the Pacific we've traced him to is huge. We'll find him, Chris."

"Michael," Lisa murmured awkwardly, "I don't like you

raising false hopes." At forty Lisa Jagger was still a beauty. She wore her platinum hair in a shoulder-length layered cut; her eyes, a clear and drowning blue, were artistically made up, and her skin retained a smooth, soft glow of youth.

"Don't you want to hope, Lisa?" Michael inquired softly.

Caught off guard by her brother-in-law's gently insinuating tone, Lisa floundered. "Of course," she said quickly, then snapped, "You think I'm hoping he's dead, Michael, but you're wrong! I believe I'm closer to Kyle than either you or Chris! I'm his wife . . ."

Estranged wife, Mike Jagger thought as Lisa shrilled along. He knew very well that Kyle's eagerness to return to the States at the first possible moment had been to put an end to the charade that had gone on for years.

"And if you're thinking that I do really wish Kyle dead because of the divorce plans we played with, you're terribly, terribly wrong!" Lisa managed a very heart-tugging cry. "We've discussed divorce, yes, but . . . we'll never really do it. If we could only talk now, we could have a reconciliation. I can't really let Kyle go . . . nor he me . . ."

Oh, Christ, Mike thought with disgust as Lisa sobbed on. Reconciliation! He doubted if his brother had touched her ten times in as many years. Was Chris falling for his mother's histrionics? he wondered. No, a glance at the boy told him that although he was too well bred to insult his mother openly, Chris was no fool. He didn't even glance Lisa's way, but turned his attention to his uncle.

"Do you really believe Dad will be found?" he asked eagerly,

"Yes," Michael said adamantly. "I'm going to look for him myself," he added. "The company's pilots are good, but this is something I have to do myself."

Chris had been idly pacing the spacious drawing room, staring blankly at the oriental carpets. Now he stopped, and stared piercingly at Michael. "I'm going with you."

Michael shook his head with a soft smile, looking so much like Kyle that Chris felt his heart catapult. The brothers were very much alike, not so much in actual looks, but in manner, the twist of a smile, and the light of the eyes.

"You need to be here, Chris. Your father needs one of us to be running the company." Michael Jagger didn't want the boy with him if what he discovered was debris and bodies.

"I don't think either of you need to go," Lisa protested, afraid her strong-willed son would insist upon going anyway. "That producer the woman passenger was having an affair with has called out all kinds of special rescue fleets. Surely if they can be found . . ." Lisa was disgruntled to find both men ignoring her.

Chris was looking very mature again, no sign of fear or tears on his handsome face. "I'm going to go tell Gram you're off to look for Dad yourself, Uncle Michael. And then I'm going in to the office."

With a smile Chris left his mother and uncle.

Lisa glanced plaintively to Michael. "You will let me know as soon as you find . . . anything?" Her beautiful hands trailed possessively over the fine brocade upholstery of the mahogany sofa that faced the massive granite fireplace. "I do love Kyle, you know."

"Do you know, Lisa," Michael said, finally leaving the windows to approach the woman. He hunched before her. "I don't know if you love Kyle—I doubt it very much. I'm not even sure at times that you love Chris, but I do believe you would dearly love a reconciliation with my brother. You're getting older now, Lisa. And your failed love affairs are talked about all over. And you know, Lisa, I even think you always preferred my brother. You just thought for too long that you could do anything to him. But he never was a man you could step on, Lisa. I think we both know that. And I also think he's going to come back absolutely furious that you didn't sign the divorce decree yet." With Chris out of the room, Michael felt himself well capable of telling Lisa exactly what he thought. He was too sick and worried himself, too afraid to handle what acts she had to put on.

"You're a fool, Michael Jagger!" Lisa hissed. "They can't even find a trace of debris! Kyle is dead!" Tears formed in her eyes, and they were real tears. Lisa was confused. She knew Kyle's feelings for her bordered on hate, indifference, and disgust. She knew all the courtesies extended her over the years had been for Chris's sake. She knew that even now she sat in the Jagger home, playing court, because of her son.

But for all that she had done, Michael was right. There was no other man in the world like Kyle Jagger. Though his death would leave her in a far better position than the promised divorce, she didn't know what she really wanted. She did want to believe that Kyle was alive somewhere with all his vibrance, that he would fall in love with her again, that she would be the only woman in his arms.

But that was unlikely. And freed from her at last, Kyle well might marry again. And Lisa thought she just might prefer him dead, so she could dream of him, rather than know another now called herself his wife, slept in his bed, became mistress of his home.

"You wait and see, Michael," she hissed venomously, "if Kyle is alive, there will be no divorce. I plan to take my rightful place as his wife once again."

"Really?" Didn't Lisa know how much Kyle had confided in him? Michael wondered. Sure, Kyle had given in to Lisa's demands many times. For Chris's sake. But Chris was a man now. "I don't know," Michael said lightly, rising and pulling the front page of the newspaper that covered the crash off the end of a marble coffee table. "If he is alive, then so probably is his passenger." Michael couldn't prevent a teasing twinkle to his eyes. "And his passenger is quite a woman . . ."

"Oh, shut up!" She snapped. She didn't need Michael's opinion of Skye Delaney's attributes; during the past weeks, Lisa had studied every word in print about the woman. She rose and took a cigarette from a handsome ivory-inlaid box. "Don't forget Kyle's companion is going hot and heavy with that producer. And even if she and Kyle were to play a bit, he would never be serious . . ."

Michael laughed despite his deep fears. "Dear, dear, Lisa! Who are you trying to convince?" He turned his back on her, striding across the polished hardwood floors and smart oriental carpets with a snap to his feet that denoted purpose. "Good-bye, Lisa. I'm going to see my mother, and then I'm off. I will find Kyle. And I'm not too sure he's going to be pleased to find you at Montfort waiting."

Michael missed the calculating look that Lisa quickly hid by lowering her lashes. "I won't be at Montfort waiting," she said cryptically. "That is, if you do find Kyle . . ."

Seven

Inland the mosquitoes were bad. Cursing as he slashed at the insects attacking his flesh, Kyle continued his perusal of the jungle anyway.

Yesterday he had found the plane's log. He could quit searching, but it had given him something to do, something to fill the long days.

His nights were filled.

Kyle tried to force his mind from Skye, tried to concentrate on the abundance of trees and grass that flourished on the island. But no matter what, a vision of beguiling amber cat eyes came to him.

Skye no longer made any pretense of denying him. She had even come to him the next night, oddly thanking him; then, as darkness had fallen, she had teased him, telling him she had promised to get even.

He had watched warily as she had moved toward him straddling him, running her fingers through his chest hair.

He had watched the perfection above him, the heave of beautiful, full, rounded breasts, rose-tipped, proud above a lithe, thin torso, an incredibly slender waist.

And before their lovemaking was over, he had told her that he loved her.

She had stiffened momentarily before becoming consumed in their fire again. He knew she didn't believe him. They were words easily said in the heat of passion. And he didn't know if he meant them himself. He knew that he wanted to possess her, that he wanted her in his bed every night—be it a bed of sand or silk—that he wanted to care for her in a way he had never taken care of any woman.

But was it love? He had disdained the emotion for so long. And the relationship that had come to them physically had stilted their speech. She came to him in the night, and if she didn't come to him, he would take her. He never tired. And he was fully aware that he could always create arousal, elicit a sweet response, a passion deeper than any he had known, a beautiful, wonderful passion, so earthy, so heavenly intimate.

A fine sweat broke out across his brow. Strangers by day, lovers by night. He wanted more. He wanted her by the light, he wanted her to repudiate her past, the home she dreamed she would return to, the man she probably thought of and cherished by day.

He would never let her return, but how would he stop her?

I will, he assured himself. I will stop her. If he had to kidnap her and isolate her and surround her with guards, he would keep her.

It might not be easy, he reminded himself, and the flash of desire that accompanied his thoughts made him dizzy. He found a boulder protruding from the grassy floor and sat upon it, noting as he breathed deeply that his darkly tanned torso was slick with a cold sweat.

She had told him once that she was afraid of a pregnancy. She hadn't mentioned it again, and she had come to him willingly time and time again.

Was she an ostrich with her head in the sand? If so, the better for him. There were no lies between them.

They both knew the potential consequences of their torrid stay upon the island.

And he would continue to make it as torrid as possible.

A flash of pain jackknifed him. It was all so ironic. His first marriage had been forced on him by a pregnancy.

He was in the Air Force when he met Lisa. He had always loved flying, and the Air Force would train him and offer him the education he couldn't otherwise afford. It was at a dance off base.

At nineteen, and in uniform, Kyle Jagger was devastating. He'd been around a little, of course, but was still in no way prepared for Lisa Alden.

Her dress that night was flame red. It dipped low enough to reveal half of high, pointed breasts.

And she came straight to him, requesting a dance.

When she danced, she swayed, she moved against him, she tantalized with her eyes, she seduced.

And late that night she taught him things he had yet to know. It was a cheap hotel room, but it was a night he would never forget. He discovered in the morning that she was the daughter of one of the town's leading industrialists. And he also discovered, upon returning to base, that half his company had been beguiled into hotel rooms with her.

But he enjoyed Lisa. Base was dreary. Lisa, although capable of cruelty, was fun. She asked for no promises from him, she was beautiful, she was there.

And she began to see him exclusively. And then she began to tell him that she loved him. And before she could begin to make him nervous, she told him in tears that she was pregnant and her father would kill her.

He wasn't in love, but he had been involved. He had enjoyed her thoroughly. He was obligated, and so he married her. And he intended to make his marriage work, to give it a complete go.

He was startled when his son was born over a month ahead of time. He had thought to question.

And then he realized how completely he had been used. He knew from the moment Chris was born that the boy wasn't his. But even then he said nothing, not a word to still the nervous questions that now finally came to his wife's eyes.

The child wasn't at fault. He was a beautiful, husky, healthy baby boy. And when his tiny fingers curled around Kyle's, Kyle ceased to care. He lost what liking and admiration he had had for his wife, and turned all his attention to the child he would claim.

Maybe it wasn't entirely Lisa's fault. Maybe she realized she had lost the man she had come to love and need through her own treachery. And she was struck with the terribly sad realization that the truth would have stood her so much better. Kyle could forgive. If she had come to him honestly, he would have married her anyway. They would have had something.

Three months after their marriage, they were entirely estranged. They lived in the same house; they slept in the same bed; they hardly ever touched one another.

Lisa started going out at nights. Kyle was stationed in Europe, and she suddenly announced that she wanted to enter her father's business. She spent most of her time in the States. The care of the infant Chris, then the toddler Chris, fell to Kyle. He would come home every night, dismiss the sitter, and care for his son himself. He knew Lisa slept around; he just didn't give a damn. He was finding his comfort elsewhere on the few occasions when he found time to form friendships. He was a very busy man, even then creating the foundations for his company as he worked late into the night, long after Chris had fallen asleep.

Kyle went to work for a major airline when he returned to the States. He asked Lisa for a divorce. She refused him, telling him tearfully how the child, who loved him, would be hurt. Kyle claimed he could get custody. Perhaps he could have. But he didn't want Chris lacking a mother, no matter how worthless she was proving to be. They bought a house, a large house with several bedrooms. Kyle couldn't bear to sleep with her anymore.

He spent his free hours with his son, and working. Lisa was constantly gone, also working with her father. She very seldom made a meal, she was seldom there when Chris needed her. Yet she continued to claim she loved her son. And Chris did love his beautiful, vibrant mother.

Kyle tolerated his living situation as he slowly created Executive Charters. His younger brother had by then acquired his pilot's license, and together they flew the first flights.

Executive Charters took off. The company was well out of the red in its second year.

Kyle bought the mansion outside of San Francisco. More and more jets were purchased, more and more pilots hired. At thirty he was surprised to find himself a millionaire.

He brought his mother to live at Montfort. And he offered Lisa an extremely handsome settlement to give him at least a legal separation. She accepted. But she returned to Montfort often to visit—rather than take Chris away, she explained. And so she kept a suite of rooms at Montfort, and made it almost her home, much to the chagrin of Michael Jagger. He had seen his sister-in-law in action a few too many times. But he said nothing. Kyle didn't care what she did, so long as Christian wasn't hurt. And Michael was vaguely aware that Kyle, badly burned, had no intention of marrying again. Lisa was his shield; she kept all his affairs safe, his mistresses at bay.

But then Chris had reached his twentieth birthday and
no longer needed to be protected. Kyle's feelings about
a divorce began to change. And apparently Lisa, too, began to realize that occasionally seducing Kyle didn't im-
prove his opinion of her. The idea of half a fortune being
entirely hers began to look better and better . . . She had
no power, no influence over Kyle and she knew it.

Kyle drew a ragged breath and brushed his fingers
through his hair. The sun had begun to sink as he had
been lost in painful memory.

He didn't really hate Lisa. He could still remember how
lovely she was, how vibrant. She was spoiled, she was pampered. She had definitely used him. What he felt now was
pity. He could still remember the last time they had been
together. She had come to his room and something had
stirred within him. She was made right, and she had all
her moves down pat. But it had all been mechanics, re-
sulting in simple release.

And Lisa had thought she had something back. The
next day she had begun to lord it again—queen for a
day. He knew her, he knew she was incapable of not being
a user . . .

A dry, bitter laugh escaped Kyle.

Skye had called him a user. But of course she couldn't
know. He would have stayed with Lisa, probably even remained faithful, if she hadn't sought companionship elsewhere first, left him continuously. Marriage had, at one
time, meant everything to him. It was a vow.

Time had warped his ideals, and emotions. So now he
didn't understand himself. He only knew that he couldn't
let Skye go.

He stood then, thinking of Skye. He wanted to be back
with her, even if awkward silences reigned between them.
Night would fall.

Night—hell! he thought with a grin subtly streaking

across his features. He wanted to change things, this afternoon would be as good a time as any to start.

He whistled as he returned to camp, unmindful now of the mosquitoes that followed him. As he broke from the grass, he saw her, legs outstretched to the tide, torso balanced on the palms of her hands as she looked out to sea. He increased his pace, jogging silently across the sand until he was upon her, eliciting a startled cry from her as he pounced upon her, encircling her into his arms and rolling with her across surf and sand. He felt the vital warmth of her body, the feminine softness of her as her breasts were crushed to his chest. Her eyes were slightly alarmed, wide as he rolled her on top of him. Then she was turning a beautiful shade of pink as he slid his hands beneath the remains of her blouse and pulled her head down to savor her lips. He felt the pounding of her heart as he drank deeply.

When he released her she fumbled up, hands splayed across his chest, lashes lowered. He knew the ardor she gave him embarrassed her at times; she tried to ignore it by daylight, just as she tried to hide her mind and soul from him.

"I've missed you," he said huskily.

"Don't be ridiculous!" she murmured primly, struggling against his arms until she realized she was stuck. "You've only been gone a few hours."

"I missed you within ten minutes!" He laughed.

Skye finally opened her eyes fully to look down at him. He looked marvelous. He was deeply tanned now, and the muscles in his chest and shoulders were clearly defined, each visible and delineated. The auburn beard upon his chin was growing nicely. She had trimmed the ragged edges with her sewing scissors. And now, gently grinning from ear to ear, his eyes sparkling mischievously; his entire face was extraordinarily handsome, young, teasingly seductive. Skye shuddered slightly. He had become her whole world. She was so in love with him that he was part of her being. And yet she had to hold back something. So often he was distant, sometimes hard, utterly unapproachable. She couldn't allow herself to forget for one minute who he was, in real life. She had his passions, as he had hers. But it was infuriating to know that he knew all too well that he could touch her, and she would surrender, forget her own past, plead that he take her.

She was like a pet, cared for, pampered, ordered about at his convenience, forgotten when his mind went elsewhere . . .

He whispered words of love, but wouldn't he do that for all his mistresses?

Skye felt herself blushing again and pushed against his chest. "Kyle . . ."

"Do you know, Ms. Delaney," he informed her, refusing to let go, "you don't know how to play."

"I beg your pardon?" Skye murmured uneasily.

"Play. Take things easy. Enjoy yourself."

Her face was growing very hot. How could he say such a thing? Dear Lord, they had played continually.

He was working at her buttons. "Kyle!" she protested.

"I want to see you," his voice, in itself, fanned her flesh electrically.

"You've seen me!" she gasped.

"I want to see you in daylight. I want to look at you and look at you . . . and look at you . . ." Her blouse was open, but suddenly he pulled away. "Take it off for me, Skye."

She trembled, her eyes lowered. "I can't," she whispered.

"Please." It was soft, so soft; it compelled.

Eyes downcast, she slipped the garment from her arms.

"Everything," he urged. Skye could feel his devouring gaze, and despite all that had passed between them, she trembled again as she undid her bra.

She was, Kyle thought for the zillionth time, perfection. Her breasts were perfect, so firm, yet so soft . . . the nipples that provocative shade of deep rose. His breathing quickened and he said huskily, "Everything, Skye . . . please."

She rose above him, confused, suddenly aware that he was subtly changing their relationship again. He was asking more of her than he ever had before; he was asking for her trust, and in so doing, setting himself up for a certain amount of vulnerability.

She wanted to reach out for him so badly.

Standing over him, she shed her shorts.

As if her nerve endings had suddenly been given a sensitizing drug, she could feel everything acutely—the heat of the sun as it played upon her, the rush of the cool ocean air, the flow of the surf over her heels and toes. But more than any real sensation, she could feel Kyle's gaze. She opened her own to him, and the spasmodic shivers that had assailed her became shudders that contracted the muscles of her stomach in a heat of longing.

He watched her for a long, long while, scanning her from head to toe, the expression in his eyes dark yet gentle—all the reward she could ask for loosing all inhibitions. It felt good, she realized with a sudden little thrill. Good to stand naked beneath the sun, good to feel the sand of the earth with every fiber . . . good to allow the breeze to caress her flesh . . . good to feel the appreciation of his eyes . . .

Kyle finally rose, dropping his cutoffs. Skye felt her lids lower as he came to her, laughing softly.

"Why look away now?" he murmured, his hands falling to her shoulders. "Don't you like my backside anymore?"

"Of course," Skye murmured, then stuttered, "that was before . . ."

He laughed again huskily, then began to plant butterfly kisses over her face, hedging her lips. His lips seared her down to her shoulders, creating moist streaks over the hollows with his tongue. Then he sank to his knees before her; his tongue sought her navel, the contours of her hips. The fire was so great that she cried out, digging her fingers into the breadth of his shoulders, convulsively moving them to his hair. Still his kisses moved on until her cries and moans were incoherent pleadings.

He bore her down to the surf. The foam teased her thighs along with his arousing fingers and lips. The pleasure was so intense, so achingly sweet, it was almost unbearable.

And then his lips finally met hers along with his explosion within her. The heat of the sun mingled with theirs; the relentless pounding of the ocean was their rhythm, the lash of the waves, the incredible wash upon wash of sensation. And when it was over, it was the surf that cooled them, the sun that benignly blessed them with its warmth.

Skye was at peace, and yet she was torn. Basking in his arms was bliss; she had never known such a feeling of total belonging, of such wonderful, fulfilling satiation. At the moment their disaster was a paradise, their solitude a gentle miracle.

But the storms would come again. Sea and sky would rage destruction, perhaps eventually death. She feared with a trembling terror that they would be stuck on the island eternally, yet she was beginning to fear with an equal ardor a return to civilization.

Here Kyle belonged to her. While she as yet could not clearly remember the planes of Ted's face, and while her own business became less important, she was well aware that Kyle was restless. His mind was often on his business, she was sure. And more. She had often watched him covertly when his eyes were off to sea, when she could feel that he was totally lost in his past.

Who awaited him? she wondered. And, despite his

words, did he perhaps miss the wife he claimed to have no love for. Or were there others? A mistress he gave to as he did to her, a woman he loved, a woman she replaced physically.

She realized he was watching her again. Leaning upon an elbow, he seemed contented. The warmth remained in the lime of his eyes. He smiled as her eyes met his. He ran a gentle finger from the cleft of her collarbone to her navel.

"I don't think there are words," he said softly, "to tell you how wonderful you are."

He laughed as the eternal blush filled her cheeks and her lashes lowered. "Un-unh!" he teased. "Look at me."

She did so.

"I want you to be entirely at ease," he told her softly. "I want you to be as comfortable with me as you are with yourself . . ." He caressed her as he spoke, fondling her breast with fascination, as if he never tired of exploration.

"I am at ease with you," Skye murmured, tensing again to his touch. Words quavered on her lips. She wanted to tell him that she loved him, but she didn't dare. He said so only in moments of passion.

He was on his feet suddenly, pulling her up. "Let's go swimming."

And then they were in the water, and Kyle was teaching her just how much fun it could be to play. He touched her again and again in the surf; she touched him back, she learned to stare and touch in return, heedless of the daylight, bold and brash and knowing. She laughed with him as she never had before; she made love in the water, able to stare into his eyes all the while.

But late that night, curled together in the hut, she softly asked him a question. "You're anxious to get back, aren't you, Kyle."

He was half asleep, pleasantly inhaling the clean scent of her hair. "Of course," he murmured drowsily. "My whole life is back there. Don't worry," he added, believing she needed the assurance he didn't feel himself. "Rescue will come." Then he stiffened slightly himself, barely controlling the harshness of his cross-questioning. "You must be very anxious to get back, too."

Skye couldn't possibly understand his meaning. He had just told her that she wasn't any permanent part of his life . . .

"Yes, I'm very anxious to get back," she responded. "My entire life waits, too."

A sudden fury hit Kyle. "Don't hold your breath for tomorrow," he said, not hiding the gravel now. "We may be here a long, long time."

His arms were tight around her; they were almost cruel. Skye felt tears burn behind her eyelids. She had allowed herself a foolish mistake; she had allowed herself to forget he was K. A. Jagger.

And she had become his island toy. He was a man of strong desires and needs, and he would play at his whim. He was well aware that his toy hadn't the strength to resist him.

A single hot tear trickled silently down her cheek. She had allowed herself to become the mistress of a man whose mistresses she scorned.

He was searching again, although he had no idea of what he searched for.

Skye was sleeping when he left her. Upon their ragged sheets she had been a beautiful sight, her sleek limbs tanned and elegant. Her hair, too, was touched by the sun; it was fanned out in platinum splendor around her delicate features.

The irrational anger that had struck him the night before returned to him. Without bothering for a drink of water, he struck off into the island, hoping to ease the tensions that assailed him.

And today he was to make a startling discovery.

He was about a hundred yards from the spot where the plane had exploded, and he didn't even see it at first. He knew he was upon it because his toe struck it, hard with the fervor of his stride.

It was a case, a metal case. Scorched and scarred, but obviously bomb-proof. It had survived the explosion.

"What the . . . ?" he murmured, surveying it, testing the cool metal with his fingers. The case was squat, no more than a foot and half by three, but its depth matched its width, and when Kyle attempted to lift it, he found it surprisingly heavy. It's made of steel, he thought. He was able to pick up the case, but it was like lifting weights.

He set the case back down, studying the catches. There were three, below and flanking the handle. Each catch was some type of lock.

Kyle picked up a rock and began hammering away at the catches. He didn't know how long he pounded. His hair and skin were wet from his exertions; beads of perspiration slicked the breadth of his shoulders and trickled miserably through the growth of his beard.

His huge rock cracked before the first catch. But he sensed a give and scouted the ground for a second rock. Under normal circumstances, he thought vaguely, it would probably take a herd of elephants to snap the catches. But the force of the explosion had given him a chance.

He went through four more rocks before snapping two of the lock catches. Another two rocks—and timeless persistence and determination—and the third catch gave.

And then the case was open. And what met his eyes stole his breath in a sharp intake.

Gold, its brilliance blinding beneath the sun. Small bars, five pounds, he decided as his fingers automatically

reached to lift one. But there were many of them. Fifty
to seventy pounds in all and stamped. Issue bars of the
Australian government? *They had to be.*

His mind ticked away even with his shock as he calcu-
lated the worth of his find. A small fortune. And then he
made a second discovery. The depth of the case was de-
ceptive. It was double walled in the same steel. Something
else had been brilliantly secreted into the case, and as he
realized that it was unlikely that even his herd of elephants could break the steel of the inner case, he felt a
new outpouring of perspiration bead his features, and
then turned cold, very cold.

The entire thing had probably been brilliantly engineered. Set indestructibly into the false bottom and lining,
Kyle was sure there would be a tracking device—maybe
two or three. It couldn't possibly be lost, couldn't possibly
be removed.

Kyle suddenly began to wonder if the hydraulic failure
of his plane hadn't been planned. Wondering led to being positive that that was the case.

And that being positive led him to wonder again. How
had the gold gotten aboard his Lear?

His thoughts fell instantly to the woman who already
held his wrath this morning, the designer who dealt in
gold. He thought of the innocence that combined with
the sensuousness of her amber cat eyes. His only passenger, solitary passenger, the only other human being to
come aboard the plane after checkout.

Anger exploded in his mind. His plane, his company,
he had been used.

With tight lips a grim line against the auburn bush of
his beard and the bronze of his face, he made his way
painstakingly back to their shelter, the case feeling more
and more as if it weighed a ton as he hefted it high on
his shoulder to plod his way through the sand.

Kyle stormed into the hut, body sleek with sweat, muscles strained and taut. He heaved the heavy case down beside the sleeping girl, undaunted from his fury as the sudden thud next to her ear awakened her, sending her startled eyes wide open with alarm, her torso jerking upward in panic. She saw him, saw the case, met his eyes, her own pleading confusion.

She was lovely as she looked at him, her fair hair splayed around her shoulders, falling provocatively over her naked breasts. But her very loveliness increased his wrath. He had been used once by beauty and innocence and he had done the right thing—the honorable thing.

But now he felt sick. His pain was gut-wrenching. He had fallen in love with her.

"I found something I think you were missing," he said harshly.

Skye desperately tried to unmuddle her groggy thoughts. Strange, was her first coherent realization, yesterday she had felt so natural with him. But now, with him glowering down at her, clad half respectably in his cutoffs while she had on nothing, she felt vulnerable, stripped of everything.

"I don't know what you're talking about," she murmured, scrambling to retrieve the sheets from beneath her and wrap herself in them. Anything to shield herself from this scowling stranger who had the power to rend her limb from limb.

"What am I talking about?" Her words had further incensed him. Mindless of her feelings, her state of dress or undress, he reached down with both hands and wrenched her to her feet by her shoulders, glaring relentlessly into her eyes. The sheet fell to the sand, but he ignored her gasp. "Gold, Ms. Delaney, I'm talking about gold. Funny, but it was on my plane. And I didn't put it there. Stolen gold, Ms. Delaney.

Skye's eyes fell to the case with horror. "I didn't put it there!" she protested desperately. "I—"

"I can only assume that you were working with some-one," he rasped heatedly. "And I'm also assuming you know damned well someone will come to this island. Your accomplice will be looking for that."

"Don't be absurd!" Skye grated, tilting her head de-spite the pain of his tense grip upon her shoulders. "Why would I . . . why would I have to—dammit, I'm not sui-cidal!"

"The way I see it, Ms. Delaney," Kyle continued tersely, "you're not suicidal. I don't think that at all. I think you've been betrayed. You were just the lackey—the one who was supposed to get the gold aboard the plane. You were perfect, known by the government, perfect creden-tials. A businesswoman who frequently comes in and out of the country—very respectable. But apparently your ac-complice didn't intend to do any sharing. I think the Lear was supposed to go down—in fact, I'm damned sure now that the hydraulic equipment was tampered with. No, you're not suicidal. You must have been every bit as shocked at the crash as I. Betrayed. Your accomplice got you to get the gold out of the country, but, you poor dear, he—or she—never intended to share. You should have never gotten into smuggling, Skye."

"How dare you!" Skye demanded in full temper. "I'm not a smuggler! I have more than sufficient income of my own! I didn't bring any gold aboard your plane," she said in a scathing tone. "All my purchases go through the government! If there was something aboard your plane that you didn't know about, it was lack of efficiency by your own company. And how do I know you didn't know anything about it? You could have been a smuggler as well as I. Perhaps that's why Executive Charters has done so well so quickly."

He was tempted to strike her. He pushed her from him, and winced as she lost her balance and fell to the sand. He didn't know what to think, his emotions were clouding his mind. Why was he in such a wrath? If he had found the gold yesterday, he wouldn't have told her. He would have thought that it would have frightened her. And yet here he was today, accusing her.

She was the only other person aboard the plane.

But he did believe that the plane had been tampered with. Might she have been involved in something that could cost her own life? The depression she had fallen into that day had been real. She had been ready to give everything up until he had brought her back to life with his needs and desires and, yes, caring, needing, specifically, her.

"Skye—" He reached a hand down to her.

"Don't!" she snapped, cringing away from him.

He turned on his bare heels and left her hunched in the hut.

It was some time before she could get herself together, but Skye finally managed to stop the ridiculous flow of tears that drenched her cheeks despite her insistence that she should be furious, not broken. He thought she was a thief. He could take her, hold her, laugh, make love to her with tireless energy.

And then he could become an absolute stranger. A power she couldn't touch.

When she emerged from the hut, he was nowhere to be seen. She forced herself to eat, although the overabundance of coconut she was consuming was beginning to make her sick. It went down like cardboard.

Still, Kyle didn't return.

She spent part of the day collecting water, determined to survive without him. But as the dreary hours passed with painstaking slowness, she became more and more agitated.

I'm a coward, she told herself morosely.

And she was a coward. As night fell, she began to shiver. She managed to get a fire started, but it was weak. Kyle hadn't been out with his spear, so there was no fish to eat. Only by severely lecturing herself could she force more fruit into her system.

She had never felt such miserable confusion. No matter what he thought, she wanted him near her. Despite his harshness, despite the cruel things he had said to her, she knew she loved him still. She knew why he had easily had so many mistresses, she knew why his wife clung to the thread of their marriage.

And she knew that if he came back, she would fall at his feet and beg that he believe in her and just allow her to be near him, anyway he chose it to be at all.

"No," she whispered aloud to herself. She had to cling to something. Pride was all she had. She couldn't bear to think of herself as a clinging, begging woman . . .

"I'll go to sleep," she told herself. "And when I wake up, it will be day. I'll be all right."

Tossing and turning, and fighting waves of terror, she tried to sleep within the little shelter offered by the hut. But the island seemed to come to life that night. She could hear things rustling through the trees, she could feel things crawling on her; the ocean seemed to set up a wail that threatened and howled.

Skye grit her teeth against her fear. She counted sheep all the way up to one thousand. She shifted position endlessly.

And she didn't dare open her eyes. She knew her poor fire was dying out.

It was exhaustion that finally claimed her. But not even sleep brought the release she craved. Her dreams were more torturous than ever.

Steven was there. He kept screaming out that it was dark. He kept pointing over her shoulder, and telling her that more darkness was coming. It would claim them, it would bury them, it would take them to hell. Night birds, dark and red-eyed, assailed them. Their screeches tore the black skies asunder. They were in her hair, they tugged and pulled, their screeches turning to demented laughter.

"It's so dark! It's so dark! Help me!" Steven screamed.

But she couldn't help him. She was screaming herself. She was fighting off the birds with the hell's-fire red eyes. She was pleading that they leave her alone. She fought and flailed and screamed and screamed.

"Skye."

Her eyes flew open, but she was still fighting madly. Her eyes were glazed, fogged, and she trembled with a terror she still couldn't control.

"Skye." The voice was soft and soothing. Her hands and nails struck against flesh, but he held her patiently. She finally became subdued, crying softly as strong arms encompassed her.

"It's all right, I'm here," the voice soothed over and over again. "And the fire is going again, Skye. It isn't dark anymore. I'm here, my darling, let me hold you."

"Kyle," she choked in a panting gasp.

"Yes, I'm here."

"You left me," she accused him softly in a daze.

"I'll never leave you again."

His fingers stroked her hair comfortingly. He could feel her shivers, he could feel the cold clamminess of her skin. She made no protest but sat still dazed as he stripped her clothing from her. He brought her down beside him.

Something of what had transpired between them entered her mind. "No," she murmured.

"I'm just trying to warm you, babe," he murmured, and his strong arms and powerful frame came around her.

He was warmth, and he was strength. His heat radiated to her, and she finally stopped shivering. She wanted the feel of his smooth skin against her; she buried her head into the mat of his chest.

"I'm not a thief," she murmured, a touch of indignation in her voice.

He smiled at the soft, reproachful hurt in her voice.

"I know you're not," he said soothingly, enveloping her more thoroughly. Desire sprang into his loins as his manhood brushed between her thighs, but he contained himself, making no movement. He had come to comfort her; he had come at her first cry. His feelings for her went beyond anything so natural. He had only stayed away because near her, he couldn't think. He had hurt her; he couldn't take her.

But she shifted, parting her thighs, sliding against him. "Make love to me, Kyle," she murmured. Only then could she be warm, only then would the nightmare be vanquished entirely.

He couldn't take, but he couldn't refuse to give.

And long after he had filled her with warmth, exhaustion, and peace, he lay awake.

Tomorrow he would have to tell her what the repercussions of his discovery might be. They no longer needed to fear drug smugglers. Someone more deadly would be looking for gold.

Eight

"You're making absolutely no sense to me," Skye said warily. Kyle had apologized for yelling at her, but not for accusing her. There was a subtle difference there, she thought bitterly. "If someone was trying to steal gold, why tamper with the plane? What good would their gold do them on the floor of the Pacific? And nine out of ten that's where the plane should have gone down."

"I believe there is some type of tracking device attached to the case," Kyle explained quietly, idly poking at the morning fire. "The case has a false bottom and false sides. Something important is concealed. And our thief is probably an expert diver. He would know the general vicinity in which we would lose power. He would have planned carefully." He switched his gaze from the low flames to Skye. She had taken to combing her hair the customary hundred strokes every morning and every night before the fire, which made him glad of his gift. He loved to watch her, and he loved the feeling of domesticity. He lit a cigarette as he watched her through the smoke haze that rose. They were definitely becoming creatures of habit. He was down to two a day—one of which was always with her as she combed her hair in the morning. It dawned on him awkwardly just how comfortable—barring quarrels and that strange distance they both kept—it was becoming to live with her.

Skye stopped combing and chewed uneasily on an edge

of the tortoiseshell. "Then why hasn't this thief appeared yet?"

"What? Oh." Kyle inhaled deeply and exhaled slowly. He shrugged. "There could be a number of reasons. One, he might be waiting for the turmoil of our disappearance to die down. Two, he might be waiting for the turmoil of the gold's disappearance to die down. Three, he might have a job he can't just leave without creating suspicion."

Skye bit harder on the comb, trying to quell the shivers of deadly apprehension his tale elicited. "So," she said quietly, "you believe that eventually the person who engineered the whole deal will appear."

Kyle nodded.

"So you think we're in danger."

"Yes."

Skye stood angrily, tossing her comb into the sand near the fire and planting her hands on her hips as she glared down at him, the firelight catching the amber of her eyes and giving them a dazzling gleam. She was shaking, she was afraid, and the only way she could deal with it all without going crazy was to throw it back to him.

"What are you saying? Why are you telling me this? Someone is going to come to this island with the belief that we're dead and the intent to make us so since we're not, and you're simply sitting there telling me that is the way it is! And you calmly tell me that yes, we're in danger, and all you can do is smoke your stinking cigarette!"

Goaded by her tone, Kyle stiffened and rose slowly, approaching her until he stood an inch from her, towering over her. For a moment it looked as if he wished to strangle her, and Skye had to swallow to keep herself from backing away. She wished she could take back her words. He was trying to explain a situation to her, but she was so frightened and so frustrated. There wasn't a direction in which she could possibly look that would offer any type of an answer . . . any help.

"I'm sorry, Ms. Delaney," he said with steel in his voice, "I intend to do all the chivalrous things, but I can't carve out a gun for you from a coconut shell, only take the first bullet."

"Oh, God," Skye gasped, covering her face with her hands.

Kyle was immediately struck with remorse. Christ, he should be handling the situation better. If only he were sure she was all she looked and claimed to be.

What did it really matter? he wondered. He had called the rules of the island; he had wanted her, he had taken her. A tic tightened in his cheek. He wanted her still, forever. She belonged to him now; he would cherish and protect as well as possess. Didn't she know that? That he would happily die before allowing a hair on her head to be harmed? He reached to tell her so, but as her hands moved from her face, courage was burning in her eyes. "I'm sorry," she said curtly, backing away from him now. "Perhaps you can tell me what we might do."

"Skye," Kyle said with a long sigh, "I didn't tell you any of this simply to scare you. You have to be prepared to watch everything. You can't go running after a ship like you did—"

"The day we saw the drug smugglers," Skye interrupted impatiently. "I know that. You told me then we'd have to be careful. But . . ." She swallowed again. "This is different, this is . . . is . . ."

He finally saw the slight quiver to her lower lip. "This is worse," he finished for her quietly, "and it's serious. But it's not the end—you just have to know where we stand. And"—he finally smiled for her, longing to reach out and touch her—"I do have a plan."

"What?" He saw the relief in her features. She was relying on him. If only he were invincible, he thought.

"We're going to get off the island."

She understood him immediately. "A raft?"

"Ummmm."

He didn't need to touch, she came to him. "Oh, Kyle, can we? Do you think we can build one that will get us somewhere?"

He smiled again, captivated as always as he stared down into her eyes. Her hands, petite and soft, were against his chest. He brought his arms around her and gently dipped to kiss the tip of her nose.

"Yes, we can do it."

Suddenly he crushed her to him, his fingers entwined in the silk of her hair. He would get them off the island, but he would be damned if he would let her go then.

He released his hold and she raised her head, her eyes meeting his with confusion.

"Kiss me," he commanded her, stunned by the harshness of his voice. He felt a shiver ripple through her lithe body, saw the flare in her eyes. But the flare was touched by the passion that could rule her and she complied, lacing surprisingly strong slender arms around his neck and raising her head to his. Her lips met his fully, parting at the fullness of his, meeting him with a staggering volatility. The sweet heat of her mouth was his, the fiery vibrancy of her delicately voluptuous form. He held the embrace, tongue thrusting deeply, consumingly, as if to meld with her for all time, for moments of a hell's-fire eternity. Something about the hot, vibrant passion she gave him was reassuring; he finally released her, meeting her open eyes. "The arguing stops here," he told her. "We live together, we love together, we trust together."

Skye nodded, loath to bring her arms from his neck. Oh, God, she thought desperately, if only . . . if only she could stay with him and have him until they turned old and gray. She wouldn't care if they never left the island, if she lived all her days at his side, listening to his velvet voice, feeling the ripple of muscles beneath her fingers. "The arguing stops here," she murmured. They didn't really argue so much, did they?

"And no more prim Ms. Delaney."

"What?" Skye's brows furrowed in a frown.

"We're going to be careful, Skye. We're going to build a raft. But in the meantime, we're not going to stop living."

"I don't know what you mean."

He smiled enigmatically and traced the outline of her lips with a gentle finger. "I'll show you later," he murmured. "For the moment we have a raft to build, right?"

"Yes." Skye returned his smile. "We have a raft to build."

By late that afternoon Skye was wishing they had long ago decided to build a raft. She enjoyed spending the time with Kyle, being with him constantly, working at his side. The hours passed like quicksilver. She learned which trees were most buoyant, which vines would create the strongest ties. She ventured farther into the plateaued ridges of the island than she had ever dared before, and listened contentedly as Kyle explained how the action of volcanoes and earthquakes had charted the Pacific. He told her about the islands he visited, about peoples, places, and things. He kept her laughing half the day. The only note of seriousness came when he told her they were going to attempt to camouflage the hut so that they could see before they were seen. Skye silently helped him with a thatching that Kyle assured her would blend their living quarters with the island from any distance.

"I must compliment you, Ms. Delaney," he teased when they were done with work for the day.

"Oh?" Skye had an itch on her cheek and she rubbed it against his shoulder.

"You haven't been at all prim."

"No," she agreed, appreciating the smooth tension that rippled from his shoulder to her face as she rested against him.

The sun was slowly setting. Its rays were majestic shades, delicate shades. The sand was bathed in a soft mauve haze while the sky was streaked with vibrant violet and magenta. The ocean was turning a mysterious indigo, whimsically tipped by the foam of rising whitecaps.

The breeze was strong, fanning the natural paradise, shaping shadows with the dipping palms. A breath that was pure magic was in the air.

"You were going to show me something," Skye murmured lazily against the taut skin of his back. "Something about living."

"Ummm . . ." he murmured in return.

He spun suddenly and caught her in his arms, assailing her with slow, heated moist kisses along her shoulder, lifting her hair to allow his lips to wander sensuously to the nape of her neck and back to her earlobe. The soft whisper of his breath, then the grazing of gentle teeth and the touch of his tongue, sent her into quivering spasms as waves of sensation washed over her.

"Kyle . . ." she murmured, burying her head against his chest, feeling and loving the brush of coarse hair against her cheek.

He moved back from her, holding her shoulders. The fire he had stoked just moments before leaped high and Skye could clearly see his fine profile, chiseled to be arrogant, formed to be proud, against the radiant colors of the night. His lips were full and sensuous, easily tightened, but easily forming a smile, easily touching her with such volatile results.

"Kyle," she murmured again. She was coming to know him so well that she could feel him with every fiber of her body, a body acutely attuned to his . . .

She *was* coming to know him so well. And yet, she

thought, a chill steeling her, she *didn't* know him at all. She didn't know him off the island, she didn't know the man he was in real life. Even now he could close himself to her, even now she could wonder what caused the fierce expression in his countenance.

He had a past; he had a life. He chose not to share it with her. And suddenly she realized that she had been glad, that she had gone to him many times ignoring the possibilities of other lives, of their situation changing.

She didn't want to change anything. She didn't want to know anything. She could and would pretend that the world outside of their rose and violet sunset didn't exist.

His fingers tensed upon her shoulders and she looked at him wonderingly. His eyes flickered now with a tense emotion she couldn't understand, and then he shook her slightly.

"Don't ever turn away from me, Skye," he said hoarsely.

She shook her head, unable to comprehend his mood. Turn away? She was waiting for his lead. Something in her silent answer, in the open depths of her amber eyes, must have been right. His mood mercurially changed. He laughed and scooped her high in his arms, his whispers throaty as he carried her fully clothed into the indigo surf.

If ever man was meant for paradise, this was he.

His laughter continued as he swirled her in huge circles within the dark, cool bath of the ocean. Her laughter rose to join his. They spun and spun as the colors intensified, as magic ruled the coming of the night. And then their laughter stopped as they looked deep into one another's eyes. Kyle was still. He finally moved to kiss her, his eyes holding hers until their lips touched, and then closing slowly.

He held her still as he strode out of the water, until

Take **4 FREE** Books!

Zebra created its convenient Home Subscription Service so you'll be sure to get the hottest new romances delivered each month right to your doorstep — usually before they are available in book stores. Just to show you how convenient Zebra Home Subscription Service is, we would like to send you 4 Zebra Historical Romances as a FREE gift. You receive a gift worth up to $24.96 — absolutely FREE. There's no extra charge for shipping and handling. There's no obligation to buy anything - ever!

Save Even More with Free Home Delivery!

Accept your FREE gift and each month we'll deliver 4 brand new titles as soon as they are published. They'll be yours to examine FREE for 10 days. Then if you decide to keep the books, you'll pay the preferred subscriber's price of just $4.20 per title. That's $16.80 for all 4 books for a savings of up to 32% off the publisher's price! What's more...$16.80 is your total price...there is no additional charge for the convenience of home delivery. Remember, you are under no obligation to buy any of these books at any time! If you are not delighted with them, simply return them and owe nothing. But if you enjoy Zebra Historical Romances as much as we think you will, pay the special preferred subscriber rate of only $16.80 each month and save over $8.00 off the bookstore price!

We have 4 FREE BOOKS for you as your introduction to
KENSINGTON CHOICE!

To get your FREE BOOKS, worth up to $24.96, mail the card below. or call TOLL-FREE 1-888-345-BOOK

Take 4 Zebra Historical Romances FREE!

MAIL TO: ZEBRA HOME SUBSCRIPTION SERVICE, INC.
120 BRIGHTON ROAD, P.O. BOX 5214,
CLIFTON, NEW JERSEY 07015-5214

✌ YES! Please send me my 4 FREE ZEBRA HISTORICAL ROMANCES (without obligation to purchase other books). Unless you hear from me after I receive my 4 FREE BOOKS, you may send me 4 new novels – as soon as they are published - to preview each month FREE for 10 days. If I am not satisfied, I may return them and owe nothing. Otherwise, I will pay the money-saving preferred subscriber's price of just $4.20 each... a total of $16.80. That's a savings of over $8.00 each month and there is no additional charge for shipping and handling. I may return any shipment within 10 days and owe nothing, and I may cancel any time I wish. In any case the 4 FREE books will be mine to keep.

Name _____

Address _____ Apt No _____

City _____ State _____ Zip _____

Telephone (   ) _____ Signature _____

(If under 18, parent or guardian must sign)

Terms, offer, and price subject to change.   Orders subject to acceptance.

KR0699

AFFIX
STAMP
HERE

KENSINGTON CHOICE
Zebra Home Subscription Service, Inc.
120 Brighton Road
P.O.Box 5214
Clifton, NJ 07015-5214

he reached the high burning fire and deposited her gently, tenderly, beside it.

"Are you cold?" he asked as she shivered.

She nodded.

"I'll warm you," he promised, still gentle, still achingly tender as he worked upon the buttons of her fraying blouse, his fingers trembling. They watched one another as he eased the fabric from her shoulders.

Skye stood then, shedding her damp shorts with innate grace. Kyle rose before her. She reached for him, sliding her fingers beneath the band of his pants. A thrill, the heat she had been promised, suffused through her as she heard his groan, felt the contraction of his stomach muscles. She held his eyes as her fingers found the button, released the zipper, held his eyes as she eased her fingers over his bare buttocks, sliding his shorts to the ground. Stepping from them, Kyle kicked them aside.

A sudden streak of gold filtered through the magenta of the dying day. It met with the glow of the fire; it covered them with a sheen of warm, provocative, glorious light.

It was paradise; it was Eden, and like the magic of Eden, they were perfect creatures as they faced one another, man and woman, tanned to that glowing silken sheen by the sun, strong and firm and lithe of limb.

Skye was sure she had never seen anything more splendid than his naked form touched by the golden sun. She closed her eyes for a dizzying moment. He was hers, but he wasn't hers. No, the night was magic. It was hers. The breeze whispered, the surf intoxicated. With a little whimper, she moved to him.

Standing on tiptoe, she planted light kisses against his lips, up the line of his cheek to his eyes. His hands splayed over her hips to grip her buttocks firmly, drawing her to him. But she held away, savoring each salt taste of his skin as she continued her kisses, grazing his shoulders lightly with her teeth, following the touch of her lips with that of light fingers. Lower and lower she moved, teasing male nipples, luxuriating in the sound of his shortening breath, in the feel of his tensing flesh. Her kisses moved downward until she dropped to her knees and his fingers traced a pattern of fire as they grazed up her spine from tailbone to nape, resting in her hair as he groaned. He tilted her chin firmly so that she would meet his eyes openly even in the burning heat of the passion she wantonly offered.

Her eyes were beautiful, he thought, and then he couldn't think. Paradise. He had been offered paradise. Sensations spread through him that were agonizingly sweet. And then his groan of delirious pleasure rent through the still, sweet air. He was drawing her to him, lifting her to lay her once more beside the flames that displayed the feminine curves and angles so willingly offered him. Insane and pulsing with desire as he was, he still had to pause. Perhaps it was only a second, a second in which paradise was forever ingrained in his mind—the giving in delicate face and fascinating eyes; the rise of firm, hard-tipped breasts bathed in the firelight; the shadows of slender hips; the beautiful long limbs that shifted with exquisite intimacy to open and accept him.

Magenta and gold exploded within Skye's mind and vision.

Kyle had never been more tender, more gentle, yet never more ardent, more wild. Her heart was seared by the crackle of the fire that seemed to rage around them; her head was filled with the glowing gold. The music of the breeze and surf touched her ears in a wild rhapsody. Kyle touched her, and touched her; all through the magenta storm that assailed them, he touched her, taking her lips, cradling her breasts, holding her hips with firm possession, rhythmically driving them tighter and tighter together, melded as one.

And when the climax caught them in an explosion of color—violet and gold and searing red—he kept on touching her.

And then he was kissing her, tongue and teeth teasing from head to toe, then taking and demanding, seeking intimacies that drove her crazy, drove her mad, drove her to cry his name and demand that he be within her again.

Sunset was indigo night, the water one with the sky. They didn't think to eat that night, nor to move to their shelter. They stayed beneath the velvet of the sky, beside the fire of paradise.

They both knew that strangely this, of all sunsets, had marked a proverbial new day in Eden.

And not even Kyle was worried. He had meant to tell her that they shouldn't have fires at night anymore, that to rest they needed the cover of complete darkness.

He knew that beyond a doubt nothing would break the spell of the night. He knew he had been granted magic, given paradise.

It was incredibly rough going. Even with his crudely created tools, Kyle was having difficulty with the raft. It was different than benches and chairs he had created for their use; the raft had to be secure, had to be completely and painstakingly safe.

Neither of them minded the time. If it weren't that she spent strange moments, assailed by chills, looking over her shoulder although she knew danger couldn't actually sneak upon them, Skye would have been happy. Happier than she had ever been in her life.

Kyle had warned her of the danger of the fire at night, and she had nodded agreement that it no longer burn. She had feared the nightmares, but the nightmares no longer came. She slept, knowing that he held her.

She frowned. That had been five nights ago . . . hadn't

it? She wasn't really sure, time had lost all meaning. Days had passed, weeks had passed. She closed her eyes, her features tense as she tried to concentrate. "Six weeks," she said aloud suddenly. "We've been here a full six weeks as of today."

Kyle paused in his efforts to hack through a tree limb. His shoulders were bathed in perspiration; he ran the back of his forearm over his brow and watched her. He looked at the pseudo-hatchet in his clenched hand and then dropped it with a casual sigh, rubbing the growth of his beard as he sat beside Skye. "Six weeks, huh?"

Skye nodded. Her hands also became still on the vines she had soaked, stretched, and soaked again, and now braided for strength. She glanced at Kyle's profile, at the way he looked out at the sea from the ridged height of the plateau where they worked.

"It bothers you, doesn't it?" she asked.

He shrugged, his arm coming comfortably around her although his gaze remained on the sea.

Of course it bothers him, Skye thought blankly. That was normal. Why wasn't it bothering her? There should have been something . . .

And then she again began to wonder why it was she could sell her very soul for Kyle and she wasn't even missing Ted. Skye closed her eyes, forcing herself to think, to search for a past that could fill her heart with a normal remorse.

Everything had always been so easy, so good. She had met him at the opening of a play and immediately been intrigued by his quiet charm, impressed by his natural manner. He was not her picture of the stereotypical producer. He had not come on to her, but flowers had arrived at her apartment the next day. And then he had called for dinner.

A picture of Ted finally filled her vision, and stayed—

warm, deep eyes, tawny hair, quietly but impeccably dressed as he stood at her door that first night.

She had been a fledgling in business then, and he had advised and encouraged. He saw her steadily, but never remarked upon the months when she would leave and spend time in Sydney. Why hadn't she ever pushed him to come? she wondered. Everything should have been there. But it wasn't. And somehow she had known. And she had known about Steven, and she couldn't talk, couldn't share, even when she knew she was going to lose her twin, the brother with whom she had an indefinable bond. The lifelong friend whom she had naturally teased and tortured, but with whom she had shared her adolescent dreams, the years of growing up, of learning to live in the world.

She was over Steven's death now, she realized. And it was because of Kyle. But it wasn't Ted's fault that he had never helped her; she had never allowed him in. Why? she wondered again desperately. There wasn't a single thing wrong with Ted. He was good, he was kind and gentle. He had been as tender and giving as a man could be.

We love where we love, she thought sadly, then gave herself an inward, bitter grimace. How profound. She should love Ted because they were free and they were right, and she shouldn't love Kyle because he really wasn't free, and he was an enigma of a man, giving so much, yet holding back, taking her, caring for her, and still at times giving her the feeling that she was a well-kept possession, kindly treated unless she tread over certain bounds.

In every relationship, she thought with a sudden bit of astute wisdom, no matter how equal, one partner held a percentage more of the power. With Ted it had been her.

With Kyle, she was forced to admit, he held the power. He knew it and would have it so. And she was forced to admit that it didn't matter, which was hard. She was proud, she was independent. She ruled her own world, or she had.

"Thinking about home?"

His query was soft. Skye opened her eyes to see that he no longer gazed idly over the ocean, but gazed intently upon her.

"Sort of," she murmured.

She sensed a tension in him, but still his reply was quiet. "We will get back." He was silent for a moment and then queried, "Why didn't you ever marry him?"

Had he known that she had been thinking of Ted? If so, had he read her thoughts? She hoped not. It would be terrifying to have him know how vulnerable she was, how she had ceased to care for anything but him when she knew well his mind still dwelt elsewhere . . .

Skye shrugged. "Is marriage so all-important?"

"Marriage is a commitment," he replied. "Are you afraid of commitment?"

Again Skye shrugged. She didn't want this conversation; she didn't want any intrusions from the real world.

"You made a commitment," she reminded him. "And look at your past years. I think my way is preferable."

"But I took a chance," Kyle crossed her. "I tried."

There was so much she didn't know. He had told her once that he had never loved his wife. Was that true? Or had he said so because he had loved too deeply. Had he retained his marriage all these years in hope?

Would she one day deny that she had ever loved him?

"What is she like?" she heard herself ask, wincing as the words left her mouth. What was she expecting? What did she want? An assurance that all was really over? That she wasn't just another of his easily taken mistresses, that his wife was a terrible creature? God, yes, she wanted him to say something, anything, to justify her losing herself, everything, becoming his lover when she knew all the circumstances. I had no choice, she told herself quickly. But that was a lie. Even that first time he had known she would accept him, give to him all the passion he had awakened.

"Lisa?" he inquired dryly.

"Yes, Lisa," she said simply.

Kyle shrugged. "She is quite a character."

What the hell did that mean? Skye wondered. And then she didn't want to know. She wanted to believe that his Lisa was a withered crone, a shrew. "Oh," she murmured, and then she realized his mind wasn't really with her, he was looking back to the sea.

"I wonder," he said idly, "how Michael and Chris are doing with the company."

"Who are Michael and Chris?"

His attention turned back to her and he laughed. "Mike is my brother. And Chris is my son. I'm sure I've mentioned him."

He started telling her about his brother, about the company, how they worked together. He didn't mention Chris again, but she had sensed the pain in his voice.

His son. Her heart bled for the boy, bereft of his father. And it also bled for herself. Chris was a part of another life, his life. Chris, and his mother, Lisa. All must be waiting, praying. Kyle belonged to them, not her.

Somehow she gave correct replies to him at appropriate times. This was what she had wanted front him. She had wanted him to open up. But she was losing more than she was gaining.

And she was so lost. She had lost Delaney Designs. She had lost Ted. And in six weeks the years of her own past were lost.

"Ohhh . . ." Kyle stood suddenly and stretched with a grimace, easing tired muscles. He reached down to give Skye a hand and bring her to her feet.

"I'm tired. Let's take a little walk and call it quits for the day."

Skye nodded, vaguely resenting herself. He beckoned; she came. Where was she? She had to grasp on to something, find herself, tear away.

No. Her heart constricted. Life was too uncertain. A past meant nothing if the prospect of any future was debatable.

She walked along by his side.

They stumbled upon the garden that night. Skye caught her foot in a root, and when she bent to disengage her toes, she pulled at the root. Something plump and orangish appeared in her hand.

"I'll be damned," Kyle murmured, taking it from her.

"What is it?" Skye asked.

"Looks like a sweet potato or a yam," Kyle replied, biting into it and grimacing at the raw taste. "It is a sweet potato." He began to pull at the various grasses and weeds around them, exposing haphazard rows of the root.

"A garden?" Skye inquired incredulously.

"Looks like it."

"But how?"

Kyle shrugged, intent upon digging clear their discovery. "Someone lived here at one time. Probably recently, if these have survived."

"You mean whoever had the Coke bottle?"

"Carrots!" Kyle exclaimed cheerfully, ignoring her question at first, and then answering, "No. Whoever had your Coke bottle was just passing by. Probably off a dinghy from a larger boat. You can't move much in here because of the reefs. No, at one time this island must have had a small population. Maybe a small group that just decided to quit civilization for a while. Who knows? People have been coming and going throughout these islands for centuries—hey, would you quit standing there and help." He stopped himself suddenly, staring at her with a broad smile. "I'll bet we could unearth all sorts of useful things buried by time and storms. And just think, if you weren't a klutz, we might never have discovered all this!"

"I'm not a klutz!" Skye protested automatically, but she was laughing with him. Then the delicious change of diet offered her suddenly jolted her stomach and she was pushing him aside to dig. "Must you just sit there? I'm starving."

The prospect of food had a dizzying effect on her. Skye wasn't even aware that her dark mood left her, and that she was living for the day.

It rained in the night, and they consumed their badly cooked but delicious meal in the hut, both feeling as if they had been treated to a feast in a gourmet restaurant. Onions had also been found between the carrots and potatoes, and the flavoring to their usually bland fish seemed the highest of epicurean delights.

Kyle broke open a bottle of Burgundy, and as the storm played around them, they rested in comfort.

The rain was further insurance of their water supply.

It wouldn't be so terrible to stay and take our chances of discovery, Skye thought, basking comfortably in the harbor of his arms, if only they needn't fear the coming of a thief. Or drug smugglers, but the drug smugglers would leave them alone if they were left alone.

And what were their chances in the Pacific? In the endless sea where storms of death and destruction could strike at a moment's notice, where deadly sharks abounded, where they could drift for eternity beneath a merciless sun, slowly draining their water supply, their lives?

In the morning she told him she didn't want to leave.

"Listen to me, Kyle," she persisted as he gave her a hard, impatient look that clearly certified her as crazy, a foolish woman who hadn't listened to or understood a single thing he had explained to her about the danger of the gold. "We finish the raft, and we take the gold out—as far out as possible. And then we dump it. If there is a homing device, it will lead straight to the ocean floor."

He still stared at her coldly. "I don't understand your sudden reticence. Don't you trust my ability to get us out of here?"

"Yes. No. I mean, I trust you, but not the elements—and we have everything here now, enough to keep us alive if it takes them months and months to find us—"

"Not," Kyle interrupted impatiently, "if we hit a dry spell. Not if one of us becomes seriously ill."

They were lying together on the sand floor of the hut. Moments ago they had been in one another's arms.

Now Skye turned from him, fighting anger, fighting a haze of tears. He didn't care if he killed them both, as long as he could try to return to the life of power he craved.

He cared for her, she was sure. He spent half their time together making love to her, whispering how beautiful she was, how he cherished every inch of her. But obviously, she wasn't enough. He couldn't accept his imprisonment with her, she couldn't make up for the loves that awaited him, even if time spent in that prison was pleasurable . . .

"Skye." He reached for her arm but she eluded him, trying to grasp her clothes. Those he managed to wrench from her. "Skye, dammit, what the hell is the matter with you?"

"Nothing," she said curtly, shrugging and moving to exit minus shorts and tattered blouse. What difference did it make if she were decently clad or not?

"Skye, I'm talking to you!"

Now was as good a time as any to reassert herself. "Kyle, I'm not in the mood to talk at the moment." She left the hut and ran blindly toward the interior of the island. She would have time. Kyle was still probably so stunned that she hadn't allowed the seizure of her clothing to upset her that it would take him some time to realize she had actually defied one of his holy commands.

Defiance wasn't worth much. Tears started to trickle down her cheeks, and then she was furious because she was crying. Oh, Lord, why did she have to feel so abnormal, why were there threats every way that she turned.

And why the hell did she have to feel so damned sick she wondered suddenly as she reached their work site of the previous day? Probably because she had glutted herself with the fresh vegetables. Under normal circumstances, she reminded herself wryly, she didn't like sweet potatoes or yams or whatever they were.

The Outer Limits. There was nothing normal left. She had stepped into a small jet and the normal world had been left behind. And she couldn't just be happy to be alive because being alive had made her think so very much, had brought her to know Kyle.

She wiped away the moisture that touched her cheeks, knowing she wouldn't cry again. The cool, unruffled Skye who could walk down the hectic streets of New York with calm purpose, heels clicking steadily on pavement, was a long way away. Perhaps she was lost forever. But this morning she was gaining a little of that woman back.

She had never been a complete coward. And now she forced herself to accept the fact that it was a fear of far more than sharks that kept her clinging to the island. And in accepting, she was ready to leave. Love, if it was real, withstood all storms. And if Kyle didn't love her, she would have to learn to live again without him.

The sweet potatoes took another acidic venture up her throat. "What I wouldn't give for an Alka-Seltzer," she said aloud to herself wryly. And then, to her amazement, bracing her shivering form with both hands upon a convenient palm, she was sick.

The truth didn't sneak up on her; it hit her bluntly,

and her first reaction was a startled amazement, and then a harsh self-judgment. What were you expecting?

Just yesterday she had mentioned idly that six weeks had passed. She had glibly talked on. The idea hadn't even entered her head.

Why are you amazed? she asked herself next. You knew from the beginning, one can't lead this type of intimate life without . . .

She pushed away from the tree and sought a handful of last night's rainwater from a nearby puddle, carefully cupping her hands so as not to include mud in what she splashed over her face. Carefully cupping her hands a second time, she drank a long, cool sip, grateful that her mind had long ago adapted to unfiltered water.

The water stayed down. The puddle, as she knelt before it, gave her a slightly distorted mirror image.

"What do I do now?" she asked her wavering reflection. Do? She laughed in silent reply. Nothing. What was there to do? The Center for Advice to Single Parents was no more around the corner than the drugstore she had once mentioned to Kyle.

It is not, "What do I do?" she thought, but "How do I feel?" And as she sat looking at her reflection, she realized that she didn't mind. She wasn't frightened that she would most likely bear her child on an island, without medical attention. She wasn't frightened that she might return to civilization and face the wife of her child's father.

She closed her eyes. It was a good feeling. Because whatever was, whatever came, she loved Kyle. And even dizzy, confused, and still a little queasy, she could accept a feeling as elemental as their lives on the island, as primitive. It was warm and thrilling to know she carried a part of him inside of her to nurture and to cherish.

Do I tell him? she wondered blankly. Of course, he had a right to know, and she had to share such a feeling even if he did infuriate her at times.

But not yet, she corrected herself. She wasn't sure. It could have been the potatoes, she could just be late. Trauma caused such things, and surely a plane crash was traumatic.

Just living with Kyle, she thought wryly, was traumatic.

A soft breeze stirred, rippling the puddle. For a moment she saw a blurred image, a picture of a chic, sophisticated woman, smart in a handsome beige business suit, heels, purse, and low-brimmed hat to complement the cool outfit. What would that woman of six weeks ago have thought if she could have had a picture of the naked, disheveled primitive now glaring down at a puddle, her lips curved in a dry, rueful smile? A ridiculous savage, ridiculously pleased with herself against all odds. . . .

"I'm not really that calm," she whispered aloud. "I think I'm still in basic shock." The worry, she knew, would come later, when her new knowledge had time to sink in. Already it was occurring to her that her diet was sadly lacking, that she didn't know a thing, that—

"Skye?"

She turned to see that Kyle had finally followed her, and that the light in his eyes was very gentle. He came to her and hunched down beside her, elbows resting lightly on his knees. "Listen, Skye," he said quietly, "you're right, and I apologize. I don't know why I argued with you. I was thinking the same thing about the danger of the raft since we began to build it. We were lucky to escape the plane wreck with our lives. At least if we stay put we know we can survive. But the raft was still a good idea. It kept us together. It kept our hands and brains busy. And I think—if you agree, partner," he said with a smile, "that the wisest thing to do is to get the damn gold off the island, rather than us."

He sighed, looking down at the ground, then continued. "I've realized that we could be a thousand miles from the nearest pinprick on a map. Like I said, I really

don't know what made me argue with you, I should have
been grateful that you realized. I think . . . I think that
you struck a blow to my ego. I'm not known to be a
bundle of cheer first thing in the morning. And I guess
it just sounded like you considered me completely incapable. Oh, damn! I'm sorry."

Skye smiled softly. "It's okay," she said. In her present
mood she would forgive him anything. And he was apologizing to her; he was, in essence, telling her—that itself
was the important thing.

He shrugged, catching her eyes. "It's not really okay—
the things I told you were real fears that I have—a
drought, sickness, but so far the island has sheltered us
well. What we're going to do is this: finish the raft, then
I'm going to take it out alone. I want to dump the gold
and the tracking device out good and far. Perhaps I'll
catch sight of something interesting after a day's rowing.
When I come back we'll discuss what we do from there.
How does that sound?"

She smiled at him slowly, realizing that she was seeing
him in a new, benign light. Then a little lump caught in
her throat. She wasn't sure she could stand watching him
leave for the sea alone in the raft. She was torn; she
wanted to go with him, but she was also filled with a
strong desire to survive, if not for herself . . .

"How . . . how do you know you'll find your way
back?" she managed to ask with only a little catch.

"Have some faith!" he chastised with a rueful grin. "I'm
a pilot, remember? I do know a bit about navigation. I
even spend a fair amount of time boating, and I promise
I won't take a single chance." He was silent for a moment.
"Okay?"

Skye nodded, a smile slowly curving her lips along with
a feeling of light-headedness. He had cared about her
feelings, granted the intelligence of her arguments. She
caught the reflection of them both then in the puddle,

and her smile became a soft chuckle. What an absurd pair they made—she kneeling naked in the dirt, he with his ragged beard and rat-trap cutoffs balanced beside her. Who would believe they had ever been executives?

She had a sudden vision of him losing that expert balance and careening into the puddle and the muck beneath it, and had to stop herself from allowing her chuckles to turn to crippling laughter. He was constantly telling her she needed to learn to play . . . to relax.

Coiling to spring herself, she gave him a full, radiant smile. "Okay," she said softly. What the hell! She placed her hands with lightning speed upon his kneecaps and pushed with all her might, springing to her feet at the same time. She stayed just long enough to appreciate his stunned expression, a rueful grin setting in as he realized he had been had. The puddle had become mud with his landing and he was sprayed from head to toe.

Laughing, Skye took off through the trees, feeling wonderful as she ran. She was quick and agile and she knew it. In actuality, the island had been good for them. They had both grown strong.

Kyle would catch her; she knew that, too. But when she thought of all the times she had been at the mercy of his superior size and strength, it was all worth it to have been at least once the victorious aggressor.

She heard his grumbled threats from the distance.

"Damn it, Skye, if you think you're going to get away with this . . ."

She had to pause for a moment to catch the breath her laughter was costing her. Then still chuckling, she took flight again. She intended to be demurely setting up for breakfast before he shook himself free of the mud and returned to extract his revenge.

Interlude

From the bow of the *Bonne Bree* Michael Jagger searched the shoreline, powerful binoculars in hand.

His eyes began to hurt with the hope and the strain. And yet he was sure this was the island.

Last week's search had entailed the use of seaplanes, and he had been sure he had seen something. Here. This had to be it. He had checked his coordinates carefully when he had realized he couldn't land the seaplane because of the huge outcroppings of coral. Ripping up his plane wouldn't have helped his brother. It would have only served to strand them both. If Kyle was alive . . .

He was alive, Michael told himself convincingly. He had seen something. And he was sure that this was the island.

Bronze flesh crinkled around the green eyes that were a unique trait of the Jaggers. He had found it. The something. Blending into the sand and green of the island. Visible now only as he sought it. Some type of a thatch dwelling. A hut.

Michael had not known his tension; he had not known his fear. But now he began to shake, he went weak with relief. Tears sprang into his eyes as if he were a boy rather than a man long past maturity.

"Ray!" He called the name of the old school chum who was the owner of the *Bonne Bree*—an enthusiastic sailor who knew the Pacific as the Jaggers knew the skies. The sound was nothing but a croak. Michael tried again. "Ray!"

Ray Thorne sprang from the cabin hatch. "Yeah?"

Michael started to beckon to him, but he suddenly froze, the binoculars still to his eyes. A smile slowly slid across his features, bringing with it his return to strength.

He hadn't seen his brother, but what he had seen made him blink furiously.

Was it illusion? A dream? Or had he stumbled upon paradise.

A wood nymph lived upon the island, a sprite. She flew across the sand like an Aphrodite through the clouds. She laughed and he swore he could hear the melodious, tinkling sound. She paused by an outcropping of palms and turned, spinning mercurially, her hair trailing the graceful swirl of her body in a fan of lightest gold to fall entrancingly over high, round breasts.

He would have been less than a man not to follow her figure, and then not to wonder once again if he hadn't sailed out of the known world and into paradise. He was sure he had never seen a living creature of such perfection. Those enticing, firm breasts, heaving with the exertion of her breathing, standing proud above a long, slender midriff, a waist that could be spanned by hands . . . hips that flared with feminine bewitchment . . . concave abdomen . . . long, long, supple legs . . .

"Michael?" Ray queried. "What is it?"

Michael dropped the binoculars with guilt so quickly that the cord that held them snapped around his neck. He swallowed, shocked that he was flushing. "I think I've found them," he murmured quickly, knowing his bearded friend watched him as if he was crazy. "I'll take the dinghy in."

Ray nodded, accepting the binoculars as Michael took them from his neck. "Don't radio anything yet. I haven't seen my brother."

Ray gave his friend a thumbs-up sign as Michael boarded the dinghy. The small motor roared into action.

Salt sprayed his face, but Michael felt nothing. The wind as he sheered the surf tore at his knit shirt and jeans, bringing the dampness of the water. He still felt nothing; he was too busy keeping a sharp eye on the coral and then on the shore. His nymph had disappeared, but that was natural he supposed. He had had the binoculars pointed far to the west and he was approaching the sand spit by the hut from dead on center. A ways from shore he cut the motor to row through the last spots of treacherous coral.

Then, bare feet plunging thick into wet sand, he was on shore.

Michael took a deep breath. Then a brisk walk took him to the hut. He saw the sheet of fabric scraps. Giddy excitement bubbled within him; he felt the world spinning. Among the scraps was a piece of cloth that could have only belonged to a captain's jacket—his brother's jacket.

He moved out of the hut, to the fire that was only an ember in the daylight. But it burned, the coals were hot.

He sensed rather than heard a soft, fleet padding against the sand. It came from the west. He turned, rising from the fire and walking back toward the shore.

And then he saw her, his nymph. She didn't see him because she was laughing—and this time he could hear the sound and it was a melody—and her head was turned as she watched for something behind her.

She saw him just an instant before she collided with him. His hands reached out to catch her, to steady her.

She wasn't a dream. She was real. He knew when his hands touched that tanned flesh that was so like silk, when he looked into amber almond-shaped eyes that flew as wide as a startled doe's. Then rose lips parted in a panicked scream that wouldn't come.

Nine

Impact with the stranger drove everything from Skye's mind except sheer panic. He had come for the gold; he had come to make certain there had been no survivors.

A scream struggled to rise from deep within, a scream that would be a cry of terror elicited from every nerve cell in her entire body. And then just as suddenly as the panic had overwhelmed her, it died. Her scream choked in her throat; it became a disbelieving gasp of confusion.

The eyes that stared down at her were just as wide as her own. They were different, and yet they were a unique color she had come to know. The face was different too, younger, perhaps it crinkled to laughter more often. It was clean shaven and still it, too, was familiar.

She had no idea that she had screamed, then choked, then gasped, until the sound of Kyle's frantic voice calling her name slipped into her consciousness.

She heard the rustle as he broke through the trees, the thunderous padding of his feet against sand as he raced, a bronze blur, to reach her. Still she couldn't look around, but stared at the stranger in a state of shock.

She vaguely felt him as he neared her and the stranger, felt the astonished end to his fervent race, felt him staring at the stranger.

And then she was abruptly released.

The stranger's eyes misted; he uttered a joyful, "Thank God—you're alive!"

"Michael!"

Skye was ignored as the brothers embraced; she felt a lump catch in her throat even as she watched them, still dazed. Michael, of course. She watched the emotion between them, the depth of the family tie, the frank, unabashed joy of their meeting. Her heart constricted; it was something she so clearly understood. Not so long ago she, too, had had a brother who had been her best friend.

"How the hell did you find us?" Kyle finally inquired, holding his brother still by the shoulders, his grin splitting his face from ear to ear against the thick auburn of his beard.

"Persistence!" Michael Jagger laughed, looking back to Skye.

It wasn't until then she actually realized she was standing naked on the beach. And then she was horrified. Civilization had returned. What had been natural only moments before was now indecent, mortifying.

Kyle noticed Skye at the same time; Michael, too, seemed to realize what she was feeling. He glanced back to his brother awkwardly, hastily complying when Kyle said quickly, "Mike, give Skye your shirt."

Michael Jagger wasn't quite the size of his brother, but his T-shirt was still tremendous. Skye slipped it over her head, miserably wishing it would cover her face. Of course it didn't, but it did hang midway to her kneecaps.

There was an uneasy silence for a second, broken pleasantly with Michael's easy laughter. "Damn! Even I can't believe yet that I've found you!"

"Thank God that you did," Kyle replied, smiling and taking over his brother's lead to ease Skye's tension gallantly. "Michael, I'm sure you must know this is Skye Delaney. Skye, my brother, Michael."

She was accepting Mike Jagger's hand, mumbling a courteous "how do you do," and feeling absolutely absurd. But there was kindness in the younger Jagger's eyes, a sincerity that welcomed her back to the world of the known with no hint of condemnation. The moments of tension were eased over.

"How is Chris?" Kyle asked his brother quickly.

"Chris is fine," Mike assured him. "He was raring to come with me, but, well, just *if* I hadn't been able to find you, or if . . ." his voice trailed away, but they all knew the implication. If he had found only remains of the plane and broken bodies . . . "Anyway," Michael picked up, "he accepted the fact that all three of us shouldn't be away from the main office at the same time. I'm sure he's had his time occupied with business, but I do think we should radio in right away. He's been deathly worried. I'm afraid Lisa hasn't helped much, wailing around the house—" Again Michael broke off, unable to prevent himself from a stupidly apologetic glance at Skye. She felt her cheeks burn. Poor Michael, she thought vaguely, trying so hard, and then he inadvertently mentions the name of the wife in front of the mistress.

"You haven't sent in a message yet?" Kyle inquired.

"No, uh . . ." Michael Jagger, despite the strength of appearance so similar to his brother's, was capable of a deep blush. "I, uh, saw Skye from the boat, but not you, and I wanted to be certain."

Kyle waved a hand in dismissal of Mike's explanation. "I'm glad you haven't sent a message yet. We have a bit of a problem." He went on to tell Michael about the gold, leading his brother into the hut to show him the case. "I think we need to get hold of the Australian authorities first and tell them what we have. Ask them how they want this handled before the world knows we've been found."

Michael was nodding agreement. He offered Skye a broad smile as he saw her, standing with arms clasped around her chest, in the exact position in which they had left her.

"I guess we'll get out to the *Bonne Bree* now, Miss Delaney," he said. "It won't be home, but I'll bet I'll be able to offer you a number of things you missed! We have a shower with nice hot water, and a freezer full of steaks. And we'll radio in as soon as possible. There is a host of people going frantic over your disappearance too, you know. Your friend, that producer, must have half a fleet out here in the Pacific searching."

Skye nodded. She was dimly aware that Kyle's face had taken on a look of granite. Why not? He was in touching distance of his high-powered world. His mind was already working on priorities, on the business of the gold and the Australians. In a short time he would be back with his son, back in his home.

Back to his estranged wife. Would they be so estranged now? Would the joy of seeing him alive send Lisa into his arms? Would his own appreciation of life renew his need of that which had been his before?

"I would certainly love a shower, Mr. Jagger," she said softly, dignified despite the baggy T-shirt and her disheveled presence. "And a steak would be just lovely." She walked past both brothers to the hut. "Excuse me, I'll just be a moment." She was determined to slip into her shorts beneath the T-shirt.

As she grabbed her shorts and listened to Kyle and Michael discuss things at home, Skye allowed her eyes to roam over the confines of the hut. They were leaving; it was over. She still couldn't believe it, couldn't assimilate that it was possible that in just days she would be walking the streets of Manhattan again, returned to her life.

As Kyle was returned to his.

She should be ecstatic. But she was gripped with nostalgia, gripped with pain. The tattered sheets reminded her of their first time together. The walls of the hut gave credence to the number of ways Kyle had cared for her, creating their world, making it livable, allowing her to lean on him, demanding, but offering security and constant protection for the taking.

She was carrying his child.

And now the question "What do I do?" had meaning. She couldn't tell him. Not now. Not until her return to civilization was accomplished, not until she could think clearly, decide what would be best.

I'm going to keep the child. She tried to ignore the voice. She really didn't know what she was going to do yet. She was so confused. Already Kyle was a complete stranger. His brother was here. Mike Jagger was real, tangible. He spoke of the real, tangible world that was Kyle's, a world in which she held no place.

Her eyes lit upon the tortoiseshell comb resting beside the remnant sheet. She picked up the comb, slipped it beneath the T-shirt and into the pockets of the shorts that had once been her crisp beige business suit. Then she collected her canvas bag and long ignored purse— normal, useful items once more. There was a real world. She closed her eyes, turned, and left the hut. "I'm ready," she told the brothers.

"Let's go then," Kyle said impatiently, taking her arm proprietorially and leading her toward the dinghy. She didn't attempt to pull away from him, but he felt her stiffen. And earlier he had seen the look in her eyes after Michael's arrival.

Kyle was confused himself. He was grateful to see his brother, grateful to know he would soon see Chris, relieved to know that Skye would be safe from those seeking things on the island, safe from further typhoons, safe from any illness that might strike.

But something else also hurt very badly—made him stiffen, made him withdraw.

He had seen her eyes.

And he knew that the magic was over.

Paradise had been lost.

* * *

Skye and Kyle were both unabashedly kissed by the irascible Ray Thorne. She had to laugh, had to feel welcomed. And then she was being courteously pushed into the ample shower compartment, assured the hot water supply was vast, and being offered a velvety maroon robe that Ray cheerfully informed her belonged to his girlfriend. She would find all sorts of soaps and shampoos and "female folderol" that belonged to his girl, Marsha, and that Marsha would be insulted to death if Skye didn't make full use of anything that she found. Skye had little choice but to grin and to swear solemnly that she would help herself, and to say thanks.

How odd it felt to bathe with perfumed soap. To feel the richness of the shampoo she lathered into her hair. She appreciated all with base sensation, marveling at the uniqueness of what she hadn't even realized that she had missed. Did losing the world make one more attuned to all the nuances of it? Of course, that was natural. Natural that she would have to readjust.

In the large mirrored cabinet over the sink, Skye found a score of toothbrushes. Apparently the *Bonne Bree* was stocked well for entertainment. Ray Thorne, she ascertained, owned the spacious yacht. And it seemed Ray Thorne, as bohemian as he appeared, was as affluent as his friends the Jaggers.

She stared at the toothbrush for a long time, running her fingers over the soft plastic bristles. Of all the things she had missed, this now was luxury—this and the mint taste of the toothpaste.

How incredible. She was thinking about toothpaste when she was pregnant and the father of her child was already moving into the arms of his family, and she was going to have to see Ted and tell him about it and that she didn't love him when he had a fleet of ships out searching for her.

Skye spat out a mouthful of toothpaste and stared at her reflection. She felt ancient, as if they had been on the island years, instead of weeks, aged beyond recognition. She looked pathetically young. Her eyes were still wide—culture shock—and the kindly, invisible Marsha was obviously a more statuesque woman than she as the soft sleeves of the robe covered half her hands and the hemline trailed to her feet. Woodenly, she plugged in a compact blow dryer and worked on her hair, but that didn't seem to help much either. Her long pale hair falling against the maroon robe was far too innocent for a woman who . . .

Who what? she asked herself with annoyance. I didn't become sultry Sadie in six weeks on an island.

Skye meticulously picked up after herself and exited to the *Bonne Bree*'s long hallway. The yacht was quite a vessel, with full-size bedchambers fore and aft. The galley and the center cabin were separated by a spotless Formica cabin, and as she emerged, she found Ray and Mike, still comfortable in cutoffs and sneakers, dipping beer at the varnished cabin table while Kyle sat at the chart desk, making use of the radio. He wasn't saying much; he was listening. Skye could hear little of what was being said over the static.

Both Ray and Michael sprang to their feet as they saw her, offering her space at the table. Skye slid in by Michael's side asking, "What's going on?" as she inclined her head toward Kyle.

"He's gotten through to the Aussies," Mike explained. "From what I gather so far, they're requesting we hold our position for the night. They'll have someone out here tomorrow. What can I get you? The galley is well stocked. Name it, and I think we can come up with it."

Skye smiled at his eagerness to please her after her

time away from the niceties of civilization. "To tell you the truth, that beer you're drinking looks just wonderful."

Ray hopped to his feet. "A beer it will be." As he hurried to oblige her, Skye turned back to Michael. "I don't understand. Why should we hold our position?"

"So that no one attempts to retrieve the gold tonight."

The answer came from Kyle. He had left the chart desk and now took Ray's position at the table, sliding around so that he sat on the other side of Skye. "Once word gets out that we've been found—alive and well—someone is going to panic. They'll know that the Board of Aeronautics will be out soon to pick up the pieces of the plane and report the cause of the crash. That someone will have to make a move quickly. This choice is yours, Skye, but they've asked that no one be notified that we're alive until tomorrow morning. They need a grace period of silence to arrive."

Skye stared blankly at him a moment, wishing he hadn't chosen to sit beside her with his arm casually draped behind her shoulder. She didn't want to give the Australians a grace period; she wanted to crawl into a hole and pretend she hadn't been found racing down a beach stark naked.

Ray graciously set her beer before her. All eyes were on her. She thought of Ted. Knowing for certain that she didn't love him didn't ease the poignancy of knowing his pain, how he searched for her, and she thought of Virginia, surely worried sick in Sydney. She thought of how badly she needed to be away from Kyle now that they were no longer a world unto themselves.

But then she thought of the wonderfully polite and helpful treatment she had always received from the Australian authorities. She thought of Steven, buried on Australian soil. She didn't want to think that she owed the Australians anything, but she did.

"Fine," she said, wishing that her voice didn't sound so weak. She took a sip of her beer and cleared her throat. "How long will it be before we . . . before I can get home."

"Not long," Ray supplied cheerfully. "A day from here is a little private island called Igua. It's kind of a hideaway for the world's more affluent. Michael flew there to meet me at the boat, so transportation will be waiting. And the Aussies have promised to inform—who is it, your sister-in-law?—first thing in the morning that you're alive."

Virginia, Skye knew, would immediately notify Ted . . . She could feel Kyle's eyes boring into her, but she refused to meet his gaze. What right did he have to condemn her for wanting to be home? He was already with those close to him. She directed her question to Michael. "Isn't it dangerous for us to sit here?"

"No." It was Kyle who replied, and she finally turned to him.

"But—"

"We're not defenseless anymore."

Skye didn't like the sound of his voice. It was hard. It held an element of cold steel, and it sent shivers down her spine. It reminded her that he was K. A. Jagger, a man who allowed no quarter.

"I don't think there will be anyone appearing," Michael said quickly, seeming to sense that tension had arisen anew. He hastily changed the subject. "Hey, Ray! I promised the lady a steak, and it's well past noon." He glanced back to Skye. "How do you like your steak, Miss Delaney."

"Medium rare"—she smiled—"and please call me Skye." It was too absurd for a man who had seen her running in the buff to call her Miss Delaney, she thought wryly.

"I'm going to hop in the shower while you're cooking," Kyle told his brother. He rubbed his bearded chin.

"Think I ought to keep this awhile, Skye? Or should it go?"

Skye tensed inwardly, forcing herself to look into his handsome features. There was a cool fire in his eyes, a challenge that she didn't understand, a hardness to his features . . . "I'm sure it makes no difference to me," she responded lightly, turning away with an attempt at nonchalance as she saw a muscle tighten beneath the hair on his cheek. She felt his eyes on her for only a moment, and then he was sliding from the table. "Mike, I'll need something to wear."

"Sure," Mike said quickly, rising to join his brother. "Help yourself, my stuff is aft. In fact, I'll come along with you and get my stuff out so that you and Skye can have the aft cabin."

Oh, God, oh, God, oh, God, Skye thought, a blush covering her face. Michael was assuming there was a relationship that could continue.

"Good," Kyle said. "Thanks."

Why hadn't he granted her the dignity of protesting? Skye wondered furiously. She opened her mouth to do so, but snapped it shut. She would sound absolutely ridiculous. She couldn't possibly deny—not after the scenario Michael had witnessed—that an intimate relationship had existed. But damn, she was being put in an awkward position.

Sighing, she watched as Kyle and Mike disappeared down the hall. Then she stood with a bright smile for Ray Thorne.

"What can I do to help you?"

Mike returned to the galley while Kyle showered and added his efforts to preparing their mid-afternoon dinner. Both men seemed determined to entertain her lavishly, and as time passed, Skye realized she was growing very comfortable. Mike Jagger had none of his brother's rough edges. He was simply straightforward and charming as he asked about the island and the hardships they had endured. Skye told him about the storm, about the drug runners she had almost hailed, about the morning Kyle had discovered the gold—leaving out all personal details.

"You're lucky to be alive," Mike said softly, peeling an onion. "It's almost a miracle that Kyle was able to land that plane to begin with."

Yes, she was lucky to be alive, and she was alive because of Kyle. A shiver rippled through her and she blinked. She had to blink to convince herself that she was on a boat, that she was cooking in a galley, that they had been found.

It wasn't so hard to believe, she told herself. She was already at ease with Mike and Ray, comfortable in the soft robe. Had it been only last night that she had slept in the sand, believing there was a possibility she would never see another human again other than Kyle?

"Kyle is an exceptional pilot," Mike was continuing. "Probably one of the finest alive."

"Yes, I believe that," Skye said softly. She didn't want to think of Kyle as a pilot. It was another reminder that today was only an awkward respite.

Michael and Ray both began to question her about Delaney Designs. For a moment Skye panicked. Delaney Designs. What was that? It had ceased to be real. Searching for food was real. Keeping a wary eye on the water supply was real. Feeling the sun upon her flesh, sand and tangled grass and mangrove roots beneath her feet . . .

Kyle was real.

Skye forced a smile and began to answer their questions. Did she look normal? she wondered. She didn't feel at all normal. Did she sound sane and reasonably intelligent? She was groping in her memory for particulars. How silly. It had only been six weeks, but six weeks composed of individual days that had been aeons; six weeks in which everything had changed.

Kyle, freshly shaven, made a reappearance. For a moment his presence, too, made Skye panic. Why? she wondered. Except for the clean line of his jaw, he looked basically the same. He still wore cutoffs—a pair of his brother's that had once been faded jeans. But he also wore a sports shirt, blue knit, with a collar.

He always moved with assurance, so that wasn't it, Skye thought as he moved toward the galley, extracting a packet of Michael's cigarettes from the labeled pocket of the shirt. He laughed as Ray mentioned that he had preferred the beard, helped himself to a beer from the icebox, and hoisted himself to sit comfortably on the counter.

He has made the transition, Skye thought, and I haven't. He has come from man on an island with life the necessity to man discovered and back in the life he knows—his life, his friends, a boat he is familiar with. He is at home.

He caught her eyes then, and she knew he had sensed her feelings. The look he gave her was a bond that could only ever exist between the two of them, a bond of things shared.

Skye smiled back tentatively; she ceased to hear the things that were being said around her.

The day passed pleasantly enough, and Skye became grateful for her own period of grace. Every little thing was a form of adjustment—holding a fork, tasting the red meat, enjoying a cup of brewed coffee after her meal.

Sitting beside Kyle in company, she was learning not to flinch when he touched her while someone else was present, learning to listen to him talk about Executive Charters, an empire more vast than even she had realized, an empire ruled by two men who sat now in cutoffs, lazy, laughing, so at ease, not executives at all.

By an apparent unspoken agreement Lisa Jagger was never mentioned. Ray and Michael, Skye decided, were probably accustomed to Kyle's being with other women. They would have thought it not only odd, but impossible for Kyle not to have formed a relationship with her when she was a female, beautiful and vulnerable and alone with him for all that time.

"Skye."

She dragged herself from retrospection and looked at Kyle. "Your eyes are half closed," he told her with a gentle smile and a trace of amusement in his eyes. "Go to bed."

"I . . . uh . . ." She glanced around the table to see that Michael and Ray were also looking at her with gentle smiles. "I'm sorry, I guess I am tired." She rose, excusing herself, longing to ask Kyle, *"Aren't you coming, too?"* But she couldn't ask him. She felt a stupid blush rising simply because the other two men knew she would share a bed with Kyle.

But again Kyle seemed to sense what went on in her mind. He rose to walk her to the aft cabin, stopping her with his hands on her shoulders as they reached the door. He brushed a quick kiss over her lips. "Go to sleep," he commanded, and she stiffened slightly at the absolute authority in his voice. "I won't be in for a while."

"Why?" the question formed on her lips.

"Because we're all taking a shift on guard duty," he informed her briefly, twisting the doorknob and ushering her into the bedroom. The door closed immediately behind her even though she had other questions, even though he had given her chills with his voice.

She had been dismissed. And she knew why. On the island survival had decreed that she be a part of everything, that she understand, be informed.

But now things were different. She had taken the role of cared-for pet again, not partner. Kyle, she knew from the steel of his voice, was hoping the gold thief would appear. He had a personal vendetta. His plane had been sabotaged, his life almost taken, her life almost taken.

And now she was afraid. She didn't like Kyle like that, so furiously cold, ruthless, determined.

Skye lay down in the ample bed and stared at the teakwood ceiling. She began to pray that the night would be quiet. She could hear the quiet rumble of conversation from the cabin, and she tried to sleep, but the pleasant state of drowsiness had left her. Her mind was back to turmoil. She worried about Kyle and the night, praying the night would end. And then she prayed that the night would never end because the day would bring them back to their individual lives, and they hadn't talked and she didn't know if she had been a mere convenience or if Kyle would care for her still when he had his choice of women, and a wife to boot.

And then there was Ted.

She finally began to drift in and out of sleep. And then her eyes flew open because she could hear conversation again, clear this time. She blinked, as if to clear the sleep fog from her mind, and then ascertained that the speakers were Kyle and Michael, and that they were on deck right above her.

"You're going to be in for trouble," Michael was saying. "I'm telling you, she's changed her mind."

"I really don't give a damn." Kyle—that voice of steel again. "I will get a divorce, she can't stop me."

There was silence for a second, then Michael again, "Maybe she can't stop you, but she can tear apart Executive Charters. And she can keep you in court for years and years."

"Why the hell is she doing this?" Kyle murmured.

"She says she loves you."

"Lisa loves me?"

Skye strained to hear more, knowing she was eavesdropping upon a private conversation, but not caring. She hadn't been able to read the tone of the last question; Kyle and Michael had apparently been moving, and they were no longer overhead. Do you care? she wanted to scream, and only by biting down hard on a knuckle could she stop herself. Tears sprang to her eyes. What were you expecting, jerk, she asked herself. A perfect ending? Lisa stepping right out of the picture, Ted kindly granting a blessing, Kyle falling to his knees to say that he did love her dearly above all others, and her telling him that yes, she would be his wife and wasn't it wonderful, they were going to have a child?

The cabin door opened. Skye froze, closing her eyes quickly and trying to feign sleep. Kyle did not turn on the light, but quietly moved about the room. Skye heard a soft rustle and knew he had pulled his knit shirt over his head. A muffled thud informed her he had dropped his jeans to the floor. She felt him as he crawled in beside her—warmth and power and a pleasant, heady male aroma.

Still she lay frozen, curled away from him, her mind dull, her eyes closed tight in her semblance of sleep.

His arm came around her, pulling her gently so that the curve of her back fit into that of his chest.

She didn't protest, but neither did she move on her own.

Seconds ticked by. He merely held her, and she was glad of his comfort, of being within the strength of his arms.

And then he began to move. His hand found the hem of the maroon robe; his fingers moved up the length of her leg slowly, drawing the robe up and up. The tips of his fingers, rough with the calluses of work but gentle, teasingly soft, began to draw exotic little patterns over the curve of her buttocks, sliding to her thighs, sliding back . . .

Skye caught her breath as the embers of fire within her
ignited instantly. Don't do this to me, she moaned inwardly, clutching the sheets as she tried to remain still.
But he continued his slow, leisurely seduction, his hand
shifting so that his circles were created low over her belly,
down to a point of torture, back up to her ribs, over her
breasts, grazing the nipples over and over again until they
hardened . . .

And surely he knew she no longer slept, if he had ever
believed that she had.

Skye bit hard into her knuckle, trying to hold back the
moan that escaped her anyway. And then the teasing was
over. Kyle's broad hand splayed over her lower abdomen,
pulling her tightly against his rising desire—a pulse, a
heat, a passionate need belied by his gentle approach.
Seduction became demand. His left hand slid over her
hip, coaxing and shifting her thigh. His breath, warm and
moist, nuzzled her neck, his teeth grazed her earlobe with
a whisper of fire.

And then he was inside her, a shattering drive that was
vibrant and alive, an electricity let loose, unleashed, undeniable. Heat radiated through her from that core; she
was at once paralyzed with the sweet feeling and sent into
a frenzy.

Her teeth ground harder into her knuckle. There were
others on the boat; she didn't want to cry out, she
couldn't even whisper. Only he could hear the sound of
her breath, the sheer, soft whimpers she forced back in
her chest.

Her fingers tightly clenched the sheet, released it,
clenched it again convulsively, moved to clasp the hand
that held her abdomen so tightly to him while their undulating, writhing rhythm possessed them in the excruci-
ating spiral of delicious reaching and reaching and
reaching.

Eyes closed, in the dark, she knew the fingers she

touched—tufts of auburn on bronze bands of iron, short, clipped, clean nails. She knew the body she blended with in liquid fire—the broad chest, the mat of hair that tapered, became thick and gold-tinted below the hips, legs that were sturdy, powerfully sinewed.

Her thoughts left her; everything left her but sensation. She could feel her own muscles, taut as they strained against his pliable, but more powerful strength. He guided, he commanded. He caught and held her through the burst of physical ecstasy and euphoria that came to them simultaneously, held her and chuckled softly when her moaned cry escaped her despite her diligent efforts to keep their lovemaking a quiet coupling.

They lay still together for a long time. Skye could feel the beating of her own heart, the pounding of his. She could feel his breath still against her nape, labored, becoming easy only slowly. He still held her belly, and although his hold became gentle, he didn't give it up, but stroked tender patterns again as they rested.

Finally he moved, leaning on an elbow and pulling her toward him, frowning at the robe bunched around her. "This thing is drenched," he murmured, "let me help you."

His eyes, in the near darkness, were bright. The contours of his face, even as he smiled, seemed harder than she knew them.

This man is forty years old, she reminded herself, the character in his face has been ingrained there, he built an empire by himself, he lived things I will never fathom.

She shifted up and allowed him to help her remove the damp robe. Still without speaking, she sank back to her pillow, watching him . . . as he watched her. He smoothed her hair back over her forehead; it, too, was damp. She looked at his fingers and realized she loved his hands, loved the way they held things, loved the way they moved when he spoke, loved the way they touched her, sometimes unthinkingly, but because she belonged to him, because he led, because he showed her something.

He leaned down and kissed her, softly but deeply, slowly exploring her mouth, tasting her tongue, her teeth, her lips.

He shifted back again, smiling, then picking up her hand. He studied her palm, then kissed it, then kissed each of her fingers one by one, taking the last into his mouth sensuously, grazing it with his teeth.

It was the match that ignited the embers within her body once again. Strange, how one little, certain touch was a catalyst.

His moist suction on her finger was that catalyst. She shuddered slightly as the sweet surge of renewed desire swept through her, but murmured a protest.

"Kyle, we really need to talk . . ."

He shifted suddenly, lowering himself over her, his legs sensuous and gentle despite their strength as he wedged his length between hers so that he could plant feather kisses over her collarbone, slide his tongue between the valley of her breasts.

"Kyle . . ."

He lifted his head, took her face tenderly between his hands, holding it firmly as he stared into her eyes. "We have a long way to go tomorrow, miles to talk. Tonight is ours."

She couldn't argue with him. She was so terribly afraid that the morrow would not give them miles, but put the irrevocable distance that was their separate lives between them.

Her fingers thread into his hair as his kiss began with her lips, moved fervently over the arch of her neck, became feverish as it touched upon her breast, swelling beneath it in instinctive response. Skye was once more busy trying to keep silent, trying to retaliate against his erotic torture, wondering how he could keep his wicked whispers so low as he breathed against her erotic descriptions of how he loved her breasts, the contours of her belly, the luscious movement of her hips.

And then, right before she gave herself up to the sensation again, she began to wonder how he would love her body when it changed, when her breasts became heavy, when her stomach filled.

She almost told him. Almost. Almost told him that her body carried his child. But she didn't. For an instant, just an instant, the salt heat of tears burned her eyes.

She couldn't tell him.

It was only a suspicion at the moment—sound suspicion, but suspicion. And she didn't know if he would be around when her body took on those changes.

The knowledge would hold him to her, and she knew it. But she didn't want him held or confined. She didn't want to be simply a responsibility for him.

She didn't want to be his mistress, and she didn't want to have a marriage like his first. Like the marriage that still tied him.

She didn't know what she wanted. Except, at this moment, she knew she wanted his lovemaking to go on and on. . . .

Ten

There were moments in that pleasant stage between sleep and awareness in which Skye thought she was still on the island. She would open her eyes, see the thatch of the hut, feel the sand beneath her, and through the door see the slow pounding surf of the ocean. She would roll and touch Kyle, or if he was awake before her, he would be near, she would hear his whistle as he poked the fire into action.

She wasn't on the island; she was on the *Bonne Bree.* Before she opened her eyes, she felt the comfort of the mattress beneath her, the coolness of the cotton sheets. Her head rested upon a soft pillow. Automatically she stretched out a hand, but Kyle was gone.

Today we return, she told herself. I can drink coffee all morning, raid the galley until I'm sick. Within the week I will be able to gorge myself with views of traffic jams, with people moving in the thousands, all knowing where they're going. I'll pick up the reins of my company again, I'll be worrying dollars-and-cents layout and designs, precious metals and precious stones.

And when I'm back, I'll be able to think, to reason, to handle everything as a responsible adult.

But all her reasoning meant nothing. When she moved, sore muscles reminded her of the night, and she was sure Kyle dreaded what the return to civilization meant as she did. He had made love to her as if there were no tomorrow, as if memory had to serve a lifetime. She was even hazy as to when she had actually fallen asleep.

There was a knock on the door and she instinctively clutched the sheets around her. But at her rather strained "Yes," the door only opened a crack.

"It's Michael, Skye," he said softly. "I'm throwing you a pair of Marsha's jeans and a T-shirt. The head's free, and we have company aboard. They're requesting your presence."

"Thanks, Michael," Skye murmured, smiling as the clothing was slipped through the crack in the door. "I'm awake, I'll be right out."

When the cabin door closed again, she leaped from the bed and quickly slipped into the offering, wishing Marsha wore bras. She really didn't feel like meeting officials in just the thin, oversized T-shirt and the jeans that threatened to slip off her. Rolling the hems carefully so that she wouldn't trip, she started to exit, then remembered her purse.

Her makeup, so useless on the island, could help her now. It could make her feel a little more together, a little more dignified, a little more like a mature woman than a castaway.

She spent less than ten minutes in the head and was proud of her achievement. She hadn't forgotten how to care for herself. It was a little thing, but somehow important in returning to reality. She heard voices as she brushed back her hair just before exiting, and knew the Australian officials were with Ray, Mike, and Kyle in the cabin. She would be seen as soon as she opened the door. For a boat this nice, she thought dryly, it should have been a two-head vessel; then she would have had the length of the hall.

She opened the door. As she expected, all eyes turned to her.

There were two Australians aboard, both clad in crisp

beige short uniforms. They sat at the table with Kyle between, clipboards in hand. Mike and Ray hovered behind
the counter, coffee mugs in hand. Kyle and the Australians rose at the sight of her. Kyle quickly introduced her.
"Skye, Sergeant Menzies and Lieutenant Griffen. Gentlemen, Ms. Skye Delaney."

Skye shook hands with the men, wondering why she
felt uneasy. She glanced at Kyle, but his expression told
her nothing.

"Well," murmured the lieutenant, the older of the two
officers, a dignified-looking man with a graying handlebar
mustache, "Shall we get started?"

Skye lifted an eyebrow at Kyle who merely offered her
a seat; Michael silently brought her a cup of coffee. She
offered him an equally silent look of gratitude.

"Get started with what?" she inquired crisply.

She was to regret that she had asked the question.

The lieutenant, who apparently did all the talking, informed her politely first that she was not required to answer questions without counsel, but that her cooperation
would be appreciated. With disbelief she realized that she
was once again under suspicion as a smuggler. *I shouldn't
cooperate,* she thought furiously, *I should make this as
miserable as possible for the lot of them.*

It didn't help to realize that it was only she they suspected. It was obvious that Kyle was in the clear. Only
millionaires make the grade, she thought bitterly. Apparently, Delaney Designs was not affluent enough to clear
her. And apparently Kyle hadn't seen fit to inform these
people that it couldn't possibly have been her.

Her voice icy, she answered questions for the better
part of an hour. Questions that drove her crazy. They
wanted to know every single thing she saw, did, or heard
before their flight left Sydney. That had been over six
weeks ago now . . . a lifetime ago. How could she possibly
remember the trivia of a day that had ended in trauma?

"You're sure you saw no one near the plane before takeoff?" she was asked for the fourth time.

"Perfectly sure," Skye reiterated, her temper rising. She tried to cool down, adding an acid, "It's a pity you gentlemen don't have a lie detector with you."

"Well, actually . . ." Sergeant Menzies began, glancing to his superior for support, "we do—"

"I think Ms. Delaney has been as helpful as possible under the circumstances," Kyle finally cut in. "She is an American citizen you know, and she deals frequently with your country. She has survived a crash landing and six weeks on a primitive island. She has cooperated fully. I think this is all we can offer."

Skye didn't know if Lieutenant Griffen decided he had done his duty, or if Kyle's words had been the influencing factor, but his attitude changed suddenly. He smiled at her, blue eyes twinkling. "Forgive us, Miss Delaney. We're dealing with a very serious situation here, and I'm afraid we can't leave a single stone unturned. Gold, as you must be aware, is a strength of our country. The richest square mile of gold-bearing land in the world is our Golden Mile at Kalgoorlie."

"I'm aware of that, Lieutenant," Skye said, trying to return his smile, but finding her jaw fixed after her third degree. "I've visited the mines in Western Australia. In fact, Lieutenant, I have spent half of the last six years in Australia, my sister-in-law is an Australian citizen, and my brother was an Australian citizen—"

"Skye," Kyle interrupted, "the officers have actually been trying to save you a trip back to Sydney. They understand your circumstances and don't want to have to call you back when you've reached the States after this ordeal."

"Oh," Skye murmured. Could they call her back? She didn't know . . . maybe she did need counsel.

"I'm sorry," she said, "but I've told you all I know."

Lieutenant Griffen rose and offered his hand. Skye accepted it warily, but the softness in the man's clear blue eyes touched her.

"Thank you, Miss Delaney. You must understand, we believe the perpetrator of this crime also almost cost you—and Mr. Jagger—your lives. He—or she—is responsible for the six weeks of your life you lost. If there is anything you can think of, please, you must let us know immediately."

"Yes . . . certainly . . ."

He smiled at her a last time, and squeezed her hand. "Good luck, Miss Delaney. Oh, you'll be barraged by reporters. We don't want this part of your story reaching the papers."

Skye nodded. There was a lot of her story she didn't want reaching the papers.

"We look forward to seeing you in our country again."

"Thank you," Skye murmured. Of course she would go back, Australia had become a second home, the whitewashed house in Sydney . . .

Sergeant Menzies followed Lieutenant Griffen out, with Kyle accompanying them. She heard Kyle's voice in answer to a muffled question from Griffen. "Yes, I'll be there, in less than ten days."

It seemed she was vindicated; it also seemed that Kyle was more determined than the lieutenant to apprehend the culprit.

"More coffee, Skye?"

It was Michael, smiling with gentle empathy.

"Yes, thank you," she murmured. She glanced at him, so like his brother, yet without the touch of hardness, the quality of steel that was so often an enigma.

"Michael?"

"Yes?"

"Is Kyle going back because he has to? Or because he wants to?"

Michael hesitated. "If they're ever going to make an arrest, Skye, they'll need Kyle's help. It was his plane that was sabotaged."

"We don't know for certain that the plane was sabotaged."

Michael poured himself a cup of coffee and sat beside her while Ray busied himself quietly in the galley. "Skye, don't you want this person apprehended?"

"Yes, yes, of course, it's just that . . ." She had known Michael only a day. She had no ties to Kyle. Could she, did she have a right to discuss him with his brother? Yes, she answered herself, because I love Kyle.

"I'm just worried," she said, meeting green eyes so like the ones she loved. "He . . . he seems ruthless where this is concerned. I'm afraid . . . I'm afraid Kyle will find this person, that he'll . . ."

"Act on rage? Commit murder himself?"

"Yes, I guess," Skye said unhappily.

"Don't worry," Michael assured her, "Kyle will see justice done, and it will be a good exercise in self-control. He's not crazy, Skye. He hasn't gotten where he is by letting his temper rule him."

"But how will they catch this person? What if no one comes to retrieve the case?"

"The thief will be found."

There it was—that tone. Michael was a lot like Kyle . . .

Except now he was smiling again. "Drink up. We're not even going to have time to offer you breakfast."

"Oh?" she inquired, startled.

"You'll be glad to hear that we're taking the dinghy out to meet a seaplane. We'll be on Igua within two hours."

She never had a chance to talk to Kyle at all—to tell him that she greatly resented his not saving her some of the misery she endured under her interrogation by the officers; to tell him that she needed to talk to him, that she loved him . . .

He was a stranger again as they left the *Bonne Bree,* and again she felt as if she had been dismissed. Did she love him? she wondered. Sometimes she hated him, when he mentally left her, when he watched her with cold lime eyes, his expression rigid.

She hated him because he could love her passionately, but he didn't seem to need her, and she had come to need him.

It was impossible to talk aboard the seaplane. Ray had stayed with the *Bonne Bree,* but Michael was with them, and the pilot of the plane, who, of course, worked for Executive Charters. And even if they had been alone, it would have been impossible to carry on an intimate conversation above the noise level of the engines.

The Pacific rushed beneath her. It was strange, but she hadn't been afraid to board the plane. Flying now should terrify her, but she hadn't been afraid at all. Maybe it was statistics—the odds against a person crashing more than once in a lifetime.

She stared down at the water. It seemed endless, and endlessly dotted with tiny islands, sometimes miles apart, sometimes one on top of another. Speaking of miracles, it had been a miracle that Michael had found them.

Skye shivered suddenly. They could have easily perished on the island, with no one ever the wiser.

A prickle of feeling brought her vision to the front where Kyle sat beside the pilot. His eyes, as she had expected, were on her. But they held no glimmer of sharing. They were fathomless, cool, assessing . . . hard lime-green. What had she done to deserve such an expression? she wondered. How was he capable of changing so easily from the night?

"There, Skye!" Michael, beside her, suddenly exclaimed. "Igua."

She could see the coastline coming into view, a beautiful place of white beach with one marked difference from the island she had just left—a stretch of handsome buildings beyond the sand, a harbor, an airstrip.

People.

People, she realized as the seaplane dipped and came in low for a landing, who were waiting for them.

"Michael," she murmured, feeling as if she were strangling, "I thought no one knew we had been found?"

"Oh, hell, Skye, I guess we all forgot to tell you with the excitement of this morning. The Australians changed their minds last night. They figured our radio contact could have been picked up by anyone anyway, so they informed my family and yours."

The Australians, she thought sadly, had had their period of grace, but she wasn't to get hers.

Before the engines had even ceased a crowd was racing toward the plane. Skye looked quickly to Kyle, but his eyes weren't on her. They were on the crowd.

And then Kyle was exiting the plane. From behind him Skye could see the reason for his haste. He was embracing a boy . . . a man . . . a handsome young man almost as tall as he, yet slender, promised breadth as yet not filled out. A dark youth, hair almost ebony, deep dark eyes alive with unashamed emotion. Skye's heart tugged painfully at the scene.

"Chris," Michael murmured in her ear, and she nodded, before feeling an icy winter chill. Two women were taking the young man's place—a lovely older woman with strong features and green eyes that surely identified her as Kyle and Michael's mother, and another woman, extraordinarily beautiful, tall, shapely, statuesque; handsomely attired in a light navy outfit that matched from silver-blond head to exquisite toe.

"Lisa," Michael supplied unnecessarily.

Skye closed her eyes and swallowed. She had not been an ugly shrew. She looked, as Kyle's entire family did, as if she were not an outcast, but truly part of his charmed circle.

And she had been encircling graceful arms around Kyle's neck.

Skye felt Michael's steadying arm around her. "I believe there's someone anxiously trying to get your attention . . ."

Skye opened her eyes again, careful not to cast her vision in Kyle's direction. And then everything happened so quickly she would never be able to sort out just what happened first.

Michael was helping her from the plane, and Virginia was there, dove-gray eyes filled with tears, words incoherent as she embraced Skye. And behind Virginia was Ted.

Skye was numb as he embraced her. She recalled all the pleasant things that were familiar, the scent of his after-shave, the touch of his tweed jacket against her cheek, the gentle appeal of warm brown eyes that lit easily to laughter . . .

He pulled away to hold her at arm's length, to look at her, to assure himself she was real. Skye met his gaze. She strained to offer him a tremulous smile; she tried to remember that this handsome man holding her with familiar arms was the man she had known and loved for four years.

But he was a stranger. His words brushed her ears but she didn't hear them. Kyle had made Ted a stranger. And then had become a stranger himself.

Skye sensed Kyle's eyes upon her. She turned, just slightly. His gaze, indeed, was upon her, fathomless. It appeared that he was going to come toward her, but his progress was halted. Lisa was attached to his arm. Her eyes, liquid and huge, were brilliant and pleading as she spoke words to him Skye couldn't hear.

Did Kyle mind that the woman hung on him like a leach? Skye wondered briefly. How much could he mind? She answered her own question with another question. Lisa was exquisite, and it appeared that she did love Kyle, did adore him.

She would never give him a divorce.

Skye caught Kyle's eyes for an infinitesimal second. She couldn't read anything but ice in them; his expression was rigid, cool, harsh. The stranger—he could take her, but she could never have all of him.

She pulled her gaze from his willfully. She threw her arms around Ted's neck, threaded her fingers through tawny hair, brought her hands to his face, pulled herself up on tiptoe, and kissed him—long, hard, passionately.

Forgive me, she thought sadly.

Skye heard a click; a brilliant flash of light exploded. The reporters were after their stories.

She disentangled herself from Ted. "Can we get away from all this, please?"

"Of course, darling, of course. . . ."

He began moving her through the crowd of jet-set curiosity seekers and reporters. Virginia clutched her other arm; they hurried toward a dark sedan and Skye was ushered in. She didn't look back.

"We've a suite at the Sheraton," Ted assured her, holding her hand as the vehicle began to move. "We'll get you settled, Virginia will stay with you, and I'll make our plans to return home. We can do whatever you wish, Skye. Stay here until you feel rested, start back immediately, whatever you wish."

Ted was good, Skye thought, closing her eyes. Was he actually missing an opening? she wondered. He was so anxious. She squeezed his hand, then glanced at his fingers. They were strong hands, just not the hands she craved to have touch her.

"Skye," Virginia murmured softly, "you are going to

have to talk to the reporters to get them off your heels. We'll arrange something. The Jaggers are all in the Sheraton, too. Perhaps we can arrange something together."

"No!" Skye exclaimed, then at the bewildered expressions they both gave her she murmured, "Please, not right away . . . I . . . I just want to settle in, then I'll make decisions."

"Of course, Skye," Ted murmured, soothingly. "Don't worry, I'll take care of everything."

Two hours later she was still soaking in a bubble bath in which the majority of bubbles had dissipated.

The water that had been steaming with heat was cold.

What was Kyle doing now? she wondered. Her stomach muscles tensed. He was in the hotel, not far away. Perhaps at this very moment he was setting aside his differences with Lisa, the mother of the son he so adored, taking her into his arms, making up for time lost over the years.

She didn't realize she had groaned aloud until the bathroom door flew open and Virginia flew in. "Skye! Are you okay?"

Her sister-in-law was usually so serene, with a quiet strength that suited her angelic prettiness to a tee, and at the sight of her gray eyes wide with alarm, her short brunette hair flying wildly, Skye smiled.

"Sorry, Ginny, I'm fine. Just pruning from sitting in the water so long."

Virginia handed her a massive snowy-white towel, and Skye wrapped herself in it as she emerged from the water.

"I haven't become an invalid you know," Skye told Virginia, who continued to watch her with worry.

"I know, I know," Virginia murmured with a flush. "I just can't tell you how worried I've been, how sick. I had just learned to accept . . . to accept Steven being gone, and then . . ."

"Hush, Ginny," Skye interrupted, impulsively hugging her and soaking her through the towel. "I'm alive, I'm here, I'm real." Virginia brushed away the beginning of tears with the back of her hand.

"Well," she said briskly, "Ted should be back up any minute to tell us what arrangements he's made. I'm sure, knowing you, that after all that time with nothing, you're dying to dress up! I picked up a slew of things from the boutique in the lobby while we were waiting for the plane to come in—" Her giddy speech was interrupted by the ringing of the doorbell. "I wonder who that is?" she said, brows arched. "I doubt that Ted would ring."

"Go find out," Skye said. She laughed as Virginia still appeared to be lost. "Ginny, answer the doorbell. I can hardly do so in a towel."

Giving her a sheepish grin, Virginia left the bath and exited the adjoining bedroom, closing the door behind her. Skye followed her out of the bath and glanced at the packages lined up on the bed, then quickly began to rummage through them.

She paused uneasily and glanced around the plush chamber with the massive white quilted bed.

There were only two bedrooms in the suite. Ted, after seeing her to the suite, propping her up in the thickly cushioned sofa in the sitting room as if she were an invalid, and assuring himself that she really was healthy and sound, had left her with Ginny to check with the French authorities who governed the island and straighten out her papers.

After ordering a huge meal—she was famished—and talking with Ginny, she had sunk into the bath.

She didn't even know whose room she was in. Was Ted putting her with him? Or, suspecting that she had slept with Kyle and would need time now, leaving her to sleep with Ginny?

Her heart seemed to stop for a moment. She couldn't sleep with Ted, not tonight; she didn't know if ever . . .

Her glance moved to the twin hardwood dressers. She felt her heart begin to pound again, then she sank to the bed with relief. An assortment of very feminine powders and perfumes filled the top space of the far dresser.

"Skye!"

"Coming!" she answered Virginia's call. She could hear conversation from the sitting room, but couldn't decipher what was being said or who was speaking. The other speaker, however, was male.

She dug into the first bag and found an attractive off-white day dress with long sleeves, an A-line skirt, and full front buttons that ended at the neck in a tailored collar.

And Ginny—bless her—had been thorough. The smart shopping bag also contained low sandals to match and pretty lace undergarments, even pantyhose.

Skye hurriedly dressed, her curiosity piquing her. An official, she was sure, to welcome her back to the world of the living, to the island.

Her hand froze on the knob before she could open the door. The drone of the man's voice was familiar. It was Kyle. She was sure it was Kyle.

"Skye?"

Virginia's call caused her to jerk open the door, and she struggled desperately to control her features, to wear an expression of cool cordiality.

But the man wasn't Kyle. Michael Jagger waited for her. "Skye!" He greeted her with pleasure, taking her hands and kissing her cheek. "You look stunning!"

"Thanks," she murmured, trying to hide her vast disappointment. Kyle was not coming for her. Had she expected him to cast Lisa aside dramatically and to appear at her door to proclaim his love and whisk her away from

Ted? No, she thought, not after the show she had given him of throwing herself into Ted's arms, kissing him heatedly.

She felt a blush rising to her cheeks. What must Michael think of her? He knew she had been sleeping with Kyle; he saw her show of intense delight in another man.

But apparently Michael Jagger didn't judge. Strange, but he had become a very comfortable friend. She felt oddly as if, in some way, she knew Michael better than Kyle.

"I'm sorry I took so long, Michael," she apologized. "What can I do for you?"

Michael laughed. "I'm not sorry you took time at all, Skye. I've been getting acquainted with your sister-in-law."

"Oh!" Skye said, a smile creeping into her lips as she watched Virginia—quiet, shy Virginia—blush.

"Anyway," Michael continued, always able to make others feel comfortable, "we've arranged a press conference for you and Kyle in the ballroom for five o'clock. We told the reporters thirty minutes and that's it. Then you won't be hounded—"

"I haven't been hounded."

"Kyle had your calls diverted to our secretary. He didn't want you bothered."

"Oh," she said again. She didn't know whether to be angry or not. Even away from her, even in the arms of his family, he was running her life. A rush of misery swept over her. She didn't want to be back in the real world; she wanted to be back on the island with bark for a toothbrush and sand for a bed, back on the island where life and love were simple, basic, elemental.

"Is that all right?"

"Yes, Michael, thank you," Skye murmured. She thought he would leave then, she wanted to close herself into a room and sort her life and thoughts, hide like an ostrich.

But Michael didn't leave. Virginia, stuttering peculiarly, was offering him a drink. They sat and talked. Skye talked but she didn't know half of what she said.

Then Ted was back and she was trying to smile for him, trying to be comfortable, trying not to cringe when he touched her.

And then it was time for the press conference.

It was only thirty minutes, but it was thirty minutes of pure hell. She sat next to Kyle, so close that she could feel the heat and tension of his body close to hers.

More so than ever, he had slipped away from her. She didn't know the man in the impeccably tailored suit, yet his scent was poignantly familiar from that first day. Against the pale blue of his shirt, his face was ruggedly bronze, his eyes were brilliant, shrewd . . . condemning when they lit upon her.

Oh, dear God, she thought, floundering as his gaze turned to her as he answered a question about their food supply and diet. She had never seen facial muscles so rigidly set, a jaw so seemingly composed of granite.

It was over. They had both done well, she thought vaguely. Not a word had been mentioned about illegal gold, not a word that linked them as anything more than two survivors.

The reporters were ushered out; family was once more rushing toward them. Why do people always rush? Skye wondered. Why don't we get even a moment?

And then all she wanted to do was run. Chris was the first to reach his father, the first to be politely introduced to her. He showed her a sincerely friendly interest, and still she felt uncomfortable. He was an adult. Did he speculate about her relationship with his father? Or was she paranoid?

Chris was called away by his uncle. Ted was busy speaking with a reporter who hovered persistently by the door. Their moment had come . . .

Kyle turned to her with a dark glower. "We have to talk, Ms. Delaney."

Talk? About what? Last night had been their time to talk. Now was too late. His wife was coming toward him again with his son. "About what?" She said it aloud, bitterly.

"Us," he said curtly.

"Us?" Skye laughed briefly, a quiet sound, but dry and harsh. "There is no us. I'm leaving shortly—with Ted." Why had she said that? she wondered, praying she didn't burst into tears. She couldn't handle the situation; words she didn't mean to say were coming to her lips.

"Is that what you want, Skye?"

No, it wasn't what she wanted at all, but how could she say anything else when it appeared that he hated her and was merely taking care of her still because she had become some type of an obligation . . .

I think I'm pregnant, she wanted to wail out, but when she spoke it wasn't those words. "Yes, of course that's what I want. The island—what we had there—is over. I have my life . . ."

"Kyle!"

Skye's hushed whisper was interrupted by Lisa Jagger's soft voice. The woman was smiling as she approached the chairs where Kyle and Skye still sat, and again Skye was startled by her beauty. She appeared to be ageless; her manner impeccable.

"What is it, Lisa?" Kyle asked, his voice brittle and snapping.

"Excuse me." Lisa smiled again, apparently aware that Kyle's rarely contained anger was directed more toward a difficulty between him and Skye than toward her actual interruption. She extended an elegant hand to Skye. "I haven't met Miss Delaney yet. How do you do? Since my *husband* seems to have lost his manners, let me introduce myself. I'm Lisa *Jagger.* Kyle's *wife."*

"Dammit, Lisa—" Kyle began with thunderous irritation, but he was interrupted again, this time by an apologetic Michael needing his immediate attention to clarify a problem with flights.

"I'll be right back," he told Skye, ignoring Lisa.

Lisa shrugged and gave Skye a patient sigh. "You poor *thing.* What a miserable experience for you."

Skye twisted her lips into a meaningless smile. She had thought Lisa beautiful; she had believed Lisa did love Kyle, she had had been so perfect and charming. But her statements in private held a note that was vicious. Even as she smiled and simpered, a certain malice filled her eyes.

"It wasn't all that miserable, Lisa," she replied, her voice cool and poised. *"Kyle* is so . . . resourceful." She underscored her words with a meaningful pause. "Now, if you'll excuse me, I believe my sister-in-law is calling me."

Skye rose, wishing her height equaled that of Lisa Jagger. She began to walk away as calmly as she could manage.

"Just a moment, Miss Delaney."

Skye halted, turned slowly with questioning brows.

"Just remember, Miss Delaney"—Lisa still maintained her smile, although it was strained—"I am Kyle's wife. I'm aware you've had some type of a physical relationship with my husband, but for your own sake, don't take it seriously. Kyle has had numerous affairs." She lifted her hands in a parody of apology. "I'm still his wife. And I fully intend to remain so."

"Your marital problems are between yourself and Kyle, Mrs. Jagger." Skye's tone was crisp, her words to the point, though she wished she could die inside.

She turned once more, desperately blinking away tears. She wanted nothing more than to get away; unfortunately, she walked right into Kyle. He caught her, his grip on her shoulders punishing.

"Dammit, Skye," he hissed, the green of his eyes smoldering. "You will talk to me. I intend to see you—"

"No!" Skye protested, lowering her voice immediately and clenching her teeth to keep from wrenching away. "I will not be your mistress, a pleasant diversion you can use when it suits you until you're no longer amused," she hissed in a vehement whisper. "Let me go. Your *wife* is waiting for you."

He removed his hands from her shoulders. "Skye," he said with fierce control, "we *will* talk this out. I *will* see you alone. Tonight. We'll have the entire thing out with both Lisa and Ted."

He walked on past her, but Skye didn't doubt his purpose for one moment. Despair and bewilderment assailed her viciously. She wanted him desperately, wanted to hear all that he had to say.

But now she knew Lisa. And she knew the words she had heard Michael Jagger say to Kyle were true. Lisa would destroy him. And Skye really didn't even know just what it was Kyle felt for her.

She sought out Ted. She knew they weren't scheduled to leave Igua until morning. That didn't matter.

"I want to start home now," she told him.

"Skye," Ted murmured with surprise, "I don't think we can leave tonight. The flights are all arranged for tomorrow morning."

"I want to leave tonight! Please!" Skye insisted.

He looked very upset. The typical male with an unreasonable female on his hands close to tears he didn't understand.

"I'll try, Skye—"

"Go to Michael Jagger," she told him. "He'll arrange it."

She had the strange feeling that Michael—of all people—understood everything she was feeling, understood why she so desperately wanted to get away.

Michael Jagger did understand. She, Ted, and Virginia were off Igua by seven P.M.

Interlude

"Where are you going?"

Kyle had almost reached the door when Lisa stopped him. The Jaggers had taken a large part of the hotel's eighth floor, but every room opened to the spacious main parlor of the suite. Concern for his mother's health had brought Kyle back to the suite after the press conference; she was a spritely sixty, but he worried about her heart and the strain caused her by his disappearance, then the joy created by his return.

But now she was sleeping. And he intended to accost Skye.

He paused and turned coolly back to Lisa. "Out, Lisa. To see Skye."

A baby grand sat in the center of the pleasant parlor. Lisa ran her fingers in idle chords over the keys.

"She's gone."

"What?" He took several menacing steps toward her, his face a dark twist of anger. "So help me God, Lisa, if you've done anything—"

Lisa was bright enough to realize that she had pushed her husband one too many times in the past. He had never been physically violent, but he looked as if he might throttle her now. She unwittingly lifted her hands in self-defense and said quickly, "I haven't done a thing. Your loving brother arranged a flight for her." Lisa had been about to add, "and her party," but the look on Kyle's face precluded any further explanation on her part.

Kyle stopped dead in his tracks, jaw constricted with pain. Lisa watched as dark emotions rippled through his rugged bronze countenance; a shudder rent his body. He took one more step toward her and stopped, his voice in control when he spoke. "I want you out of here, Lisa. Now. I've tolerated your presence so far for the sake of your son and my mother. No more. The only communication I wish to have with you in the future will be through my attorney."

He turned to leave. "I won't give you a divorce, Kyle," Lisa called, her voice rising shrilly.

Kyle turned again. He was still calm. "Why, Lisa?" he demanded quietly. "Why are you doing this to me?"

"I won't let you marry that woman," Lisa said, emotion again making her voice shrill although she had intended to sound disdainful. Silence followed her statement and she repeated it. "I won't let you."

Kyle took another pantherlike step toward her. "Are you jealous, Lisa?" he inquired, his voice deceptively soft. "You shouldn't be—you're still very beautiful. Free me, Lisa, and you'll also be a very wealthy woman in your own right."

Lisa made the mistake of misreading his tone. She slid from the piano bench and slipped her arms around his neck, pressing against him. "I'm not trying to be cruel, Kyle. It's a mistake. You'll quickly find her boring and be miserable. You're back in the real world now. I want us to give it a go again, Kyle."

He didn't protest her embrace, but neither did he respond to it. He smiled ever so slightly and lifted a brow. "I see. You're telling me that you love me."

Lisa widened her eyes and pouted her lips prettily. "Of course, Kyle." She brought a finger up to touch his lips. "Remember how good it could be, Kyle. It can be again.

I'll show you . . ." She pressed even closer to him, allowing a husky sexual tension to drift slowly away in the aftermath of her tone.

Kyle caught the hand that touched his lips, secured the one that clung around his neck, and very nicely but firmly placed them back by her sides and stepped away.

"I'm sorry, Lisa, but no, I don't remember how good it was. Ever."

"Kyle—give us a chance . . ."

"I gave us every chance in the world." He sighed tiredly. "I accepted Chris; I forgave you all your lies. I spent at least five years being a model husband. It wasn't enough for you, Lisa. You wanted to keep my name, but you also wanted everything else that walked in pants."

"You've been sleeping with other women for years . . ."

"Yes, I have. I don't deny that. But do you know what the sad thing is, Lisa? Neither of us ever cared. In fact, right now, I don't believe you'd care if I continued sleeping with Skye. Just as long as you could still be Mrs. Kyle Jagger. Well, I don't want to live like that anymore. I want to marry Skye. I want to be a faithful husband; I want a faithful wife."

"She's gone home with her lover!" Lisa spat. She had the pleasure of seeing him wince, of seeing every muscle within his dangerous frame tighten. Inwardly she shrinked, but her courage was bolstered by her knowledge of the man. He would never touch her now; he would be afraid of his own wrath.

"Perhaps," he said finally. "But the future remains to be seen. And Lisa, I will divorce you."

"You'll be destroyed trying," Lisa promised in a hiss.

"I'll take that chance. And I'll also give you fair warning. I'm going out. When I return, I want you gone. If you're still here," he added so pleasantly that she didn't dare doubt him, "I'll have you removed. Do you understand?"

He didn't wait for her answer. He left the room in search of his brother.

It took him twenty minutes to find Michael, which was probably good. By the time he found his brother—Michael was sitting in the Lotus Lounge drinking a Scotch as if preparing for the confrontation he knew must come—Kyle's temper had cooled. He knew that Michael had also decided Skye was a very special lady, that he had acted to save her from pain—and from whatever Lisa might have up her sleeve.

Kyle stared at his brother for a minute, then pulled out the chair opposite him. Michael warily returned his brother's stare, then released a pent-up breath as Kyle sighed, lit a cigarette, and motioned to the cocktail waitress.

"Scotch, rocks, please."

Michael drained his glass. "Make that two."

"Two doubles," Kyle corrected.

The cocktail waitress left. "Kyle," Michael began, "I'm sorry. From the moment I saw her on the beach I knew she was different. She deserves—"

"Everything," Kyle interrupted, waving a dismissing hand. "I'm not angry with you, Michael. I was, but I'm not." His face twisted into a dark scowl as he added, "However, don't ever mention how you saw her on the beach to me again. Come hell or high water, I'm going to marry her, and I'd just as soon my brother not keep reminding me he's fully acquainted with his future sister-in-law's anatomy."

Kyle was serious; Michael had to laugh. "Hey!" he protested. "I'm only human."

Kyle gave him a dry look but didn't comment further. Their drinks arrived. Both brothers took good swallows. Then Kyle became all business.

"I want you to get hold of McVicar and McVicar. Tell them I want every possible loophole in a marriage explored, and that while they're exploring, to get something started. I want out—no matter what it costs. Lisa can't really touch Executive Charters—not the way it's incorporated. Next, I want you to get hold of the O'Reilly people. I want to know every move Skye is making in New York. And I want someone out in Australia on this gold thing. I'm heading back out there myself until I hear from McVicar and—Michael, are you listening to me? What the hell is that grin for?"

"I don't believe it. You're actually going to have someone spying on Skye?"

"You don't approve?"

Michael laughed. "I sure as hell do approve. You're serious about all this, aren't you?"

"What the hell did you think?"

"Nothing," Michael said quickly. "Nothing. I'll follow everything to a tee. And I'll damned well be rooting for you."

"Only one thing could stop me."

"What's that?"

"Skye," Kyle said softly.

Eleven

July 23, New York City

"I should have never let you go to Australia alone when Steven was dying. I kept telling myself that he had just taken a turn, that he would respond to treatment and pull through. I don't think I ever believed it myself, but you didn't push, Skye. And I was relieved. I was being selfish, and I knew it. My excuses were reasonable on the surface, but inside I knew I didn't want to face tragedy with you. I always wanted things light, easy. I wanted to be with you when you were laughing . . ." Ted's voice trailed away with a deep misery as he paced before the plate-glass windows that led to Skye's terrace—hundreds of feet above the busy streets below.

Skye, curled into the corner of her plush white sofa, closed her eyes, her fingers nervously kneading a deep maroon throw pillow. Don't do this to me, she silently pleaded. Please don't bare your soul to me . . . now . . .

"Ted," she said softly, awkwardly, "you didn't do anything wrong. I really didn't know that Steven was . . . was actually dying until I got there. And it was all over a year ago." She had known this moment was coming, and she had dreaded it. Ted had murmured about a serious talk all the long journey home. And now they were home. He had left her alone in her apartment when she had mur-

mured she was tired from jet lag. He had left her alone
for two days.

She no longer needed time to acclimatize to her home.
She no longer needed time to sleep.
She no longer needed time to adjust to global changes . . .

Ted stopped his pacing and knelt on one knee before
her, taking her hand into his. The sincerity in his dark
eyes seemed to touch her, to fill her with pain. "I did
everything wrong, Skye. You might not have known for a
fact that Steven was dying, but I still think you knew the
kind of crisis you were facing. You needed me, but you
were too strong to say it and so I pretended not to understand it." He stopped speaking with a rueful smile,
but lifted a hand to shush her when she would have answered him. "I have to tell you everything, Skye. I was
relieved when you said we needed time before marriage.
I didn't want the commitment, I didn't want to be legally
tied down. I liked things the way they were, easy, no responsibility."

"Ted," Skye was finally able to protest, "you're apologizing and you have nothing to apologize for! You've always been wonderful to me. We've both always been
happy with the way things were."

He shook his head. "I was always first, Skye. Me and
my stupid shows." He kissed the palm of her hand, then
slid beside her on the couch. "I want to change that,
Skye. I want to marry you, I want to be with you through
everything."

He saw the tears start to form in her eyes and wrapped
his arms around her, drawing her close. "Isn't it something, Skye? When we think we've lost something, we realize how much that something means to us. You. When
I heard your plane was lost, I wanted to die. I realized
then that I loved you more than anything in life. Say that
you'll marry me, Skye . . ."

He kissed her forehead with gentle lips. Skye looked

up into his eyes. Tears still hovered in hers, but they didn't fall. They seemed to congeal, as did her body with a cold pain. She didn't want to hurt him, oh, God, she didn't want to hurt this wonderful man . . .

He lowered his lips then and kissed her, holding her tight. Skye felt the kiss touch her, and yet she felt it as if she were an onlooker. It was a fine kiss, a practiced kiss, one offered with the tender emotion of love. She could respond to it, she could easily murmur a yes to his proposal and fall completely into his embrace until his gentle ministrations stirred her. They could so easily make love, and it would be pleasant. But all the while she would be closing her eyes and imagining another touch, another man.

Skye drew away from him. Someday she would have to forget Kyle. She would have to learn to live and to love again. But it couldn't be with Ted. He loved her, and she could only hurt him, cause him more pain.

"I can't marry you, Ted," she told him, wishing she could cry, wishing she could touch him and make him understand how much she did care about him . . .

He saw the tears in her eyes; he saw the pain. He stood, and stared at her as she stared straight ahead. He bit into a corner of his lip and walked back to the plate glass, staring sightlessly out into the dark night beyond.

He finally spoke. "I know you were sleeping with Jagger, Skye."

Skye was jolted. Her eyes sped to his back as he stood facing the window. He had spoken so quietly, but with such certainty. Her problem of how to tell him was solved.

For a brief second she wondered with bitterness how everyone seemed to know. To Michael Jagger, of course, it had been obvious. But Lisa . . . and now Ted? It was as if she wore a placard on her chest. I was sleeping with Kyle Jagger.

Or had she really changed? Did something in her eyes,

in her manner, decree that she had fallen under the spell of a man who was a walking embodiment of a power anyone could sense, anyone could feel?

She didn't say anything. What could she say?

Ted kept staring out the window. After a moment he started speaking again; he hadn't expected an answer.

"I understand it, Skye, at least I think I understand it. You were alone. Jagger is certainly a fit specimen, and I don't mean that as bitterly as it sounds. He seems to be a decent person. Very decent. I suppose I even have to be grateful, and I am. He kept you alive, he kept you well."

Skye heard the soft whistle of his sigh, saw a hunch, then a straightening to his shoulders. "I know you slept with him, Skye. I understand it, I accept it. I also hate it. I can't help it, but I don't ever want to hear about it." He finally turned to look at her and she realized from the naked expression in his dark eyes that he was pleading.

If I could only undo this, she thought, if I could only go back in time. I could have been everything he wanted.

She swallowed, dug her nails into her palms, bit the soft inner skin of her lips. Her words came in a rush anyway; her tears fell. "Oh, God, I am so sorry. So very, very sorry. I can't marry you."

"Skye," he began, moving swiftly toward her.

Skye stretched out her hands, palms outward. "Don't, Ted, please don't.—" She struggled for something to say and then blurted out, "I'm pregnant."

His first expression was that of a man who had been hit with a brick he had seen coming but had stupidly stared at it. But then he collected himself quickly, and came to her despite her protests.

"I don't care, Skye. I love you, I'll love your child."

She cried then as she had never cried in her life. Great heaving sobs that racked her tiny frame. He tried to hold her, he tried to soothe her; it all only made her worse, and all she could finally manage to say was, "I still can't marry you, Ted."

He held her in a soft quiet. After a while he murmured, "You're in love with him, aren't you?"

"Ted," Skye garbled, "you are wonderful, you're everything anyone could want—thoughtful, kind, warm, gentle, good."

"But you're not in love with me."

"I do love you—"

"Hush. I believe you, I know that. But you're not *in* love with me. Please, Skye, don't look like that. It's my own fault. I had four years. Jagger only had six weeks. If I'd had any sense, I would have married you four years ago. I would have been with you."

They were both quiet, staring out the glass into the night. He still held her, a gentle grip, one of comfort.

"I'll still marry you, Skye, if you wish, if you want the child to have a father." He hesitated only a second. "Jagger is married."

"I know," Skye said softly. "And thank you, but no."

"What are you going to do?"

"I don't know yet. Go back to work for a while," she told him with a rueful smile. "Then maybe I'll go out and stay with Virginia for a while. Long enough for the public to forget me."

"Jagger will find out."

Skye shrugged. "I'll have to handle that if and when it happens."

"You know an abor—"

"I couldn't."

"I didn't think so."

Again a silence reigned between them, but it was a comfortable silence, marked by a friendship that had risen in the ashes of what almost was but could never be.

Ted rose to leave. He kissed her forehead. "Call me if you need me. I'll always be there."

Skye nodded, her throat too constricted for speech.

He reached the door.

"Ted."

He turned. There were tears in his eyes. Why had she stopped him, prolonged this agony? "I'm sorry, Ted. I'm so sorry."

He gave her a rueful, strained grin. "Don't be sorry. Don't be anything but Skye—honest, warm, and beautiful. You can't help your feelings, honey. You love him. You can't change that, and I can't change that. Not now, anyway. But later, if you want to try, I'll be around."

He was gone. Skye stared out the plate glass for hours. She prayed that he would find a woman who would give him all the love he deserved.

And she wondered achingly what kind of a fool she was to give up a man like him for the emptiness that the future promised.

Unless Kyle did care for her, unless he loved her, unless Lisa gave him his freedom . . .

Unless, in short, a miracle occurred.

September 26, San Francisco

From his office window Kyle could see the bridge glimmering beneath the sun. He stared at it, thoughtfully chewing the nub of a pencil. When he had returned from the island he had spent a month in Australia, and now, for the past month, he had been trying to contact Skye. She had spoken to him only once—very coolly. She had asked after his family, then his *wife*. He told her his family was fine, he assumed Lisa, too, was well.

"She *is* still your wife?"

"Yes—but—"

He never had a chance to continue. Skye had excused herself to answer another call. She had never returned to the line.

Since then he had spoken with her secretary a dozen times; he had heard the recorded message on her answering machine another two dozen.

But now he was going to wait no longer. His sources had informed him that she was no longer seeing Ted Trainor. When he finished the interview he must now handle, he planned to contact Trainor himself, then fly to New York. She wouldn't come to a phone, but by damn she would see him. She would have to because he'd gag the damn secretary and break down her office door if he had to.

Kyle's intercom buzzed. He flicked a switch on the left side of his large oak desk.

"Yes?"

"Mrs. Jagger is here, Mr. Jagger."

"Send her right in," Kyle said grimly.

He stood while he awaited Lisa. She entered with all the flair he might have expected, seeming to float on the breeze of expensive French perfume, her hat sporting a lilac feather, which he assumed must be chic. Her hair was coiffed elegantly; her manner was assured.

"Hello, Lisa," he said calmly, pleased that he would be the one with the bombshell for once. "Thank you for coming."

She closed the door behind her, paused dramatically, then moved gracefully across the tan soft pile carpet. Kyle was a man of simple tastes. One contemporary sofa in a tawny shade to match the oak of his desk flanked it. Lisa seated herself, watching him.

"I was summoned," she murmured sarcastically. "So I'm here." Lisa slowly drew off her gloves finger by finger. "I believe you've heard from my attorneys? I'm contesting any action." She smiled very prettily. "I believe the differences in our marriage can be reconciled."

Kyle smiled, equally pleasantly. He took his seat behind the desk once more and tapped the pencil he had been chewing against his desk. "I've heard your response from my attorneys, Lisa."

"I hope you haven't called me here to threaten me, Kyle? That wouldn't sit at all well with a judge."

"Lisa, I have to admit I've actually thought of strangling you and accepting the consequences as well worth the deed. But no, I haven't asked you here to threaten you. This is a very polite warning. You don't want a divorce; I don't think we have to go through one. You see, I believe I can have our marriage annulled."

"Annulled!"

"That's right, annulled. You see, Lisa, marriage is a contract. A contract can be broken when there has been misrepresentation on either side. As in the wife having full knowledge she is carrying the child of another man and refusing to mention that fact—"

"You wouldn't!" Lisa's calm was broken; she was on her feet, her beautiful face contorted in a twist of rage. "You wouldn't! That would make Chris . . . that would make Chris . . . No! You can't do it! You'll never get away with it. We've been married for twenty years. No judge in the world will give you an annulment."

Kyle knew he had to maintain a dead calm. He had to carry out the world's finest bluff. "Don't count on that, Lisa. I wouldn't be attempting such a thing if my lawyers hadn't advised me as to the feasibility."

"You wouldn't do it to Chris. I know you wouldn't. He would know then that you weren't his father, and I don't believe that you would do that to him—or yourself. You don't want to ever take any chances on losing Chris—"

"Chris is twenty years old, Lisa. He's an adult. He's old enough to make his own choices—"

"And he'll choose to hate you if you have him legally declared a bastard!"

Kyle gripped the undercorner of his desk. Beneath his tailored business suit, muscles were tense. He gripped harder. He couldn't fly into a rage . . . "Lisa, I was the one who was there when Chris took his first steps, when he said his first word, when he woke up in the night with bad dreams . . . Oh, what's the sense of going on? I think Chris might understand."

"He's still my son, Kyle. No matter what you did when he was young, he'll hate you if you throw me out and have him declared a bastard. And I'm still not terribly sure you can do it!"

"Lisa, you're acting like the vestal virgin spurned. You forget—Chris was witness to any number of the things you did. You weren't particularly discreet. You never hid your affairs from him." Kyle broke off with an exasperated sigh. "I don't want to argue with you, Lisa. The past is over. I don't want to hurt you; I don't really want to hurt anyone. But I want out. Think about this. If I succeed with an annulment, you wind up with nothing. If you sign the papers that will get us out of this marriage in a matter of two months, you'll get half of my personal assets. The choice is yours."

"You're bluffing, Kyle."

"Am I?" He raised a brow at her with a polite smile.

Yes, he was bluffing. Or was he? At this point he didn't know himself. He had thought about this confrontation for endless hours. He loved his son with his entire being—what he contemplated was almost an irreverence. Chris was *his* son. It was the pain of a deep and twisted knife to even consider using a threat that involved Chris. . . .

But it was the only threat he knew. And a threat was nothing more than words. Dear God, what would Chris think if he knew? Could he lose his son? Kyle wondered.

Blood meant nothing to Kyle, but would it mean everything to Chris?

No, Kyle thought, his faith in the boy was justified.

But what would Chris think? What would he feel?

Oh, Chris, I don't ever want you to know. Forgive me for even threatening. In reality, I can't even contemplate your knowing the truth, much less hearing that I'm willing to make you a bastard.

Yes, it was a bluff.

But Lisa couldn't know that. She had to believe that he meant every word that he said.

Perhaps Lisa had been reading his thoughts. She smiled as she watched him and repeated, "You're bluffing, Kyle."

"Am I?" *Cool,* he warned himself. He raised a brow at her with a polite smile. The pencil still lay on his desk. He picked it up and casually played with it. "I'll give you exactly two weeks to make up your mind. Have papers signed by October 10, or I'll have you in court for annulment proceedings."

Lisa rose, staring at him with challenge. "What is your hurry, Kyle? Has little Skye given you a time limit?"

"I haven't seen Skye since Igua, Lisa. This is my choice."

"I see. Skye won't see you until you're free. Pity, Kyle, because you're right. I don't care if you sleep with that woman. But I guess she covets the title of 'Mrs.' herself. I don't intend to let her have it. You can fight me until you turn blue in the face, Kyle, and I'll still keep you in court for years. I'll even go for a stake in precious Executive Charters. So where does that leave you? She won't be your mistress. Although I must point out that if she did care for you—and not affluence and power—she would be with you, don't you think? But you can't give her what she wants. And so you have to sit here while she winds those pretty little legs around that producer's—"

"Get out!" The pencil snapped in Kyle's fingers; his

attempt at calm was lost in a roar. He stood again; Lisa had sense enough to do the same and back slowly toward the door.

"Hit you where it hurts, eh, Kyle?" she threw out.

"I don't care to listen to your vicious and vulgar mouth, Lisa. I repeat myself, *get out.* You've got your choices. Now leave before I solve all our problems by breaking your neck."

His voice had regained quiet control. It held a deathly quality that moved Lisa. She stalked quickly to the door and set her hand upon the handle before casting out a last warning. "Try to bring her back, Kyle. See if she's worth everything you're going to have to go through to have her. See if she does care enough about you to sleep with you. And you'll discover she's just another warm body. You'll tire of her when you start to see Executive Charters torn to shreds—"

She broke off abruptly, pulling the door wide open as Kyle began to take steps toward her. Beneath the bronze of his face was a white anger. Muscles twitched in his jaw; his lips were a tight line more grim than the coiled tension of his stalk.

"I'm leaving, Kyle. Just remember what I've said."

She was out; the door closed. Lisa was no fool. She knew she had pushed his patience to the limits.

Kyle stopped where he was. He closed his eyes, willing the painful fury to ease from his body. He stood dead still for several seconds, slowly breathing with regularity.

He returned to his desk, stared at the reports of the fruitless search for a clue to the gold heist, stared at the papers piled high on his desk awaiting his signature.

He saw nothing—except the vision Lisa had planted in his head. Skye . . . naked . . . seductively smiling . . . arms reached out . . .

He threaded his fingers tightly through his hair, pressed hard at his temples.

He flicked on his intercom. "Jennie, tell Michael I'm leaving in an hour—clear me through to Kennedy. Then get me through to New York City. A Mr. Ted Trainor. Whatever you have to do, get him on the phone. Hold all of my other calls."

"Yes, sir."

Kyle forced himself to turn his attention to the business on his desk. He scanned purchases and routes, scowled, set problems aside, set his signature to what he approved. Time ticked away, and he didn't stop.

The intercom buzzed. "You're through to Mr. Trainor, Mr. Jagger."

Kyle didn't hedge with his conversation.

"Trainor?"

"Yes?" The reply was slow, suspicious.

"I'm coming to New York. To see Skye. It's my understanding that you two are no longer seeing one another. Is that true?"

There was a long hesitation. "Jagger, that's none of your business—"

"Why?"

There was a hesitation again. "Mr. Jagger, Skye is my friend. I'm afraid if you want answers, you'll have to get them from her."

"I just wanted you to know that I am coming. And that I do intend to see Skye."

"I can't stop you, Jagger. You should have seen her before this. But I'll tell you something. I asked her to marry me. She refused . . . because of certain circumstances. But take care of her, Jagger, or I'll still be around."

"Just what does that mean?"

There was a long sigh. "You have to talk to Skye, Jagger. I'm not at liberty to say more."

"All right, Trainor." Kyle paused for a moment. "Thank you."

There was silence on the line. "You're welcome," Ted said finally.

Within an hour Kyle was headed east.

September 26, New York City

Skye glanced up as Lucy Grant breezed into her office, perplexity written on her round, friendly face. Her graying hair was frizzled as if she had literally been trying to pull it out.

"Skye, honey, I know you're busy with the Rathstadt designs, but Mrs. de Vintner is driving me crazy! She said she expected her Egyptian earrings to be twenty-four karat, and I've tried and tried to explain about the weight but she won't listen to a word I say."

Skye laughed and set her pencil aside. "I'll talk to her, Lucy. What line?"

"Oh-seven," Lucy said gratefully. "I know secretaries are supposed to save the boss from the hassles, but honestly, honey, this woman—"

Skye waved a dismissing hand. "I know Mrs. de Vintner. Go on ahead and see if you can contact Mrs. Rathstadt. This will be ready for her to see this afternoon."

Lucy exited with a sigh of relief. Skye picked up the phone, cordially inquired about Mrs. de Vintner's health, then proceeded to explain that the drop earrings that reached almost to Mrs. de Vintners shoulders had to have hoops of eighteen-karat gold. The copper alloy within the hoops strengthened them. Twenty-four-karat gold could not sustain the heavy pull of the earrings, which, combined, were an entire ounce of gold. Mrs. de Vintner was finally appeased. Skye hung up the phone, rested her forehead in her hands, then stood and stretched, rubbing her lower back.

She moved to her window, leaned against the pale blue

draperies, and stared to the street, so far below. The people busily moving about looked like hordes of ants. It was only early afternoon, but the cars were creeping along, congested in an eternal traffic jam.

She grew dizzy staring down, and closed her eyes to fight a wave of nausea. She was so tired. The doctor had promised her the miserable sick feeling would leave her soon, but "soon" couldn't be soon enough. Her pregnancy wasn't even apparent yet, but damn, she could feel it! She was thin, so there was already a soft swelling to her belly, and she was finding herself more and more frequently touching that little swell. She might be half crazy, but she was already in love with the little life she carried. The love made up for all the discomfort. But not for the loneliness.

She bit into her lip, thinking of all the times Kyle had called. Each time she heard his voice, growing angrier with every recorded message, she was tempted to pick up the phone, to tell him that she needed him, that she loved him, that she didn't care about anything except that he be with her.

But she didn't pick up the phone. She would dig her nails into her palms to steel herself. She had made her decisions. If Kyle had really cared for her, he would have come . . .

And she didn't want him because he felt obligated. She didn't want him going through strain and misery to rid himself of Lisa, when he would only be trapped into another marriage of obligation like the first that had been such a disaster.

Skye left the window and returned to her desk, trying to concentrate on her design. Concentration wouldn't come. She closed her eyes again. It was pleasant to daydream. When she closed her eyes, she could remember the clean breezes of the ocean, waking to the sound of the surf, feeling sand between her toes, knowing Kyle was near and that their entire existence was for one another.

She opened her eyes. She had to be half crazy to be wishing herself back on a deserted island, struggling against the elements.

She sighed. In another month she would go to Sydney and leave the business of Delaney Designs to Lucy. Virginia had been gone a month now, and Skye sorely missed her company. In Sydney she could find anonymity while planning her life and still keeping busy with the actual work of design. . . .

Skye stared back down at the Rathstadt design. The dress swept the floor in luscious folds, but the neck was bare, the cleavage was low, held by thin straps. Mrs. Rathstadt wanted her jeweled accessories bold and striking. And Mrs. Rathstadt was a stunning regal-looking woman. She would be able to carry the boldest design with a flair.

Skye set a transparency over the original drawing and set to work. The clear neckline would allow for a heavy gold collar, with an emerald pendant to catch and accent the rich green of the gown, which would be of the finest Chinese silk.

Skye was startled from the concentration she had almost achieved as Lucy burst back into her office. "Skye, I'm terribly sorry, but this gentleman insists on seeing you . . ."

For a split second Skye's heart seemed to constrict, to skip a beat. She was sure it was Kyle, he had finally come, and she should be upset because she didn't want to see him because things could never work out, but she was so happy because she just wanted to see him again, to stare at him and have all that he was refreshed in her memory.

The man wasn't Kyle.

He was a nondescript little person in some sort of a drab uniform. He wore a badge.

"Miss Skye Delaney."

"Yes, I am. What—"

An envelope was stuffed in her hand. The little man turned as quickly as he had come and disappeared through her office door, closing it behind him.

Skye stared after the man, looked at a stunned and very upset Lucy, then back to the envelope. Shrugging, she opened it. Legal terms began to swim before her eyes.

"What is it?" Lucy demanded.

"I'm not sure," Skye murmured with confusion. "It seems I'm being subpoenaed to appear in an Australian court!"

"For what?"

Skye frowned and bit her lip. She had never discussed the gold discovered on the island, not with Lucy, not even with Ted or Virginia. With her thoughts constantly occupied with memories—and admittedly bitterness—she had almost forgotten the gold. She had known Kyle had returned to Australia, but he had never said anything about the gold. Of course, she had never given him a chance.

"I'm not really sure," she murmured in reply to Lucy. "Hey, Luce, get Harry Dunbart for me right away, will you?"

A half hour later Skye was thoroughly furious, frustrated, incredulous—and ready to cry with sheer disbelieving self-pity.

"I'm an American citizen!" she spat, throwing the offending envelope with disgust on her desk. "I crashed in a damn airplane, I was marooned on a stinking island not knowing if I would live or die, and now this! Because some baggage clerk is claiming that case went on board with my luggage! I should have sued Executive Charters and Jagger for every penny they were worth—"

"Skye, calm down," Harry Dunbart soothed, rubbing the bald spot on his temple with agitated fingers. "Executive Charters has nothing to do with this. And you're not actually being accused of anything. They want you for further questioning."

"I don't want to answer any more questions! I was a victim in this entire thing! I—"

"Skye," Harry interrupted, "I understand, and you're right. But victims often suffer. And I'm afraid if you don't appear for this hearing, you might wind up being extradited, and your refusal to cooperate could look very bad. Skye, you were planning on going to Sydney anyway in a month. I'll make arrangements to be with you as soon as possible."

"In other words, Harry, you're saying I have to go."

Harry rubbed his bald spot with such a worried vengeance that Skye began to fear he would shortly bare bone. "I'm a corporate attorney, Skye, I'm a little over my head with this thing. But yes, I think you have to go. I'm going to find the best possible person to represent you. We have a few weeks—"

"No, Harry, I'm going today. From Virginia's I'll be in a better position myself to try to understand what's going on. We'll meet in Australia."

"Skye, that's insane, you don't have to leave today."

"Well, I am. I'm too disgusted to do anything else!"

Harry left unhappily, promising to be thoroughly prepared when he reached Australia. Skye called Lucy in and told her to make arrangements so that she might leave immediately.

"Immediately? Skye, the airlines—"

"Call Executive Charters," Skye said bitterly. "Their motto is 'Anywhere at any time!'"

The New York offices of Executive Charters were almost as large as the home group in San Francisco. Skye was able to arrange a flight out within two hours. She boarded a Lear uncannily familiar to that which had landed her in the South Pacific not so very long ago.

But the pilot was a cordial, middle-aged man with pleasant powder-blue eyes and a crinkling smile, not the vitally intense male with the searing green gaze who had once barely swept his eyes over her before taking his seat for a flight that would prove to be the most catastrophic detour in her entire life.

Away from her office, away from a view of all others, Skye closed her eyes and leaned her head back against the plush rest. It wasn't fair. Oh, God, it wasn't fair. Her existence had been torn asunder. She was pregnant by a married man. But she had learned to cope, she had known where she was going.

But now this. It just wasn't fair, it wasn't fair. Tears slipped beneath her closed lids. She wondered if Kyle would have to appear in Australia. And she wondered if he would prove to be a witness for the defense—or for the prosecution.

Lucy Grant's day hadn't been going well at all. She was worried sick about Skye, exhausted from the whirlwind of her employer's hasty departure, and nervous silly over the responsibility she had been handed. Mrs. Rathstadt would be in shortly to okay the design Skye had barely finished. Thank God it was nearly time to go.

Lucy began to clear her desk and to put things in order for the next working day. She began to collect meticulously a sheaf of invoices, then gasped and tossed them all high into the air as the outer door slammed inward and a man barged in like a tornado.

"I'm here to see Ms. Delaney," he announced in a harsh bark, ignoring the mass confusion his abrupt entrance had obviously created.

Lucy was tongue-tied as she stared at him. She had never come across a person exuding such an energy. He was a strikingly handsome man, but that fact could almost be overlooked. She could feel a power from him, something that compelled, something that radiated a vital heat from a muscular form with the lithe agility of a lynx.

She stared into his eyes, green eyes, searching for words in the confusion of his overwhelming appearance. He was just a man, she thought, tall, excessively attractive—but that aura.

He was Jagger, of course; Lucy finally stumbled to her senses and realized. She had seen his picture when Skye had been found; she should have known the voice instantly from having refused so many of his calls.

Lucy finally managed to close her mouth. "She isn't here," she stuttered.

"That's exactly what I expected to hear," he said with impatience, brushing by her to the door marked, Skye Delaney.

He entered the inner office, searched it in a hurry, returned to Lucy. "Where is she? She isn't going to hide out any longer. I'll find her, and if I don't, you and I will sit right here until she returns."

Lucy's eyes widened. Of course, he thought this was another ploy for Skye to avoid him . . . "Oh, Mr. Jagger, she really isn't here!" Lucy exclaimed. And then she went on to tell him that Skye had been subpoenaed and had stormed out to catch a flight to Sydney.

"Dammit!" he murmured, obviously shocked by the news. "I have a dozen people on this thing and I didn't hear a thing about Skye being recalled . . ." His voice had changed; he appeared frustrated and worried, but he offered her a rueful smile. It was a devastating smile, Lucy thought. Skye was a fool, even if he did have a wife.

"Listen, miss," he began.

"Lucy," she interrupted. "Lucy Grant."

"Lucy," he corrected, another devastating smile lighting his rugged features, "I'll help you collect these papers"— he began to gather the scattered invoices together—"and you get on the phone to my New York office. Tell them Kyle Jagger wants a fueled Lear ready in thirty minutes. And that I want to be cleared to Sydney. Wait—on second thought, tell them I want a pilot. Mathews, if he's available. I don't want to arrive exhausted."

"Yes, sir!" Lucy replied, responding to his natural authority with even more than her usual efficiency. "Please, sir, don't bother with the papers. I'll be able to handle them just fine . . ."

He was gone with the swift, determined step that had brought him. Lucy put through the calls, then sank into her desk chair, ignoring the invoices, forgetting all about Mrs. Rathstadt.

She had just been touched by an earthshaking force of nature, felt the fringes of a tornado—the stuff of daydreams.

She wondered vaguely if Skye was aware that she was loved by this particular green-eyed tornado. And then she began to hope fervently that problems and chaos could turn to the stuff of dreams.

Twelve

September 28, Sydney, Australia

"I'm very sorry, Mr. Jagger," the young officer apologized with sincerity. "We did try to contact you, but you were already in motion yourself. Our telegram about Miss Delaney simply didn't reach you. And the hearing is still two weeks away. We haven't charged her with anything yet."

"But you do believe you will be charging her, after the hearing, don't you?" Kyle demanded. He had decided to discover exactly what was going on with the prosecutor's office before contacting Skye, and now he was finding out with a sinking heart that a case was being made against her. Damn, he felt furious and helpless! He had spent weeks here working on leads that turned up nothing. He had checked the banks, the customs authorities, the airport—nothing. And now an obscure baggage clerk had come up with the sworn statement that the black case had gone through with Miss Delaney's luggage.

The young officer nodded unhappily. "I believe she will be charged, sir. International smuggling is a very serious offense—"

"She didn't do it!" Kyle snapped, then regretted his abrasive haste. The desk officer had little to do with the case. "She certainly wouldn't sabotage her own flight," he amended more quietly.

"No, sir, we believe an accomplice was involved. I mean"—the officer swallowed quickly—"Miss Delaney is certainly innocent until proven guilty . . ."

"She's innocent and will be proved innocent," Kyle said grimly. "Thanks," he told the officer. "Tell your lieutenant I'll be back to see him in the morning."

"Oh, yes, sir, Mr. Jagger, I'm sure he would have been here if he had known you were coming."

Kyle nodded briefly, turning to leave the crisp, clean office. Whereas fall had been approaching in New York, spring was coming to Australia. Even in the busy downtown section, flowers were in abundance. Unfortunately, Kyle had little time to ponder upon the beauty of the day. He was intent upon bringing his rented Volvo across the Harbour Bridge to the secluded suburb where the directory had listed the residence of Virginia Delaney.

A chill gripped him as he drove. The authorities were following the same logic he once had. Skye had been the only passenger on the plane.

She wasn't guilty. He knew she wasn't guilty. But if there was something, anything that she knew . . . Had she been used in any way? Should he actually be confronting her now?

Whether he should or shouldn't didn't matter. He hadn't seen her for over two months, and she had plagued his mind every hour, every day of all that time. He suddenly realized he was nervous. Two months had put the breach of time between them, and besides that they had problems that appeared insurmountable. It was more than possible that Lisa would call his bluff; he could never hurt Chris. Somehow he would have to try to hold Skye through bitter months, perhaps years, as he battled Lisa.

None of which would be consequential if they didn't solve the problem of the gold.

* * *

Dressed in a white flannel robe, Skye lay dispiritedly before the fire in Virginia's living room, watching the flames as she idly rubbed her fingers over the soft fur of her sister-in-law's Persian cat, Muff. She couldn't remember ever being so depressed or tired in her life, unless it had been that day on the beach.

She didn't want to remember that day on the beach. It would remind her of Kyle. And then she would ache with missing him. Then she would remember that he had thought her a smuggler, too, that she was in Australia with everyone thinking her a common criminal, and that he had probably known what was going on all along and hadn't come to her defense.

Gold. She closed her eyes against the warmth of the flames that burned in that color. How she hated gold. She had crashed because of gold, she had feared for her life because of gold, she had fallen in love with Kyle and become pregnant because of that same gold, and she was here now, sick and miserable, wondering if she would face incarceration for what remained of her youth—all because of gold.

Maybe if she didn't feel so terrible she could care more. As it was, she felt as if she had been drained of the will to fight.

The doorbell began to ring and she listened to it listlessly. Then she remembered that Virginia had gone out shopping. Skye still listened, not caring. Whoever it was would go away. But the noise continued, and finally, when the persistent buzzing threatened to give her a headache on top of all else, she struggled to her feet and passed through the cozy living room to the entrance foyer and flung open the door.

Simple instinct upon seeing the thunder in Kyle's face caused her to back away and to attempt to slam the door. He caught it with a single hand and pushed it back inward. "No way, Ms. Delaney. You can't hide behind an answering machine now."

Skye froze as she watched him close the door behind himself. Her fingers were clutched around her robe, pulling it more securely. Even in dreams she hadn't remembered him so formidable, quite so tall, quite so broad, so sleekly, powerfully rugged . . . nor had she remembered an expression quite so threatening . . . so determined . . . so relentless. And yet he appeared almost casual. He seemed relaxed, arms crossed as he leaned against the door, watching her with that cool, assessing gaze. Why not? He was in the door. If she moved he could catch her in a single step. And what was more, he had the advantage of being immaculately and handsomely dressed in a lightweight fawn suit. She was a wreck, her dress the soft robe, her hair carelessly disheveled . . . He had planned on finding her; his appearance was a shock to her.

She bit her lip and mentally straightened her spine. "Kyle," she murmured with a biting trace of sarcasm. "Come in."

"I'm in," he replied grimly. And then he breached the step between them, taking her by the elbow and leading her back to the living room as if it were his home. "Where is your sister-in-law?"

"Shopping. She'll be right back."

He raised a brow and practically pushed her into the sofa, choosing to pull a straight-back chair from the nearby card table for himself. He planted it in front of her, straddled it backward, and set his elbows over the high back. "I doubt if she'll be right back, and that's just as well. We have a lot of talking to do."

Skye stared at him, wishing her feet weren't bare, wishing she were respectably, attractively dressed, wishing she had makeup on, wishing she had anything as a bit of self-assurance. Was this really the man she had shared intimacy after intimacy with for days on end? Damn, he was such a stranger—so hard, so cool. And still she wanted to reach out and touch the fabric of his jacket; his scent was so familiar. She wanted to crawl into his arms . . . but his face was not one that invited her touch. They had been lovers once, now they were familiar strangers.

"I want to know every single little thing you know about that gold," he told her, his gaze intense. "Every movement you made the day of our flight. Anyone you dealt with. Anything that might give me any lead to any information about the gold."

Skye didn't like the tone of his voice. She did stiffen. "Why don't you just ask me when I stole it?"

"Did you?"

"Go to hell."

She saw a tightening in his jaw, but no other reaction to her dull statement. "I need to know everything, Skye. I'll get you out of this, but I need to know everything."

Rising, she eluded the hand he stretched out to stop her. "Don't worry, Mr. Jagger, I'm not intending to fly the coop. I'm hardly dressed for an escape." She walked over to the fire and leaned tiredly against the marble mantel, talking into the flames. "I don't know a damn thing about the gold. I went to the airport straight from here. I never saw the black case until you threw it at me in the hut. And by the way, hello, and yes I'm fine."

"You're not fine," he said shortly, ignoring her dig, "You look like hell."

"Suspected smugglers do look like hell, didn't you know?"

She hadn't heard him move, and yet she knew he was behind her. Still she was startled, completely taken off guard, when his arms slipped around her and his hands splayed over her midriff, moving quickly upward to cup her breasts, then descending to stretch over her belly.

"Kyle, let me—"

"When were you intending to let me know?"

"Know what?" she gasped, struggling against his clasp. But his hold was rigid; his voice, whispered in her ear, was level but harsh.

"Oh, come on, Skye! I lived with you night and day for six weeks! I suspected the moment I saw you, I knew for sure when I touched you."

"Kyle," Skye said quietly, "will you let go of me, please?"

He released her, taking her place by the mantel while she returned to the couch. "You weren't intending to tell me at all, were you?" he demanded with curtly suppressed anger.

"I really don't see where it would have made any difference."

He didn't rush to her side, he moved there slowly with purpose, tilting her chin with a firm finger so that she couldn't escape his eyes. The cold wrath she found in their depths was chilling.

"Why? Were you planning an abortion."

Skye didn't blink or waver. "No, I wasn't. But what makes you so sure this is your child?"

He smiled, but it wasn't a sight to ease her chills. "You refused to marry Trainor—you haven't seen him since you returned to New York. And you haven't seen any other men either."

"How the hell do you know?"

"I had you watched and I spoke to Trainor."

"You bastard! How dare you have me spied upon!"

Kyle shrugged, leaned back, lit a cigarette. "I had to know what you were doing."

"If you wanted to know what I was doing so badly, you should have come to New York. You seem to pop around the world on whim—cross-country should have been nothing."

He raised a mocking, curious brow. "I see. You're bothered that I didn't drop everything to follow you in the middle of the night?"

"Don't be ridiculous." Skye lied with applaudable indignation.

"No, I suppose not," Kyle said with a dry trace of bitterness. "But do you know, Ms. Delaney, I would have followed you. My brother brought to my attention the fact that I had a few problems of my own to solve before accosting you."

"Oh? Have you solved them now? Or are you here because of the gold?"

"Skye, I didn't know a damn thing about your being involved in this until I reached New York and found you gone. I spent a month here—a wasted month—hoping something would turn up. I spent another month catching up on a sadly neglected business—and struggling with my personal life. A month, I might add, in which you refused to speak with me."

Skye lowered her eyes, turning her attention to Muff, who had decided to slide against her legs seeking affection. She picked up the cat, feeling the beat of her heart quicken. He had been coming after her anyway . . . She caught a corner of her lip with an eyetooth. Ted! He had said he had spoken with Ted. When? What had Ted told him? Had he known about the child and sought her out because he did know? "Did Ted call you?" she inquired, attempting to sound casual.

"I called him."

"Why?"

"To tell him I was coming after you."

Skye turned to look at him again. It was impossible to read his granite expression. "And what were you going to gain by coming after me?"

"I was going to take you home with me—to San Francisco."

A bitter gall seemed to rise in her throat. "To be your mistress for all the world to see, Mr. Jagger? No thanks."

"Now you're being ridiculous. I intend to marry you."

A laughter that she couldn't control bubbled from her. It was bordering on hysteria, but she simply couldn't help it. "Oh, Kyle! The last I heard, bigamy was definitely outlawed in California! Or were you hoping your wife wouldn't notice?"

"Dammit, Skye!" He crushed his cigarette out and grabbed both her hands, dragging her so that her face was just inches from his. "Personally, I don't find this amusing. You knew soon after the crash that I was filing for a divorce—"

"Which you obviously haven't gotten!" Skye interrupted, flying to equal fury to counteract the tears that threatened to rise.

"I'm doing the best I can!" he exploded in return.

"Obviously your best isn't good enough!"

With a muttered oath he dropped her hands, rose, and paced to the mantel, hands rigid in his pockets. "I never would have thought it, Skye, but you are a hell of a lot like Lisa. Screw all else, just go for the name. Well, don't worry, you will get the name. We have to be married now, as quickly as possible. There's the child to think about."

Skye blanched, first at the reference to Lisa, then at his insinuation that their marriage—should it ever take place—would also be for the sake of a child. "Who ever implied I expect to marry you?" she said, straining to make her voice more than a sick whisper. "I told you once I was quite self-sufficient."

"You also told me once that a child deserved both a mother and father who wanted it and loved it. Were you lying then, Skye? Is everything about you a lie?"

"No—" she began to stutter, but then she sensed him behind her again, cutting her off as he placed his hands around her head, half gently as he teased her hair with his touch, half as if he wished he could crush her skull . . .

"Do you know, Skye, I never did know what you felt for me. On the island I could have sworn that you did care. But then we were alone, I was your survival. It's a pity that you don't love me. If you did, you wouldn't mind coming to San Francisco. You would trust me. You wouldn't care if others put labels on your situation."

Skye winced. His fingers had moved to massage her temple; their touch was controlled, but she could sense the power and the tension. Oh, God, she thought, closing her eyes, seeking for an answer to give him. She didn't care what others thought, she feared he would change his mind. He wanted her now, he was determined to marry her. But she had known other women who involved themselves with married men. And in the end perhaps the wife, perhaps the pressure, perhaps a combination, killed the strongest love. With Kyle it would be even worse. They had so much to lose . . .

Kyle wasn't waiting for an answer. "It's a pity that you are going to mind, Skye, but you are coming home with me."

Again, Skye began to laugh. She really didn't seem to have any control over herself. "Oh, Kyle! How can I come home with you? It appears right now as if I'm going to be having this child in some Australian prison!"

He paused for a long moment. "I'm going to get you off the charges. And then you're coming home with me."

She was tired. Too tired to argue. She wanted to crawl into his arms and tell him she loved him and she didn't care about anything as long as he was there and she could leave her life in his hands. But that tension was still in his touch. She wasn't sure if he loved her, desired her, or hated her. "Yes," she said quietly. "You get me out of this, and I'll come home with you."

She felt his fingers tighten. "Like I said, Skye, don't

worry. You will wind up the legitimate Mrs. Jagger. I have a card to play against Lisa if the situation becomes desperate."

"What?" Skye inquired.

"At the moment it's none of your business."

Startled and hurt to the quick by his hard, bitter tone, Skye snapped back, "It's none of my business because it doesn't exist!"

"It's none of your business because it could seriously injure someone else!" Kyle thundered. She almost cried out because his grip, threaded now through her hair, was so tight. Seeming to realize what he was doing, he released her. "Don't push me, Skye," he warned in a hiss. "I'm tearing my life apart for you and I'm really beginning to wonder if it's worth it. You act the part of the callous bitch with even more flair than Lisa."

No! she wanted to cry, but the word froze in her throat. It was all wrong. He had come after her, they were discussing marriage, they were discussing their lives, and it was all wrong. There hadn't been an embrace between them, a note of tenderness . . . Somehow, they had started on the wrong track, and now, though she wanted to, she couldn't touch him, couldn't fling herself into his arms, couldn't tell him she loved him . . .

She heard his steps as he walked toward the entrance foyer.

"Kyle . . ." She had to repeat his name because her voice was so weak. "Kyle!"

He paused and turned toward her.

"Where are you going?"

"To work on clearing you of the charges." He raised a curious and very sardonic brow. "That is the deal, isn't it? I clear you—you come back with me. Even if it is as my *mistress* for the time."

Skye was so startled by his bitterly mocking tone that

she didn't reply. He smiled with no humor, turned, and left.

The next two weeks of her life became a living nightmare. She spent hour after hour with Kyle's attorney going over and over every move she had made before leaving Australia on that ill-fated day in June. The senior McVicar, along with an Australian associate, was handling her case. He was a kindly man, gentle with her, but she had faith that he could argue a case with the best. His sharp blue eyes missed nothing; he picked up on any statement for thorough explanation, no matter how trivial it might seem to Skye.

Kyle attended every session, but he kept a rigid distance from Skye. The only time she saw him was with Mr. McVicar—cold and aloof across the room, his attention entirely on the proceedings.

Skye couldn't really see where any of it was doing her any good. It was going to be the word of the baggage clerk against hers.

Three days before the hearing Mr. McVicar suggested she agree to a sworn deposition before the prosecutor's office for New South Wales. Skye agreed, feeling sure in her innocence she could say nothing to condemn herself.

She wasn't nervous, but righteously angry. Still, as the questions went on and on—ridiculous questions dating all the way back to her first trip to Australia—she began to tire. The attorney was pleasant, cordial, and polite, but painstakingly thorough. After three hours Skye thought she was either going to scream or to die.

It was at that point that Kyle, silently sitting in the background, chose to interrupt. He excused himself to the prosecutor and court reporter who were well aware of who he was and the nature of his connection to the case.

His presence for the deposition hadn't even been questioned. His interruption was politely accepted.

"Ms. Delaney agreed to come here to provide all the assistance she could. She has also offered to participate in a lie-detector test. Gentlemen, she has been here for three hours. I think you should tie up your questions. The lady is pregnant, and I don't think a continuation at this point is necessary, and very well may be hazardous to her health."

An end was immediately put to the deposition. Skye was given a polite and solicitous apology.

She wanted to die. She had known from the concerned—but speculative—eyes that turned to her that all were aware the child she carried belonged to Kyle Jagger.

She waited until they had left the law offices behind—until she and Kyle were alone in his rented car—to challenge him heatedly.

"Don't ever, *ever* do that to me again!"

He paused, key in ignition, to study her with apparently surprised interest. "Do what, Skye? Pretty soon your condition is going to be very apparent."

Skye closed her eyes and leaned back against the seat, bringing her palm to her temple. It was true. Virginia already knew, although she wasn't saying anything. But then Virginia was already fond of Kyle; she had taken a liking to him from the moment they had met after the rescue.

But didn't he understand how she felt? It might be the eighties, but it was still a man's world. Kyle didn't appear concerned in the least that he had fathered a child out of wedlock. She couldn't help but cringe when curious, knowing eyes lit upon her.

"Are you ashamed of carrying my child, Skye?"

"No. I—You just can't possibly understand. Forget it."

"I didn't want you sitting there any longer under strain.

You're thinner now than you were on the island, and that can't possibly be good for the child. If you don't want to take care of yourself for yourself, think of the baby."

Skye sighed. "I do think of the baby. It's just rather difficult at the moment. Oh, dammit, Kyle! Can't you see how everything has changed for me? Before the island I was an entirely independent person. My life was ordered, it moved in the direction I pleased. Now my business is in chaos, I'm seriously suspected of smuggling, and I'll shortly be notorious for my affair with you! I've been reliable, dependable, and respectable all of my life. Can you imagine what it feels like even to be suspected like this? And if I do go to trial, by then I'll be . . . I'll be—"

"Stop it, Skye!" Kyle interrupted harshly. He jerked the car off the road just before the Harbour Bridge. For a second he stared at her with exasperation as she stared ahead at the glitter on the water and the bustle that was the busy bay. She wouldn't look at him and he muffled a curse, snapped on his lighter, and lit a cigarette.

He exhaled slowly. "Skye, you're not going to lose your business. I have offices all over the world and I assure you I don't spend time in all of them. You can work in San Francisco as well as in New York. I don't believe you're ever going to go to trial. You haven't even been officially charged with anything. And by the time you're as big as a house, we'll be married."

She would have been all right if he hadn't touched her. But when his hand came around her neck, gentle and firm, massaging away the tension, she burst into tears. Kyle flicked his cigarette out the window and pulled her into his arms, brushing her hair from her forehead soothingly. "It's going to work out, Skye, I swear it will."

"I'm so scared," she told him, stuttering into his lapel.

"I'm so scared. I never imagined I could wind up in prison and now I can hear the jail bars clanging in my mind."

"Shhhh . . ." he whispered. "Maybe it's not as bad as it seems."

As he held her, gently rocking beneath the brilliant sun of Sydney, he became determined to stop it all. He knew her strength; he could well remember the spirit of the girl with whom he had survived a crash and the hardships of survival on an island with nothing.

But no one could be strong through everything. And Skye was dangerously near a breaking point.

He held her until she was cried out. Then he silently drove her home, delivering her to Virginia.

"I'm fine," Skye said, refusing his assistance as he tried to walk her up the flower-bordered path to the house. "I'm sorry. I didn't mean to fall apart all over you."

"You're not fine," he informed her, sweeping her into his arms and carrying her the rest of the way. When Virginia opened the door, he briskly carried Skye to the couch and set her down. "Don't let her up for the rest of the day," he told Virginia. "And Ginny, get her to eat something, will you? She's going to lose that baby if she can't keep some weight on."

"Kyle!" Skye half snapped and half wailed.

"I'm sure Virginia is well aware of the entire score," Kyle said, silencing her. "Quit acting like a damned ostrich, Skye."

Virginia nodded gravely. "I'll watch her, Kyle. I'll fix her some lunch and make her take a nap."

"A nap!" Skye protested. "I'm an adult. I don't need to have my lunch fixed—"

Kyle bent over her and kissed her lips, silencing the rebellious outflow. "Shut up, will you, Skye?" he murmured, moving away. He smiled at Virginia and left.

Skye fell silent. She ate the soup and sandwich Virginia prepared for her.

The kiss had been the first sign of affection Kyle had shown her since they left the island. Maybe it meant that there was hope.

Virginia appeared with a pillow and blanket and tucked the latter around Skye as she lay on the couch. She sat opposite Skye and picked up her yarns and crochet needle, saying nothing.

"Virginia?" Skye said softly.

"Yes?"

"What . . . what do you think of all this?"

Virginia set her needle aside. "What do I think? Believe it or not, I think you're lucky." She waved a dismissing hand as Skye's look intimated she was crazy. "I don't think for a minute that you will be charged. And I do think that things will work out with Kyle. You stumbled into a horde of problems, but you also stumbled into an incredible man. And, oh, Skye! Despite everything, aren't you excited about the baby?"

Skye colored slightly but nodded. "Yes, I guess I am."

Virginia picked up her crocheting. "Booties!" she said cheerily. "Skye you haven't a thing in the world to worry about. As soon as Kyle walks into a room, you know he'll take care of everything. He's a man who always gets what he goes after . . ."

Virginia rambled on. Skye clutched her stomach as she had done so often lately. Yes, it was possible that Kyle would take care of everything. But then where would she be? What would she be? An obligation who dragged him down, who, in his own words, was tearing his life apart . . .

She twisted into her pillow. Still, she was excited about the baby despite all. It was pleasant to dream about the child, about a life shared with Kyle.

Except that he barely touched her anymore and the hearing was still to come and he was still married to Lisa.

Beautiful Lisa. When faced with his stunning wife, and

the awkward form Skye felt she would soon have, where would Kyle's choices lie? To have Skye, Kyle would have to wage a war.

To have the lovely Lisa would be easy. No war . . . no long and tedious court battle.

Eventually Skye slept, dreaming that an avenging angel came down from the heavens and permanently attached a paper bag over Lisa's face and mouth.

He had to find the way to clear her.

He had promised. He had bargained.

And she was pregnant.

He closed his eyes and felt his forehead grow clammy. He was pleased. Pleased, hell. He was thrilled. It was what he had wanted, a way to bind her.

But now he was desperate. Damn Lisa, damn her to hell.

Chris . . .

He had used threats regarding Chris. And they had been a bluff. But were they now? Because he had to be free.

And Chris was all he had.

Shudders began to rip through him and he swallowed down a gulp of Scotch. What the hell was he going to do? He couldn't really hurt Chris.

He could talk to his son.

No, he couldn't take that chance. He had to take the chance. No, he had to win. Damn! Lisa was his mother. She had to care! Surely she would believe that he would carry through his threat if he played it far enough, and she would then give him his freedom.

Chris was his child, but so was the baby Skye carried, the baby he had hoped would exist . . .

Oh, God, what the hell was he going to do?

Day by day, he warned himself. Day by day.

Pressure Lisa until she gives . . .

Talk to Chris . . .

No, he's going to have enough to handle. The divorce, accepting Skye, accepting a brother or sister . . .

No, he told himself, Chris will have no problems with acceptance. I forget that he is my son, that he is a man, that he has grown with a sense of conscience, of caring, of giving . . .

I can't possibly hurt him.

I have to do something.

I have to make Lisa give.

Take it a step at a time.

And the first step was the one he had to worry about now. Skye. He had to clear Skye. Force other things from his mind so that he could concentrate his full efforts on the seriousness of the dilemma that desperately needed to be cleared. It was a critical situation.

Oh, God, was he tired. His mind whirled and whirled and with each dead end the ache in his temples became more agonizing.

Something about the baggage clerk . . .

The phone rang and he picked it up wearily. "Jagger here."

His tiredness left him instantly when he heard the voice of the private investigator he had hired. The man was excited. He had found the taxi driver who had driven Skye to the airport on June fourth. The man was eagerly ready to swear that Miss Delaney had not carried any luggage other than a canvas tote bag and beige Gucci suitcase.

Controlling his own excitement, Kyle asked, "How can the man be sure? How can he remember one woman after all these months?"

"I'll bring him right over," the investigator offered, "and then you'll understand."

Ten minutes later Kyle was listening as a balding little

man with earnest brown eyes spoke to him, nervously twiddling his cap in his hands all the while. "I remember this little lady clear as day, sir, because we happened to be talking about her work. Such a charming little thing, so soft-spoken. I knew she was class right off, sir, and she was as nice to me as she might be to a duke, she was. After I asked her what she did for a living, I said I'd sure love to have an extra nice necklace for my wife—our silver anniversary is coming up—and Miss Delaney drew me a beautiful sketch, right there in the cab. And then she gave me her business card, and said to call collect if I decided I wanted the piece, and she gave me a little wink and said not to worry too much about the cost because we could work something out easy. I never tried to call her, sir, I heard about your plane disappearing." He paused a minute, eyes on his cap. "But I never did hear anything about this gold business—not till this man here"—he pointed to the nondescript private investigator—"came looking for me. I would have spoken up before now if I'd have known she was in any trouble. I sure am sorry—"

"Don't be sorry, Mr. MacDonald," Kyle shook the man's hand. "I'm in your debt." He turned to his investigator. "Tom, get this man down to see the lieutenant. Just tell him what you've told me, Mr. MacDonald. And don't worry, I'll compensate you for any time—"

Mr. MacDonald drew his small frame to a dignified posture. "I don't need compensation, Mr. Jagger. Not for doing my duty as a citizen and helping out that nice Miss Delaney."

Kyle smiled. "Thank you then, Mr. MacDonald." He waited until the little man was out the door and then called back Tom Keaton. "Tell Lieutenant Griffen to meet me at the airport, and, Tom, see to it that Mr. Mac-Donald gets a nice necklace for his wife. Put it on the expense account and you and I will settle later."

Keaton nodded, and left with MacDonald. Then Kyle was out the door himself. He was beginning to feel both elated and ill. The baggage clerk was a liar. The baggage clerk was also an employee of Executive Charters . . .

Kyle remembered the statement given by Jake Henry he had read. "I sure don't like to think that lovely lady could be a thief, but she had that case with her when she came through. She came in with a big, heavy suitcase, a canvas bag, some kind of a ladies handbag, and that very metal case. I didn't think a thing of it—I'm not a customs agent, you know, just a clerk . . ."

He could remember the statement almost word for word he had read it so many times. Soon after that came the damning sentence. Someone had obviously asked how she had managed to carry it all.

"Oh, ah, the lady wasn't carrying her suitcase. She had her cabby with her . . ."

Kyle left the car in a no-parking zone, treaded steps with which he was well familiar, and moved to the area designating the space of Executive Charters. He had to slow his steps consciously, to breathe consciously, to force himself to smile, appear easy.

Jake Henry was working. "Hi, Jake." Kyle leaned easily over the counter and smiled at the saturnine little man. He had to fold his fingers together; he was dying to reach out and press his hands around the man's throat . . .

"Hello, Mr. Jagger, sir. Are you taking a plane out? I haven't heard anything about you coming—"

"No, no, Jake," Kyle interrupted, still smiling. "I just came by to see you. I wanted to ask you a few more questions about the Delaney woman."

"Oh." Jake Henry smiled agreeably, but Kyle sensed a change in his demeanor. A fine film of perspiration was already appearing on his forehead.

"Jake, you said to the police that Ms. Delaney had a

cabby with her when she brought her luggage in. Would you recognize the man?"

"Oh, ah, I'm not sure, Mr. Jagger. That was more than four months ago now, and you know, I see hordes of people every day. There's always cabbies around, you know?"

"Yeah, well, Jake, we've found the cabby."

The man was sweating profusely now. He ran a finger around the back of his starched white collar.

"Oh? Do you think the cabby will remember right? A cabby sees even more people and suitcases and such than I do, you know, sir?"

"This cabby remembers, Jake." Kyle suddenly dropped his relaxed pose. He reached across the counter and gripped the man by the lapels. "Listen, Jake, this thing burns me, man, it burns me real bad. Not only was my company used, my plane used, but it was almost my life that was taken and that of a lady whose life means even more than my own. Now smuggling is bad, Jake, real bad. But murder is worse. I don't think you're a killer, Jake, but I do think you know how that gold got aboard the plane. Now listen real good, because this is what is going to happen. You're going to turn yourself in *and* you're going to give the police the name of your accomplice. Because if you don't, you won't only have to worry about the Australian government thinking you were the one guilty not only of smuggling but also attempted homicide, you're going to have me thinking you're guilty of attempted homicide. The court will give you a chance. I won't."

Jake Henry was shaking like a leaf blown in winter. His face had turned a mottled purple. He gasped only once in protest. The look in Kyle Jagger's eyes convinced him that thirty years in a penitentiary would be preferable to the treatment he would receive from this man.

"I didn't touch the plane, Mr. Jagger, I swear I didn't touch the plane. I didn't know anything about the plane being touched—I just figured there'd be some plan to pick up the stuff in Buenos Aires. I swear I didn't touch the plane . . ."

Kyle felt his fingers tightening on the man's lapel. He had never felt such a black rage in his life. Beads of perspiration were breaking out on his own brow while what felt like a chill was gripping his muscles, fogging his mind, tensing his grip. He took a deep breath; he was beginning to shudder . . . He had lifted Henry above the ground until his toes scraped . . .

"Jagger, please, for God's sake!" Henry begged in a breathless garble.

Kyle dropped the man, biting down hard.

"Jagger!"

Kyle turned to see that Lieutenant Griffen had arrived. He looked at Griffen tiredly, then finally spoke. "Mr. Henry here has another statement to make for you, Lieutenant. I believe it will agree with the new information you've received from Mr. MacDonald." Kyle turned back to Jake Henry abruptly, filled with disgust. His voice became very quiet—deathly quiet. "Who fixed the plane, Henry?"

The little man switched his eyes nervously from the lieutenant to Kyle. Even with the authorities around it was apparent he didn't trust the latter. He licked his lips nervously. "I don't know anything about the plane being fixed—"

"You're a liar, Henry," Kyle said, his eyes pinioning the man.

"Smithfield!" Jake Henry suddenly babbled. "Ted Smithfield, the mechanic. The whole plot was his idea, Mr. Jagger. He threatened me, I had to go along. But you're not going to find him; he lit out right after you were discovered on the island. He knew the Aussies would keep someone there . . . he knew he'd never recover the gold. I didn't want in on it. I didn't. Smithfield said that if I didn't get the gold on the plane, he'd get me. I swear, Mr. Jagger."

Kyle turned from the man in disgust, sure he would feel the urge to throttle the man again if he stared at him any longer. Walking slowly from the scene, Kyle could hear Griffen reading Henry his rights. The sound began to grow dim. My own employees, Kyle thought, and I threw that gold at Skye on the island as if she were the lowest of thieves . . .

Kyle had come within five feet of his rental car when Lieutenant Griffen hailed him. "Jagger!"

Kyle stopped and waited.

"I intend to extend my apologies to Miss Delaney, Jagger," the lieutenant began, "and I want to extend them to you, too. Of course, we'll still need you to fill out a few forms, and I'm sure you'll want to know when Smithfield is apprehended, but you can be out of here in a maximum of three weeks. And, of course, we'll cover any of Miss Delaney's expenses."

"Lieutenant Griffen," Kyle interrupted. "Neither Ms. Delaney nor I need expenses covered. Executive Charters was used in this; I'm responsible for Executive Charters. And I'll stay to fill out all your forms. Then I want to go home. I'll take a trip back when you catch Smithfield. I have a few other affairs to handle."

"Okay, Jagger. Listen, I really am sorry about Miss Delaney."

Kyle paused, feeling his temper rise again. "Skip it, Lieutenant. You were doing your job."

The lieutenant kept apologizing, going over the evidence. Kyle slid into the car, waved, and headed back out for the Harbour Bridge.

He wanted to get to Skye.

Virginia opened the door for him, looking uneasy.

"Skye is cleared," Kyle said.

"Wonderful!" Virginia said, but she didn't look as if

she had received news that wonderful. "Skye is still on the couch. Go talk to her and I'll fix some drinks.

Kyle walked through the foyer and paused. Skye was staring at him dolefully. He frowned. She looked like a little urchin huddled in the blanket, her hair spilling around her, her cat eyes narrowed. His heart took a little lurch; despite the baleful glare she was giving him, the mass of her spilling blond waves and the grace of her position touched the desire he had been ignoring through the intensity of the past days.

"You're cleared," he told her.

Her expression changed to one of surprise, wary disbelief, and then incredulous joy. "How?" she demanded.

Kyle sat across from her in the chair Virginia had vacated, idly moving the crochet items. He fingered a half-made bootie as he talked, telling her about the cabby, about his trip to the airport, telling her about Henry, about the man they still had to apprehend. "So you're clear, Skye. Entirely clear. We have to stay on to fill out some paperwork, but that's it. All over. We go home to Montfort."

The expression of joy that had been Skye's vanished.

"What the hell is the matter with you?" Kyle demanded. "First Virginia, now you. I just told you that your biggest worry in the world is over and you're looking at me as if I'm asking you to dig a grave and crawl into it."

Skye straightened on the couch. "I really don't see how I can go to Montfort with you. Your *wife* just called here."

"Who?"

"Your wife! You remember her—Lisa Jagger." Oh, God, Skye thought, she sounded so shrill. She couldn't help herself. She took a breath. "Lisa called here about a half hour ago. She said to tell you something about calling your bluff. She was just charming. She apologized very sweetly to me, but said she was sorry, she does love you, and she doesn't intend to sign a thing. She also thought it only fair to warn me that she didn't think a child such as myself could possibly hold your interest and—"

Skye broke off, closing her eyes, clenching her teeth.

"Go on," Kyle growled.

"And . . . and that as soon as you tired of me in bed you would come to your senses and realize a little sport wasn't worth your empire. Or your 'bluff.' Whatever that means."

Kyle stood, hands in his pockets as they so often were when he was angry. He returned Skye's glare.

"And you let Lisa's phone call bother you?"

Skye finally lowered her gaze. "Kyle, I really don't think it's a good idea for me to go back with you. If you've only been bluffing her, then you aren't taking any stands against her. Solve your problems with her. I'm grateful, very grateful, Kyle, for all that you've done for me. But—"

"But *nothing!* I'm leaving here exactly three weeks from today. You're coming with me. That was the deal. Damn you, I'll hold you to it if I have to drag you by the hair."

Skye bit her lip, looking down at her fingers. "Then use what you have against Lisa, Kyle. What can I believe if you have a way to free yourself and you refuse to use it?"

Kyle froze, locking his jaw as he stared at Skye. His "bluff" was his son. And he wasn't terribly sure he could stand to inflict that kind of pain on Chris, to disown him publicly. What if Chris didn't understand? There had to be another way.

But he couldn't, wouldn't, lose Skye, or the child that she carried that was also his.

He reached down, took her face between his two hands, and stared into her accusing, but tantalizing cat's eyes. "You're going to have to trust me," he said, and his voice was hard. He released her. "Three weeks, Skye. Be packed and ready to leave in three weeks. Because I am threatening you now, and I will carry out my threat."

He turned, brushing past Virginia, who was holding a tray of champagne glasses, and he left without another word.

Interlude

Skye actually heard herself laugh as the suction of the tide beneath her feet suddenly caused her to lose her balance, bringing her down with little grace to sit awkwardly in the water. She had been staring blankly out to sea for so long that the water had risen without her being aware. Consequently she was fully dressed and soaking wet.

But it was warm and getting wet didn't really matter. It was a secluded beach, and she loved the area. Off the beaten tourist track, it was both forlorn and beautiful. Steven had brought her here when he had first married Virginia and made Australia his home.

And now, here, in this private place where the sea birds cried and the surf lulled with its endless encroachment upon the sand, she had actually laughed.

But her laughter was short. Oh, Steven, she thought, if only you were here! What would you think of Kyle? He has demanded that I go home with him; he gave me three weeks. . . .

But in all that time, Steven, he hasn't seen me, he hasn't even called. He's married, Steven. He says that he wants to marry me, but he has some kind of a hold over his wife and he refuses to use it! Is he playing me along, Steven? I should really tell him to go to hell. Lisa said she was calling his bluff, and it appears she has been able to do so rather well. . . .

I've never met anyone like him, Steven. He orders me about, and for some absurd reason, he's getting away with it. I have to tell him to go to hell! If I have any pride at all, that is exactly what I should do—refuse to be dragged to his home and displayed before his family. He's telling me to turn my entire life around! And he's the worst damned chauvinist I've ever met. Imagine me, Steven, of all people, with a man like that. . . .

He doesn't know that I love him, Steven. And I don't think that I dare let him know. He thinks that I'm after his name, his position. He thinks that if I loved him—according to him—I would go with him willingly. But I'm afraid, Steven. What if he does tire of me? I don't want to be like Lisa, not a wife, but an obligation.

Then there's my pride. This is the first day I've been out. The reporters are finally beginning to leave me alone.

A chill gripped Skye. The thunder of the waves began to intensify; the breeze whipped against her face and she balanced to her feet again, toes gripping the wet sand as she hugged herself. She had known her twin so very well, for a moment she could almost envision his face, hear in the wind the exact reply he would have given her.

Pride? What is pride, Skye? You love this man with all your heart, and you're going to let pride stand in your way? No, Skye, use your pride. Go to him with pride. Let your pride and dignity be the things that will see you through.

Skye closed her eyes and felt the water and air around her. Then she hugged her arms around herself and turned from the surf, pausing only to retrieve her shoes before she left the sand of the beach behind her.

She disappeared just moments before the man who had filled her thoughts walked down to the waves from the north rather than the south, and stood just a short distance away from where she had been. It was a secluded beach, but it wasn't so strange that he had chosen the same place to come for solace. Their minds and their hearts worked alike, even when they couldn't touch, or even talk.

A secluded beach would always be reminiscent of her.

He observed the surf, but he didn't really see it; his eyes were far away, full of turmoil. Tomorrow, he was thinking, would she be there? Or would she have flown again? She had every right to do so. . . . He had said terrible things to her. He had pushed and bullied her. She wasn't like Lisa, not a damn thing like Lisa.

He was afraid, afraid as he had never been before. He loved her so much that now his hands began to sweat. He had left her with an ultimatum. He had left her in anger. And he hadn't dared talk to her, because with her he lost all control.

So he stayed away.

Would she understand if she knew his son was at stake?

Or would she care? Was marriage everything to her? It seemed so.

Did she still love Trainor? And had she only refused to marry the other man because it was his child she carried?

Kyle's fists clenched harder and harder until the clipped nails dug hard into his palms. He didn't feel them. Nor did he hear the lonely cry of a gull, or the monotonous pulse of the surf.

The sounds were merely echoes of his mind.

He had wanted Skye to carry his child. Now she did. But what he had so desired now left him with a bitter dilemma. Would she come with him only because of the child?

Would she come with him at all?

Why had he been so horrid to her?

I'm afraid. And I'm vulnerable, and I don't know how to handle it . . . I can have anything in the world, except for the one thing in the world that I want . . . And I don't know what the hell I'm going to do. . . .

Kyle turned away from the surf, having never really seen it. He absently dusted sand from his jeans, unaware that his leather shoes were soaked from the waves. As he left the beach and approached his car, his figure drew many an eye from the street, but he was oblivious to it.

He was entangled in the dilemma of his own mind. And he could think of only one answer.

He had to maintain the position of power. It was all that he had.

Thirteen

November 3, San Francisco

It might have been easier if Kyle *had* seen her during the three weeks of his ultimatum. If he had called, if he had whispered a single endearment, if he had once given her the support of saying, "I love you."

As it was, she entered the cathedral-ceilinged entranceway of Montfort exhausted and feeling like an unwanted visitor. Even during the long hours of travel that brought them home via Tahiti and Honolulu, he had barely spoken to her. A glance in his direction as they moved into the house sent her into a state of panic she could barely control; she wanted to turn and run into the night, anywhere that was away.

I don't know this man! her mind shrieked. I know about him, I know that he is strong, that he is determined and unwavering in his pursuits, but it's that strength that takes him away from me, allows him to close himself off. . . . Dear God, I *really* don't know him, his touch on my arm is cold, his expressions could be chiseled from stone. It is impossible that I lived with him for six weeks entirely alone, entirely free; it is impossible that I slept with him, that I carry his child . . .

"Kyle! Skye!"

"Dad! Skye!"

"Kyle! Skye!"

Apparently the entire Jagger household had been alerted to their arrival. As soon as the door opened, Michael, Chris, and Kyle's mother were upon them. Skye froze for a second, her feeling of ridiculousness overwhelming her. But right after clapping his brother on the shoulder, Michael Jagger swept her into an encompassing bear hug. There was chaos at the door, everyone talking at once, and then Kyle's mother, her eyes brilliantly happy, was taking her arm.

"You poor dear!" she exclaimed, walking Skye past the immense curving oak stairway with the elegant balcony that looked down on the marble floor. "I do hope he's fed you! I know you must be dead tired, but I've arranged for some tea. We didn't get to really meet in Igua. My sons can have atrocious manners at times. My name is Mary."

"Mother," Michael interrupted cheerfully. "We didn't have much chance to introduce you two on Igua, if you'll recall."

"That's hardly an excuse!" Mary Jagger scolded with a laugh.

Skye was half listening with a bit of awe at the enthusiasm of her acceptance, half scanning the graceful mansion where she had been brought to live. She had been led to a gracious drawing room with high carved ceilings off the grand entranceway. The fireplace was granite, the highly polished Victorian sofa and chairs that surrounded it were mahogany, handsomely upholstered in a beige and peach brocade. The floor was a parquet, but here oriental throw rugs added warmth. bougainvilleas curled from various end tables; a collection of Royal Doulton figurines filled the one curio cabinet. Although the room was in no way cluttered, and despite its size and immaculateness, it seemed in itself to offer hospitality. Maybe it was the cheer of the fire, or perhaps the cozy-looking window seats that sat before the bay windows.

"Have a seat, Skye, here by the fire." Mary Jagger released her arm and indicated a high wing chair. "Would you like tea or coffee?" She moved to a handsome tea cart that sat—obviously awaiting their appearance—in front of the fireplace.

"Tea, thank you," Skye murmured.

"Michael? Chris? Kyle?"

"Coffee, Gram," Chris Jagger said, "But you take care of Skye, I'll get Dad and Uncle Mike their coffee."

It was absurdly like any homecoming. While Mary cheerfully questioned Skye on all sorts of trivia—How was the weather in Sydney? Didn't she just love the Governor's mansion? Did she miss New York? She shouldn't, they were having a freak early snowstorm and the temperatures had been horrendous according to the news— Kyle stood by the granite mantel. He looked well there, Skye thought when she covertly glanced his way, master of the realm and all that went with the title. Kyle engaged in a rapid-fire business discussion with his brother and son.

It was shocking how easy it all became. Chris Jagger, who she had been dreading to confront the most, didn't seem to find her appearance disturbing in the least. When he occasionally caught her eye, his smile was friendly. His deep brown eyes, so unusual for this family, held a warmth that surprised her. Skye had seen him with Lisa; it was evident that he loved his mother. And yet he seemed willing enough to welcome her into his home. In fact, no mention was made of Lisa at all. Nor, with all the care given her, had her own condition as yet been mentioned. She had spent her last week in Sydney shopping for a suitable wardrobe, and the loose but attractive blouses she had purchased minimized the change in her appearance, but as Kyle had foretold, it didn't take a very astute eye to determine she was pregnant.

"Dad"—Chris Jagger's voice suddenly broke through

other conversation in protest—"I don't want to go back to the university in January. I've been doing tremendously in your absence, ask Uncle Mike. And I can fly with the best of your pilots—"

"Oh, dear, here we go," Mary Jagger said in a low, apologetic aside to Skye.

"There's more to the business than flying, Christian," Kyle said firmly. "You need facts and figures, policy and politics, geography and language. And you enjoy school, Chris, I don't understand this sudden turn against it."

"I'm not against it, Dad, I just don't want to wait. And I believe it's a justified decision. Ask Uncle Michael. I've really been a help."

Kyle glanced at Michael with raised brows. "He's been handling the European rerouting by himself. He's been making some damn good decisions, Kyle," Michael said.

Kyle turned back to his son. "That isn't the point, Chris. I've always been proud of your abilities, pleased that you love the business. But you have to realize all the responsibilities that our business entails, how many people the world over make their livelihood through Executive Charters. It's an incredible responsibility, Chris."

"I know all that, Dad," Chris said with commendable patience. "And I am going back to school. All I want to do is take the rest of the year off. Get some more practical experience. And"—he paused for a moment, glancing apologetically to Skye—"I want to be here when the baby is born. I never expected a brother or sister at my age. I'd like to be around for the event."

Skye felt as if she had suddenly turned into some type of brittle substance. If she moved a muscle in her face, her entire countenance would crack and fall apart. The room had fallen silent. Only Chris Jagger seemed to be totally unaware of his faux pas. Still intent upon his purpose, he turned politely to Skye. "Please help me, Skye," he said, a rueful smile twitching the corner of his lip. "When is the baby due?"

Michael spoke up, clearing his throat first. "Chris . . ."

Skye sensed another sound, a warning growl beginning to rumble from Kyle's chest. Oh, no, she thought desperately, aware that the awkward blow he had delivered her was not intentional. She didn't want to be the cause of strife between Kyle and his son. That the young man didn't seem to resent her in the least was a miracle. She forced herself to reply quickly, straining to be natural. "The baby is due around the middle of March, Chris." There, she had said it. The sound of her voice had been a little weak, a little squeaky, but it had come out with a forced twist of her own lips, a semblance of a smile . . .

"See, Dad," Chris said triumphantly, pleased he had proved his point. "If I go back in January, I'll be in L.A."

"Spring break is right in there," Kyle said.

"Dad—"

"We'll continue this discussion in a little while. I also want to see what you've done with these new routes. But right now I want to take Skye upstairs. It has been a long day for her."

Kyle—whom Skye could have sworn had entirely forgotten her existence since their arrival—was staring at her with a deep and thoughtful gaze. The brittle feeling became more pronounced. She felt caught in his gaze, at a loss for words in her situation.

She was crazy. She shouldn't be here. How many times during the last few weeks had she considered disappearing? Defying his ultimatum? Despite the kindly acceptance of his family, including his son, her position was preposterous. She was still his mistress, his pregnant mistress, and she was sitting beside his mother, talking to his son.

"Oh dear! Of course!" Mary Jagger said with a gasp.

"Skye, we didn't mean to keep you down here so long. Kyle, your luggage is already up."

Skye felt Kyle beside her, reaching proprietorially for her elbow. She was rising, feeling color rush through her. She still couldn't think of anything to say.

"Good night, dear," Mary told her. "We'll talk in the morning."

"Night, Skye," Michael said.

"Good night," Chris said, dark eyes upon her. "Work on him for me, will you, Skye? Dad says you need to transfer your own business here, and I can really be a help to you too—"

"Chris!" Kyle interrupted with a growl.

Skye managed another brittle smile. "Good night."

Kyle didn't say a word to her as he propelled her from the drawing room and up the seemingly endless oak stairway. Each step took her closer to the panic that seemed to rise easily within her. *I really don't know this man, I don't know him . . . he is a stranger . . .*

They walked along the beautiful balcony until they reached a door near the end. Kyle pushed the door open and propelled her in, snapping on the light.

For a moment Skye stood still, surveying the room. It was large, very large, as all the rooms at Montfort seemed to be. A huge four-poster bed with a rich maroon quilt dominated the far left of the room; before it was a thick fur rug and against the back wall was another massive fireplace, also of granite. A low coffee table of natural wood sat before the fire, flanked by high stiff-backed chairs. Large, masculine-looking dressers sat across from one another nearer the entrance and a second door, partially ajar, exposed the tile of a bathroom. A heavy walnut wardrobe spanned the far right corner of the room, sitting near floor-length draperies that were drawn now against the night.

Skye could sense Kyle behind her, watching her. Her

feeling of panic was suddenly overwhelming. Again her mind seemed to sound like a broken recording. I don't know this man, I don't know this man.

"This is your room," she finally murmured stupidly.

"Yes. Any objection?"

Yes, she wanted to scream. It's been more than three months since you've touched me, really touched me, and in all that time we've barely spoken, except when necessary. I can't, I can't do this. I can't just step into this room and pretend that those three months haven't been. I need something from you, I need to know you again, I need to know that you saved me from a prison term and are fighting for me because you love me and not because you're a man of obligation expecting your child. I need you to talk to me, to say things, explain things . . .

"I'm waiting, Skye," Kyle reminded her, his voice cool. "I repeat—any objection?"

What is the matter with me? she thought. I'm an affluent woman in my own right, I own my own business, I'm sophisticated and worldly . . . Still, she couldn't look at him. She could actually feel him behind her although he didn't touch her—a radiating heat . . . a power that was a stranger.

She stared straight ahead at the low burning fire. "No."

"I believe Lottie has already unpacked our things. Just look around for whatever you need. There's a whirlpool in the bathroom, but don't set it too hot. You shouldn't be in too much heat. I'll be back up in about an hour."

He paused at the doorway. Skye still couldn't look at him. She finally nodded, and he left, closing the door behind him.

Skye was shivering. She walked to the fire and stooped before the low flames, rubbing her hands together. Why the hell am I so nervous, she wondered. Things were really working out beautifully. Even Chris Jagger, whom she had been sure would despise her, was treating her as if she had long been a family member, as if her place in the household were assured.

The fire was warm, the room was warm, but still she shivered. And then the question that was really bothering her came to her mind. Why didn't I tell Kyle that yes, I do object to being in this room?

Because I don't, she had to admit sadly. I can't reach him, I don't understand him. He's hiding something from me and withdrawing because of it, but still I want to be with him, I want whatever he can give me.

She stood and left the fireplace, tentatively going through drawers until she found her own things, neatly folded away in the smaller of the two dressers. She selected a sheer peach gown, bit her lip, and returned it to the drawer, exchanging it for a floor-length gown of lightweight blue flannel. The woman he had desired on the island had been slender and agile. She might not be as big as a house as of yet, but her body had taken on awkward changes. She knew she wanted Kyle, she literally ached for him, and part of her nervousness was anticipation. But suddenly she didn't want him seeing her. She began to see herself as a sad distortion, misshapen and graceless.

She was struck by the terrible urge to go running down the stairs and to tell Kyle she didn't want to sleep with him. She started up a new wave of shivering, then halted herself, calling herself a few prime names. I can't possibly be this much of a coward! she chastised herself, walking with purpose for the door that led to the bath. She even uttered a gasp of delight as she entered the room. It apparently ran the length of the bedroom to the hallway, but had a private entrance only. And it was far more than a bath. The whirlpool was large enough to contain a party and it was reached by symmetrical tile steps. The entire room was done in red, black, and white, from the tiles to the towels, and was composed of a separate shower, twin mirrored dressing tables, an enormous marble sink, a handsome cabinet of magazines and books, and a thick pile rug to sink one's feet into after leaving the whirlpool. Skye had never seen anything quite like it. She chuckled slightly as she set the whirlpool—temperate as Kyle had commanded. Apparently Kyle, his tastes so simple in all else, enjoyed the relaxation of bathing. Her chuckle broke off abruptly as she realized that this was another reminder of how little she knew about him. And then she was wondering pensively if the talcs and perfumed bubble baths had been set upon the racks that encircled the whirlpool for her use, or if he had shared the whirl- pool before with Lisa. A pang of jealousy hit her and she bit into her lip. She was a fool to feel jealousy; she had entered into her relationship with him with her eyes open. But she couldn't help wonder if Lisa and he had played here as man and wife.

Sighing, she eased into the water and allowed the rush around her to ease the tension from her body. She could certainly never complain about lack of creature comforts at Montfort. Still, it was hard at times not to remember the simplicity of the island.

She had almost restored her spirits when she emerged from the huge tub and sank her feet into the plush pile rug. But while reaching for one of the Burgundy towels with the monogrammed J, she caught sight of herself in one of the mirrors and once more bit into a lower lip that was now turning raw.

I look horrible . . . she thought, and no matter how harshly she chastised herself for being immature, no mat- ter how she tried to convince herself that pregnant women were supposed to be beautiful, she knew the truth. She looked horrible.

Dropping the towel, she shimmied into her gown with haste although she stood alone. And then she tore from the bathroom and out to the bed, wrenching away quilt and sheets and diving beneath them. She had forgotten the light. She jumped out of bed, flicked it off, and dove back in, her heart thumping terribly. Kyle wouldn't turn on the light. She could remember his courtesy on the *Bonne Bree* . . . The fire was still burning, of course, but its gentle glow still left the corner of the room in shadow.

Executives don't act like this, she told herself. But no logic could change her tremulous feelings. Oh, God, she thought, how could I be having a child when I am acting like one.

Still, she lay with her mind in a turmoil, praying first that Kyle would return, assume she was sleeping, and leave her alone. And then she would feel, from deep within her, a burning for his touch, a touch that was now only sweet memory.

Skye heard a click at the door and instinctively closed her eyes. He would enter, she knew, quietly—quietly shed his clothing, quietly climb in beside her. The four-poster was immense; they could easily sleep side by side with over two feet between them.

She became abruptly aware that Kyle hadn't walked in quietly in the dark. Her eyes clenched more tightly in an involuntary reaction to the bedside light.

He walked directly to the bed, gently tugged the sheets from her clenched grasp.

She opened her eyes.

"You weren't sleeping," he told her, lips quirked with amusement.

"No," she admitted, meeting his gaze.

He sat down beside her, brushed the stray strands of hair from her forehead, leaned down and kissed her—so gently at first, grazing her lips lightly with his, setting upon them more firmly, beginning a slow exploration.

And Skye was hungry for him. His slightest touch set off an eagerness within her that was almost shameful. Her lips parted to his, accepting the moist heat of his demanding tongue, drawing it in, dueling with it, her lips clinging to his. Her arms rose around the breadth of his shoulders, her hands seeking the vitality beneath the coarse material of his jacket with which they had once been so familiar. She felt the tension, the wonderful play of muscles; her fingers crept to feel the hair that fringed at his nape over his collar, into his thick hair, to clasp his head to hers.

The kiss ended breathlessly as he drew away. He was smiling tenderly at her, enjoying the wet puff of her lips, the fan of her hair in disarray over the pillow, the rise and fall of her breasts as she returned his stare, her eyes wide, dilated, her breathing shallow . . .

His right hand tenderly touched her cheek, moved over the flannel on her shoulder, down over her hip, feeling the soft shape beneath the material. Then he found the hem of her gown and his tantalizing touch began an upward motion, sliding slowly, suggestively over her calf, upward to bare her thigh, seductively persuading the flannel from her body.

"No!" Skye suddenly caught his hand with her own, chewing her lip nervously. He ceased his motion, frowning slightly and raising an arched brow. "Skye," he said, his voice low but firm, "surely you understood that coming here with me, accepting this room, meant that we would assume a normal relationship. I do intend that we have one. And I don't intend to let you back out now. I'm afraid you had your chance, if that was your desire. But it's too late now."

She wanted to say something but she couldn't. She was looking desperately for the self-assured woman who had thought nothing of telling him exactly where to get off when they had met under the tense circumstances of the crash.

He rose suddenly and walked to the mantel, stretching his fingers out to the fire. He turned back to her. "I don't understand, Skye. Don't you want me?"

His gaze caught her and compelled her. Skye found her voice. "Yes," she said softly, "I do want you."

He still wore the puzzled frown. "Come here, Skye," he said, his voice that of gentle but firm command. And yet his voice was not what moved her. She had answered the call of his magnetic eyes long ago; she did so then, barely allowing herself time for thought as she slowly left the bed and walked to him, her eyes never leaving his. She paused directly before him, only then leveling her gaze to the crisp cotton of his shirt and the rough tweed wool of his jacket.

This time his fingers threaded into her hair, arching her neck, drawing her head back. His eyes held hers until their lips touched again, his mouth taking hers now with growing urgency, his teeth gently tugging, his tongue tasting the outline of her lips with a fever, driving again to seek the recesses of her mouth. The room began to swim before Skye; she clutched his chest, hands splayed across the sinewed strength, feeling the heat beneath the material. His fingers trailed down her spine, massaging her back, reaching to cradle her buttocks, to draw her up, press her against his heated length. Wave after wave of sweet, aching sensation washed through Skye. The need within her, spreading like the rays of permeating heat from the center of a sun, was so strong that she moaned with the lock of his kiss still upon her lips. She was barely standing on her own.

He set her from him suddenly, the dark intensity of rising passion hardening his features. He began working at the buttons of her gown, his eyes on his hands as his fingers touched the fabric near her collarbone.

Skye's fingers curled convulsively into the material of his jacket sleeves. Beneath the tweed she could feel the rigidity of his arms. "Please," she murmured, pleading breathlessly, not sure herself at first for what she beseeched. "Please, Kyle. the light . . ."

His fingers had finished with the last of the buttons, just below her breasts. His eyes returned to hers. They held a clarity, a tender understanding, but still he shook his head. He slipped his hands into the opening of the gown, sliding them to her shoulders and forcing the gown along with them. It fell to her feet with a soft rustle.

Kyle set his lips against her shoulder, against the hollow of her collarbone. His hands moved to cradle her breasts, then he moved back again, his fingers now tracing the blue veins that faintly trailed over the swelling mounds.

"I'll be very gentle," he promised, his tone a velvet caress. And then he proceeded to uphold his vow, caressing her breasts with the utmost care, bending to encircle the nipples with his tongue, moving his mouth with sensuous warmth in an easy suctioning action. His kisses moved over her ribs. "You taste so sweet," he told her in a muffled whisper, "so sweet . . ."

Skye had no reply for him. He had fallen to his knees, his hands roamed softly from her breasts to the swelling of her belly, his kisses covered the expanse. Her hands clutched his shoulders, the fingers gripping hard, the nails digging into fabric. "You're beautiful," he told her then, "I can't tell you how very . . . very beautiful you are to me . . ."

"Oh, God, Kyle, please!" Skye moaned, her fingers clenching his hair convulsively as lips moved lower, covering her thighs, finding the moistness, the heat, that clearly defined her beseeching to them both. He shifted, bringing his kisses slowly up the same path, ending with her lips as he swept her high in his arms and brought her easily to the huge four-poster. He shed his own clothing quickly, then gently lifted her thigh to allow himself entry between the embrace of slender legs.

Time and distance were forgotten. He had given her the life within her; he was the life within her. She had ached for him so badly, for so long, that tears formed in her eyes with the ecstasy of his entry. Skye arched high against him, losing herself to the undulating surge of rhythm.

In those moments he was a stranger no longer. He was the man she had come to love. Each driving thrust, every touch of his body, was an elemental reminder that he was the man who had taught her what it meant to love completely, to give, to need. And as they writhed in the united fever of desire, she knew little else except that he was the one man in her world with whom she had known the rapturous pleasure of total intimacy—the man she could see, touch, and openly shudder with pleasure before in the full splendor of light. He could create within her flames that burned so high they knew no bounds.

His rhythm intensified. Whereas he had been staring into her eyes, he closed his own and crushed her against him. That which had begun slow and tantalizing no longer sought to delay and to encourage complete capitulation, but demanded with furiously pulsing force. Skye shuddered, feeling his release, soaring with her, clinging to him and holding tightly as waves of aftershock kept her quivering in his arms. His weight remained against her, and it filled her with contentment. Moments later she felt him smoothing her hair and she snuggled to adjust to him. Her eyes were closed and she kept them so, drained and drowsy, easing to a gentle sleep.

When she awoke, the room was dark. Only the glow of the low-burning fire in the grate bathed them in a soft gold light.

Skye leaned upon an elbow and studied Kyle. In sleep his features relaxed; it was startling to see how handsome and ruggedly chiseled his profile was. And yet it was also easy to see the tiny lines around his eyes, the only indication of his age. Her gaze slipped to his shoulders and chest. The tone of individual muscles was visible even in this state. The dim golden light cast a glow upon his body, clearly highlighting the tautness of the bronze skin, the perfection of the form beneath it. Her gaze moved downward. His belly was flat, concave, except for the ripple that indicated taut muscle even there . . .

She stretched out a hand, stroking all that her eyes saw and exploring even further. Soft but coarse tufts of body hair, long, sinewed legs, not even his toes were free from her scrutiny.

She returned her vision to his face to find him staring at her, a smile curled into the corner of his lip. She hesitated a second, flushing a little despite all that had passed between them.

"Please," he murmured teasingly, "don't let my conscious participation stop you."

Skye stared at him a second longer. She lowered her eyes but returned his smile. And continued her enticing exploration.

The room was brilliantly alight with the dazzle of morning when Skye awoke again. A little groggily she blinked and stretched out an arm. Kyle was no longer beside her.

"Good morning."

She glanced up to see him expertly flipping the ends of his tie. A lazy smile started to filter into her lips, but it was quickly halted as he began to speak to her brusquely.

"I'll be gone today and every day for the next several weeks—things to catch up on. I've arranged rooms within the house for you to create an office or workshop or whatever you need. Arrange whatever you want. My mother will show you around, Chris can help you later. The house is completely staffed, so you needn't worry about anything. It's unlikely that you would answer a phone, but if you should, and if the caller should ever be Lisa, you are not to talk to her. She does call to talk to Chris, and, of course, that's fine, but *you* are not to say more than 'hello' to her. Is that clear?"

Skye felt her body stiffen with a certain shock as she stared at him with disbelief. What had happened? He was a stranger again, knocking out orders with autocratic authority. He had showered and shaved, and dressed in one of his perfectly tailored suits, and once again she didn't know him. She reached for the sheets and drew them to her chin. "Why are you afraid to have me talk to Lisa?"

"I'm not afraid to have you talk to Lisa," he said impatiently, stopping by a dresser to pocket keys and change. "She's going to do everything in her power to get under your skin, and I just want to halt problems before they arise. She said a few things on the phone to you once and you were ready to run scared."

"Dammit, Kyle!" Skye murmured bitterly. "It wasn't a matter of running scared! She said she would call your bluff and she obviously did! You refuse to—"

"Damn you, Skye, don't!" He moved swiftly to the bed, bending to grip her shoulders. He shook her and she knew from the rough touch of his hands that she had truly infuriated him. "Stay out of this! It's none of your business."

She clenched her teeth hard so that tears wouldn't spring to her eyes. "It is my business. I—"

"You will wind up Mrs. Jagger. But don't pry, Skye. Stay out of this—and don't, I repeat, don't talk to Lisa."

"Why? Am I going to hear something I won't like?" Skye hated it when his features closed to her, when he put on his "Mr. Executive" suit and challenged her, especially when she was clad in nothing but sheets, when her hair was in wild tangles and her body still sore from the ardency of his lovemaking. She felt at a disadvantage, reminded that he was forty years old, years her senior, an affluent and powerful man who had forged his destiny and roved the playgrounds of the world while she was still in grade school. It reminded her of Lisa's mockery: "You'll never hold his interest."

"Tell me something, Kyle," she demanded, determined not to display youth or weakness. "Is there something I should know about Lisa? You've supposedly been separated for ten years, but she appeared on your arm at Igua. Has she slept with you here, in this bed?"

He hesitated, his eyes hard on her, and Skye blanched. Why had she asked such a thing? The answer was one she didn't want to hear.

"She has slept here!" Skye hissed.

"Lisa was in this bed once—almost a year ago," he told her with marked irritation. "Don't start on my past, Skye. It has nothing to do with us. Besides, I could start asking you a few questions. In fact, I think I will anyway. You tell me about Ted. I know you refused to marry him—commendable morality, you wouldn't marry him while carrying my child. But what about your stay at Igua? What about that hasty return home?"

Skye smiled with no humor, lifting a brow imperiously. "I consider that none of *your* business."

She didn't like the dark tension in his face one bit. His fingers tightened around her bare shoulders, and despite herself she flinched. "Skye . . ." he warned harshly, shifting and pulling her along with him so that she lay on his lap, staring into eyes that glittered dangerously.

"You should know, Mr. Jagger. You, after all, were having me spied upon!" He tensed again and she lost her nerve. "I haven't . . . I haven't . . . Ted hasn't touched me since long before the island."

"Thank you, Ms. Delaney. That bit of honesty was nice and refreshing. And now I'll tell you about Lisa. She had rooms in this house until Igua. I told her there to get out of our suite, and she moved her things out of here before I returned. She didn't spend that much time here,

and I really didn't care if she was here or not. I tolerated
a lot because of Chris. I do not love Lisa, and I guarantee
you I certainly do not want Lisa in any way. Now that is
all that I've got to say. You are going to have to trust me,
but stay away from Lisa, and keep your nose out of the
divorce. There is someone I value very much—yes, Skye,
as much as that child you carry—who could wind up hurt.
I love you, but I'm warning you—keep out of this!"

He stared at her a moment longer, and Skye returned
his stare, clenching her muscles, catching the skin of her
lip. He returned her to her pillow and walked out.

She could have risen. She could have called after him
that she didn't understand, and that as long as she didn't,
she couldn't stay.

But she didn't. She watched him leave without a word,
torn between the uncertainty created by the vehemence
of his enigma and the little thrill that coursed through
her. He had said he loved her. It wasn't said with tenderness, or even passion. It had almost been an offhand statement.

But it was one she had been longing to hear.

Fourteen

The view from Twin Peaks, as Michael had promised, was absolutely breathtaking. Gazing to the east as the fresh wind whipped her cheeks, Skye could see all of downtown San Francisco laid before her; she could see the Bay Bridge and the Golden Gate.

Michael touched her shoulders. "See there—all of Oakland, and there, way over there, that's Marin County."

Skye nodded, appreciating the view, appreciating the fresh crispness of the air. "It is beautiful, Michael. Thank you very much for taking me up here."

"I thought it was about time you got out of the house," Michael said a bit gruffly. He set a supportive arm around her waist. "Come on, now I'll take you for some great seafood down by the wharf."

"That sounds great," Skye said quietly.

They were both quiet for the drive into town. Skye feigned a great interest in the scenery, but her mind was really fixed on Kyle. She had been in his house for thirty-six days—she could have probably counted the actual hours too—and the situation between them had done nothing but grow more tense. It was probably her own fault, she thought with a wince. Her first day had been so nerve-racking. She had spent at least four hours on the phone with New York; Chris had come home to help her and he had been marvelous, but he made her feel, oh, so terribly awkward; the house staff of five had all met her with very straight faces yet curious, speculative eyes. She was strung like a piano wire by the time Kyle appeared in their room well past midnight. All she could remember by then had been their quarrel—and his autocratic attitude.

She had curled away from him, felt his tension, heard him coldly remind her, "Do you remember, Skye, you promised once never to turn from me."

Yes, she had promised that, but that had been on the island, before Lisa had become a tenacious leech, before she had known that Kyle could free himself but refused to do so, before she had had to feel like a wanton idiot because his son quietly helped her with no words of reproach but a peculiar look in fathomless dark eyes.

"It was rather foolish for either of us to make promises, wasn't it, Kyle? We both seem incapable of keeping them."

He had sworn beneath his breath, turned from her. And then she was sorry, very sorry, but it was too late because the foot of space between them had become a mile and she was so alone, so very alone with her back straight and stiff.

They were both too passionate, too sensual, to allow their quarrel to stay within the bedroom. The next night he slipped his arms around her firmly and she retaliated by locking her fingers around the nape of his neck . . . parting her lips hungrily for his kiss. The nights became theirs, but the days remained barren, cold battlegrounds where they spoke with cool cordiality if at all. And Kyle took to staying away longer and longer, seldom even dining with the family.

Skye buried herself in the work of transferring Delaney Designs. Whereas Kyle was constantly gone, Skye clung to the house. She was loath to encounter a reporter who might find her condition a juicy tidbit to spread across the gossip pages.

But this morning Michael had come to her workroom and gruffly insisted she accompany him out. It was evident that he was clearly irritated with his brother's cool treatment of Skye and determined to make amends himself. And now that she was out, it was good to be away . . .

Michael expertly parked his little Ferrari. The scent of the wharfs was with them, tangy salt air, delectable aromas of different things from a multitude of dockside restaurants. Seabirds called and soared as Michael helped her from the car.

"Believe it or not"—Michael grinned as he led her toward a rustic-looking building that somewhat resembled a shanty—"this place is quite beautiful inside. Their specialty is a shrimp au gratin that is just out of this world."

"Sounds lovely," Skye said, and thirty minutes later she discovered that Michael hadn't overrated the food one bit. They were seated by the window overlooking the Bay and she was feeling better than she had in ages—light, carefree, and young, as if none of the clouds that had brought forth her present situation had ever existed.

Skye leaned across the table, smiling at Michael. "Thank you, Mike, for today. I can't tell you how much I'm enjoying it all."

Instead of smiling in return, as she had expected, Michael frowned. "You needed to get out, Skye." He hesitated a moment, staring at his wineglass. "I know how hard this all is for you, Skye. And I don't really know how to say this, but I wish I could make things easier for you and Kyle. His behavior at times is deplorable, I know. But he does love you, Skye."

"Does he?" Skye asked with bitter cynicism. "Oh, Michael, if he does, what is the problem? Why is he hedging on his divorce? He barks at me constantly while checking every move that I make, but lets Lisa walk all over him!"

Michael took a long sip of his wine, then swirled the liquid in his glass, watching it as he spoke. "Skye, Kyle doesn't even speak with me about this. I think I know what is going on, though, and he's really between the devil and the deep. Bear with him."

"Michael, if you know something, please tell me," Skye said. "I'm trying to bear with everything, but when I don't even know what your brother is thinking—"

"I really can't tell you anything." Michael interrupted miserably, "I know it's hard under the circumstances, but please try to trust Kyle. I think that if he really felt you were with him all the way, he'd be a lot easier to live with. He needs your support."

Skye took a sip of her wine and lowered her eyes. Was Michael right? If she took the step, told Kyle she loved him and that she didn't care when their marriage took place, as long as she knew that he loved her totally in return, would he learn to trust her, confide in her, come close to her again?

She smiled slowly. "Okay, Michael. I won't question you anymore. And I'll give your suggestion some real thought."

"Good." Michael clicked his glass with hers. "Now, I wanted to ask you about something else. Wouldn't you like to ask your sister-in-law to California for a while?"

Skye glanced at Michael with surprise, then chuckled. "Does that mean *you* would like me to ask Virginia to San Francisco?"

Michael shrugged and bit his lip sheepishly. "Yeah," he admitted. "I guess that's exactly what I mean. I—uh—" He paused, looking pained for a moment. "I'm sorry, Skye, maybe I shouldn't have said that. Kyle told me about your brother. I understand you were twins, very close. I don't suppose—"

"Michael," Skye said with a firm smile, "I'll be happy to have Virginia here—and happier still if you and Virginia want to see one another. When Steven was alive, Virginia adored him. She was a wonderful wife. She is a lady full of love and devotion, and Steven himself would be the first to wish her happiness now." There, she thought, that was so easy to say—and mean. All because of Kyle. He had allowed her to accept Steven's death, he had lifted her fear of the darkness. He had really done so many wonderful things for her, and she had never told him . . . she had never risked saying "I love you."

Michael's eyes were twinkling. He lifted his glass in another salute. "Steven was a lucky man. He had a beautiful wife, and a magnificent sister, too."

"Thanks." Skye started to laugh, but her chuckle died in her throat. Everything about her froze.

She couldn't believe the vision before her eyes. Kyle was walking into the restaurant, escorting Lisa, beautiful and statuesque as ever. Her silver-blond head was tilted back, rose lips were pouted in a smile, laughter tinkled lightly from them.

"Skye, what is it?" Michael, with his back to the pair, twisted just in time to see Kyle seating Lisa. "Oh, Lord," he groaned. "What the hell is that brother of mine doing? This is my fault—I should have never brought you here, I know Kyle comes here for lunch . . ."

Skye wasn't listening to Michael, because at that moment, Lisa's eyes rose to meet hers. The older woman's gaze swept over her torso, turned dark and malicious. Kyle saw that Lisa was looking at something and turned with a frown to see Michael and Skye.

Skye met his gaze with shock; she was further stunned to realize vaguely that she had never seen his face more drawn, more taut, more hard.

But Skye couldn't hear what Kyle was hearing—Lisa's voice, a venomous hiss. "So that's it, Kyle, your mistress is pregnant. That's why you're willing to be so generous. Well, you're crazy, now I'll certainly never let go."

"Shut up, Lisa," Kyle said curtly, scathing her with his eyes. Then he left her abruptly, striding with pain and purpose toward Skye and his brother.

Skye was regally on her feet before he reached their table, with Michael quickly hopping up to join her. "Don't, Kyle," she warned in a quiet hiss as he began to reach for her. "Don't! Don't touch me. Michael, please take me out of here."

"Skye—" Kyle impatiently reached once more to take her arm.

"Kyle," Michael interrupted softly, "let me take Skye home. We're really not in the best of circumstances . . ."

Apparently Kyle judged his brother's decision wise. His eyes didn't lose a hint of their frigidity. They seared into Skye's. "All right. I'll be there myself shortly."

Skye had to look up to meet his eyes, but she returned his piercing glare with a royal dignity. "I'll be gone, Mr. Jagger."

Michael was moving swiftly to escort Skye out, but Kyle managed to get a whisper to her ear alone. "Don't think of leaving, Skye. I'll find you wherever you are. You have no right to walk out on me without understanding—"

"Right! There is no right where we're concerned. Go ask your wife, Mr. Jagger. She'll tell you. Men have no rights where their mistresses are concerned."

"I have every right to you, Skye, that child is mine. And I will find you—"

"The law—"

"Won't be able to stop me. You be there to talk to me, or when I find you, *you'll* find yourself abducted and living on another deserted island."

Skye gave Michael an inquiring gaze. "May we leave, please?"

They were leaving the restaurant. Skye walked without haste, coolly disdaining the eyes that were upon her with a simple pride that eroded even Lisa's complacency. It wasn't until she was closeted with Michael in the Ferrari that she began to shake.

"Skye . . ." Michael began.

"Please, Michael," Skye begged. "Please, let's not talk." She didn't want to cry. She couldn't cry. She was going to return to Montfort and pack her bags. Nothing, nothing Kyle could say would change her mind.

Kyle returned to his table, but he didn't sit down. "Lisa, as long as I live, I'll never forgive you for this outrage. I fully intend to tell Christian about today, although I'm sorry I must because you are his mother. But I want him to understand why I don't ever want you to call the house, and why, if you are ever seen, with just one foot on the property, I intend to call the police and have you forcibly removed. I'm also going to file for the annulment. No bluff this time. I'll tell Chris the truth myself."

"You're a fool, Kyle Jagger," Lisa said, lowering her voice with a touch of a quaver. "She won't have you unless it's marriage, and you're like a lovesick old man—too old. If you succeed with this marriage, you'll get to spend your years wondering what young buck your wife is bedding with—"

"No, Lisa," Kyle said calmly, "that was my marriage with you."

He turned on his heel and stalked out of the restaurant, damning himself all the while. He'd been insane to make the polite attempt to reason with Lisa one last time. There was no reasoning with her, and now Skye was furious. More than furious, she was humiliated. And he hadn't been able to do a thing. She would be trying right now to walk out of his life, and God help him, he really couldn't stop her and so he was making matters worse with absurd threats.

I could strangle Lisa, he thought bitterly.

Kyle drove the hills and winding roads of San Francisco at a foolhardy pace. He thought of the cool, controlled dignity with which Skye had left the restaurant. He thought of how much he loved her, how much he needed her there at night, how he loved to feel the growing rise of her belly, how the strange innocence of hers was a unique and tantalizing contradiction to the insatiable passion he could create within her.

He ground his teeth. Outwardly, he could handle Lisa's taunts. But she knew where to strike. At the absurd age of forty Kyle was finding himself the victim of a gut-ripping insecurity. Was Lisa right? Did Skye think him old? Did she ever envision a younger man when he held her in his arms? Did she wish herself back with Ted, a man almost a decade his junior?

His facial skin, already so taut that it hurt, tautened further. Marriage. She wanted marriage. And more than anything in the world, he wanted to give her marriage. If she only loved him . . .

She didn't love him; not even in the greatest throes of passion could he get her to say those words.

Kyle jerked the car into Montfort's circular driveway, not even bothering to shut the door as he stormed into the house. He was thankful no one was present to see his thunderous climb up the staircase, or to hear the sharp retort of his bedroom door as he slammed it behind him, immediately accosting Skye as she threw things haphazardly into her luggage.

"What do you think you're doing?" he roared, catching her arms.

She didn't fight him; she went limp, staring at him with her beautiful amber cat eyes completely devoid of emotion. "I'm leaving."

Everything within Kyle went to war. His heart was thumping furiously, his muscles twitched. He fought for deep breaths. "No, you're not."

"Kyle," Skye said with that same lack of emotion that was in her eyes, "I have never been more humiliated in my life. This situation is never going to change. That woman leads you around by the nose. She publicly labels me a . . . a . . . oh, never mind, and you do nothing about it!"

"What did you want me to do? Bloody her lip? Break her jaw?"

"No," Skye said. "I just want you to let me go."

Kyle released her and walked to the door, leaning against it and crossing his arms. Skye went to another drawer and drew out a handful of stockings to toss into her suitcase.

"I can't let you go, Skye," Kyle said softly. "That child is mine."

"Then we're at an impasse, aren't we?" Skye queried lightly. "Because I do intend to leave. I waited to talk to you, which is what you requested. Well, we're talking. And then I'm leaving."

It was ridiculous; they were at one of the most critical points of their entire relationship, but as Kyle watched her move with precise, fluid, and determined grace, he could think only of how much he wanted her. Her pregnancy, if anything, had made her even more desirable. Her delicacy was still with her; the curvature of her breasts had increased. Her hips had remained slender, and the rise that was his child didn't at all detract from a lithe shapeliness that was eternally hers. He wanted to talk; he found himself returning to her, halting her in mid-stride, and forcing her into his arms. His lips descended upon hers; he felt the flare of response, but then she was pulling away, murmuring, "No." He held her still. "This can't change things, Kyle."

"I want you," he told her, eyes piercing hers darkly. "Now."

"Kyle, no—"

"We're at an impasse, you say," he told her harshly, hands rising so that his fingers might thread through the sides of her hair and force her gaze to remain locked with his. "That means it's time to strike a bargain. I'm sorry about today. Very sorry. I can't change it. But if you'll stay, I'll play that card against Lisa. No more bluff."

When the words were out of his mouth he wondered at what he had said. Chris, he thought sinkingly, what have I done? But I'm cornered, I owe this child as I owe you. I never meant it to become real, but I am cornered, backed against a wall.

And for just a second he knew too that Skye couldn't be blamed. She had gone through enough for him.

And then he was thinking again that it was she who cornered him; and he hated her for the devastation she was causing his heart, but more than anything he loved her.

Skye watched him with wide eyes, fighting tears. Dear God, didn't he know she didn't want to leave? She didn't want to force him against a wall, but she would rather take their child and herself somewhere far away from Montfort than be asked to play second place to Lisa's legal status as Kyle's wife. At least she would still have her dignity, if not Kyle's love. She forced herself to sound harsh and skeptical. "How do I know you mean that?"

"I don't lie."

Skye felt faint. Why can't we really talk? she wondered, gazing into the enigma of eyes that had gone dark and demanding with a hint of bitter cruelty, giving away nothing. I know that I am forcing your hand, she thought painfully, but Kyle, I have no choice. I can't keep living like this. You won't explain. What can I believe?

It was so hard now to remember the days on the island when they had laughed, played, so easily in the surf.

So hard now with this tension mounting between them.

Love and hate and bitterness growing . . . their bodies
hot with anger as if they were about to fuse in passion.

She could never forget his touch. Certainly not now,
not when she could feel the response in her blood simply
because he was near. Locked in his embrace she could
feel him too thoroughly, feel that she was his, that this
hard man, who now shared so little of himself, was hers.

The fainting sensation was becoming stronger. She was
ready to beg out, to back down. But she couldn't. She had
come this far. Whatever he thought of her, she had to force
the issue. Now. Bargain, as he said. Use anything . . .

"All right," she said, forcing her voice to be cold, calculating. And then she had to swallow, but she fought
valiantly to retain the callous ice of her words. "You use
whatever you have to to get free of Lisa, and I'll stay."

His touch upon her suddenly froze; his expression
tensed. He was looking beyond her rather than at her.

She was handing down the ultimatums . . .

She was asking him to sell his soul . . .

And at the moment he didn't have it in his power to
deny her.

Skye had no idea of what went through his mind as he
stood there for what seemed an eternity, holding her in
a vise of steel. He had made a promise to her, but now
it looked as if he intended to back down. . . .

Or did he? He wasn't letting her go, but he looked
honor-struck. What had she asked of him? He looked as
if she had asked him to bring her someone's head on a
platter.

She couldn't know that to him her demand was even
worse. That his mind and heart was torn between her
and his son, and the terrible, unquenchable fire that
raged through him at the moment.

Chris, forgive me, he begged.

What will I do? How will I explain? Do I come to you
first? Or do I rush right ahead? Will you despise Skye and

this child because it will be my natural heir? I will love this child, Chris, but never more nor less than I love you . . .

What have I promised? Dear God, will my son ever forgive me? Have I forfeited my right to his love because of this woman who haunts my blood? I love her, too, heartless bitch that she can be. And God help me, but at this moment, I must have her. She is a fever. I have lost all control; I would sell out to the devil himself. . . .

When his eyes returned to hers, they burned with something bitter and harsh, their blaze frightening.

His lips, rough and bruising, took hers. She clung to him, resenting his force, but powerless against it as an equal fire took hold of her senses and she matched the torrid hunger of his demand, raking her fingers through his hair, pressing against the vibrant strength of his chest and thighs. She felt the touch of his desire pulsing against fabric; sweet need took over and her tongue sought his lips, his mouth; her teeth grazed his flesh with a fevered abandon.

He swept her high into his arms and strode swiftly to the bed, heedless of her clothing as he disrobed her. Buttons went flying from his shirt as he impatiently discarded it. And then he was hovering over her, fitting his body to hers.

"You do want to be Mrs. Jagger rather badly, don't you?" he asked with bitter harshness.

Of course, Skye's mind cried, because I love you.

But she didn't say it, she didn't even think it for long. She gasped with the violence of his entry; then the fire was an explosion and she, too, whirled into oblivion as storm after storm of sensation swept her away to the frenzied land where all she knew was the sweet, sweet seeking of ecstasy and rapturous release.

* * *

It was Skye who rose. He had tried to hold her, but she slipped from his arms and raced into the bathroom, locking the door behind her. Today she didn't give the whirlpool a glance, but jumped under the shower. The cascade of the water was what she needed to ease her sore body and tumultuous mind.

A flush rose to her cheeks even beneath the furious assault of the water. He thought that all she cared about was his name, a legitimate position. And that the love she couldn't withhold from him was nothing but a bargain.

But how could she tell him otherwise? He left her no room, no opening. He showed her none of his feelings, no clue to his thoughts. And though he had agreed to do what ever terrible thing it was that he had to do to Lisa, today had all come about because he was with Lisa. If the battle between them was so bitter, why had he been so cordially and politely escorting her to lunch?

That, actually, was the question of the hour.

Skye wrapped herself in a massive towel and left the shower behind, determined in her present mood to question Kyle, to force it all out on the line.

But when she strode with purpose to the bed, she froze, chagrined. Kyle was sound asleep.

She was annoyed enough at first that she considered waking him by snatching his pillow from beneath him and smacking him over the head. How the hell could he sleep after their bitter words and volatile coupling? She reached for the pillow, then paused. He looked so tired. The tiny lines around his eyes appeared deeper. Her fingers hovered over the hair on his forehead, then she pulled them back. She couldn't wake him, but neither could she touch him . . .

Skye dressed quickly in a pair of maternity jeans and a sweater and slipped quietly out the door. She wanted to think, away from Kyle, away from his gently sweet mother, away from the curious household. She sped quickly down the staircase, not wanting to run into Michael, if he were still home, or Chris. Apparently everyone was busy. The staircase and entryway were empty.

Skye threw open the door—and walked straight into Chris Jagger, who was just entering the house. "Hi, Skye." He smiled. But his smile faded. It seemed he sensed the turmoil locked in the depths of her amber eyes.

"Hi, Chris," Skye murmured uneasily. Oh, Lord, she thought, of all the people she didn't want to see now.

"You look like you're trying to escape," Chris said. It was meant to sound like a joke. It didn't.

"I was just going for a walk," Skye said.

Chris hesitated, watching her with those deep brown eyes that were always so hard to fathom. "Would you come for a ride with me instead, Skye?" he finally asked.

"Oh, uh, Chris . . ." Skye hedged. "I, um, I really wanted a few minutes alone . . ."

"Please, Skye," Chris said with quiet sincerity. Skye found herself studying his pleasant features. He was a decidedly handsome young man, and if he hadn't inherited his father's looks, he had certainly inherited his father's calm and controlled manner. He could persuade you with the power of his eyes.

"You've been quarreling with my father," he said, a statement gently voiced, not a question. "I'd really like to talk to you. I don't mean to butt in, but I think I'm the one person in the world who can help. Please, let's get out of here and talk."

What did Chris really think of her? Skye wondered fleetingly. He was always polite, carefully courteous, solicitous to an endearing degree. But what was he really thinking all the time? Did he resent her? Or was his offer to help sincere? His devilishly dark good looks suddenly reminded her she was only six years his senior. Did he, like his mother, believe his father was merely infatuated with her? Did he, too, think she could never hold Kyle's interest?

And at the moment just what did she have to lose?

"Okay, Chris. We'll go for a ride."

He spoke only casually as they drove, pointing out certain landmarks, talking idly about precautions now taken in building against earthquakes. He turned the radio to soft music, and they wound around the hills and zigzags of the city, Skye found herself relaxing with him.

He parked beside a quiet jetty looking out over the bay. "Come on," he told her. "I'll show you one of my favorite spots."

It was a beautiful place. Gulls cried high overhead and the breeze from the bay felt fresh and good. Chris stared out to the water. He was quite a figure with his tall, straight posture, the wind whipping his dark hair back, leaving a strong profile to be clearly seen. He turned back to Skye, standing a few feet behind him, and chuckled slightly.

"I wish you would relax," he said with a wry grin. "I didn't ask you out here to toss you into the bay."

Skye flushed and joined him, seating herself on a rock. "I didn't think you wanted to push me into the bay, Chris."

"But you don't really know what to think, right?" he asked.

"Right," Skye admitted. She sighed, then decided to deal honestly with him. "Chris, you must resent me. Your parents are waging war because of me, and you've been an only child for twenty years. The sole heir of quite an empire—one you've obviously worked for as well as your father and uncle ha—"

"Skye!" he interrupted her, a trace of amusement in his eyes along with real surprise. "Why should I resent you? You're not the reason my parents are waging war— they've been doing that for twenty years. And I surely don't resent a sibling! I honestly think it's wonderful. Believe me"—he chuckled—"I'm not greedy. My father is worth several fortunes. He could have a dozen children and leave each one an empire. Besides, I love my father. I've never thought much about inheriting things. If he didn't have two cents to rub together, he would have already given me far more than I could ask."

He was sincere, Skye realized, with a pang. No wonder Kyle so adored his son . . . "Thank you, Chris," she said quietly, "for telling me this."

He shrugged, obviously wishing not to become emotional. "I should have spoken with you long ago. I just really didn't know what to say, and that's not really what I brought you out here to tell you anyway."

"Oh?" Skye murmured.

He glanced at her, pausing and studying her as if wondering how to begin. He shrugged again. "I told you, Skye, I don't really mean to butt in. It's just that I can't help but see things. I know you're miserable and uncomfortable, and I know that my father is having a hell of a bad time. I also know that he loves you—really loves you, although, granted, he behaves like a bear half the time. A polar bear." He grinned.

Skye had to return his grin. "I'm sorry, Chris, that this is so evident. You shouldn't have to be involved, to suffer. I know it must be hard on you seeing your father and mother—"

Chris waved a hand in protest, silencing her. "I'll start with this, Skye—I love my mother, she is my mother. But I don't know why she is doing this to my father. I'm twenty, Skye. Plenty old enough to understand things were over between them years ago. Old enough to see and accept the faults in those I love. Dad has given Mom everything for years—for my sake, which was okay as long as Dad wasn't hurt. I know you can't understand why he claims to love you and does nothing against her." He paused for a long moment, biting his lip with a frowning uncertainty. "I know he doesn't tell you anything. Don't ask how—I just know. Because I know who my dad is protecting—me."

Skye shook her head. "I don't understand, Chris. I—"

"Kyle Jagger isn't really my father."

Skye stared at him, stunned and confused. Kyle had told her he had married Lisa because she was pregnant. He adored Chris, how could his son not be his . . .

"It's true," Chris said dryly, "but here is where we start getting our wires crossed. I know that it's true, and my father knows that it's true. My mother obviously knows. But they don't know that I know. My father has always tried to protect me, and I haven't known how to tell him it isn't necessary."

"Chris," Skye murmured, "how do you know? I mean—"

"For one, Skye, I can count. My mother was pregnant when my father married her. Which of course doesn't prove anything, but, Skye, look at me! I'm as dark as a Spaniard. And kids pick up things. Believe me—I *know.*"

"Chris," Skye said awkwardly, "I'm sorry . . ."

"It's nothing to be sorry about," he said nonchalantly. "A biological factor doesn't change a lifetime. My father was the one who cared for me, even when I was very young. He was always there. The only reason I'm telling you this, Skye, is because I think I'm your holdup. My father has probably threatened to take my mother to court because of me. I imagine my mother doesn't believe him. And Dad is left in a fix."

Skye closed her eyes miserably. She thought of all the times she had pressured Kyle, she thought of the terrible bargain she had just forced from him, and she thought of how very, very tired he had appeared. All this time, if she hadn't been afraid to offer love, she could have trusted him. She could have been beside him, with him, instead of being another front that he had to battle. Kyle had always been there for her—on the island, in Sydney. She knew now that he had always loved her, and that she had offered him little in return except a bitter choice: his son or her.

"Oh, Chris . . ." Skye murmured. And then she couldn't help herself. She started to cry.

"Oh, Lord, Skye," Chris muttered with typical male helplessness. "I didn't mean to upset you. I was hoping to make things better." He sat beside Skye on the rock and awkwardly slipped an arm around her shoulders, trying to comfort her.

"You did make things better," Skye finally murmured. "It's just . . . you made me realize a few things about myself." She wiped her eyes, and smiled at him through glazed amber eyes that were remarkably beautiful. "Again, Chris, thank you," she said very softly.

"Hey," he replied lightly, "all I did was let you in on something you should know."

They stood together and Skye looked out over the bay. "This really is a beautiful place."

"Yes, but I think I'd better get you home."

"No, Chris," Skye said suddenly. "I'd like to get you home, then borrow your car."

Chris raised an eyebrow.

"I'm going to go see your mother, Chris. Don't worry, I'm not going to say anything about our conversation— that's all between you and your parents. I just want to tell her how I feel—and hope that I can avoid problems for all of us in the future."

Chris looked quite uncertain for several moments. Finally he sighed. "Okay, Skye, I guess you know what you're doing."

As Skye dropped Chris off at Montfort and took down his mother's address, she sensed his unhappiness. She called him back to the car before he could mount the steps to the door. "Chris," she told him softly. "I know you love your mother. I know I'm asking you to go out on a limb for your father and me. I promise, I'll remember that she is your mother and that you do love her."

Chris nodded with a grimace. Skye pulled out of the drive and Chris stood on the steps, making up his own mind as he watched her go.

From the bedroom window Kyle, too, was watching Skye drive away—in his son's car. He stared upon the scene with a curious frown etched into his features. What the hell was going on? And why the hell had he done something so foolish as to fall asleep? Damn, maybe he was getting old. He had been tired and worried, he had found contentment with Skye, even amidst turmoil. But they had needed to talk. He had meant to tell her . . . something. Anything. Something to alleviate the harshness and brutality of his words and actions.

Where the hell was she going? Had Chris agreed to help get her out? He knew that even his son wondered why he was so brusque with the dignified beauty he had brought to his home.

No, Skye wasn't leaving. She had agreed to stay. He had forced her into a bargain, forced her into his bed.

And he had sworn to play his last card.

Kyle turned briskly from the window. He left the bedroom and strode down the stairs and into the drawing room—and straight to the wet bar for a large Scotch. The fire was burning. He sat before it, gulped his drink, and set the glass on the coffee table. He raked the fingers of both hands through his hair. Face it, old man, he told himself, you've handled everything like hell. And what do you do now? How can you turn one son into a bastard, but how can you let another be born one? And what about Skye? How can you live without her now?

"Dad?"

Kyle jerked back to a straight position. "Chris, where did Skye go?"

"I'd rather not tell you, Dad," Chris said apologetically. "I think Skye is going to want to tell you herself."

"Oh?"

"Yeah . . ." Chris walked into the room, straight to the bar. "I think I need a drink."

Kyle glanced quizzically at his son. It wasn't like Chris to hedge. He wanted to demand an answer from Chris about Skye, but he also knew his son. Chris would never divulge a confidence.

"What's up?"

"I want to talk to you."

Kyle watched Chris as he poured himself a drink. He walked to the mantel with a straight Scotch, and despite the dilemma that weighed down upon him like a thousand bricks, Kyle felt a dry smile come to his lips. Chris might not be his blood, but he was his son. He stood as he did, thought as he did, made decisions like a man.

"We haven't talked about this much, Dad. But I want to say a few things. I think you know I like Skye. She's more than beautiful—she's kind and sweet and very strong in a way I don't think either of us could ever really understand. I admit, I kind of watched her at first. I was afraid she might be a fortune hunter—she is young. I don't care about your fortune, but I do care about your happiness."

"Chris," Kyle interrupted with a bit of a growl. "I'm glad you like Skye. And thank you for worrying about me, but don't. I'm not in the middle of doddering senility—not yet. And I believe I've known a few more women in my lifetime than you."

Chris laughed. "Sorry, Dad, I didn't mean to imply—never mind. I'm trying to get at a point and I'm not doing it very well. I'm going to start over and"—he raised a hand—"don't jump down my throat until I finish." He took a sip of his Scotch. "Like I said, Dad, I got to really like Skye. To be blunt, I've spent far more time with her than you have—outside of the bedroom."

"Christian!" Kyle bellowed, rising.

"Dad, I asked you not to interrupt. I'm being blunt."

"Well, don't be so damned blunt."

"I'll try. Anyway, I didn't like the way you were treating her. She came tearing down the stairs today to get out of the house—and away from you. So I decided to take her out, for your benefit. I wanted to tell her why you were being such a monster."

"Oh?" Amazed, Kyle stared at his son. "Chris, in the future my affairs are none of your concern. I don't appreciate your interference, even if you were attempting to vindicate a monster."

Chris appeared undaunted by his father's lecture. "I interfered because this isn't entirely your affair. I have this strange feeling I know exactly what the problem is with the divorce. You can get out of your marriage to Mom, but you won't because you might hurt someone— me. I want to tell you to do whatever it is you have to do. I know you aren't my father."

Kyle's knees buckled beneath him. It was a good thing he was in front of the sofa because he found himself sitting. He pressed his forehead into the palms of his hands. "Chris," he groaned. "oh, Lord, I never wanted you to know . . ."

"Dad, please." Chris's voice was raspy but level. "Dad, I've known for ages. I never said anything to you before, because there never was any reason. But now I think you need to know that I know . . . I want you to marry Skye. I want you to be happy. And"—his tone tightened—"if that means publicly disclaiming me, I want you to do it."

Kyle stood and walked to his son, placing his hands on his shoulders. "Chris, I never wanted you to know that you weren't my son because you are my son—no natural child could have ever meant more to me. I love you, I've loved watching you grow. I was proud of the boy you were and I'm proud of the man you've become."

Chris had meant for the confrontation with his father to go easily, nonchalantly. But he saw tears in his father's eyes—in the eyes of the man who had raised him, the man he had seen as a pillar of pride, strength, and dignity all his years.

And he couldn't hold back his own tears. He was crying as if he were a child, and he had come to his father with his first, terrifying nightmare.

The two men embraced; it would be a draw to decide who held the other with more fervor. "Ah, hell," Chris finally stuttered in a groan, pulling away from Kyle. "I'm supposed to be a damned adult . . ."

Kyle laughed and unashamedly wiped the moistness from his face with the back of his hand. "So am I," he said dryly, and then his features again became tense. "I meant what I said—you are my son, Chris."

"I know that, Dad, that's another reason I've never tried to discuss this before."

Kyle pulled out a cigarette and lit it. He placed a hand on the mantel and stared into the fire. "I can't tell you anything about your natural father, Chris, I don't even think your mother could—"

"I don't care, Dad." Kyle looked at him and he smiled. "Honestly. I suppose I should be curious about learning all that, but honestly, I don't care. Dad, all my life you've been with me, you've put me first." He paused. "That's why I want what is right for you now. Do what you have to do. You can't hurt me."

"Chris," Kyle said uneasily, "we're talking about your mother."

"Yeah," Chris said unhappily, "I know. And I want you

to explain to me everything that's happened. About this divorce business."

Kyle sighed deeply and looked at his son. Chris was an adult. More of a man than many he knew . . .

"Okay, son, I'll tell you what's going on. In the best legal terms I can. But remember, I haven't made any decisions yet, and I don't want you trying to influence me. There are things I really don't want to have to do . . ."

Chris sat down with a smile. "Who me? I wouldn't think of trying to interfere."

Lisa recovered from her first shock at seeing Skye, smiled imperially, and invited her in.

Lisa had moved into a lush apartment. Too lush, Skye thought. The room appeared frilly and cluttered.

"If you've come to plead your case," Lisa said, still smiling, "I'm afraid you're wasting your time. Kyle is still my husband. That makes you"—she raised an elegant brow—"at best, in the nicest terms, his mistress. You will understand that it took me by surprise to see you . . . quite far along in the, uh, family way."

Skye was surprised that she could return Lisa's stare with amusement rather than rancor.

"The child is Kyle's? I mean, are you sure?"

"The baby is Kyle's, Lisa. I'm quite sure." She might have reminded Lisa that she was the one who had apparently deceived him with another man's child. But that child was Chris, and even if it weren't, Skye wasn't feeling hostility.

"Well, if this is a plea to my better nature for the sake of the child," Lisa said bluntly, "forget it."

"Lisa I would hardly be here to plead with you."

"Good. If you've made the foolish mistake of becoming pregnant by a married man, I'm afraid that's your problem. Really, in this day and age, there was no reason . . ."

Skye dropped her smile. "Lisa, I didn't come here for an apology, to plead, or to beg. Or to exchange moral barbs. I came because I want you to know that I don't care what you do. You can drag this divorce out for as many years as you wish, and it won't matter a hair. I love Kyle. I'll live with him on any terms for the rest of my life. You think he'll tire of me. I don't. I believe he loves me. And I couldn't care less about his age, Lisa, or mine. It's something that's never even come up between us. I don't care if my child is illegitimate. He or she will have both parents' names on his or her birth certificate, and I'll never be ashamed of anything I one day have to tell my child. I don't know why you're fighting this, Lisa, but I don't care anymore." Skye wound down as she realized Lisa had lost her imperious, assured stare. Instead, she was beginning to look ghastly.

"Why are you trying to hold up the divorce, Lisa?" Skye asked.

Lisa hesitated a moment. "Because I love him, too."

Skye rose. "I'm sorry, Lisa. Very sorry. But I didn't create your problems. Your marriage was over long before I met Kyle. And I love him more than my own life. I don't intend to leave him."

Skye turned to leave. Lisa called her back.

"Skye—wait." Lisa clenched her eyes shut tightly for a moment as Skye returned. She opened her eyes and studied Skye. "I assume Kyle has told you something about Chris?"

Skye returned her stare, pausing. "I know," she said softly, finding compassion, "that Chris is not Kyle's son."

Lisa gripped her wrist, suddenly desperate. "He wants to go for an annulment, Skye. Please don't let him. Think of what it would do to Chris! He might say he didn't care, but it would be public knowledge . . . it would be horrible . . ."

Skye gently extracted her wrist. "He won't go for an annulment, Lisa. He loves Chris."

Skye was shaking as she left Lisa's apartment. And drained.

Fifteen

"So, why was Skye running out of here today?"

Kyle lifted a bleary eye to his son. He was on his sixth Scotch. Chris was on his fourth. Kyle had explained every legal procedure he had open to him, and the two had openly discussed all options. They sat with feet propped on the elegant coffee table, ties loosened, tailored appearances in dishabille.

"That," Kyle said dryly, "is something I do not care to discuss." Good Lord, he thought, I'm getting drunk. So why not? I lost my son; I regained my son. And it's been a hell of a day . . . Lisa attacking Skye, Skye trying to run out . . . "And speaking of Skye," he suddenly growled to Chris, "I think it's about time you tell me where she is!"

"Right here."

Kyle heard the dry voice from the doorway. He and Chris immediately tried to sit straight, like guilty teenagers. It was no good. She approached them with high-arched, imperious brows, noting with an amused disdain the condition of the father and son.

How was it possible, Kyle wondered defensively, for such a small woman to create such a regal presence. He was suddenly vulnerable, suddenly frightened. He stood, managing to waver only slightly as he took up a position at the mantel. "Well, well, Ms. Delaney. Welcome back to Montfort. I would have given you about another ten minutes, and then I would have set out to see that you lived up to your side of the bargain."

"Dad!" Chris gasped.

"Stay out of this, Chris. Where the hell have you been, Skye?"

Her brow rose a shade higher. "Out, Mr. Jagger."

"Out where?" Kyle thundered.

He was stunned to have his demand answered with a tinkle of melodious laughter. "Taking care of business," she replied with a wink at Chris. "And the business went very well." She walked straight to Kyle, a slow step, graceful, light. She stood on tiptoe and wriggled her nose slightly as she planted a little kiss on his lips and laughed again, leaving Kyle dumbfounded.

"Scotch, huh? What brought on this little overindulgence?"

Chris cleared his throat. "Dad and I were talking, Skye. We got a little carried away. We, um, well, we, uh, had some rather serious things to discuss."

"Oh," Skye murmured, her eyes leaving Kyle's for a moment.

"I told him to go for an annulment, Skye," Chris offered, his words a bit slurred.

Skye returned her eyes to Kyle's. "No annulments," she said clearly. "And no bargains."

"What?" Kyle demanded roughly, taking her shoulders between forceful hands. "What's going on here?"

"Dad, I told Skye this afternoon what I told you."

"Oh, Lord," Kyle began, but he was suddenly interrupted by another intervention—Michael walking into the room. He had the same question for all of them. "What's going on here?"

"A couple of drunks!" Skye said dryly. "Michael, I'll take care of Kyle. Can you get Chris to his room? And someone should tell your mother that dinner will be a bit delayed . . ."

Before anyone could protest, Skye was leading Kyle from the drawing room. "Think you can make the steps?" she asked impishly.

"Of course I can make the steps!" he roared. "And when I get up them, I'm going to damn well want a few explanations."

"Really?" Skye murmured. "Well certainly, Mr. Jagger. You'll get all the explanations you want."

But she had no intention of answering him immediately. With their bedroom door closed behind them, Skye began to move briskly. "A good soak in the whirlpool is what you need, Mr. Jagger," she told him, leading him with efficient steps to the bathroom where she set the jets into action and turned with purpose to strip his loosened tie and methodically work at the buttons of his shirt.

"Skye—"

"I'll talk to you after you're in the tub!" she informed him.

He scowled and warily stepped away from the gentle fingers that were such a tantalizing touch upon his flesh. Glaring at her, he dropped his trousers and briefs and stepped into the whirlpool.

"I'm in the tub," he announced. "Now come over here and tell me what's going on."

Skye smiled and moved to the rim of the deep sunken tub, only to lose her smile to a gasp as she realized Kyle certainly wasn't as inebriated as she had thought—he snaked out his hand and caught her arm. "Now, Skye, I'd appreciate an explanation."

"You already know most of this," Skye murmured. "Chris told me you weren't his father. And that you were protecting him. I never realized, Kyle, I couldn't understand . . ." Her voice was catching in her throat, and he was still staring at her. "I decided to go see Lisa myself. So I did."

"What," Kyle asked hoarsely, "did you say to Lisa?"

Skye lowered her eyes. "I told her that I loved you, and that I didn't care how long she dragged out the divorce. I told her I would live with you as long as you wanted—"

"And did you mean it?"

"I—"

"Look at me, Skye. Did you mean it?"

Skye lifted her eyes to his. "Yes," she said softly, her voice very steady. "I meant it."

"Then come here and tell me that."

Oblivious to the fact that she was still fully clothed, Skye moved into the shallow jetting water and into his arms. She slipped her arms around his neck and smiled into his eyes, feeling the gentle comfort of his hold around the small of her back. "I love you," she said. "And I'm so sorry, Kyle."

"Don't be sorry. Just tell me you love me again. You've never said it before, Skye."

"I love you," she told him. He kissed her gently, massaging her back, moving his hands under her sweater to touch her swollen abdomen. "I love you, Kyle, so much," she said again, after she had caught her breath. "Oh, Kyle, why didn't you just explain to me about Chris?"

Kyle smoothed her damp hair. "I couldn't tell you about Chris, because of Chris. No one knew—except Lisa, myself, and Michael. My mother doesn't even know, Skye, and I didn't think Chris knew . . ."

"It makes no difference to him, Kyle. You are his father."

"I know that, Skye. I know that now." He smiled at her. "And I finally know that *you* love me."

Skye lowered her eyes, raised them again. "It's rather difficult to tell a man you love him when the majority of the time he behaves as if you were the enemy."

"I didn't know how to keep you, Skye. I thought that

you still loved Trainor, that you were only with me because of the child—"

"Ted!" Skye exclaimed. "Oh, Kyle! It was all over with Ted, not because of the baby, but because of *you*. I loved you, Kyle. I couldn't go to him. Even when I believed there was no way you could escape Lisa, I couldn't be with anyone else. And then, when you came to my rescue in Sydney, I still didn't know how you felt. Especially when you found out about the baby. You were so hard, Kyle. You didn't speak to me unless it was in connection with the gold—"

"Skye." Kyle laughed. "I wanted to speak to you, touch you, hold you—attack you! But things were rather tense, if you recall. And you weren't behaving as if you were dying for my embrace. I didn't think Virginia would appreciate an assault in her living room!"

"No, I guess not," Skye murmured, burying her face into the wet slickness of his neck. "Oh, Kyle, I do love you!"

"Honey, I love you. So much that it was driving me half crazy."

"Oh, Kyle, it really doesn't matter."

"I wish I could have been there. I never wanted you to talk to Lisa because I didn't want you hurt."

"Oh, Kyle, nothing can hurt me as long as I know you really love me. I was so afraid of your marriage! I didn't want you marrying me just because I was pregnant . . ."

Kyle chuckled softly. "I'll let you in on a secret. On the island I was hoping you'd become pregnant. In fact, I worked rather hard at it. A pleasurable task, of course!"

"Why you . . . you . . ." Skye sputtered, searching for a suitable name.

Kyle laughed. "You'll think of something, I'm sure. But don't resent me for it too much. I didn't know if we would ever get off the island at the time, and if we did, I assumed I would be divorced within a few months. It never occurred to me that Lisa would change her tune." He frowned suddenly. "I'm worried, Skye. This court action with Lisa may take us ages. I want to be married before our child is born. I know how much it means to you. You know, Skye, an annulment just might be faster."

"Don't be ridiculous," Skye protested.

"It was a bargain I made with you," Kyle reminded her.

"We don't need bargains anymore, Kyle. And I really don't care how long the divorce takes. Just as long as I know that you won't wind up hating me because of what I'm doing to your life. Or tiring of me—"

"Tiring of you! If I were given a hundred lifetimes, Skye, I could never, never tire of you."

"Oh, Kyle . . ."

He kissed her again, his touch with the flow of the water gentle and reverent . . . and stimulating. She moaned as the deep tenderness of his kiss suddenly swirled into something more erotic along with the driving pulse of the jets. The hands that touched her began to join with the wild cascade, as he tenderly helped her to remove her clothing.

He broke the kiss for a moment, lifting her high, bringing her down over him. He smiled as he held her around the rib cage, his thumbs free to graze her nipples.

"One last question for the moment, Ms. Delaney," he said, his eyes brilliant. "Are you sure you want to get tied up with an old man?"

Skye's eyes widened with surprise. Then she laughed. "I just love the elderly sort," she murmured huskily.

"Good," Kyle returned. "Another question—"

"You said just one."

"So I did, but this is extremely pertinent. Do pregnant ladies mind the fathers of their children making love to them in whirlpools?"

"I certainly don't propose to speak for all," Skye answered him, her eyes—the intriguing topaz eyes that had bewitched him so long ago—heavily lidded and enticingly sensual, "But this particular pregnant lady would just love the father of her child to make love to her in the whirlpool . . ."

"I think," Kyle murmured, "that we'll be very late for dinner."

"And I think," Skye returned, adjusting her body to his with a shudder of pure pleasure, "that absolutely no one will mind."

Then neither was thinking. The pulse of the whirlpool carried them away in its steaming tempo . . .

The ringing of the phone was strident. Jostled from a luxurious sleep by the sound, Skye burrowed closer into Kyle's shoulder, wishing the noise would stop. They had stayed awake so late last night . . . deciding to have dinner in their room, lighting the fire, relaxing before it on the thick rug and slowly sipping hot cinnamon brandy while they talked and talked and made love again and again.

The phone kept ringing. Kyle groaned. "Why isn't someone answering it?" he muttered, as he groped for the receiver on the nightstand without opening his eyes.

"It's probably too early for anyone to be up," Skye murmured drowsily in return, settling comfortably against his chest.

"Hello," Kyle muttered tonelessly into the receiver. Skye was suddenly jostled from her pleasant position as Kyle sat bolt upright in the bed, his eyes miraculously sharp. He was doing most of the listening, but as Skye frowned in question to him, he shook his head, his expression tense; he wasn't ready to be interrupted.

What was it? Skye wondered, worry quickly dispelling the contented laziness that had been hers. Her frown deepened as she listened to Kyle utter a stunned "Why?"

and then several yeses, and then, right before clicking down the receiver, a "Fine!"

"What?" Skye demanded, forcefully tilting his chin toward her. "Is something wrong?"

Kyle started laughing suddenly, slipping his arms around her and drawing her so tight that she could hear the sound rumbling deep in his chest. "No! My love. Something is *right!* Very right! That was Lisa's lawyer. She has decided to sign the papers today."

Skye struggled against him, raising herself off his chest with her palms to stare into his eyes incredulously. "Why did she suddenly agree?" Skye demanded. "I told her yesterday you'd never go for the annulment."

Kyle smiled, his eyes very tender as he touched her hair, and then drew a soft line over the fine bone of her cheek. "You also told her you were staying no matter what. Don't you see, Skye? Lisa would never let on to you, but she knew then that she had lost. You weren't just another woman to come and go. You were a permanent fixture in my life—Skye, you are my life! Lisa knows I'll eventually get a divorce. By agreeing now, she'll come out of it a lot better."

"Oh, Kyle!" Skye leaned down and brushed his lips with a feather kiss. "You mean it's all over?"

He frowned, nibbling a corner of his lip. "No, Skye, it's not all over. It's still going to take time. But it will be a couple of months now, not years, which she might have been able to drag it all out to. It won't be all that long, darling . . ."

Skye laughed and slipped her head back down to his chest, running her fingers through the coarse tufts of air. "I told you I don't care, Kyle. I'm happy that it's going to be a little easier at long last, but it still doesn't matter. I will wait, forever . . ."

"Hey!" Kyle said, nudging her. "Are you going back to sleep on me? After news like that?"

"Well, we didn't get any sleep last night," Skye reminded him.

"Lord!" he groaned. "Where's your sense of romance? Ah, hell, I guess I'll just have to have enough for two."

But Skye was laughing as he rolled her over. Her arms slipped around his neck. "Oh, Kyle," she murmured, eyes shining, "I do love you . . ."

February 28, San Francisco

Skye laid down her pencil and rubbed her eyes. She had fully intended to devote her concentration to the bracelet sketch, but intent and action were two different things.

She stood and stretched, wincing at the dull pain in her lower back. It was being very persistent today.

She walked to the bay window and looked out upon the lush landscaping. Spring was coming, and she was glad. She had loved Christmas at Montfort, and winter had been beautiful. But though she was happy, winter had been a time of waiting. Kyle had been asked to return to Sydney in January—Smithfield had been apprehended and Kyle's testimony had been necessary for the trial. He had gently refused to take her with him—the trip was too long and her doctors would not be pleased. She had not wanted Kyle to go; it was over, she had told him. And she had worried about his temper and his anger and he knew it.

"I'm not going for revenge, Skye," he assured her. "But the man would have killed us without blinking an eye. I have to make sure he's put away. Think of what he could do to others."

And she had agreed, but it had been hard waiting for him to return. But his trip home brought a very pleasant surprise for both Skye and Michael—Kyle returned with

Virginia. And on February tenth, very quietly, Virginia became Mrs. Michael Jagger.

Skye smiled with the memory of her conversation with Virginia. Her sister-in-law had told her, "Skye, I'll never forget Steven, he'll be a part of me all my life . . ."

"Virginia!" Skye had laughed, "Don't be absurd! I'm thrilled about you and Michael. I get to keep you as a sister-in-law! Steven will always be a part of both of us—a cherished part."

Skye knew that both Virginia and Michael had wanted to tactfully delay their wedding until after hers. But living in the same house had been very difficult for them. And Michael, at thirty-five, didn't consider himself particularly young.

The dull pain suddenly shot across Skye's midriff, making her gasp. She frowned, considering calling the doctor. She wasn't due for several weeks.

Skye grimaced, shrugged, and returned to the chair by her desk. The pain went away, a band that constricted, slowly let loose. Skye picked up her pencil again, but she didn't even glance at the paper. She nervously chewed on the eraser.

Today was it, the end of waiting.

At this very minute Kyle was in the courtroom with Lisa. He would return today a free man.

Skye dropped the pencil and began to pace the room. She could have gone, but she hadn't wanted to be there. Only Michael had gone with his brother. Chris, like her, had preferred to be absent. And Mary Jagger and Virginia had decided that this, of all days, was the one when they wanted to take over the kitchen and create some type of Polynesian delicacy Virginia had discovered on her honeymoon.

I think I'll go downstairs, Skye decided. She had wanted to be alone, but now she wanted company.

She threw open her workshop door and headed across

the balcony to the stairs, only to pause before taking the first step. The same pain, not quite as strong as the first, assailed her. She held her breath, clutching the banister. How long had it been since the first? Fifteen, twenty minutes? A little more than that . . .

As she stood waiting, the front door flew open. Skye watched as Kyle strode in, his footsteps sharp and assertive on the marble. He paused in the entryway. As if by instinct he raised his head, saw Skye, and smiled, his eyes brilliant and warm, his grin spread handsomely across rakish features. Skye smiled in return, her heart taking on the little flutter she still felt after all this time at the sight of him. He was all male today, devastatingly masculine as he tilted his chin in her direction, hands on hips, legs spread, broad shoulders emphasized by the tailored cut of his dark charcoal sports jacket.

"It's all over," he told her. He lifted a beckoning hand. "Come here."

Skye sailed on down the staircase and into his arms, wincing a bit at her awkward angle as she kissed him. She wasn't actually big as a house, but she often felt like a small elephant.

Kyle smoothed her hair and whispered softly in her hair, "Tomorrow, darling, we'll apply for our license."

Skye drew away from him and grimaced. "I'm not so sure about tomorrow, Kyle. We may have to wait."

He frowned, encircling her shoulder with his arm as he led her into the drawing room. "Why should we wait?"

"Because I think another Jagger might be making an appearance today."

Kyle came to a dead halt. He whirled her around and narrowed his eyes as he demanded, "The baby? Today? Are you sure? It's early yet?"

Skye laughed. "Well I've never done this before, you know, but I think I'm sure."

He held her close. "I wanted us to be married . . ."

"Oh, Kyle, it really doesn't matter."

He drew back abruptly. "Yes, it does matter. When did you start thinking you might be in labor?"

Skye frowned, perplexed by his anxiety. "Not long ago. Half an hour at best."

Kyle was suddenly propelling her onto the sofa. "Just sit tight, Ms. Delaney. You are going to be Mrs. Jagger before the baby is born!"

"You're crazy, Kyle!" Skye told him, half laughing and half frowning, "It's impossible, there are laws in California—"

Kyle was headed for the phone. "But not in Nevada. Let's see, we have at least six to eight hours. Time to fly, acquire a license, step into a notary's, make it back . . ."

"Oh, no, you don't!" Skye flew to her feet in alarm. "Kyle, I don't think you understand! I'm in labor."

"No problem. I'll fly us right out of here—"

"The hell you will! I'm not sitting in the back of one of your planes by myself, wondering if I'm going to deliver in a Lear!"

"Skye"—Kyle covered the mouthpiece of the phone with his hand and spoke patiently—"I have been through this before. You aren't going to deliver for quite some time. It's your first child—" He broke off as someone answered on the other end of the line. "Jagger, here. I want a plane cleared to Las Vegas in fifteen minutes. Yes. Thanks." He hung up and dialed again.

"Kyle!" Skye persisted. "You're crazy! Who are you calling now?"

"Dr. Hammond. He can check you out, and then I'm sure he won't mind a little flight, a little diversion from the day-to-day routine."

"Kyle, I'm nervous! I'm not sitting alone, even with the doctor, while you fly—"

"I'll fly!" a voice from the doorway interrupted.

Skye spun around to see Michael leaning in the door-way, a mischievous grin planted on his features.

"Michael!" Skye wailed. "Help me talk him out of this harebrained scheme. Don't sit there aiding and abetting him!"

"What's going on?" Virginia suddenly appeared, slipping her arms around her husband's waist. Skye could already hear Kyle joking with the doctor on the phone.

"Virginia, they are both nuts. I think I'm in labor and they want to fly to Las Vegas so that Kyle and I can be married."

Virginia's pretty eyes widened and she smiled. "That's not nuts, Skye. It's wonderfully romantic!"

"Oh, Lord!" Skye moaned, sinking back to the sofa. "Isn't anyone here sane?"

Kyle hung up the phone. "Dr. Hammond's on his way. If he says it's okay, Skye, are you game?"

Skye stared at him a long time, shook her head incredulously, and finally smiled. "All right, Jagger. It will serve you right if your child is born in the back of a damned plane!"

Dr. Hammond, an old Air Force friend of Kyle's, assured them both that yes, Skye was definitely in labor, but in the very early stages. "If you stayed home, Skye, I'd have you walking for more than half the day anyway." He grinned. "I rather like this idea. I'll be with you all the way."

And so they were shortly flying to Nevada, Michael at the controls, Kyle holding Skye's hand, Virginia, Dr. Hammond, and Chris, whom they had picked up at the airport, all chattering away in the passenger seats. Then Kyle and Skye acquired a wedding license and then they were before a notary.

I must be the only bride in history to have to gasp out

a yes, Skye thought as a vicious pain assailed her right in the middle of the ceremony.

But then it was over, and she realized with a bit of awe as Kyle kissed her that she was finally, actually, Mrs. Kyle Jagger.

The pains grew intense as they flew home. Kyle tried to keep her mind occupied; he firmly instructed her in correct breathing. "Come on, Mrs. Jagger," he soothed, allowing her to grip his hand with deathly pressure, "It isn't that bad!"

"Of course it isn't!" Skye snapped sourly. "Not for you anyway, I'm the one having the baby!"

Kyle chuckled. In fact, he was finding the entire thing a bit too amusing. When they finally reached the hospital, he took his place as assisting father without a qualm. He was so calm and cool—and annoyingly authoritative—that Skye would have gladly clobbered him at times. Time was beginning to wear at her resistance to the pain, but the more frantic she would become, the more Kyle firmly assured her, forcing her to breathe instead of give way.

She was ready to scream, praying someone would shoot her, when Dr. Hammond finally announced they were ready for the delivery room. And still Kyle held her hand, still he assured her.

"Easy, Skye, it's almost over."

"That's easy for you to say!" Skye moaned in a strained whisper. "You're not on this table!"

"That's right," he grinned. "Women are designed for babies!"

"Jagger—you always were a damned chauvinist!"

"And you always were an opinionated little witch—a beautiful little witch, of course. Now shut up and push!"

And then it was all worth it. Her daughter was born with a hearty little wail that could hardly be described as feminine.

And Skye was able to laugh and smile and lie back with

contented exhaustion, filled with a wonderful ecstasy as she watched her husband—yes, her husband!—dip his infant into a soothing bath after gamely agreeing with Dr. Hammond that he didn't mind cutting the cord at all. She was grateful then that Kyle had continually talked her out of anesthetic. She would have missed this moment, seeing his gentle, adoring handling of their child, seeing his eyes as they turned to her, feeling the love that bound them as three as he placed the baby into her arms . . . feeling his kiss on her forehead as she awkwardly relied on instinct to bring her tiny daughter to her breast . . . hearing his words . . .

"She's beautiful, Skye, absolutely beautiful. Thank you, Mrs. Jagger." He leaned closer in his hospital greens. His eyes were a deep shade of tender mint, dark and tender. "Thank you," he whispered again, "thank you my love, my wife, my life . . ."

With their child greedily huddled close to her and Dr. Hammond tactfully turning his back, Skye offered her lips to her husband, shivering with incredible happiness.

Epilogue

June 4, the South Pacific

A dozen seabirds, splendid as they soared against the ceaseless green and brown backdrop of island foliage, carried on wild squawked conversations. The sun blazed down on the glistening shoreline; a startled crab danced along the sand in a comical side step.

On the horizon sat the *Bonne Bree*, and pulled to the beach, the dinghy that had brought humans to the shore of this particular paradise.

Kyle Jagger stood tensely poised by a coral outcrop, his eyes sharply following the lazy swimming of a small fat grouper. His tree-branch spear was raised high in his hand—dripping water from several fruitless previous attempts to score the fish.

"I am going to get you, fish," he threatened with low-toned authority. He plunged. The fish sidled by. "Okay, fish, so far, you've been lucky . . ."

"Kyle!"

He waved an impatient hand toward the shore, sighed, then glanced over the water to his wife.

"I've almost got it," he lied.

"Kyle!" Skye moaned, "We don't need the fish! We have a cooler full of steaks for tonight!"

"That's not the point!" he called back. "I want this fish!"

He studied the movements of the fish again, heedless of the time elapsing. He was about to plunge again when he was detoured by another call. "Kyle!"

He glanced to the shore. Skye, hands on trim hips, blond hair blowing in the breeze, stood in cutoffs and knotted shirt, arched brows portraying exasperation. "Just a minute more!" he vowed.

"Okay," he threatened the fish. "Your luck is coming to an end. I couldn't have completely forgotten how to do this! Now stand still, buddy, one last time."

"Kyle . . ."

The call was different this time. There was a husky, sultry tone to it.

Kyle turned to the shore. She stood as she had before, feet firmly planted in the sand, head tilted back, hands planted on her hips, hair flying like spun gold in the breeze . . .

Except now she stood naked and proud beneath the sun, a bold goddess, beckoning.

He stared at his wife, at her shapely slender form, the sun glistening on lightly tanned, soft flesh . . .

A shudder gripped him, sending shock waves of heat through him even as he stood in the water.

A smile curved her lips, touching exquisite amber cat eyes with an enticing glimmer of sweet, seductive promise.

Kyle grinned, dropped his tree-branch spear, took one last look at the fish. "This is your lucky day, fellow," he murmured.

Then his eyes returned to those of his wife. He began a slow, sure walk from the water, holding that amber gaze.

Gold had brought him to this paradise once. Golden beauty had brought him back. And would bring him back again, and again, and again. He knew, as she did, that every year they would leave their world behind—the hustle, the strain, even the tiny daughter they adored—to return to this place, to be alone, uniquely together, special lovers remembering, savoring, creating new moments of paradise.

She walked with lithe, fluid movements to meet him, and beneath the sky and sun, within the temperate blue water, he reached out and touched the woman who was the gold of his life.

Put a Little Romance in Your Life With
Hannah Howell

__**Highland Destiny** 0-8217-5921-3	$5.99US/$7.50CAN
__**Highland Honor** 0-8217-6095-5	$5.99US/$7.50CAN
__**Highland Promise** 0-8217-6254-0	$5.99US/$7.50CAN
__**My Valiant Knight** 0-8217-5186-7	$5.50US/$7.00CAN
—**A Taste of Fire** 0-8217-5804-7	$5.99US/$7.50CAN
__**Wild Roses** 0-8217-5677-X	$5.99US/$7.50CAN

Call toll free **1-888-345-BOOK** to order by phone, use this coupon
to order by mail, or order online at **www.kensingtonbooks.com**.
Name _____
Address _____
City _____ State _____ Zip _____
Please send me the books I have checked above.
I am enclosing $_____
Plus postage and handling* $_____
Sales tax (in New York and Tennessee only) $_____
Total amount enclosed $_____
*Add $2.50 for the first book and $.50 for each additional book.
Send check or money order (no cash or CODs) to:
**Kensington Publishing Corp., Dept C.O., 850 Third Avenue, 16th Floor,
New York, NY 10022**
Prices and numbers subject to change without notice.
All orders subject to availability.
Visit our website at **www.kensingtonbooks.com**.

The Queen of
Romance
Cassie Edwards